Summertime Friends

a novel

HANNAH HAMRICK

Please be aware that the following content warnings apply:

- Panic attack description

- Discussion of death of a relative (cancer)

- Explicit sexual content

ISBN: 979-8-9907095-1-5

EBOOK ISBN: 979-8-9907095-0-8

Book Cover by Rachel Sierra, www.rachelsierraart.com (@Rachel.sierra.art)

Editing: EJ (EJL Editiing)

To the girls who feel as if they'll never be enough, you are.

To Dad, the first person who taught me that second chances can be a form of love and compassion. Your heart for loving and serving others was contagious, and I hope that this book is a small glimpse into everything you taught me about championing those around me.

Playlists

Scan to listen to the *Summertime Friends* playlists.

Some of my favorite songs included are:
Would've, Could've, Should've – Taylor Swift
Ribs – Lorde
The Good Kind – The Wreckers
I miss you, I'm sorry – Gracie Abrams
4ever – The Veronicas
Want You Back – HAIM
Friends – Francis and the Lights, Bon Iver
Lips Of An Angel – Hinder
Hanging By A Moment – Lifehouse
Hope Is a Heartache – LÉON

Prologue
Liam

One Summer Ago

My muscles gripe as my shoulders shake from the breeze blowing across my back. When did it get this cold out?

It dropped to the twenties on previous nights, but it feels at least ten degrees colder than that. When dressing earlier, I knew I should have exchanged my short-sleeved cotton ribbed henley for a long-sleeved shirt. I'm sort of a baby when it comes to the cold.

The temperature is abnormally low for June. I think we've been spoiled during the day with cloudless blue skies and highs of 40°C. We came in from surfing midday for lunch and overheard strangers mention that a cold front was coming from the north. They spoke confidently as if they were meteorologists or above-average pros at the weather app.

Security takes an extra moment to check my ID before letting me in the pub. He's probably not used to seeing a London ID in downtown San José, Costa Rica.

I can barely take a step in here without colliding with someone. It's packed.

Callum and George are already here. They secured a circular booth in the back corner of the place. They texted me earlier to let me know. Moments later, they sent a *kind* follow-up text, including a photo of a girl on George's lap—no surprise there.

We've been here—this pub, this table—every night since we arrived four days ago. On our first night here, we stumbled by, had a proper good time, and have been back every night. No surprise again.

I nod to my best mates as I walk up to the table. They're in a chat with three women, too preoccupied to even notice I've arrived. Two brunette twins with dark brown eyes sit on either side of George. The other, a redhead with hair bobbed at her shoulders, has her hand caressing Callum's upper bicep. Her bright pink nails clash with his orange polo, which unfortunately appears straight out of the fifties.

"Oi." George finally recognizes that I'm here. "This one's for you," he tells me immediately, thumb-pointing to the brunette to his left.

"Feels as if they might both be for you." I raise one eyebrow at him.

He lifts both of his brows, his eyes darkening with an idea.

"Reckon, we could be up for something new tonight?" he asks me.

I snuff a laugh at him. One of the twins whispers in his ear, and a devilish smile stretches across his face.

"Ask Callum," I joke. George and I look over at him. The redhead is now in his lap, distracting him from the idea that's bouncing around. "Too sore, anyway," I add.

Truthfully, I am sore. I wiped out on my board earlier, and I can feel the bruise forming across my back. But what I don't say is that I'm not in the headspace.

I slide into the booth, the faded maroon linoleum creaking underneath me. One of the brunettes, Mila, I learn her name is later, edges closer to me.

She's hot, not oblivious to that. And unlike her sister, she seems gentler and not as much to handle.

I don't make a move to get closer or talk to her.

Usually, I'd devour this. The attention. The feel of her touch.

Usually, I'd read her intentions, calculate my every move and word to make her sweat for it, egging her on until I get to reward her later, on her back or all fours, panting for more. There's an art to a hookup, and any other night, I'd be up there compared to Michaelangelo.

George tosses me a glance. I shrug.

"Li!" Callum slurs. He only refers to me as Li when we've been out drinking. "About damn time you showed up."

"About damn time you come up for air to notice," George jokes, playfully patting Callum on the arm.

"Where have you been?" Callum asks me.

"Had to take a call." It comes out extremely matter-of-fact. My eyes meet with George and then Callum. A warning within them that says it all—'do not ask me again.'

She never sets me off like this. Shit, she hasn't set me off in *years*.

She didn't even do anything tonight to set me off. I did.

With only a few more days left of our holiday in Costa Rica, the idea of being in the same city as her again looms over me.

We took our annual summer holiday early—June instead of July. After seven days here, I'll fly to Chicago to spend the summer. Hayes Hotels, my hotel line, is expanding to the States. After years of establishing myself in the Greater London area, I'm ready for this.

Expanding to the States was always part of the plan. At first, New York was our initial choice, but that changed after my summer with her.

She lived in Chicago. She *lives* in Chicago.

So, Chicago became the five-year plan.

I was on the phone with my realtor in Chicago before coming out tonight. Elizabeth, a commercial agent, had called me to confirm showings for next week. We reviewed my budget and timeline for locating an office. Elizabeth is also helping Callum and me find a long-term place to live. Hotels are incredible, but I didn't want to be living out of one for months at a time. Plus, if everything goes as planned, we will split our time between Chicago and London.

She found a place in the Loop. I had to hang up on her quickly, my brain tuning out everything she said about the place and area. I had never been, but I knew the area. I asked her to email over the details, and I'd get back to her.

The next hour was a blur. I slumped in the chair behind the desk I'd been working from.

I wondered if she still lived there—in the Loop, not Chicago. I knew she still lived in Chicago. At least, that's what her social media showed the last time I checked before I unfollowed her. Seeing her in my feed hurt. I'd fixate on her smile and remember that, at one point, I was the reason she smiled—and the one that caused her to stop. She looked happy, which made me happy, but also jealous that she was no longer smiling because of me.

I sat there, letting myself stew in the memories, trying to decide whether I should contact her to tell her I'd be there. Ultimately, I decided against it, instead working up the energy to go and meet the boys. I might have let her down, but I wouldn't let them down.

George and Callum don't ask about her anymore. I think she lives in the past for all of us as a faint summer memory. But she isn't only in the past for me.

And I know they pick up on that tonight.

"Negroni with an extra shot of gin, man," I order from the waiter when he circles back to take orders. "Thanks."

I'm hopeful that this will help turn my night around.

It doesn't.

Two more rounds of drinks don't help either.

I sat there like a scene out of a movie. Everyone around me moving fast while I'm frozen in slow motion.

George leans over the table and claps his hands.

"Alright, ladies. It's been beautiful, but it's time to go. Put your drinks on his tab." George points at me. "And have a lovely evening."

Their amusement drops, cross about the end of whatever they assumed the night would go. With a few huffs and sighs, they exit the booth. George and Callum don't move as the women climb around them, but I slide out of the booth to let them exit.

"Now tell us. What's wrong?" Callum asks.

"Is this about Chicago?" George asks, narrowing Callum's broad question.

They both stare at me, already knowing the answer.

I nod.

"Do you still love her?" they ask in unison.

"I think I always will."

1

EMERSON

Now

"Honey, come check out these windows," Brandon's mom, Laura, calls him over. "You could put florals in the window or have the curtains pulled together, but I don't think they should be open to the public."

Brandon walks over to her. Leaving me and Josie, the event coordinator, who has been giving us a tour for the past two hours.

When scheduling the tour today, they confirmed it would last an hour. We aren't even halfway through, and we've doubled the time. Brandon's mom stops every four steps to study the placement of an outlet or ask irrelevant questions.

I don't say anything because she's paying for the wedding. That, and I learned my lesson the first time I tried to make a decision.

"Did you have a date in mind?" Josie whispers to me.

"No," I reply.

"Our first available Saturday is in December, but—"

"Oh no. No. No. No!" Laura is rushing toward us, hands frantic in the air. "I will not be having a wedding in winter."

How the hell did she hear us? Josie glances at me. Eyes flared with precaution for what to say next.

"What season are you thinking?" I ask Laura, careful of my tone.

"Emerson, how could you even think about getting married in the winter?" Laura shakes her head at me with a concoction of sheer disappointment and curiosity about how her beloved son could be marrying a brainless girl like me. I seek Brandon for backup, but he's not even paying attention. "Summer." She turns to Josie, ignoring me and the fact that I'm the bride. "They will be getting married in the summer."

"Unfortunately, we are completely booked for this summer. When we return to the office, I will check out available dates, but it will have to be next year," Josie says calmly and directly.

Laura releases a dramatic sigh. "I suppose that's fine."

Suppose? Tell that to her feet.

She stomps off to the other side of the ballroom to examine who knows what.

"I don't mean to be rude, but how are you putting up with that?"

I shrug. "He's worth it." I think.

Josie nods and moves us on to the next part of the tour.

She speaks clearly, highly educated on the space and offerings. Every question Laura has, even the strangest of questions, Josie doesn't show if she's flustered. Each answer is respectful and intentional in trying to keep Laura at bay.

It's impressive. I could learn a thing or two from watching her. Josie, I mean, unless we are talking about things not to do, then Laura.

We make our way back to the office to review the final details. I space out during this part. Doesn't matter. I lost control of making decisions the minute I said 'yes'.

He's worth it. My earlier words echo in my head. Brandon is worth it, right? He has to be.

Brandon silently assures me, as if he read my mind, squeezing my right hand, which is resting in his lap. He has to be—we're getting married.

Sitting beside him, I peek at my left hand—a three-stone ring. The center stone is cushion-cut and set between two other diamonds. The band is silver, with smaller stones winding around it.

Beautiful, don't get me wrong; however, it is not my style.

I'm not a fan of silver. Laura is, which means Brandon is.

Our relationship revolves around his mom, as if she is his puppeteer. Two months after introducing me to her, he proposed to me at his family's lake house in Michigan. We were there for a family reunion last June, and it was my first time meeting his extended family. Brandon and I had been together for five months at that point. Discussions about forever hadn't even happened. The publicness of his proposal overwhelmed me, and I didn't know if I saw a future with him.

But who says no to a proposal when it's in front of their entire family?

I said yes. We've been engaged for a year, and it sounds like we'll be engaged for another.

I question myself: Why go through with this? There are several reasons.

Brandon is sweet and treats me well enough. We have a good time when we are alone, trying new restaurants, watching classic black-and-white films at small theaters, and always laughing. Always laughing.

That's what I enjoy most about our relationship: never a dull moment.

Plus, he's pretty good in bed, which always helps.

"Mom, why don't you let Emme and I talk about the venue and let you know?" Brandon finally speaks for the first time in four hours.

"I'll give you three days." Laura glances between the both of us. "Or, Josie, is there a way to hold the date temporarily? I would hate for *Emme*"—she hates the palindromic nickname—"to take too long to make up her mind, and we lose that Saturday in June."

My jaw drops as I stare at Laura. I turn to Brandon to see if he'll stick up for me and call out his mom for the audacity to say that. He's silent again.

Frustration boils in me. But what's new in the matter?

"I can." Josie types away on the computer. "It does require a deposit. I can make it refundable for the next seventy-two hours, but after that, it will become non-refundable."

"Amazing. Did you hear that, Emme?"

"Yes, Laura," I say. "Brandon and I will let you know." My voice is as sharp as a razor.

Laura exchanges her black card and other information with Josie while side-eyeing me.

"Do you mind if we take off, Mom?" Brandon asks.

She nods. Not even saying goodbye to us as we get up to leave.

"Mind a walk down Michigan Ave?" I ask Brandon.

He nods, lacing his fingers with mine.

We walk in silence for a mile or two. The silence between us is awkward, and I hate it. In the moments of silence, my worries about us fundamentally as a couple and our future take over. Is this how it's going to be forever? Is this something I can do forever?

"Coffee?" Brandon uses his head to gesture to the door we are about to walk past.

"Yeah."

He opens the door for me, kisses me on the cheek, and asks me to get him an iced mocha while he uses the restroom.

It's surprisingly empty in the shop this afternoon for a Tuesday. Only a handful of people are scattered about on laptops, working or talking with friends. That would be us if we didn't have to take the day off work because of wonderfully thorough Laura.

A short line forms behind me as I order our coffees.

"One black coffee and one iced mocha, please," I order.

"Sixteen or twenty-four ounces?" The barista asks.

"Sixteen for both, thank you."

I tap my card to pay and move out of the way for the next customers to order.

Scrolling on my phone, I check Instagram to view Natalie's story. She's been away again on another brand trip. I tap on her profile picture and am instantly transported to Amsterdam. Videos of her biking alongside the canals. A collage of photos showing off the clothes that she's modeling and a video of her squeezing a metal boob coming out of the brick road in the Red Light District. A recap of the previous days—as I know, she landed home earlier today. I reply to her story with a series of laughing and heart emojis.

There's a tap on my shoulder when I hear my name.

"Emerson?" a deep, rough British accent tickles my ear.

2

EMERSON

Now

I could recognize that voice anywhere. It could be the year 2074, and I would. It has its own wavelength and frequency that I used to believe was unique to me.

I can picture my name on his tongue. The way his mouth forms each syllable, holding on to the last one longer than the others. There is a bit of intrigue and confusion this time, but even with that, the sound of my name coming from his mouth is as if I'm being welcomed home.

But it couldn't be him. This is only my mind playing a trick on me.

He's in London. I'm in Chicago.

That's how we left it three years ago.

"Emerson," he says again. *It is him.*

A hand comes to my back, patting it a few times when I realize I'm choking on my saliva. I haven't even laid my eyes on him, and all the oxygen has been sucked out of me.

"Are you okay?" Brandon rushes over to me.

"Yeah—I'm—I'm fine," I squeak out.

Brandon gives me a once over, then glares up at the man standing behind me, whose hand is still on my back. He shifts his focus between me and Liam.

Delayed, my body shudders under Liam's touch as I register the sensation of it. It's the carefulness but familiarity that has me unsteady.

Liam's hand drops from my back.

"Emme, who is this?" Brandon asks me.

"I'm Liam Hayes." He reaches out his hand to Brandon. "An old—*friend* of hers."

Friend. Huh. *Do not roll your eyes, Emerson.*

Brandon shakes Liam's hand as he takes up residence next to me. I can't help but notice and fixate on the way Liam said friend as if it was foreign.

"Oh. She's never mentioned you. When did you two know each other? Were you pretty close?" Brandon lies.

I gulp, grabbing both of their attention.

"Years ago," I say.

"Met when she was traveling in Europe," Liam says at the same time.

"Your trip with Nat?" One of Brandon's brows raises as he asks.

"Yup."

The three of us stand there, staring at each other. I can tell by the statue that Brandon becomes; he's putting together the pieces of who Liam is to me. I told Brandon briefly one night about a guy I had a summer fling with after he interrogated me with questions about the people I've been with.

Fling, huh.

I nervously reach up my hand, tucking a strand of hair behind my ear. Liam's eyes catch my ring.

"You're engaged?" He's shocked.

My eyes shift to where my hand is lingering on the side of my face. My ring is sitting right in my peripheral vision. I flick my gaze back to Liam and then to Brandon.

He steps closer, looping an arm around my waist and pulling me in for a kiss.

Liam's shoulders tense as he watches us.

"Have been for a year," Brandon says.

"Wow. Congratulations—I'spose," Liam says. The shock on his face is gone, and his demeanor turns sad. The sparkle of his blue eyes dull as I watch the disappointment flare in them when he glances at my ring again.

I drop my hand, shoving it into the pocket of my jeans. Trying to hide away the reminder to each of us that this could have been us in a different lifetime.

"These are our coffees." I move to the pickup counter. Brandon steps around me, grabbing both of ours. He doesn't say anything as he makes his way toward the exit.

Turning back to Liam, I peer at him. His appearance is the same, but older. He's exactly the way I remember him.

"I'm sorry?" My voice is unusually meek. I don't recognize it.

I don't know what I'm apologizing for. I don't know if it's because I'm engaged now or because of how we ended all those years ago.

"Don't worry about it. I'm happy for you," he tells me.

"Okay." I take in the sight of him one last time before following after Brandon, who is standing at the door watching our interaction.

I'm a few steps away from him when he calls out my name again.

"States."

I turn back to him. "Yeah?"

"It's great to see you." For the first time since he tapped my shoulder, Liam smiles at me.

"You too." I mirror his smile. I turn back around and hurry to the door.

"All good?" Brandon asks me as I reach him.

"Of course," I lie. He leans in to kiss me, but I turn my head, and his lips land on my cheek. He pulls away and glances over his shoulder to where I know Liam is standing, and then we leave.

3

EMERSON

Six Summers Ago

"This is ridiculous! Emme, did you even book two beds?" Natalie snaps at me.

"Yes, Natalie, I did." Is she serious right now? It's almost midnight. We're both tired from the fifteen-hour train ride from Barcelona—I knew we should have flown.

"Then why is this happening *again*?" The emphasis she puts on again makes my eyes roll to the back of my head. "I trusted you to book all the logistics."

"Do you want to see the booking confirmation?"

I flash her my phone. The confirmation email already pulled up before we even checked in. Two beds, city view. In bold, right at the top. I booked the same type of room in every city we are traveling to.

Natalie huffs, rolling her eyes, and turns away from the counter.

The lovely, older woman working the concierge desk has already apologized proficiently after informing us they only have one king bed and city view room available. If we wanted two beds, we would have to substitute the city view for a street view. I was about to agree to that offer when she told me it was all cars and garbage on that street. I opted for the king bed and a better view. We could share a bed. We have several times in our friendship. Plus, I don't need another Natalie episode when she wakes in the morning to the site of garbage.

"Natalie, did you hear me? Is that okay with you?" I try to wrangle a final agreement from her before I take the keys from the concierge.

"Whatever. I'm tired." She's on her phone trying to connect to Wi-Fi as she spins on her heels and trudges toward the stairs. "Let's just go to the room."

I turn back toward the concierge. "I'm sorry," I quietly say to her. Dropping my shoulders, I remove the keys from her hands. Rolling my suitcase behind me, I follow Natalie up the stairs.

Natalie doesn't speak to me as we unpack our bags and prepare for bed. Brushing past each other in the bathroom. An annoyed glare when we both reach for the last hanger in the wardrobe. The silent treatment is extremely childish, but I'm used to it.

After what happened in Rome, I should have triple-checked and reconfirmed all of our hotels. Barcelona, we were in the clear, but I can guarantee that if it happens again after tonight, I might not make it back alive from this trip.

Even though I booked the correct accommodations—these are mistakes I wouldn't make—the hotels are changing our reservations. It's still my fault. I know this is letting her down.

And I hate letting Natalie down.

I hate letting anyone down.

Nat releases a dramatic sigh as she climbs into bed. My trusted telltale code for 'I'm disappointed in you.' She's had it since we were ten.

Kicking her feet at the covers, she wiggles her way into the sheets and pulls them up to her chin—only a mess of blonde curls sticking out on the pillows.

"I'm sorry," I say to her as I climb into bed on the other side and turn off the glass lamp on the bedside table.

She doesn't respond verbally. She rolls onto her side, away from me.

The disappointment in myself outweighs the tiredness I feel at the moment. I lay there in the dark, listening to the sounds of Natalie already fast asleep. Question after question consumes my thoughts. One after another, keeping me up.

How can I make this up to her?

Why do I always disappoint people?

How can I make sure this doesn't happen again?

We have four weeks left in our eight-week Europe trip. Besides the extremely minor, easily fixable one-bed situations, there haven't been any other hiccups.

It's probably been the best four weeks of my life. Hers too.

I was initially hesitant when Natalie approached me with the idea of spending the summer in Europe after we graduate from college—two months, no one else. It confused me why I was hesitant. Europe with your best friend is practically every girl's wildest Pinterest board dream.

Natalie proclaimed it as our last hurrah before we officially had to become adults.

As she laid out her idea, a.k.a. the Pinterest board dream, it all sounded ridiculously irresponsible. We needed to accomplish too much before we high-tailed ourselves out of our small Midwestern town in Indiana to Chicago. But to Natalie, all of this was ridiculously fun.

And here we are.

But that's how our friendship has always been. Natalie, the cool, confident, carefree spirit—no worries, no problems. And me? The opposite.

Growing up, we were always sunshine and a storm cloud.

Natalie Thomas and I met fifteen years ago when we were seven. Her family moved in four houses down from ours in the cul-de-sac. I had lived on Wellington Court my entire life. Growing up, our section of the neighborhood didn't have any other girls. I either had to play with the boys, which they hated, or keep to my books and Barbies. I wasn't thrilled when my parents told me someone moved into the old Peterson's house. It was fairly easy to assume it would be another family of boys.

Imagine the expression on my face when my parents dragged me to introduce myself. The teal blue front door opened to a blonde little girl smiling directly at me. Squeezed against her chest was a

Barbie—the same one I had been playing with before we walked over.

My eyes were big, but my toothless smile was bigger.

"Hi! I'm Natalie! This is Lilly, my Barbie." Those were Natalie's first words to me ever.

She unclasped one of her hands on the Barbie and waved. Her parents were walking toward the front door to greet us.

"I'm Emerson," I shyly replied with an encouraging nudge from my mom. I kept flicking my eyes from her to the ground to my parents. I didn't want my excitement to come off too strong and scare her away. I came to learn that nothing could scare Natalie. She was—is fearless.

"Can I call you Emme? I like Emme better." Natalie replied with a big toothless grin. She was missing both of her front teeth. Informing us that she had lost them last week, and that's how she got her Barbie. Her tooth fairy was awesome.

We've been inseparable since.

She's the best friend turned sister that I never had.

When I was thirteen, I asked my parents why I had no siblings. They told me they knew my life needed a place for Natalie. They were right about that, but even then, my intuition didn't believe that was their real reason. That same month, my dad left my mom and me. . . but that's another story for another day.

It didn't take Natalie long to convince me to go on this trip, and it never takes her long to convince me of her ideas. I need to see her happy.

I just needed to confirm the logistics. *Ironic*.

I let out a soft huff in the bed, reflecting on the memory.

That was March. Three months later, here we are. College graduates and already halfway through our trip.

***

My alarm goes off at seven.

Waking up this morning, I was reminded why I booked two beds at all of our hotels. Natalie is the worst sleeper. She tosses and turns all night, losing complete control of her body movements, and doesn't know how to stay on her side of the bed.

I'm on the edge of the king bed with a sore back. In her conquest of the bed, she kicked me square in the back.

I try to roll over but am chained to my spot by one of her legs draped over mine, the full weight of her lower body holding me there. Natalie's torso, though, is twisted the other way.

As I take in her form, a silent laugh escapes my mouth. How is that comfortable? Another laugh, not silent this time, escapes. I hope this isn't how she *sleeps* when she has a non-platonic sleepover.

I try to get out of bed without waking Natalie.

Gently and as quietly as possible, I grab her ankle to push her leg off me. Successfully, I give myself space to get out of bed without waking her. Flinging my legs over the side, I slide my feet into the soft hotel slippers. Three sizes too big, but they might be my favorite part about hotels abroad—slippers that are to die for. Turning off my alarm, I stand up and head to the bathroom.

"Good morning, Lisbon!" a sleepy Natalie shouts.

In the bathroom mirror's reflection, I can see both of her arms stretched out above her head, making a giant V. I ignore her, closing the door until it's only opened a slim crack so we can talk.

"Are we still going to Sintra today?" Natalie yells.

"Inside voice Nat. People are sleeping," I try to remind her.

"That's not my problem. They should wake up then." She does her witch laugh.

"The tour leaves at ten," I tell her.

"What time is it now?" she asks.

I flip my phone over on the white marble counter, pressing the side button.

"It's only seven. We need to leave in two hours to arrive at the pickup location on time."

"Emme," she groans. "It's summer. We are on vacation. We are in Europe! Why are you up this early?" Miss overdramatic in full effect this morning.

"You know I can't sleep past seven, ever."

"You would if you'd—"

"Don't even finish that statement, Nat," I cut her off.

Natalie's laughing from the bed. Her contagious laugh carries into the bathroom, and I join in. "Whateverrrr. I'm going back to sleep. Beauty calls for it."

When I exit the bathroom, she's cocooned once again in the bed. This time, the covers are pulled all the way over her head, and pillows, including mine, surround her. She fortified herself in the middle of the bed. Beauty sleep must be protected.

This is my favorite part of the day.

Indeed, my body can't sleep past seven. But I also don't let it sleep past seven.

I love mornings. I love the peacefulness and opportunity to seize the day before the world awakens. The slowness calms my mind.

I also love traveling and spending time with Natalie, but being with her or anyone else twenty-four-seven can be daunting. After our first week, I learned that if I booked a tour late enough in the morning, I could have a couple of hours to myself, doing whatever I wanted while Natalie slept.

Most of the time, I just walk around the city. Find a café. Read by a park or the water. Take photos of the scenery or architecture. Never anything fancy or riveting, but enough to keep my sanity.

Slipping out of my pajamas, I pull out a hunter-green linen dress to put on. I pair the dress with my usual pair of chunky, black Converse. Standing in front of the full-length mirror, I check myself out, using my hands to flatten out the few wrinkles in the linen.

The sun has tanned my skin slightly, enhancing my few freckles and giving me a couple of new highlights in my hair—the lighter brown contrasts with my dark chocolate-colored hair. My fingers twirl the end of one of the braids I slept in. I take my hair out of its braids. Naturally, it's thick and wavy, making it, at times, uncontrollable. I use my fingers as a brush, combing my hair and giving one final peek in the mirror.

There's this urge to look. . . presentable this morning, and I have no clue why.

4

EMERSON

Six Summers Ago

I'm panting after walking around Lisbon for the past forty-five minutes. The triple digits of miles we've already put in thus far aren't helping my legs on the hills that make up the city. For the first time, my legs burn. I figured that all the walking and time spent on the StairMaster this semester would have prepared me, but I was unfortunately wrong. And out of all the unsolicited advice people gave us for the trip, not one single person ever mentioned how hilly Portugal is.

I need a break and a coffee.

I reach the top of an incline on my way back to the hotel, remembering that there was a cute café close to where we were staying.

It wasn't directly at the top, I think. I swear it was up here. Maybe it's another block or two? I'm not positive, or good with directions, but I do know I have to head in this direction no matter what.

Across the street, I finally catch a glimpse of it. I sigh with relief.

Outside, there are six metal, small patio tables for two along the slant of the cobblestone road. In between the tables are off-white umbrellas that complement the pale pink building and painted tiles behind it, creating shade for the people sitting at the tables. It's early, but without a cloud in the sky and the torrid heat wave, they are needed.

The table furthest to my right is an older couple. The gentleman's attention is focused on his wife. Her skin is dark and wrinkled from age, and she's squinting at the paper she reads aloud to him. With her nose in the paper, she fails to notice that he isn't listening. He's gazing at her with a smile, ear to giant ear, looking utterly captivated by her marvel.

I watch them for a few moments, making up a story about them in my head. One where love is more than enough and can span decades. Their type of love, if that's what it is, is one you can't decipher if it's fifty years old or brand new. His countenance, though, tells you a million stories and ways he loves her.

Too bad love is a joke. Or at least it is for me.

I release the air I was holding in.

Discreetly, I take a photo of the couple on my Canon. Dropping the camera back into my bag, I hurry across the street and head into the shop.

At the front, I order a black coffee to-go.

"An American who doesn't want an iced coffee?" She, too, must not be from here. There is no hint of a Portuguese accent, but her Boston one sticks out. "Impressive." The barista eyes me as if I'm an anomaly.

"It could be a hundred degrees out—" as it is supposed to be today. "But I will always want a hot, black coffee." I shrug casually, trying to pretend that I'm cool or something.

"My girl. Coffee is individually brewed. It'll be five to ten minutes."

I pay for the coffee before finding a seat at a table near the front. Pulling out my book, I set it on the table before me.

I haven't had much time to read between school, work, and life this year. I brought four books with me for the trip. All of them have been sitting on my to-be-read shelf for too long, and I plan to finally read them this trip.

But I'm distracted.

The coffee shop is alive inside—a whole world of its own. It is vibrant and full of energy, bouncing from one patron to the next. I don't close my book but use it as a facade as I relax into the chair and allow myself to absorb everything around me.

Maybe I won't need this coffee, and this place will be my caffeine injection.

My eyes tour the shop. They make their rounds of the people, the vintage decor, and a hand-painted mural before they are met with a pair of blue-gray eyes. Eyes that remind me of the ocean before sunrise. The blue is there, calm, eager to reflect the sun that is about to cross the horizon. You see one color at one second before it fades or brightens to another. His eyes work precisely that way. Piercing me, so bright, but I can't look away.

I take it back. Those eyes are like a buzz to the system.

Zooming out my gaze from its hyperfixation on his eyes, I take in the most attractive male I have ever seen. His short brown hair is unkempt but tamed. Long enough that you'd be able to run your hands through it, but short enough that it's still professional. A cut jawline with a dusting of facial hair. His shoulders are broad, and there is little left to the imagination of the muscles that must be taut underneath his white button-down shirt.

I try to stop myself from memorizing all of him, capturing mental photos, when he catches me gawking.

The left side of his mouth lifts into a smug smile, making me fully aware that he knows exactly how attractive he is.

And his smile. Damn.

I bet I'm not the first girl this morning that he has found staring at him. . . and I won't be the last.

He doesn't break my stare. Something about him and the heat of his gaze causes a coating of sweat to appear on the back of my neck.

With impeccable grace, not breaking eye contact, he lifts his mug to his lips.

My curiosity takes over, the imagination gate wide open. I wonder what it would be like to be that cup. His lips are on me instead—the ones that make up a smile reserved for God alone. His lips are full for a male and a delicious shade of pink-red.

I blink.

Our locked eye contact breaks as I hear the barista call out my order loudly as if she'd already called it. "Black coffee to-go for the American."

I swiftly stand up, push the chair back I've been sitting in, grab my book, and walk up to the counter to grab my coffee.

Turning back around, I find his eyes are still on me.

He didn't stop watching me.

I glance down at my outfit, checking to make sure my underwear isn't showing or that I didn't step in dog poop.

Nothing. Everything is in place.

"Thank you." I smile at the barista over my shoulder before leaving.

With my arm outstretched, I open the heavy wooden door to leave and glance back at the place. I don't need to search to know exactly where he is. Like a compass finding north, there he is. He's still watching me. My face doesn't falter from its indomitable position.

Turning my head back toward the exit, I push it the rest of the way open and walk out.

My body is buzzing. Fueled by the coffee I'm sipping, that place, and the thought of him, the remainder of the walk back to the hotel feels quick.

"Where have you been?" Natalie is frantic. She's rushing around the room, getting ready, throwing clothes out of the wardrobe, and trying to figure out what to wear.

"On a walk. I wanted a coffee."

"And you didn't think to bring me back one?"

"Here." I hand her the cup even though I know she hates black coffee. "You should wear what you have on. It's nice."

She takes one sip. "Blah."

Natalie hands the to-go cup back to me.

"I thought something happened to you or that you were going to miss our day trip!" she huffs while lacing up her shoes, grabbing her purse from the table, and adding lip gloss and her phone to its contents.

"Yeah, you appear concerned. Almost as if you would have gone without me."

"I wasn't going to have both of us miss it. Whatever, you're here now. Are you ready?"

5

LIAM

Now

I watch Emerson and Brandon as they leave. His arm around her as they walk down the street. She tenses up when his hand settles on her shoulder, a subtle jump that spills her coffee.

Through the windows at the front of the shop, I see her peering back at me. Over her shoulder, her brown hair covers part of her face, but I can tell her eyes are searching for mine.

I find them.

She doesn't smile. She stares at me with a haunting expression, her eyes singing the sad song that has become us.

Her gaze leaves mine and turns back to his. She nods to whatever he's saying, and I watch as their image fades into the street.

Have you ever had a moment in your life that you fixate on only to realize that it's a fantasy that won't come true?

Seeing Emerson again is mine.

Emerson Clarke is every fantasy of mine. Ever since I saw her six years ago, I knew that I wanted her. Instant attraction and crossed paths, a pull to her as if she was the moon and I was a tide. Pushing and pulling me how she needed until we lost all sense of gravity.

She's the one person who holds a part of my heart and doesn't even know it. All those summers ago, I tied a piece of me to her, hoping it would connect us forever.

It did, but not in the way I wanted or ever imagined.

Thinking about her doesn't hurt how it used to. The sting of us hurting each other has scabbed over, healing into a scar. One I wear proudly across my chest.

I grab my coffee off the counter and leave. I'm supposed to be meeting Natalie, my—well, I don't know exactly what she is to me. Friend? Girlfriend? FWB? We never labeled it.

I haven't defined anything since Emerson. Haven't exactly been attracted to anyone in that capacity since her, except for maybe Natalie.

We met last summer, coincidentally the week before I came to Chicago. It was great having someone to show me around the city. She and I fell into an easy friendship and routine while I have been living between here and London.

She's the first person I could see the slimmest potential future with since Emerson.

I pull out my phone out of my back pocket and text her.

Meet me at my place instead.

Nat: Everything okay?

Yeah

Nat: See you soon!

I share a condo with Callum here. Typically, we aren't here simultaneously unless there are full team meetings or we are meeting with a potential acquisition. Four-bedroom, four-bathroom, two-story condo in River North. Modern black kitchen with an open concept in the dining and living rooms. The place overlooks Lake Michigan with floor-to-ceiling windows on both floors. The bedrooms are upstairs. Callum and I each claimed one, turning one of the extra rooms into a dual office and the other into a guest bedroom.

Sitting at my desk in our office, I can't shake the sight of Emerson out of my head. I try blinking, closing my eyes to wash away the image of her, but closing my eyes is even worse. It's there that I see her even more vividly.

Her chocolate brown hair is longer than I remember, cascading in waves down her back.

Her eyes—my favorite eyes in the world. With the looming summer thunderstorm, her eyes were a sharp-cut piece of Jade. Her eyes always favored storms. The grayness of the sky enhances them, brightening them as if they were lights beckoning you to them—my personal version of the light at the end of Daisy's dock in *The Great Gatsby*.

Anytime there's a storm, and in London, the odds are high, I think about her eyes. I wonder who they behold. Is there another person in her life? Do they make her happy? Do they treat her right? Do they love her?

I suppose that's the one good thing that can come from seeing her again.

There is someone else, and I have to infer yes to all the other questions because she's engaged. *Emerson's engaged.*

I should be happy for her, but I'm not. I know I told her I was, but that was a lie. How are you supposed to be happy when you always thought it would be you at the end of the aisle she walks to?

Never in my fantasies was there ever someone else.

I hear the front door close shut.

"Liam?" Nat calls out from down the stairs. "I'm here."

"Coming." I press send on the email I've been staring at since I got home and head downstairs to meet her.

She's quite ravishing in a purple sundress, bronze skin, and blonde curls tied back.

I round the stairs and walk over to her.

"Is everything okay?" she asks again. Her gentle eyes wander over my face, trying to catch a glimpse of whatever is happening within me.

"Now it is."

I lean in and kiss her.

6

EMERSON

Now

Today sucked. Laura kicked it off beautifully with a reminder that we have one day to decide on a venue, and everything else decided to follow suit. Dropping my lunch, stepping in gum, and missing my workout. Ending the day with an engagement shoot should make it better, but it doesn't.

They never do.

I don't know why I torture myself by being a wedding photographer as a side gig.

My last fling got one thing right, kind of, when he called it with me. He told me that I don't know what love is or how to love. I'm slightly, like 63 percent impossible of love. I should honestly come with my own set of fine print and an asterisk next to the word love. Then, anyone who gets to know me can go to the bottom of the page and understand what they can expect from me.

I love a lot of things.

I love books. I love Chicago. I love my friends. I love black coffee. I love biking to work. I love meal delivery services. I love being behind the camera!

I understand love and its existence outside of it being romantically toward another person. That unconditional bullshit is fake. It's a construct to make companies, i.e. Hallmark, money, fooling people, as in Laura, into overpaying for something that inevitably ends in misery. It's made up to be all romance novelesque. Sure, those have happy-ever-afters most of the time, but there's always someone getting heartbroken in the process, and I don't want that to be me *again*.

This sounds terrible, being engaged and all, but in my own strange way, I have a form of love for Brandon.

Scrolling through the photos I captured in the past hour, I glance up at the couple.

"Blake, these are stunning. Seriously! You picked the perfect location for this." I smile at my coworker, Blake, who is standing a few feet in front of me.

Blake giggles. Not in a cute little girl way, but in a light, airy laugh that warms the cool evening air.

"I've been dreaming of doing my engagement photos here since I was seven, coming into the city. Luckily, Ben—" She glances at him. "Thought the location was perfect *too*," Blake sarcastically says the last part. She squeezes Ben's bicep playfully.

"Yeah, luckily, Ben thought the location was perfect." He speaks in the third person. His laugh is a sign that says, 'I didn't get an opinion on where my engagement shoot would be. . . or what to wear.'

Blake lovingly smiles at him.

Four months ago, Blake Murray began working at Nelson and Moore, a full-access marketing agency. She coordinates the photo and video shoots needed for campaigns.

She came rushing into my office this morning, worrying and acting as if the end of the world was happening. I freaked out, thinking something was falling through with one of our products or shoots. No, it was the end of her world because her photographer bailed on them tonight and for their wedding. She begged me to step in—on her knees, begging me. Blake even offered to throw in an extra $2,500 since it was last minute.

Even though I was at my capacity for the year, I couldn't fathom her without one. I said yes.

Wrapping up, the three of us walk to the park entrance while the sun is in its final moments of setting over the city. I take my equipment bag off my back and begin putting away my camera.

"How long will it take to get the gallery back?" Blake asks.

"The full gallery usually takes about two weeks. . . unless Margot throws any extra work my way; then it'll be about three or four." She appears slightly disappointed by that. "But I can send over a sneak peek of ten shots by the end of the weekend?"

"We'd love that. Thank you," Ben jumps in.

"I'll handle Margot. Let her know about your priorities." She fake cracks her knuckles as if she's ready to throw a punch.

Ben and I laugh at her.

"I don't think Margot will see your wedding as my priority."

"You barely see your own wedding as a priority."

"Blake." Ben gives her a stern look.

"I mean, if she isn't prioritizing her own, she could prioritize ours." Ben sighs next to her. She turns to face him. "Honey, I'm kidding!" She isn't. "Sort of. I just—I can't wait to marry you, and now I'm excited for the pictures, and it's getting real."

He kisses her nose softly. "I know. I can't wait to marry you, too."

"Alright, love birds. If that's it, I've got a train to catch home."

"Emme, the first weekend in November works for you, right?"

Laura would cringe knowing they are getting married in November. She would cringe at almost every part of their wedding, including me being their photographer. We can't dare to have someone who is only part-time.

"Mhmm. I already checked, and I'm not booked for that weekend. Let me know if you want a second shooter or not."

She glances at Ben to get his opinion. He shakes his head.

"I think we are good unless you need one. Up to you! I'll send over the details again via email, and can sign a contract or whatever if you need."

Watching Blake and Ben interact tonight was different from other clients. Typically, I can put blinders on and focus on the task, but I know them and am a living participant in their love story. It makes me think about my own from all those years ago and if this would have been us had that summer never happened.

I don't think I'll ever know.

"Oh! Before I forget, how should I pay you? I didn't ask earlier," Blake says.

"I'll-" I stutter, my mind catching on to the reminders of him.

I wish I never met her.

Liam's words from that summer ring in my ears. Louder and more frequent since I saw him a couple of days ago.

I didn't believe the words he said. I didn't want to. He was hurt, my fault, but then he weaponized it to hurt me back. I try to bring myself back to the present moment, standing in front of Blake and Ben, but instead, I'm standing in his place. Then, in the restaurant. Then, on the street while he cries out my name. I think a part of me is always there, straddling reality and the past. Gravity tries to pull me toward the present, but how can it be when a piece of me, maybe the one that matters the most, is always with him?

"Send the contract when I get home. There will be a link in it for payment. If you have any issues with HoneyPot, text me," I finally say.

"Thank you, Emme. We greatly appreciate you stepping in," Blake says.

"You're welcome."

"Ready, love?" she asks Ben. He hooks his arm around her shoulder and leads her toward their car.

Zipping up my gear pack, I watch them. An aching sense of longing chills my veins.

How did they figure it out? Why aren't they screwed up?

During their shoot, the way they looked at each other was magical. Each kiss, little peeks when the other didn't see, and handhold was as if you ripped it right out of a fairytale. Even though I was there, they acted as if they were the only ones that existed at that moment—and for each other. It reminded me of the couple at the café in Lisbon. Somehow, I know in forty years, that will be them. Ben won't ever stop looking at Blake as he did today. And her the same.

The excitement in my eyes dries out as I think again about how they figured out love. I'm almost twenty-nine and—well, I'm engaged to someone I don't think I've ever loved as I should.

As they continue down the path to the parking lot, Ben is now holding her hand. Twirling her around as they walk. Quickly, I assemble my camera and take a few more shots of them. Zoomed in, blurry movement, candid. The exact type of photo I know will have Blake squealing.

***

I missed the train home and didn't want to wait for the next one. From the back seat of the Uber, I texted Natalie.

> Miss you. Catch up on Love Island with you soon?

She didn't reply. She's on another brand trip.

Natalie was one of the lucky ones who started posting content early. Before blogs were even popular and you had to use those built-in Instagram filters. Her favorites were Sierra and Ludwig.

Two years after we moved to Chicago, she dropped out of law school to be a full-time influencer. At the time, that word, or job, I guess, wasn't even a thing, but now she's become a household name.

Even with the popularity she's gained, I love that her brand is still the same. She's still the same Natalie I met when I was seven. However, now she's also the person you go to for all things travel and fashion. Her 875k followers can attest to that.

It's almost midnight, and sleep hasn't found me yet. I tried reading a book, but my mind couldn't focus on anything other than Liam.

My phone buzzes, and for a split second I hope it is him. It's not.

Natalie: I'm back on Tuesday.

Natalie: Come over on Wednesday?

KK, see you then.

7

EMERSON

Six Summers Ago

Standing in the Leonardo di Vinci International Airport baggage claim, Natalie turned to me. "Promise me that this is our summer."

"Of course," I told her.

"No. *Our summer*. No parents. No rules. No boundaries." She dug through her purse and pulled out a crumpled-up piece of notebook paper. "I created one of these for each of us last week. A bucket list—"

"You mean our itinerary?" I cut in.

She scrunched her nose and shook her head. "No. This is a girl's bucket list! Like the ultimate best friend list? Things we should do while we are here."

Natalie passed me the list. My eyes went expressive reading it.

"Boys?" She shrugged. "You're joking."

She stared into my eyes, grabbing onto the top of my shoulders. "I am completely serious. See this face."

I laugh at her. She's trying her hardest to be serious, but Natalie's never been one for serious faces or seriousness. It's as if her face won't let her express anything but a smile.

She's always been little Miss Sunshine. From head to toe, she glows. Light blonde hair that's mere inches from her butt and curls for days. Legs up to her brown eyes. Golden skin, and now that it's summer and we've spent our days outside? Game over for the rest of us. She's a walking European goddess.

She is a magnet for eyes. Naturally, everyone's eyes and bodies gravitate toward her. It happened in high school, and college was no different. She pretends that she doesn't recognize how beautiful she is, but seeing as I'm her best friend and know her better, she knows. She enjoys it. She weaponizes it into a currency for her benefit.

It's easy to fall for her. No one is immune to her.

Me, on the other hand? You'd be lucky to win a smile from me.

It's one of the reasons I enjoy our friendship. We are complete opposites, and it can be quite a puzzle when trying to understand us, but we work.

Natalie's made good on her bucket list for us; honestly, it's impressive.

I have—*not*.

Natalie tells me I need to loosen up and that my standards are too high. I don't disagree. But what's wrong with having high standards? After my dad walked out on my mom (and me), I got scared that I wouldn't be enough. I wasn't enough to keep them together; how would I be enough to keep any relationship together? Natalie is an outlier.

Years. It took years for my parents to become amicable with each other. They had split custody of me, which my mother's lawyer had to fight for. Claiming a parent should never abandon their kid when my dad was willing to give me up with the marriage. Those years of being required to visit on weekends and holidays were a battle. I wasn't truly welcomed in either home. Like a broken record, I thought I was the scratch. Maybe if I had been a better daughter, they would have loved me enough, and that wouldn't be how I spent the rest of my life growing up.

It broke something in me—the idea of love. My parents instilled in me that it was fake and non-existent. This preconceived notion flowed into my other relationships. I'd let myself get close to people, try to be everything they'd want, and when things got close enough that someone might love me or me them, I'd mess it up.

Actually, I don't think it's high standards at all. I think it's childhood trauma.

I'm drawn out of the memories when Natalie asks me what type of wine I'd prefer. I point to the glass on the menu.

"Tomaremos uma taça verde e uma taça de rosa," Natalie orders in her best extremely broken and over-enunciated Portuguese.

Natalie also thought we should try to learn the language in *every* country we travel to this summer. It's not a bad idea; it's a great idea. We downloaded Babble. On the flight to Rome, we spent hours of air time trying to pick up the basics. Doing the same on each train or plane ride between places. We lost ourselves to giggle fits over how badly we pronounced words. As much as I'd love to share our accomplishment in becoming bilingual, we are rather unfortunately unsuccessful unless you consider saying 'more wine' and 'where is the bathroom' a success.

We arrived back in Lisbon from our tour to Sintra and Cascais. Before going to the hotel to change for the night, we stopped for drinks at the wine bar down the street. It's quaint. The walls covered floor to ceiling in bottles. Dim lights and wooden family-style tables line the middle of the place, and there are a few employees who I think might own the place.

"Obrigado," Natalie says.

"We'd also like a charcuterie plate. Any combination works," I quickly add before the waiter walks away. "What? I'm starving. We didn't eat anything while we were out, and our liquid diet isn't cutting it for me today."

"Yeah, same. My head would be as light as this rose if I didn't eat."

She picks up her wine glass that was quickly delivered.

"To being best friends forever. Salude."

I playfully roll my eyes at her, smiling. She's too cheesy, but I love that about her.

"Salude." We clink glasses and drink. "How are you feeling about the move?"

"Better than I feel about law school." Natalie drops her shoulders. "Me? A lawyer?"

Most people think Natalie is stupid—a stunning, bimbo blonde. While she might not be street smart and a girly girl to her core, she's wicked intelligent. She starts law school at the end of August after being accepted into Northwestern's law school on early admittance. She won't admit that she's nervous, but she's going to kick ass. I know it.

"Do you remember setting up a courtroom in my basement? We'd use Barbies and whatever dolls we could find as the jury?"

"How could I forget? I'd make you take the stand and pretend to ask you questions."

"You were good at it, too. Nine years old and already commanding a courtroom. I used to think you'd research techniques or watch *Law and Order* secretly after your parents went to bed."

I take another drink of my wine.

"I think I'm just good at getting people to do what I want." Natalie pretends to sweep something off her shoulder.

I cough-laugh on my wine. "True."

She nods in agreement. Picking up her phone, she tosses it at me, then picks up her half-drunk wine glass.

"Snap a picture of me? For my blog."

I take the picture and a few extra candid photos which she loves.

"Here." I hand her phone back to her. "I think you were destined to be a lawyer, Nat, and you will thrive at law school."

She smiles up at me, the compliment reflecting off her. "Thanks, Emme."

We didn't make it back to the hotel that night to change for dinner. Or dinner.

We spent the rest of the evening at that wine bar, talking about how life will be when we return home and dreaming up our next chapter together in Chicago. We move three weeks after we return. Natalie in law school, and I'll be a Creative Assistant at a marketing agency. We've already lined up a cute two-bedroom apartment in the Loop. It's closer to my job than campus, but Natalie doesn't mind.

Those hours sitting there together felt as if we were teens again—fifteen and inspo boarding about our lives right now. It's hard to believe we are only months away from making it all a reality.

I'm proud of us for reaching this point as individuals and as best friends.

8

LIAM

Now

I rub my hands over my brow, letting out a frustrated sigh.

"No, that's not right," I say through gritted teeth.

Everything with our Chicago expansion has been great, perfect even. Callum and I spent the last year building out our office, hiring, and laying the groundwork here. In addition to buying, redoing, and opening a hotel. As expected, we've encountered a few road bumps, including the difference between British and American work culture, but we've been flexible and pivoted as needed.

"Mr. Hayes, we are only following the agreed upon marketing plan," a woman in her mid forties tells me.

We hired a local agency to run marketing for our hotel here in Chicago. With rounding out our first year in the States, we weren't ready to bring in a marketing department in-house or lean on ours in the London office. Our account manager, Savannah, has been out on maternity leave for the past month and a half, leaving us with this woman who has been anything but delightful to work with.

"It's bloody rubbish." My accent is thick with irritation. She watches my mouth, trying to read my lips, I assume.

"What he's trying to say is that the campaign doesn't fit the demographic we are going after," Ben Campbell, our Director of Operations, tells her.

"And what demographic is that?"

"Young, millennials, new adults. Think twenties to mid thirties. The type of people who travel and want their stay to be part of their Instagrammable moments."

"This?" I hold up the folder of images sitting on my desk. "Is not that. This looks like something our parents would stay at."

"Is that a bad thing?" she asks.

"No." I take a deep inhale because she is right. It's not bad, but it's not our intended customer. "It's not what we want."

"I think we may need to read into ending our contract." Ben nods at her, taking the blow of severing this relationship.

Her demeanor is somber and reflects disappointment. The work Savannah oversaw was pristine. Always on time and always exactly what we envisioned. I account for part of our instant success from the work Savannah has put in.

"Savannah will be disappointed to hear about this," she tells me pointedly.

"I'll speak with her directly. Maybe, if she's lucky, we will poach her to come work for us when she returns from leave. That would solve the problem of having to work with you."

I try to return the folder to her, but she swipes it away. "Keep it. Make sure to show it to whoever you hire next as an example of what not to do."

She turns on the balls of her feet and storms out of my office.

"Have a great day!" Ben calls after her. Always quite nice, that one.

I slump into my chair. Resting my elbows on the glass desk and bringing my hands to my face.

"That was unfortunate," I huff.

"Care to explain your rash anger and decision-making there?" Ben takes a seat in the chair on the opposite side of my desk.

"No."

"Callum won't be happy about this," Ben tacks on.

"And? His name isn't the company."

He rests his hands in his lap. "Alright, Liam. What's up?" he asks.

Emerson is what's wrong. I can't get her out of my mind, and the more I think about her, the angrier I get at her—and myself. I misled myself for a year after not seeing her that first month. I thought I was in the clear, that there were enough people in Chicago that I would never run into her, but seeing her has me completely undone.

"I have a lot on my plate and mind right now," I reply to Ben.

"Anything I can do to help? Or do you want to talk about it?"

"You do not need to be bored with my personal life. But I do have back-to-back out-of-office meetings this afternoon. Can you handle finding a new marketing agency? Compile a list of three to four options and email them to Callum and me by the end of the day. We don't have time to waste with the hotel opening in September."

"I can do you one better. My fiancé works for another agency here. They work primarily with beauty and clothing brands, but their work is ingenious. I'll call Blake and see if they are taking new clients."

"Great." I'm packing up my bag to head out. "I would prefer you to research other options still and we can review tomorrow morning at eight. Callum will need to video in. Have Marissa clear his schedule."

"Alright, boss," Ben replies.

9

EMERSON

Now

It's Monday, again. I've always enjoyed Monday—a new week, new opportunities, but today, I'm dreading it.

Friday night, Brandon and I got into a fight after I told him that I didn't want to get married at the Waldorf. He went on a tangent about how it'll upset his mom and that she has been working painstakingly on this wedding, and that I need to be a tad more respectful. I laughed out okay and hung up the phone.

We didn't see each other all weekend.

I ended up editing all of Blake's engagement shoot. Staying up all night on Saturday and then most of Sunday night, too.

This is what used to happen after I thought about Liam Hayes.

I'd find something to throw myself into. Distracting myself until I can climb out of the Liam-shaped hole in my life, trying to find a part of me that he didn't touch in some way, and back into reality.

It hasn't happened in almost a year, but this weekend, it was as if the hole became a canyon, and there was no way out.

I tell myself I shouldn't feel this way, that it's been three years. But also, it's *only* been three years. And is there even a time frame for when you are supposed to get over the only person you've ever been wildly in love with?

Reality hit this morning when the gear shift on my bike broke.

I called Brandon, but he was already at work.

And I was already running late for coffee with Chloe. There was no way I had time to drop it off at the shop.

I left my bike in my apartment's bike storage and sprinted to catch the brown line into the city.

Peering out the window as the train bumps along the track, I question why I haven't decided to move back downtown. I hate commuting.

Money isn't the problem. I make enough now, finally. After years of hard work, I'm finally a Senior Creative Director. Between that and the weddings I shoot, I can afford more than a shoebox—at least a size eleven one-bedroom in the Loop.

I simply love living in Lincoln Park. I love my old apartment with the exposed brick and high ceilings. I love the neighborhood—how I can walk to the farmers' market every Saturday, enjoy coffee at one of the six local coffee shops, all within three blocks of each other, and sit outside on my four-by-four metal patio, reading a book in the sun while people-watching. If I didn't love it the amount that I do, then I would have moved last year.

I get off the train at the station before the stop for my office. Two blocks east and a few extra minutes from my building is the Tipsy Bean, my favorite coffee shop.

Walking in, the aromas instantly fill my nose, making this Monday turn around. What completely revives it is the friendly face waving at me from the couch opposite the door.

"No bike this morning?" Chloe asks me.

I roll my eyes and catch her up to speed on the events of my morning.

People dream about being best friends with their coworkers. Chloe Henry was that dream for me. She no longer works at Nelson and Moore, but that didn't stop us from our Monday morning coffee dates—a routine that has been going almost five years strong.

Chloe was hired a year after me, and at the time, our desks were right next to each other, even though we were on different teams. She works in events. Our paths crossed for the launch of a new lip gloss for Second Chance Beauty. I was blown away by her ability to command an event from planning to execution. We became best friends shortly after. Once I introduced Natalie and Chloe to each other, the rest was history.

Chloe left the company after being recruited to work on the Natural Cosmetics event team as their Head of Events. Her role requires her to travel extensively domestically and internationally for launch parties and brand trips with influencers. Chloe planned Natalie's trip to Costa Rica last summer.

"When did you land?" I ask Chloe, passing her an iced oat milk latte with a splash of honey. I sit in the opposite corner of the couch, tucking a leg underneath me.

"Late. Took the red eye, so after midnight."

"How was Denver?" Chloe was visiting her boyfriend, Seth, this past weekend. They met during a previous work trip there.

"Ten out of ten. A peak weekend." She winks at me, taking a sip out of the metal straw.

I laughed at her dad joke even though it was terrible. But that's Chloe for you, black-cat personality laced with quick 'dad-wit.'

"Seth wanted to hike the Rocky Mountains. We spent all day Saturday there, and I swear my legs are still sore from the miles. I think he forgets that my daily walk to work isn't climbing mountains."

"You don't walk to work," I remind her.

"Right."

"I'm sure he made up for it later, though."

"A full. . . leg massage was required as payment. Did you get my picture of the pepperoni pizza I sent you?"

"Yes! I was practically drooling. Had to order pizza for dinner."

"Beau Jo's!" She uses her hand to do a chef's kiss. "I wasn't sure anything could be better than Lou's or Parlor, but this beats them both. They make in-house honey—it's gotta be because of that. I already told Seth he's required to figure out how to mail a pizza here. My life will never be the same after this pizza."

"Okay, Miss Dramatic," I tease her.

"Excuse me, but that title is reserved for Natalie and Natalie only." Chloe and I both giggle at the comparison.

"You met Seth's college friends, right?" The question comes out slightly more hesitant than I would have preferred. Chloe was nervous about meeting them leading up to the trip.

"Yeah. They were. . . they were great. A lot of fun. It's impressive that he's still close with that many of them. I barely have two friends left from college."

"And whose fault is that?"

Chloe rolls her eyes at me. "Whatever."

She dated one of her friend's boyfriends, whom she had a crush on since freshman year after they had broken up. He made the first move and asked her out. Chloe asked her friend if it was okay—girl code, ya know. The friend said she didn't care, but she did. Spread rumors about Chloe, calling her a cheater and other terrible names. It isolated her from the group.

"Anyway. I haven't asked Seth yet, but I'm itching to know if they like me. As much fun as they were, I'm nervous they didn't," Chloe gushes on with outlandish reasons why she fears they didn't.

"Chloe, stop! There is no reason for them not to love you. Seth does, right?"

"Yeahhhhh." She's quick to the 'I love you' trigger with people, but Seth even beat her.

"Then don't worry about them. Seth isn't a bad judge of character when it comes to the company he keeps, girlfriend included." I give her a reassuring smile. "When's the next time you'll see Seth?"

"Next month in San Diego," I remember now. "Meeting his parents." She pauses, swishes her head side to side like the thought in her head. "Do you think we are moving too fast? Everything feels. . . I don't know, feels. . . perfect." She appears embarrassed to say that out loud. "But—" That's why. Chloe releases a large sigh, her whole body molding into the couch. "I don't want to get my hopes up. I've never felt this way before. Remember how you were with that London guy? That's how it is with Seth. There is this undeniable attraction and connection. . . but what if it's only hyped up in my head?"

I remember all of it too well because those feelings aren't simply memories.

I imagine my friend feeling for someone the way I felt about him. It makes me happy thinking she's found someone, but it also makes me protective. If she knew the truth, would she say it was the same? How could she when, at one point, Liam and I were a supernova about to explode? Instead of creating our own galaxy, we collapsed into a black hole.

And now that he's back, all of those emotions have me like a dog. Searching for the bone that they buried in the backyard. Liam dug himself into me, and I can't remember where or how to get him out. It's there, a part of me forever now.

My heart squeezes. Eyes go soft.

I set my mug on the coffee table right before a small tremble ripples through my hands. Today would be the day I spill on my white blouse.

Chloe recognizes the expression on my face. Before I can respond, she cuts in. "Em. Oh, I'm so sorry. I didn't mean to bring him up."

"This isn't about me. I'm fine." *I'm not fine,* but now's not the time to monopolize the conversation. "Do you think it's going too fast?"

"I don't know." She plays with a string on her sleeveless blazer.

"You might want to figure that out. Before the parents, yeah?" I say it with personal experience and regret.

That's the first time that thought has crossed my mind. *Do I regret everything with Brandon?* It all happened much faster than I expected.

Chloe nods.

"The only people who get to determine whether it's too soon or too fast are the two of you. Love doesn't come with speed limit signs. The two of you set the speed. You are the drivers of your relationship together. Speed up, slow down—who cares?"

"Right. Yeah, right. I needed that reminder. It's easy to fall into the pressures of those around you and think you need to catch up or fall into their demands. I want to enjoy where we are at." Chloe squeezes my knee. The red in her cheeks dissolves back to the color of her blush, and she's back to herself. "I think we are going sixty-nine miles—"

I raise my hand to stop her from continuing. "No need to finish that comment."

She smirks and finishes off her latte.

10

EMERSON

Six Summers Ago

Natalie is unusually awake before me. Prior to waking up, I had heard her phone go off but assumed it was social media notifications, and she forgot to turn her volume off.

Her loud footsteps rushing around the hotel room woke me.

"Natalie, is everything okay?" I ask.

She's grabbing her suitcase out from under the bed when there's a loud thud.

"Hit my head on the bed. I'm fine!" She's rubbing the back of her head, hand tangled in her curls. "That was Mom. My grandma died."

I shoot up into a sitting position. Grabbing my phone off the charger, I see that I have missed calls from my mom and hers.

"I'm sorry, Nat."

"I'm booked on the noon flight out of Lisbon to Chicago. My mom is going to pick me up there this afternoon," she tells me.

"Do you want me to come with you? Do you need anything?"

"I would have booked two flights if I did." Her tone is snippy, catching me slightly off guard. "You are staying. Please finish out our trip for me."

Climbing out of bed, I walk over to where she is opening the wardrobe, wrapping my arms around her in a tight embrace.

We spend the next hour packing her bags together.

Throughout the morning, at breakfast and in the Uber on the way to the airport, I kept asking Natalie if she was positive that I should stay. Despite only meeting her grandma once, Natalie is my best friend, and I'll always be there for her. Natalie, annoyed, assured me that I was capable of staying without her and I shouldn't worry about being alone—I wasn't worried about that. She only requested that I send a postcard from the remaining destinations and live as she would.

With a final reassurance and a sad smile on her face, she closes the Uber trunk at the airport.

"Give your mom and dad a hug for me," I tell her, giving her another hug.

"I will." She squeezes me back. "Don't miss me too much."

***

I'm lying on a ledge in Miradouro das Portas do Sol. A park in Lisbon that is sandwiched by the city. If you look one way, you can see out over the city and into the ocean. The other direction is restaurants and shops. Beyond that is more of the city rolling up across the hills.

The sun is beating down on me, crisping my skin more than it already is. My hair is flowing out from under my head, slightly damp from sweating, nestled on my tote bag as a pillow. A book in my hands, the smell of the salty water and paper fills my nose as I read. Slowly, and some sentences twice because I'm distracted by the sounds around me. I can't help it. The tram bells ringing, coming to its next stop. Birds flying in the sky. People, lots of them, talking and laughing. I wouldn't call it eavesdropping when I tune into what they are saying because it's in a different language. I can see people passing by in my peripherals, some stopping to pull out their phones for pictures or sitting on the benches.

All of it slowly becomes white noise.

I read for, I don't know how long, easily two or three hours. It was long enough that the sun was dipping in the sky and no longer directly above me.

Sitting up enough to reach into my bag to check for news on Natalie's flight, my body tingles as if someone is watching me.

Turning my head to the right, there on a bench about ten feet away from me sits—no, is that the guy from yesterday? I squint my eyes, trying to get a better look. He has a book in his hands, but based on the orientation of his head, I suspect it's unread. Straightforward toward me, not down at the book.

I can't confirm if it's him, but the smile he swiftly flashes eerily resembles the one from the coffee shop.

Before I have a chance to stare any longer, he gets up. Tucking the book under his armpit, he pushes his sunglasses to the top of his head through a mess of dense brown hair.

It's him.

"Take a picture next time. It'll last longer." His voice is husky, a mellifluous ruggedness to the British accent.

"I could say the same to you," I retort.

He laughs. It's deep and involves his entire upper body. "Okay, States." Turning on the balls of his feet, he walks away.

Annoyed, I slam my book shut.

His gaze leaves a buzzing sensation that I can't shake.

I take off after him.

He's quick; after a few blocks, I've lost him in the crowd. I should turn around and leave, return to the hotel, and forget about him.

He didn't sound like he was from here, so what are the odds I'd ever see him again? None. Then why is it that after seeing him twice, I'm becoming obsessed with the way that he looks at me?

He has the type of eyes that should come with trigger warnings such as 'Don't get yourself involved, or you'll end up hurt'.

But when he stared at me yesterday and today—I determined that was what he was doing on the bench. It was in a way that no one had looked at me before.

Lost in the depths of the remnants of his stare, I run directly into a barrier separating the sidewalk and the street for cars to drive on.

That's going to leave a mark.

A hand reaches out to catch me before I slam into the bricks. It wraps around my forearm, and another comes to my back.

My eyes catch on the tan skin stretched across muscular hands. Can hands be muscular? I don't know if I've ever actually noticed or paid attention to hands before. The palm is soft and warm except for the area right below the fingers, which is rough. Small calluses scratch my skin, sending goosebumps up my arm.

"Do you work out your hands?" I ask aloud, with no filter on my brain or mouth and no care about who the hands belong to. *Shit, Emerson, that's embarrassing.*

"Flattered, but no," a husky voice says.

It's him.

I lift my head to meet his. "They're rather muscly."

"Some would say they're large."

"And hard."

My response sits there between us.

Realization of what I just said hits me. My cheeks heat, and I know they are turning an unfortunate shade of magenta, bypassing a flirtatious blush.

"That is how I am often described." He doesn't falter in his tone.

Oh my gosh, he is not helping here. I burst out laughing. I don't know if it's because I'm embarrassed at the interaction or that, from where I'm still positioned, my eyes easily find that part of him.

I don't mean to, but I can't help myself.

Why did I think it was an intelligent decision to chase after him?

"Are you okay?" He checks me out from head to toe.

"I am perfectly well." My tone is sharp and sour as I stand up.

"Sure about that?"

I roll my eyes at him.

"Positive." I try to take a step forward out of his touch, but it's impossible because of how many people are bustling past us. "Do they also describe you as a stalker?"

"Pretty sure you are the one who followed me."

"After I caught you staring at me for the second day in a row?" He tilts his head, raising his shoulders nonchalantly. "Is something wrong with the way I look?"

"That's a roundabout way of asking if I find you attractive."

"I don't care what you think about me."

"The answer would be yes."

I jolt backward. "Yes, something is wrong, or yes, you think I'm attractive?"

"Get dinner with me, and you can find out."

"I have plans," I lie.

"With me?" He grins. Damnit. I've been thinking about his. . . eyes, that I completely forgot about his smile.

"No." I shake my head.

"Why not?" He appears disappointed.

"I don't know you."

That's not exactly a good excuse, Emerson. Many people go out without knowing each other. That's the whole point of first dates. . . but this isn't a date, right?

"And I don't know you, States. But we could." I can't escape the fact that this is the second time he's called me that, but I can bury it.

I shift on my feet. Left to right.

"If you change your mind and decide you want to know me. Garbinus." He checks his watch. "Eight. I'll be there."

"I won't," I say and leave for my hotel, letting him watch me again.

11

EMERSON

Six Summers Ago

Following the directions on my phone, I'm walking to a bar that the waitress recommended. She said it was her favorite place in Lisbon to go at night. The walk is short, only about eleven minutes.

There's a short line outside the place. It's barely even ten, and the bar is packed. I'm barely able to walk through the door and to the bar without being pushed or having a drink spilled on me.

"What can I get for you, amorzinho?" the bartender asks me as I approach the bar after pushing through several people.

"Posso tomar uma taça de vinho," I reply in my best try at Portuguese. I give him a soft smile, hoping that helps.

He shoots me a surprising grin. "Que tipo você gostaria?" What type would I like? Huh, maybe I am better at this than I thought. *Go me!*

"Surprise me?" I reply in English this time. "Sorry, I don't speak much Portuguese."

"Aproveitar," he says. Reaching forward, I take the glass he returns with.

Taking a small sip, I'm surprised by the freshness of it. "It's good."

I set the glass on the bar, digging into my purse for euros. I hand over my money to the waiter, but he swats it away and winks.

Catching the confusion on my face, he flicks his head over his right shoulder, gesturing to my left.

I'm still confused. The bathrooms are in that direction. "Oh no. No, thank you!" In front of my chest, my hands wave no. I think I'm flattered by the offer, but kind of. . strange?

"No. No." He shakes his head, letting out an apologetic laugh. "He paid." The bartender points to someone.

"Oh," I say with recognition of my misunderstanding.

I turn my head slowly in the direction he pointed.

Are you shitting me?

There, over my shoulder, I catch a pair of blue-gray eyes, an irresistible trouble-making smile, and a raised glass.

Running into him again turns something in my gut. It's like a dusty, old light switch. The one you'd find in your grandparents' basement that has a chain that you pull. When it's not been used in a while, you have to tug on it a few times to get the light to turn on. His proximity is pulling on that chain.

What's in my gut, though? I'm not positive.

Embarrassment that I didn't show up for dinner? No.

The awareness that he's somehow here? No.

That I enjoy the way he looks at me and the way it makes my pulse surge? Maybe.

That something dormant in me is thawing? Also, maybe.

This is why I didn't show up for dinner. Whatever these reactions are, I don't want them.

I turn my head back to face the bartender.

"Thank you," I mouth. An anything but delighted smile plastered on my face.

Picking up the glass of wine, I ignore the mystery man and pull to him to find a place to sit.

Across the bar is an open table. I slide into the booth side, which gives me the perfect view for people watching.

My entertainment is quickly ruined when the chair is pulled out, intentionally loud. He doesn't need to try to get my attention; he's already captured it.

I stare straight ahead, not giving in to him, at the hand grasping the chair. They are strong, large, hard hands. I would know; they were on me earlier.

I swivel my head slowly, viewing the golden skin jutting from the cuffed sleeve. A slow perusal that moves to his shoulders, broad like his chest. His shirt is unbuttoned at the top, revealing no hair and only bare golden skin.

Then to his face.

His eyes darken when ours meet.

"Is saying thank you after someone buys you a drink not common in the States?" he asks me.

He finishes pulling out the chair and sits down. The table shakes under his touch as he pulls himself up against it, as close to it and me as possible.

I run my tongue over my top teeth, not breaking our stare.

"So you are stalking me," I say.

"You didn't show for dinner." He pretends to sound wounded.

"I told you I wouldn't."

"Your mistake."

I laugh. "I'll make sure not to make that one again."

He lets out a small but full-body laugh. I can see it reverberate through his shoulders and chest. Places I don't need to be watching and ideas I shouldn't be thinking about. My imagination is becoming without restraints for this man. Never in my twenty-two years has anyone consumed this many of my thoughts.

"Updating that mental picture you took earlier?" He smirks, as if his plan is working perfectly. "You're cheekier than I thought. I like it."

"And you're cocky."

"Ah. You noticed."

My cheeks heat the way my core does at the memory.

"How do you know I'm from the States?" I ask as a way to steer the conversation—and my brain—in a different direction.

"Thought I was stalking you? Perhaps that might be something I would know then." He's baiting me.

With my mouth in a line, I pinch my eyes as if I'm a cat figuring out its prey. He isn't prey, heavens no, but he could be—rather delicious prey, too.

"Right." I play along even though I deduce the actual answer, which is the café. I'm realizing we are alike; he is observant, too. "You ruined my afternoon. Are you planning on ruining my night, too?"

"States, let's get one thing straight. You'd know if I was ruining you—"

I can see where he is going, and that's not what I meant. Cutting him off, I lean slightly forward, clarifying, "I'm not sleeping with you."

"Wasn't assuming that." Yeah, right. "I'm Liam."

"And I'm leaving. Enjoy the table." I throw back the remainder of my wine. "Thanks for this."

I set the glass on the table and, with a flick, push the glass toward him. I get up and pass by him, close enough that our shoulders brush. Before I can get away, his arm reaches out and captures my elbow. My head jerks over my shoulder and down at his hand on me.

"I won't enjoy it unless I'm enjoying it with you." He looks up at me, his eyes hypnotizing. Despite the terrible pickup line, I get this strange feeling that he might be sincere. "One more drink and I promise to—"

"Leave me alone," I finish the statement for him.

"Wish that was possible," he mumbles to himself. "It's just a drink, States," Liam says with more oomph this time.

Our eyes are locked. A non-existent staring contest that neither of us wants to be the first to break. Everything in me wants to leave, shake off his touch, and walk out those doors. But everything in me also wants to sit back down.

Because I don't think it's just a drink.

"One more drink won't hurt you," I hear Natalie say in the back of my mind, like she's watching me on a secret camera. I know she wouldn't walk away, nor would she let me if she were here. She'd be living for all of this.

You promised her you would enjoy yourself. And what could go wrong with spending an hour with him?

"Fine. One drink."

He drops his hand from my arm, and I take three steps backward, sliding back into the booth side of the table.

"So—you got a name, States?"

"Emerson. I'm Emerson Clarke."

12

LIAM

Six Summers Ago

She didn't show for dinner.

I found myself quite disappointed in the fact. Not that I should have expected her to show. She warned me, but a guy can dream, right?

That's what she feels like—a dream.

I never thought I'd see her again in a city of three million people and tourists. Ever since yesterday, I haven't been able to get her out of my head.

But then I saw her today, again.

Hours ago, laying in the sun on a stone wall overlooking the city and ocean. Her head propped up on a bag, a book in her hands. I'd never seen someone look that serene and equally alluring at the same time.

The way her chocolate hair fell behind her, waves flowing out on the stone. Even from where I was sitting, I could tell she wasn't wearing any makeup, not that she needs it, anyway.

I sat on the bench, a novel in hand, reading her between sentences. A pestering itch to know her, to be close to her. She looked over at me, a hauntingly angelic smile on her face, and damn if that didn't do something to me. My veins singe at the memory of her smile.

Who smiles that big while reading? She does.

It fell away as she drew her mouth into a straight line and told me to take a picture.

If she only knew the amount of mental pictures I took. I'd be seeing her in all my favorite dreams now.

And maybe those dreams might come true tonight.

Her eyelids flutter. Emerson does her best not to show any other emotion except for leave-me-the-fuck-alone.

Whatever gloss she painted on tonight is reflecting in the light, drawing my eyes to her lips. Her tongue darts out of her mouth, wetting her lower lip. It makes them shimmer even more, and my blood rushes lower, turned on by everything that wicked tongue could do.

It doesn't take long for one drink to become three, then four. Each drink loosening her walls.

Emerson is like an iceberg; what you see isn't everything. What you should be afraid of is under the surface, just as the depths of her are more dangerous than this icy front she's putting on.

I don't know why... someday, I plan to ask, but tonight, I count myself lucky that she's even showing it to me.

A comfort between us settles in quickly, and I fret that with one wrong move, it will be redacted as quickly.

There isn't an arrogance to her like some beautiful women. Don't get me wrong—Emerson is a sass, but in a funny, protective, captivating way that makes me want more of it. Every time she talks, I'm captivated by what she says and how she says it. Her lips move with such precision that I wonder what they'd be like on me.

I watch Emerson intently. I can't take my eyes off her. Lost in a daydream of everything I want to do with her, but also simply lost in this moment with her.

I wonder if Emerson realizes how amazing she is.

In the time we've been talking, the bar has slowly transformed into more of a club. The center of the room has become a dance floor, lights are dimming, tables have all moved to the outskirts, and a DJ is now located in a corner booth.

"I think the two guys behind you are trying to get your attention," Emerson says, gesturing over my shoulder.

Behind me, George and Callum are on the dance floor with girls in their arms. George points at me. Or is he pointing at Emerson?

Definitely her. He raises his eyebrows toward the both of us and then turns his finger to beckon us to join them on the dance floor.

"Oh." I turn back to her. "Those are my friends. They want us to join them out there, but we don't have—"

Emerson cuts me off, surprising me with what she says, "Sounds fun. Let's go."

She stands up, leaving her drink on the table. Without asking, she takes my hand, pulling me to my feet and behind her as we make our way to Callum and George.

I interlock my fingers with hers, curious to see if they'd fit. Like a key in its lock, they do.

We're almost at the center of the dance floor when she stops. I bump into her. She turns to face me, placing her other hand on my chest.

"Warning. I am not a good dancer." She hesitantly chuckles.

Emerson meant it. She is quite terrible—no coordination, no control. But she left out that she doesn't care that she is bad.

From beside the guys, I watch her spin in a circle, tossing her hair over one shoulder, when her eyes lock with mine.

I don't know if the alcohol provides liquid courage or if this is always her, but the way she moves is even more magnetic, pulling me to her. I join her, mimicking her ridiculous dance moves.

George and Callum flash us caviling glances, but I don't care. Judgment is the last thing on my mind right now, from them or anyone in the place.

At this moment, nothing else matters but her. All I see is her. All I feel is her. All I want is her.

At this moment, there isn't anyone else here but us. All I see is us. All I feel is us. All I want is us.

I don't think I ever want this to end. And I don't know if my mind means tonight or whatever this bond I feel with her is.

I pull Emerson to me. Up against my body and wrap my arms around her. I rest my chin on top of her head. Pressing a soft kiss to the top of her head, the smell of coconut and macadamia nut fills my nose. It's warm and savory. Which I imagine she is. Emerson isn't a sweet girl, not someone I want to indulge in but savor forever. Leaning down so that my head is level with her ear. "Do you want to get out of here?" I ask her. Quiet enough that only she can hear me, but loud enough that my question doesn't get lost in the music.

"Liam—"

My stomach drops at how she says my name for the first time.

"You'd be much happier leaving with any other girl here," she says frankly. An invisible barrier rises between us. "I'm not that type of—"

"We don't need to sleep together," I blurt out.

"It's not that," she says.

"Then what is it?" I find her eyes and search them.

"It's that. . . the way you just looked at me."

"How am I looking at you?"

"Like you want to fall in love with me," Emerson says.

13

EMERSON

Now

"Can you tell me again about this new client?" I ask Blake. "No, never mind, just the project. I know Margot said it was a hotel brand."

Blake runs through the inquiry Margot briefly discussed with us this morning as we walk to lunch at The Cleopatra. The restaurant opened in February on the first floor of a boutique-style hotel opening in early fall.

The meeting was supposed to include an onboarding manager for new clients, but she was already booked for this afternoon. Margot asked if I could attend the initial meeting since I will manage the entire marketing plan and account.

Chicago is warm with blue skies. I didn't mind the excuse to get out of the office for a little or have lunch at The Cleopatra, a restaurant named after my favorite historical figure. I've been dying to try it since its grand opening, but reservations are hard to come by, and the wait is consistently two hours or more.

The restaurant features an extensive wine list and shareable plates. The tapas are from various cuisines, including two Egyptian foods, even though everyone forgets that Cleopatra wasn't Egyptian. Natalie went in March and said it was the best tapas she'd ever had.

"Did I tell you that Ben works for them? That's why they reached out to us," Blake informs me.

"Explains why we are branching out from consumer products."

"Trialing," Blake corrects me.

"Let's be real. Margot is probably jealous she didn't find the client herself. It is inevitable that we'd branch out."

"About time, though. I've always thought we were missing out by chaining ourselves to consumer goods." She sips on her iced matcha.

"That makes us experts in what we do," I challenge her.

"I suppose." She shrugs. "If I were to start my own company, I wouldn't specialize in one thing. How can you be the best at all of it if you don't work with all of it?"

"Are you thinking about leaving?" If she is, this is news to me. Blake appears happy and dedicated to anything that crosses her desk. I would never have suspected she would want to step out alone.

"Oh, no." She's hesitant. "Not at all." Blake cuts her head in my direction. Trying to quickly assess my level of buy-in before revealing more of her secrets to me. "But if I did, would you come with me?"

"I'm not sure." Yes, is what I want to tell her. I would risk it and go with her, I think. Maybe, finally, be behind the camera full-time instead of directing it.

"Don't tell anyone I said that or have the smallest glimmer of an idea. Please."

"What idea?" I wink. "Your secret is safe with me, I promise. Back to our current project. I am excited about it. The ideas are brilliant. This is the type of place I would stay at when I used to travel with. . ." I trail off.

Liam.

When I would travel with Liam during the summer.

"I know. The owner is brilliant. He's only been working in Chicago for about a year. Ben says that they're working to acquire three more properties. Another here and two others in New York."

The thought gears turn in my head.

"Hayes Hotels, right?"

"Yeah!"

"How long has Ben been working for them?" I ask suspiciously.

It could be a coincidence. It has to be. The only Hayes in the hotel industry I know is in London, not Chicago. But also said Hayes always wanted to expand outside of Europe. And said Hayes was in a coffee shop last week.

"He was their first employee. Well, technically, second. Callum was first."

It's not a coincidence, and it all clicks.

I stop walking. My feet stuck in their place. Blake is a few strides in front of me before she realizes. She stops and turns around to face me.

"Does he work for Liam Hayes?" I ask.

"Yeah! Do you know him?"

My face falls flat. All the oxygen gone from my lungs. I ignore her question.

"You said a *year*?"

"Yes. . ."

"This company has been here a year." I point to the ground. "In Chicago? A year?"

"Yes." Blake gives me a weird look. "Em, is everything okay?"

"I don't know if I can take this meeting." I swing my tote bag forward, one of the two straps resting on my forearm, pulling out the folder and my work iPad. I pass them to Blake. "Do you think you can take it?"

"Um, sure." Flustered, she takes the materials out of my hands. Fumbling with her matcha in one hand, she tries to tuck them into her too-small bag, with the top of the manilla folder and iPad sticking out. "Are you feeling okay?"

Knowing that he's been here for a year has me sick to my stomach.

"No. My breakfast isn't sitting well. I think I'm getting sick."

I take a deep breath, and the air fills my lungs, having the opposite effect.

Blake watches me with sympathy. She shifts on her feet uncomfortably.

"I've never taken a client meeting by myself before."

"Ben will be there, yeah?" I say between breaths. Despite their lack of support, I have to breathe. I force myself to; otherwise, I know where this is heading.

"Yes," Blake says.

"Blake, you are talented, and your people skills are unmatched. You have nothing to worry about going in there. Review their inquiry and campaign questionnaire first. Then, review how our campaign planning works, the timeline, costs, and where their engagement is required. When you are done, let them ask questions. Jot everything down. Liam might initially come off as intimidating, but that's just his jawline and gaze. Don't let it fool you; he's a softy on the inside—I promise."

"I've met him a couple of times, but do you know him?"

"More than anyone realizes." My voice drops.

"Did you two date or something?"

No, we didn't date. No, we were never in a relationship. But I loved him. I loved my best friend.

Liam is always going to be someone to me.

Liam is always going to be the boy who showed me the first glimpse of love. A taste of what it would be like to be happy with someone else.

But no, we didn't date, but we were good at pretending we were.

There are days when I wish it was because of him—and believe me, he is at fault. No one is perfect, not even Liam Hayes. But it's my fault. Even when I thought I could bet on myself—on us, I was wrong. I couldn't get to the point he needed. I couldn't be the girl—the love—he thought I was.

"No, we didn't."

"Then why are you avoiding the meeting? Are you even feeling sick?"

"We have a history I'm not ready to revisit." I give Blake a quick synopsis of said history. Her understanding was comforting, and she agreed to cover my absence.

I understand that this isn't professional and that I should separate personal from business, but this feels way too personal. Blake said Ben reached out.

Did Liam know? Is he using work as a ploy to reenter my life? There are a lot of questions floating around in my brain, making their way to my mouth, but I withhold from asking them.

"I'll take care of it," she says softly. Blake smoothes out her pencil skirt with her left hand.

Instead of facing one old friend, I face another—my panic, my anxiety. The most intimate relationship I've ever had has probably been with them.

The first time I experienced this was the summer of my thirteenth year. At first, they were more common. I forced myself to become good at hiding them. My mom, or Natalie, never knew. In college, I saw a therapist who taught me techniques to master my triggers and work through an anxious episode.

By my junior year, I was healed—that's what I used to tell myself. Managed. Under control. Conquered. My panic attacks and sleepless nights became rare. They stopped—sort of. They weren't controlling me, but there was always the slightest concern that they'd return.

Then I met Liam.

My grasp on control slipped the further I fell for him. With each step I took toward him, my inner monsters took two—more like three or four. They caught up to me and drained every ounce of love, possibility, and strength I had.

Then vanished—going back to therapy helped—till today.

I'm not sick to my stomach over food.

My head is spinning, and my vision is speckled.

I know what will happen next, and he is the last person who should see it or can help.

"You've got this," I reassure Blake—and maybe myself.

14

LIAM

Now

I'm sitting on Natalie's couch when she informs me that her friends are coming over to catch up on Love Island. The UK version, not to be confused with the American version, which is disrespectfully not as good.

"Did you ever think about going on the show?" she asks from the kitchen as she sets out an array of chips, dips, and a charcuterie board.

"Never," I tell her. "We applied for George a few years back, though. Made it through the first two rounds of interviews."

"What was the reason he didn't get cast?"

"I don't actually remember. I'll text him and ask."

"But really, you never thought about it?" I shake my head no. "You're hot enough." She winks at me.

"Never been interested. Plus, I've been tied up with someone." She points at herself jokingly.

I smile at her, and she smiles back.

"Is this you officially asking me to be your girlfriend?" She comes to sit on my lap. Bare legs sticking out of a pair of tiny cotton sleep shorts thrown over the side of the couch. And an oversized Chicago Cubs sweatshirt that smells of cherries.

"Natalie."

"I know. I know. You don't do labels." She mimics me from when I first told her last fall after she brought up the conversation for the first time. We aren't exactly exclusive, but we aren't precisely not exclusive. I don't sleep around as I used to; work consumes too much of my time, but no part of me wants to be committed to just anyone. "I still don't understand why. Are you ever going to tell me about the girl who broke you?"

"You seriously want to hear about her?"

"Maybe." She drags her bottom lip between her teeth.

"Fine." I sigh, and she squeals, excited that I'm giving in to her.

"We were together for years. Thought it was going to be forever, and then one day, she told me she didn't love me."

"That's hardly the details, mister."

She pushes my chest with her pointer finger. I rub the spot, pretending she hurt me.

Natalie is dainty. A good bit shorter than me, and her figure is petite. With her in my lap right now, I bring my hands to her waist, and the two overlap as I encircle her.

"What do you want to know then?" I ask her.

"Was she beautiful?"

"Natalie—"

"I know I'm beautiful. Shit, I'm hot and probably more attractive than her. So you can tell me if she was beautiful, it won't offend me."

Her confidence is impeccable. And she is hot, but it's the hotness that you sort of expect when someone is an influencer or model and life is out there for others to judge.

But who Natalie is asking about? That girl is the most beautiful in the world and is in this city somewhere. It isn't even her physical beauty that I was attracted to all those years ago. She has the most beautiful heart and soul. She doesn't reveal it often, but I found myself as one of the lucky ones to see the beauty inside. She's absolutely, properly devastating in the best way possible.

When I saw her the other day, it was like that morning in the café. My heart skipped a beat, and a blast of yearning and attraction blazed through me. *Emerson is still the most beautiful girl in the world.*

I close my eyes, not wanting to see Natalie's reaction, while I say, "Yeah, she is."

I open my eyes, and Natalie looks at me skeptically. She's picking up on the present tense of how I described Emerson. Without a word, Natalie climbs off my lap and heads back to the kitchen. She opens a bottle of wine, pours herself a glass, downs it, and pours another.

I guess that's the end of that conversation.

I should feel guilty about not asking her to be my girlfriend. We have fun together, but giving it a label, actually committing to her, feels like I'm cheating on Emerson. Obviously, it's not. And she's engaged now. The general idea of being committed to someone else feels like final closure from her. I'm not ready to feel as if I've entirely lost her or the idea that someday we'd return to each other.

After seeing Emerson happy with someone else last week, you would think that it would have been the sign that I could let go, cutting all of my ties to her for good. A part of me desperately wants to. A part of me still wants her and can't fathom letting her go—ever.

My post-heartbreak system has worked for years. I'll see other people. A few chats or nights and then move on to the next. Expectations clearly set beforehand that this can't go anywhere.

It's worked between Natalie and me for the past year—at least, I thought it was.

An hour later, her friends arrive.

Her friend Chloe is the last to arrive. "Em's going to be late. She had to pick up her bike from the shop."

"Rosen-awful couldn't do it for her?" Natalie rolls her eyes.

"I know."

We crowd into Natalie's small living room. It is as if a rainbow had thrown up in it. Color and artwork are everywhere. The number of items in the space makes it appear even smaller than it is. She has a two-seater sofa and two chairs—enough space for four. There are seven of us here. I sit in front of her, between her legs on the floor.

We're into a second episode of Love Island when someone knocks at the door.

"Kam, can you get that?" Natalie asks her friend, who is sitting in the white chair closest to the door.

She gets up and opens the door. I hear the sound of a bag dropping on the counter. Kam returns to the chair, and the brown-haired female who just arrived is behind her.

I tense in between Natalie's legs. Quickly removing my head from where it's resting against her bare knee.

"Emme, you made it!" Natalie claps gleefully.

Emerson stares between Natalie and me, between where I'm sitting and back to me. Her face is emotionless, but I know by the small furrowing of her brow that her mind is racing.

Emerson licks her lips. Her cheeks turn bright red. I watch her shoulders rise and fall with the deep breath she takes.

"You've got to be kidding me." She mouths to herself, gaze dropping to the grainy hardwood.

She turns and rushes down the hallway.

"Em—" Chloe calls out for her.

"You know Emerson?" I turn my head to ask Natalie.

From the oversized white chair opposite Kam's, Chloe watches us like hawks, observing every moment, every word, and every emotion.

"Yeah? She's my best friend."

Natalie looks at me like I'm stupid—and I am. She's mentioned her before but always refers to her as Emme or Em. In my head, I assumed that her best friend's full name was Emily, *not* Emerson. When I met Emerson six years ago, she was never anything but Emerson or States to me. How was I supposed to put the two together?

Wait.

It's all coming back to me. How could I forget Emerson's best friend's name is Natalie? I don't forget things about her. There is an entire portion of my brain that is reserved for her; storing facts and memories like that is its only function. But I forgot this?

I'm instantly disappointed in myself.

"How do you know her?" Chloe asks.

I debate saying that I don't. "Work," I go with, a nice partial lie. Emerson didn't show up to the meeting today. Her coworker informed me that she was sick.

She didn't look sick when she was standing out here, though.

I glance between Natalie and Chloe.

Natalie appears unbothered by what's happening, almost as if she doesn't care or this isn't a surprise.

But Chloe. She knows something. I think.

"I'll go make sure Emme is okay." Chloe shakes her head at Natalie, stands up, and rushes after her.

Quickly, I'm on my feet. As I head after Chloe, my socks catch on the wood floor, causing me to slip.

In the hallway, she stops me with a tattooed hand on my chest. Her eyes are closed, and her lips are turned inwards.

"You're him." Chloe opens her eyes and looks me up and down.

I nod. I'm unsure what she means, but I do my best to infer.

"My best advice for you right now is to either sit back down in the living room, not between another girl's legs, or I don't know. . . leave?"

"She's engaged," I let out.

"And I have black hair. Thank you for stating the obvious. But that doesn't matter—"

"How?"

"She still loves you." Chloe shakes her head and continues speaking, but I'm caught up in what she says. She loves me? Does Emerson still love me?

That's. . . that's impossible. To still love me means that Emerson had to love me already.

Chloe points in the direction of the living room. A herd of giggles and sighs come from the space, and I can only assume one of the boys gave a cute recoupling speech.

"Go," Chloe demands. Her dark eyes are piercing and add a quite scary fierceness to the look she is giving me.

Before following her advice, I say, "She's having a panic attack." Chloe nods, understanding my concern and warning. I walk back to the living room and sit down where Chloe was previously seated. Natalie glances over at me, but I avoid her gaze.

15

EMERSON

Now

I used to laugh at people who believed in fate. Then I met Liam, and he changed my mind. In those years, I thought that the world planned for us to meet.

That same group also tends to forget about fate's negative side—just how cruel it can be.

Is this my punishment for how we ended? Is fate's feelings upset that I moved on and found someone else, even if that person is a lifesaver to keep me from drowning in the depths of my fears? Or is this fate's cruel joke, playing on the thin string of hope that is Liam and me that I've clung to?

The shock of him being in Chicago the past year has barely settled. What am I supposed to do with this now?

Looking at him, it's not fear or confusion. It's betrayal.

"You've got to be kidding me," I mumble.

"Em," I hear Chloe call out to me. Everyone else in the room goes silent, their eyes putting me on display like a zoo animal. Shit, I must have said that louder than I thought. I shut my mouth before others fly out. I let them scream at me on the inside, trying to escape.

Liam was staring at me before I took off down Natalie's hallway. I bypass the half bathroom and go straight to hers. Both doors slamming behind me unintentionally.

I push the lock button in the bathroom and check the handle to ensure no one can enter.

The click of the lock was my cue to let myself feel it. *All of it.* Seeing Liam in the coffee shop. His company is our new client.

Him being cuddled up with my best friend. The distance and time that has separated us and how much I've missed him.

I throw up.

Several times. I empty my stomach of everything I ate today, which wasn't much since I didn't attend the lunch meeting. The white porcelain is cold against my inflamed skin.

Is this what it feels like to relapse? When you remember how good the high feels, you crave more of it, even the lows. Take anything you can get to try to feel normal again. You lose sight of all your progress, and the person you are now seems pointless without it.

All it took was seeing Liam last week for me to start to relapse.

Only for a moment, I let myself get high on the memories, high on the what-ifs, high on every way he possibly could have ever loved me.

It takes over my body. A blissful ecstasy so surreal that I forget where I am for a moment.

My breathing and heart rate are in sync at a pace too fast to be good. I have to get myself together before someone comes searching for me and before I disappear entirely in this bathroom.

I flush the toilet and walk over to the counter. Too afraid to look in the mirror, I turn on the faucet, watching the water as I wait for it to get as cold as possible.

There's a gentle knock on the door.

"Emerson?" It's Chloe.

"I'm fine," I choke out between labored breaths.

Touching my face, what I thought was sweat are tears. I didn't realize I was also crying. I swipe it away, but instead of my hand, it's his touch I feel, a phantom ghost of a memory.

That single tear becomes a stream; the next thing I know, I can replenish Lake Michigan with my tears.

"Let me in," she pleads with me.

"Walked here and had to pee," I fib.

"I don't believe you. Now, please let me in."

I reach behind me to turn the handle to unlock the door. Chloe opens the door, closes it behind her, and relocks it.

She flips my body around so that I'm facing her. "Are you okay?"

"Define okay," I joke.

"You know *know* Liam?" she asks.

I nod.

"How?" From her raised eyebrows and the uptick corner of her lip, I can see that she is connecting the dots. Chloe is figuring out who he is and what he is to me, but isn't forcing it. She's letting me keep control of the narrative even though I lost it the day I met Liam.

"Long story." I stare at my feet. Embarrassed that this is my reaction to seeing the two of them.

"I've got time," Chloe says, her hands reaching out to rub my upper bicep in lazy, soothing circles.

"Not really. Natalie will probably come soon."

"I don't think she will." Chloe cringes. "Do you want to leave?"

I think about how Liam looked at me last week—the same way I looked at him tonight—a green, ugly monster within us taking over. He was jealous of Brandon's arm around me and the ring on my finger. I'm envious that he was touching Natalie—he is with Natalie.

"I don't think you should," Chloe answers for me. "It might be awkward, but whoever or whatever Liam is to you shouldn't matter. Not tonight. We can deal with it tomorrow. Tonight, let him sweat while sitting there and seeing you happy without him."

"But I'm not happy."

"He doesn't know that."

"Did you know about them?" I ask hesitantly.

"No." Chloe shakes her head from side to side. "Promise."

"Okay. Give me a minute."

Chloe drops her hands from my shoulders. I turn back around, facing the mirror.

The water is ice-cold now. I place my hands under the faucet and splash water on my face. Using the paper towels, I blot my face dry.

"Let's go," I say. Feeling calmer and collected, Chloe and I return to the living room.

16

EMERSON

Six Summers Ago

I don't think I've ever slept that peacefully in my life. Maybe as a child, but the last time I slept through the entire night? I can't remember it.

As I wake up, the warmth of the early morning summer sun hits my face. Rays are shining through the three large windows adjacent to the bed. The emerald drapes are slightly agape on the furthest window to the left. Sheer curtains open behind them, letting in enough light to pierce my face. The warmth from the sun isn't what has ignited the rest of my body, though.

Something, or someone, heavy is draped across my stomach. Fluttering open my eyes, I look down to see his arm outside of the covers, holding on to me, pulling me into him. My mouth goes dry, and a self-loathing amount of heat dips low into my core, a prick of curiosity to the rest of who is under the covers.

Tipping my head down, I see I'm in a t-shirt that must belong to him. A wave of relief washes over me that I'm not completely naked. My legs are bare and intertwined with his.

The ending of last night is fuzzy.

I don't think anything happened except for a few too many drinks—my slight headache is proof of that. What I do remember is that once back at his hotel, Liam made us each another drink. We sat on his couch, talking about nonsense and laughing for hours. It was somewhere around two in the morning when I yawned the first time. When I leaned forward on the couch to search for my shoes, Liam stopped me with a hand on my thigh.

His touch was an electric shock to my body, waking me up.

"Planning to walk back at this ungodly hour?" he asked.

"I'm only a couple blocks away," I informed Liam. "Thank you for—"

"Stay," he offered. "I. . . I can sleep on the couch if that makes you more comfortable. I don't want you out there walking alone."

I bit down on the inside of my cheek, contemplating his offer. The tenderness and protectiveness of his request released a flurry of butterflies in my stomach.

"Okay," I said at the same time he offered to walk me back.

A pleased smile formed on his face. Any hesitation I felt about staying was instantly gone.

He showed me which room he was staying in. His two friends from earlier, Callum and George, are staying here also. I thought Liam was joking till we walked in. The place is insane. It is the largest hotel room I've ever been in. Liam motioned for me to make myself comfortable before heading into the bathroom to change.

I was looking down at my outfit when Liam reemerged in a pair of sweats and a faded college rugby shirt. My skirt and button-down shirt didn't exactly scream comfortable sleeping attire, but the idea of sleeping in only my undergarments had my core twisting.

I began unbuttoning my shirt when Liam tossed me one of his shirts from the dresser. "You can wear this," he said.

"Thank you."

My back to him, I slipped on the t-shirt, I can tell it's older, loved—another shirt from university. There's a small hole in the right shoulder and on the side by the hem. On me, the shirt is massive. It hangs down to below mid-thigh when I remove my skirt and hugs the curve of my butt.

"Did you play rugby?" I asked.

"Football or soccer as you call it. But enjoyed watching rugby and supporting the team. George played."

I turned around to face him, but Liam had already gone to the couch.

"Good night, States. Don't dream too much about me tonight," I heard from the couch in the suite's common living space. His sleepy voice was familiar, and I knew if I was lucky, I'd hear it in my dreams tonight.

Liam Hayes is a dream on both sides of consciousness.

"Good night, Liam," I whispered back.

I slipped in on the side I could tell was opposite to the one he had been sleeping on. The sheets pulled up around me. Warm, enclosed in his smell, and satisfied with tonight, sleep came easily.

At some point in the night, Liam climbed into the bed.

I should be bothered.

I shouldn't enjoy being in his arms.

I shouldn't enjoy the feeling of him up against me. I shouldn't be trying to feel him up against me. *But I do.*

I move my hips slightly.

"States," a sleepy Liam growls out.

"Mhmm."

"If you don't plan on that being in you, I'd stop moving this minute." His breath is on the back of my neck, sending a shiver down my spine and making the hair on my arms stand straight up. The combined sensation is a flame burning my body, desperate to be extinguished.

I try to move Liam's arm so that I can escape.

His arm doesn't budge. If anything, the jerk tightened his grip on me.

"Mates came back and kicked me off the couch. I hope ya don't mind."

Do I mind? An extremely attractive guy with muscles that rival a Greek statue, and a British accent that would have any female swooning over them, cuddled me in bed. I couldn't even get my last boyfriend to cuddle me during a movie. *Yeah, I don't mind.*

"Oh yeah. Y-yeah, I don't mind."

He removes his arm from me a few minutes later and got out of bed. Thank goodness. The warmth of his body was gone, leaving me with a chill. Never mind. I think I'd rather he be back in bed now.

I roll over. In the haze of last night and drinking in his delicacy, I didn't realize how tall he was. Standing, Liam has to be two or three inches over six feet easily. Compared to my five foot seven, he is a giant.

When he lifts his arms to stretch, it takes everything in me not to say 'big stretch' like my mom used to say to our dog, Buster.

Instead, I need to pick my jaw up from the ground. Probably find a tissue to wipe up the drool too.

His broad shoulders ripple first, each muscle following suit. The layers of muscles down his back narrow into his waist that dips into a pair of dark gray Calvin Klein briefs. If my ass is grabbable, his is one you could eat off.

Under the covers, I clench my legs. My hand flies to my mouth to cover it with a smack, and I pray that I don't say anything stupid or do anything foolish. The way he makes me feel has eroded my faith in myself.

Liam walks straight ahead to the bathroom. From the way his ears rise, I know he has a smug grin on his face.

I have to go. I decide to use Liam's time in the bathroom as my opportunity to leave.

Moving around the room stealthily, I find my clothes folded and on the dresser instead of on the floor in the pile I had left them in last night. The butterflies that have burrowed themselves in my stomach flutter their wings at the small but thoughtful and unnecessary gesture. Before joining me in bed, he took the time in the middle of the night to fold my clothing. You've got to be kidding me, I sigh.

From the top of the pile, I grab my leather skirt and step into it, trying to be quick. The metal zipper gets caught on my underwear and a bit of skin.

"Shit. Ow!" I say out loud. My eyes flash to the bathroom door, hoping that the volume of my voice won't trigger Liam to rush to my rescue. He would, I have annoyingly no doubt.

Tugging on the zipper in an upward movement, it doesn't budge. *Just leave it*, I tell myself. The skirt is tight enough on my waist that it won't fall.

I debate removing his shirt or not. It would be the most interesting souvenir I would bring home.

He won't miss it anyway, will he? Or maybe it'll force us to see each other again if he wants it back? *Yeah, I'll keep this.*

I style his shirt into the skirt.

There is a creak of a door opening as I buckle the black strap of my heels.

"Well. . . this is a first." His voice is still rough, but his tone is now. . . disappointed? Did he expect me to stay? "Never not slept with a girl and had her scurrying to get out of here."

Shit.

Operation get-the-hell-out-of-here is a total failure.

His disappointment clings to me, and I hate it. I hate thinking that I've somehow hurt him after his kindness and respect last night. In a matter of minutes, I made him feel like I've felt too many times before. I can't bring myself to look at Liam, knowing what I'd witness all over his face.

My brain is fighting to recover from the worst he has to be assuming of me.

"I was only kidding, States." He's leaning against the frame in gray sweatpants, no shirt, and an audacious smile forming across his face. "You sure enjoying. . . leaving?"

"No, I was going to get a—" *Think quickly, Em!* "—us coffees." *Coffee? That's your grand excuse?* "You don't want to see me without coffee in the morning, and I uh. . . probably shouldn't go out in only this." I pinch his shirt. "Ha."

"I'll come with you. Let me change." Liam glances down, my eyes following his lead.

Remember all those muscles in his back? Multiply them by about one hundred, and you will get the picture of the feast of his abdomen. He looks like Michaelangelo's *David* and *The Thinker* had a child and decided to chisel out a few extra muscles for funsies.

"Do you want your shirt back?" I gulp.

Liam glances back at me and licks his lip. "Keep it. Looks better on you," he says, disappearing into the bathroom again.

Moments later, he returns in a pair of black cargo shorts and a vintage graphic Beatles concert t-shirt—a complete contrast to the more sophisticated attire from last night. Both are just as appealing. He could wear a burlap sack, and I'd want to rip it off him.

He runs a hand through his bedhead. "Ready?"

***

We ended up at the same place where we first saw each other only two days ago. He pays for our coffees before we grab a table in the window.

"What brought you to Lisbon?" Liam asks me while blowing on the steam coming from his hot, black coffee.

"How long did we spend talking last night, and this never came up?"

"I know." He laughs.

"Celebratory end of college trip with my best friend."

He tilts his head in confusion. "But you were by yourself last night?"

"Long story short. They"—Liam's shoulders tense—"had to go home for a family emergency but convinced me to stay. So here I am, solo in Lisbon, finishing the last few weeks without her."

The brief rigidness in Liam's body is gone. "You don't appear too sad about her being gone."

"Is that a statement or a question?"

"I don't know. What should it be?"

"It's not that I'm not sad; trust me, I am. Maybe relieved is a more accurate way to describe how I feel." The honesty of what I just told him is chilling. I think I felt this way yesterday but was avoiding it. I didn't want to admit it to myself, but now I have—and to a semi-stranger, semi-guy I'm undeniably attracted to and spent an incredible, unexpected night with. "I *love* Natalie. Don't misread this. We've been together since we were children. She's just. . . we're opposites."

"How so?" Liam inquisitively asks.

"Let's say if she were here, you'd be sitting with her instead of me."

"Doubtful."

I tilt my head, narrowing in on him. Quickly, I've learned that Liam doesn't say something unless he means it.

"Anyway. This whole summer was originally her idea, but most of it was spent with her pining for others instead of seeing it together."

"And what do you call last night and this morning?"

"I was not pining after you!"

"I would love to agree to disagree, but States, even a blind man would know that you were devouring me with your eyes."

"You didn't seem to mind." I challenge him.

"I never mind when it's a beautiful woman."

"You are so full of yourself."

"You could have been." He takes a sip of his black coffee. I choke on mine. "Tell me more about—"

"Natalie." He nods. Good, moving away from that topic. I tell Liam how we met and a few stories that help paint the picture of her and us as kids. "Growing up, she was Miss Big Ideas, and I was Miss Get Shit Done. We still are. When Natalie spews an idea, they are mostly thought out. . . for the most part." I laugh a little, reminiscing. I take a drink of my black coffee. "They include photos, outfits, a diagram, or whatever she may need to convince me the idea is great. She gave me a full outline when she had the idea for this. I made it happen while finishing up our spring semester. I think that's why she told me to stay." Or at least I'm telling myself not to feel guilty about being okay with her gone.

I take another drink of my coffee, longer this time. Realizing that I'm word vomiting and should probably stop.

"How thoughtful of her to add staring at a stranger at a coffee shop to the outline. You executed that plan brilliantly."

I roll my eyes at him. "Wasn't on her outline. It was on mine."

"Oh really?" His eyebrows shoot up.

"No," I reply blankly, trying to avoid his flirting attempts.

"You shouldn't feel bad about wanting to stay," Liam admits softly and comfortingly.

"I didn't say I felt bad about it." My brow furrows slightly.

"States, your body language is saying it all. Your shoulders are tense. You keep looking down at your coffee, your brow pinches, and you keep biting the side of your cheek."

"I didn't realize you were paying that close attention to me." I really didn't, and now. . . now I want to know what else he noticed.

"Get used to it." He says it as if it's a promise. A promise I'm not sure I want him to keep.

What am I getting used to, Liam Hayes?

17

LIAM

Six Summers Ago

Sometimes, crazy is good. Great really. Every sane human is a bit crazy. And whatever this feeling is. . . it's abso-fucking-lutely, making me crazy.

My pull to Emerson is easy. Too easy that it should be wrong, but I can't get enough of it. Enough of her.

That's why it's crazy. Yeah?

Do you know what crazy leads to? Impulsive and improper, nonsensical decisions.

That's why I lied to her about today. When she told me she was heading to Lagos, I told her we were too. We weren't.

From the hotel hallway, I barge through the suite's front door. I pound on the door leading to Callum's room and follow it with a loud fist to George's door.

"Rise and shine! We're leaving in twenty minutes." My voice rings loud enough to wake other guests on the floor, maybe the whole hotel.

There's no sound of movement coming from either room.

Callum won't take long to pack; he's not as much of a slob as George. I don't even try to imagine what I'm about to see when I walk into the room he claimed. Clothes might not even be my biggest concern either.

The door creaks open. Taking in the room, it's not as bad as I expected. Clothes from the previous night everywhere, but that's it.

My eyes catch what else is thrown about the floor—a set of black lace knickers haphazardly next to a neon pink minidress and a pair of Prada heels.

"George!" He groans as Beatrix Archer's head pops out from under the duvet. The white sheet and duvet fall down her body as she sits up against the headboard. Her bare chest pointed directly at me.

"Oi, Bea, what a pleasant surprise!" I toss her a smile and George's shirt from the ground.

"Good morning, Hayes," her floral, feminine voice replies. She tosses George's shirt back at me.

"Heading to Lagos for the day. I've booked us rooms at Avenida. Train leaves in an hour," I say to George.

"Is the sun even up, mate?" George asks grogily.

"You would know, assuming that's when you two went to sleep."

George growls at me but reluctantly climbs out of bed, naked. Bea looks over at him, rolls her eyes, but leaves them on him, and watches with longing.

"Didn't realize you were in Lisbon," I tell her.

There isn't another female I know who is confident enough to pull off that shade of pink. Beatrix Archer, Bea for short, is the love of George's life, despite what he tells anyone—it's painfully obvious, though. Bea puts the *bea* in beautiful. Quite fit that one. Darker olive skin. The richest brown hair that matches her eyes. Tall, barely shy of six feet.

They met at boarding school. George and Bea went their separate ways after sixth form, but kept in touch through university. She'd appear for a weekend, and George would disappear the following weekend.

We never knew if they were ever properly together or not. They flaunted relationships in front of each other or dared the other to decide who to hook up with that night during visits—a game I hated watching because she is like a sister to me. Anytime Cal and I tried to stop it, they ignored us.

"Neither did I." George flashes her a glare over his shoulder. "Even told her last week we'd be here."

Her face pales. Her tone is raw when she responds, "I told you I wasn't avoiding you."

"Then why didn't you tell me?" George asks crossly.

"Georgie." Beatrix frowns.

"Care to fill me in on how this happened, then?" I ask.

"Left the bar last night and bumped into her on the street with another, but that didn't last long. Pointed at her, then in the direction of here."

"And I followed him." She exhales. "As if I could stay away," I hear her add on in an embarrassed whisper.

"Want to tag along? Lagos?" I ask Bea. "I miss you. It's been, what, six months since we've seen you last?"

"I appreciate the offer, but I should return to my friend. We're" leaving tomorrow anyway."

Beatrix walks to where her clothes are decorating the floor. She stops when our shoulders meet and tilts her head to kiss my cheek. "Miss you too, Hayes."

"We leave in fifteen minutes now. Get your shit together."

"Thanks for the orgasms," Beatrix says, not looking at George. Dressed, she strides toward the door, throwing a hand in the air, and waves a small goodbye to both of us. She's past the threshold of the door when she stops. A hand reaches out to grab hold of the archway. Beatrix turns her body to look back at George. It's my eye contact she finds. There is sorrow and a hint of wishful thinking in them. I can tell that someday she hopes that he finally stops sleeping around enough to only love her.

She's gone a moment later.

***

Emerson is standing at the train station, peering around curiously. It's the same curiosity that she proudly wore at the coffee shop.

"Is this about a girl?" George whispers to Callum behind me.

"I don't know," Callum whispers back.

It's not about any girl, it's about her. Emerson Clarke.

Emerson's head swivels till it lands on us. She catches me and rolls her eyes.

"Thought I was lying?" I call to her.

When we finished our coffee, we went our separate ways to pack. Within the quick walk back to my hotel, I booked rooms for all of us at my favorite place to stay in Lagos. I didn't know if she already had a place, but leaned into the assumption of no. Emerson didn't mean to, but revealed that this wasn't part of the original outline.

The dynamic between her and—shit, I can't remember her friend's name. Their dynamic perplexes me. I wonder if Emerson knows that her friend walks all over her like a doormat you've had forever with imprints of where your shoes step every time you walk on it.

"This fella thought he'd get away with running off to Lagos without us." George clamps a hand onto my shoulder.

I never properly introduced them last night, but they saw me with her. "The last time we were there. Two years ago, aye? Last year of uni, and Liam here accidentally—"

"That's enough," Callum shuts him up.

"I'm sorry," I mouth to Emerson, gesturing to the two idiots standing beside me.

She mouths back, "It's fine."

"Didn't get to meet last night. I'm Callum Sullivan." He pulls her in for a hug, planting a kiss on either side of her cheeks.

She looks up at him, a tiny twinkle in her eyes. The same twinkle all girls get when they see Callum. Same height and similar blue eyes as me. His sandy blond hair is cut close to the head. It curls when he grows it out, giving him irresistible surfer vibes. Fits that his two brothers are both professional surfers.

George pushes past, pulling Emerson in for a hug, but he stops when he sees my eyes. I look at him, daring him to touch her. He smirks and puts his hands on top of her shoulders, checking her out from head to toe.

"George Eaton." He reaches a hand to hers after taking a step back and dropping his arms from her shoulders. "The best of the three in more ways than one."

Cal and I muffle our disdain. No reason for us to stroke his ego.

George is shorter than us, reaching only six feet, something Callum and I don't let him live down. He has warm, light brown skin and the darkest brown eyes I've ever seen, except when you are close to him and see they are onyx. Flecks of gold dispersed throughout. The amount of gold honestly depends on what hair color he decides to have. At the present moment, it is a dusty light brown, the bleach blond fading away.

"I'm good for at least three good snogs when you're done with him," he tells Emerson. She laughs at him; however, her eyes aren't on him but focused on me.

And perfect timing. In a public place, I'm hard watching her watch me.

We're on the express train to Lagos. In two hours, we'll be at the furthest south point in Portugal. Lisbon is incredible, the city and history, but Lagos is a dream: the beaches, the bars, the everything.

I sat next to Emerson on the train, where we filled in the gaps from the night before. Growing up in London, growing up in the Midwest, my relationship timelines with George and Callum, how she is terrified of clowns and will never go to a circus despite how happy people tell her they are.

We spend the entire time talking, fun fact for a fun fact, and story for story. I categorize each piece of information about her, tucking it away as if it were contact information in a Rolodex. I don't want to forget a thing about her.

We arrive at Avenida Lagos Hotel.

Emerson trails me to the concierge desk. Callum and George immediately find themselves two seats and two drinks at the bar.

"Checking in for Hayes."

Behind the desktop computer, the concierge is typing away. She doesn't even lift her head to acknowledge us. "Hayes. Four ocean-view rooms. Can I have a copy of the card on file?"

"I thought we were all crashing together?" Emerson's ears are perked up. She tosses me a confused glance.

"Made an accommodation to the reservation." She goes to speak. "Don't sweat it, States." I smile down at her but catch a glimpse of disappointment. Did she want us to stay together? After this morning, I—well, I don't know what she wanted this morning, and I was too much of a wuss to even begin to go there.

It's not that I don't want to. I want to be in there.

The concierge hands my card back to me, letting her hand and eyes linger a beat too long on me. I swear I hear Emerson scuff next to me as she watches us intently.

"Three of the rooms are on floor four; the other is on floor three." She gestures to the stairs. "Stairs are there to the right behind you. Please let us know if there is anything we can do to make your stay more. . . pleasurable."

"Thanks." I give her a curt nod and ignore what she insinuates. If there's anyone who will make that stay more enjoyable, it's Emerson.

Callum and George have rejoined us, laughing between them. I hand each of them a key card. Emerson reaches her hand out, palm up, waiting for me to drop a card into her hand, but instead, I pocket hers and mine.

Spinning on my heels, I pick up her bag and head to the stairs.

"I can get that." She stomps after me, missing the handle, she grabs my hand. "I didn't pack light."

Correct, she didn't. We are here only for a night, but her bag easily has to weigh at least ten kilos. I would hate to know what her bags for the entire summer weigh. I force myself to keep laughing.

"You're acting like I couldn't lift you," I joke.

"Are you calling me heavy?" Her eyes flare.

"That's one way to flirt with her," George critiques from six steps up.

"He is not flirting with me," she says as if disgusted by the idea.

"Right. . . and we aren't oblivious to the way you got jealous when the concierge was staring at him," George says.

"Or like we didn't hear him in the shower this morning after your little 'friend' sleepover," Callum adds, air quotes friend.

"Is that what you were laughing about when you walked up?"

"Maybe," George taunts.

"Go to your rooms," I snap, annoyed.

"Yes, Dad." Callum laughs. The sounds of their feet and bags dragging up the stairs echo in the well.

"Give me my bags," Emerson demands.

"It's not heavy. I know you are capable of carrying them, of taking care of yourself, but that doesn't mean you have to. You should learn to let someone *help* you now and then."

She rolls her eyes. "For the record, I let people help quite often. I don't want *your* help." She drops her hand off her bag and walks up the stairs in front of me.

I wasn't trying to insinuate anything. I genuinely wanted to do this for Emerson. I got the vibe that she's too independent, admirable, and hot, but that doesn't mean she has to be independent all of the time.

Her words play over in my head, *'I don't want your help'* and *'like you are going to fall in love with me,'* as I follow behind her. A sting burns in my chest. I don't give a shit what she was or wasn't insinuating; I know her statement is weighted. There's something else going on behind her hidden spiky exterior.

I try to shake off the feeling by staying in the present moment, which is a pair of frayed light denim shorts that barely cover an inch past Emerson's butt. Tan legs stretch out of them, but I can't, more like I don't, avert my eyes from how the denim is secured on her round cheeks. Every so many steps, I can see the curve of said cheeks and all the blood rushes straight to my dick. Emerson halts, and I run directly into her. No doubt she can feel it up against her.

"I'm assuming I'll be on floor three."

"Uh yeah," I say to her, gaining composure. Looking at the numbers on the two cards in my hands, I note that she's directly a floor below me. "To the left."

I tap the key card against the black scanner on the door. It unlocks with a clicking noise and a green light. I hold the door open with one hand while Emerson walks in. Her shampoo invades my nose again as she walks by, leaving her bag in the hallway behind her.

"Could you get that?" She winks at me over her shoulder.

The room is minimalistic, with simple beige decor and furniture. We both walk a few more steps into it. Emerson rushes to the balcony on the opposite side of the room.

"This is breathtaking." Emerson sighs. Pushing open the sliding doors and stepping outside, taking in the beaches, ocean, and grottos that are all within view.

She turns around to face me, standing on the balcony, the cyan sky behind her, when a light breeze catches her hair, blowing it about. She looks like a beach goddess.

"Almost as breathtaking as you," I murmur to myself.

"Thank you for booking this place. . . and coming with me."

"I told you we were already planning on coming."

Emerson raises a brow. "Your friends gave you away. I overheard them cackling coming back from the bar. You could have told me you wanted to spend time with me, Liam Hayes." The smile that forms on her face is mischievous before dropping to become grateful. My body ignites with heat and sparks, and I can't help but smile that I did this to her. I made Emerson smile. "I appreciate it. You didn't have to do any of this."

"You're welcome, Emerson."

It's the first time I've used her name. The feel of it on my tongue catches me by surprise. How my mouth forms to the vibrations of the syllables. Can words have a home? Can a name belong to your mouth and only your mouth to say?

If yes, then it's her name.

18

LIAM

Now

Natalie insisted that I walk Emerson back to her place when everyone was leaving. I thought she was joking, but she wasn't.

Selfishly, I can't help but feel the urge to spend time with Emerson and be close to her again like we used to be. See if she's still the person I remember when we were. If we can still be them. Learn if there is hope for even a friendship.

Emerson, on the other hand, exudes that I'm the last person on Earth she wants to be around. I watch her leaning against the doorway, arms crossed, head tilted up, glaring at the ceiling.

She turns her head at the worst time. Looking over at us at the right (wrong) moment, Natalie holds onto my waist, standing on her tiptoes to kiss my cheek in a territorial way.

Emerson walks away.

"Make sure she's okay," Natalie tells me. I nod.

***

We take the elevator in silence. Outside of Natalie's apartment, I turn to Emerson. "Lead the way."

She spins toward the right and gestures her hand.

We walk in silence for three blocks. Before, the silence between us was comfortable. Now, the silence is meters between us.

"How have you been?" I break the silence.

"Good."

"And work?"

"Busy."

"Are you feeling better? Your coworker said you were sick."

"Yeah."

"You're a director now. Promotion?" She nods. "No surprise there. Congrats, States." My mouth lingers on her nickname.

"Thanks."

"You're welcome. How is your mom?"

"The same."

I thought I wanted whatever she would give me, but this is ridiculous. I need more. "I'll take the hint. You don't want to talk."

"That's not true," Emerson seethes with her first sign of any emotion.

"Then what States? This has been a one-sided conversation. You haven't said more than ten words. Talk. Talk to me, please," I beg of her. There isn't anyone else I've ever begged for, and this isn't the first time I've begged for her.

"I'm processing." She exhales. "You, me, now Natalie? I'm trying to figure out how this happened. I thought we'd—never mind." Emerson catches herself. She rubs her temples.

I blink, surprised she cut right to it.

"You thought what?" I ask her.

"It doesn't matter, Liam." She lets out a reluctant laugh. "None of it matters. I'm engaged—"

"I know," I grunt.

"You're with Natalie." I hold off on the urge to correct her, unsure if now is the time to confirm or deny that. "Just if—If it did—"

"We'd be the ones together," I finish her sentence. "States," I plead.

"Don't call me that. Not anymore." Her movements halt. Standing completely still, her eyes shut, she takes a big inhale. Releasing the exhale slowly. Her chest, which was moving quickly, slows with each deep breath.

I don't think her heart is racing for the same reasons mine is.

"I feel the same way," I say earnestly.

Emerson turns her head to me.

I don't know if I'm happy she's even looking at me or if I wish she didn't. Seeing the longing and hurt on her face and the color of her eyes has me screaming. Everything in me is screaming and fighting with her to speak. Give me the words I know she is holding back.

She opens her mouth, and all the hope in the world gets the best of me for a split moment. She blinks as if she's resetting herself. Reminding herself of where she is, what recently occurred, and why we are what we are. Her eyes return to their standard shade, and she shut her mouth.

The moment is over; we are back to a nauseating silence.

It takes us another ten minutes to reach her building. Neither of us spoke another word to each other.

Stopping out front, Emerson turns to face me.

"This is me," she says, licking her lips. "Thanks for walking me home. I guess we'll be seeing each other around." Her words are slow and punctuated.

"I'spose."

Neither of us takes a step to go in opposite directions.

Taking a deep breath and eyes locked on Emerson, I pass selfish as if I'm passing go on a Monopoly board and reaching greedy bastard because I want more of her time, more of her. I want to forget that there are other people involved. Pretend we are still best friends, have a drink, talk, and laugh for the rest of the night—or eternity if I was allowed—just as we did that night in Lisbon.

A small part of me believes that she feels the same way.

I suspected it all night.

Even now, the frayed string between us, we are both pulling on it from opposite ends, hoping it'll pull us together instead of finally splitting in half, unsalvageable.

I'm not ready to let go.

Not until I know. I have questions I need answers to.

But even if I get the answers—responses I'll like or loathe—I don't know if I'd be able to relinquish that small part of her I hold coveted. It's not because I still love her; it's because she was my best friend.

"Wait. Sta—" I catch myself before calling her States again. I don't even know if I should use her name. She told me once that I was the only person to call her Emerson. Is that still true? But her name, Emerson, is sitting there. My mouth still knows precisely how it should form to say it because every part of me remembers every part of her. "Can I use your bathroom? Promise to leave then."

Emerson nods.

We take the elevator to her apartment, floor twelve. As soon as we step off, her shoulders drop. She's relaxed.

"Do you enjoy living in this part of the city?"

"I do. The neighborhood is nice despite the longer commute to work. Depending on the day, I bike or take the train."

I follow behind her to her door. A chuckle escapes my mouth.

"What's funny?" Her stare is pointed.

Is it wrong that I'll take this irritated and perplexed version of Emerson over no version of her at all?

"I still think about how terrible you were trying to navigate the train the day we went to Lagos. You were insanely adamant that your side was in the right direction, just to be wrong and then have to sprint with your bag across the platforms."

"Hey! It said Lagos, I swear." Her laugh falls out, and I think my whole world stops. If it were humanly possible, I'd bottle up her laugh and open it every morning when I wake.

"Yeah, sure." I smile at her. "At least you can navigate us home now."

"I'm a lot better now. You know. . . the whole signs being in English really helps." We're both laughing now. I missed her laugh. It's the type of laugh that takes control of your whole body. Mouth wide open, belly laughs. Terribly ugly, but I love it terribly. "Natalie is the one that's terrible at it."

The comment snaps us back to reality.

What even is this reality? One with her in it, so close yet further away than ever. She's here, and I'm where? Drifting somehow parallel to Emerson, figuring my shit out with another girl? Emerson is finally in love with someone that isn't me?

The answer should be easy. But it isn't.

The answer should be us. But it isn't.

We break eye contact, both looking down at the mention of Natalie's name.

Luckily, we are at what must be her door.

I'm standing adjacent to her. Emerson digs in her bag for her keys, but I put my arm out to stop her. It lands on the door with a thud.

"Emer—"

"Why are you here?" she says breathily. Her back is to me, but I can tell she is fighting the same urge—an urge to ignore everything and fall back into us.

"Hayes Hotels now has a Chicago office. You would know that if you took the meeting earlier today."

She spins around to face me. I take a step in front of her. My other arm comes up to cage her in from the other side.

"I meant right *now*."

That's an answer I'm not sure she's ready to hear.

The entire walk home, I wished for her to say something. Anything. Curse at me, yell at me, put a spell on me, whatever—anything to show that she still cared. That somewhere deep down, despite what happened and the time between us, there is something still there. That Emerson struggled these past three years as much as I did because from where I am on the sidelines of her life, it sure seems as if she didn't.

"Why are you here?" She asks again.

"Did you love me?" I ask her.

I catch her off guard with the question. It's an answer to her question. To get what she wants to know, she has to give me what I need. *I need to know if she loved me.* Was what Chloe said earlier accurate?

"You lost the opportunity to know that. And it's not fair to ask me this now, and you know that." Emerson shakes her head. "If that's why you wanted to come up, then I need you to lea—"

"Why do you never want to talk about this, Emerson? What are you so afraid of?"

"Afraid?! I'm not afraid of anything. We were friends, nothing more."

"We were *not* friends, and you know it. I don't kiss, touch, or think about my friends as I did you."

"Okay, fine. We weren't only friends! Does it make you happy to hear that? It shouldn't because it doesn't matter how I felt about you then. . . or now. I'm with someone else!"

"Stop rubbing it in." The fact that 'Emerson is engaged' should be tattooed on my head given how many times I've been reminded in the past week about it. "Are you in love with him?"

"Don't be cruel, Liam."

Her hands come to the sides of her head. She runs them through her hair, pulling on it.

"Are you?" My mouth finds her ear. I whisper, hot breath trickling down her neck. "If you are, I'll—I'll be okay. I'll be happy for you. It might make me a prick, but I can't lie to you. There is a part of me that hopes you. . . aren't." I rest my forehead on hers.

It takes her a few moments, but she shakes her head. The movement moves my head with hers.

"Say it out loud, States."

"I can't," she whispers, looking up at me through her lashes. Her face shows that the admittance pains her to say.

I pull my forehead away from hers.

"Figured."

"What is that supposed to mean? You figured," she huffs.

"Well. . ." Just say it. Just do it. "You can't admit it now, and you couldn't admit that you loved me then because it scared you." The reins of my composure are about to snap. Her back is pressed up against the door, my arms still caging her in, but my body is closer to hers. Gravitating toward her with each word I say. "You were *finally* enough for someone. Unconditionally enough for me. So you pretended. You pretended we were some platonic fluffer of a relationship with each other. Pretended none of it mattered to you. Pretended the way I touched you didn't burn through your entire body. Pretended you weren't the person you've seen through my eyes. Pretended you didn't love me." My eyes close. I take a deep breath. Opening my eyes, I stare directly at Emerson. "I don't believe after what we had, you are capable of turning around and having something greater with anyone else. Now, please. Answer. The. Question."

"I already did." Her voice is faint.

"Not that one. My original question." It comes out as a growl.

I know the answer.

And I think I know the exact moment—not the moment I fell in love with her, which is wrapped around my bones like skin, even all these years later. But what I mean is when she fell in love with me.

We were in Tortola in the BVIs five summers ago. It was a year after we met and the second time that Emerson joined the boys and me for our summer holiday. We chartered a boat to take the six of us; Callum's little sister, Audrey, and Beatrix came with us. Without my mum around, I needed the two predominant women in my life to meet the third. I was the one to insist on the girls coming with us.

Emerson was at the back of the boat, lounging on the leather couch-bed. Wearing a dark green string bikini that made her eyes greener. She was alone but watching us. It's what she does best, a trait I don't think many appreciate. The patience to be absorbent as a sponge. I always wonder what she is thinking in these moments. I never ask. It feels quite like I'm invading a part of her mind that I'm not sure she would share.

I asked her this time, though. I made my way to the back of the boat.

"What's on that mind of yours, States?"

"Thoughts."

"Yeah? 'Bout me, ey?" She rolled her eyes at me.

"I'm always thinking about you." An admission I didn't expect.

"What about me?"

Emerson stands up, standing on the back of the bed. She turns around and gracefully dives off.

"Come in and find out," she taunted me from the clear turquoise water. From where I stand on the boat, I can see her pulling on the strings of her bikini bottoms.

I slip my shirt over my head; Emerson fixated on me from where she treads. Her eyes darken as they roam my torso. Her bottom lip curled beneath her teeth.

A moment later, I'm in the water with her. A cannonball that decks her with a splash. We swam to a nearby shore together, tucked in a cove where the rest couldn't see us. She slipped her bottoms into my pocket before hitting dry land. Emerson climbed on top of me while I lay on a flat rock with waves crashing over us. The sparkle in her eyes differed from all the others as she sank onto me. She leaned forward and whispered into my ear.

"How you could be my forever."

That's the day I knew she loved me. No matter if she never said it, I told myself she felt it.

I love that memory, but I get angry when I sit in it for too long. I let us both down by not doing anything about the emotions that were surging between us that trip—or any of our time together, for that matter.

She treaded water, waiting for me to join her. I tread in her past, afraid that I wasn't the lifesaver but the weight that drowned her.

"Yes," present-day Emerson finally confirms.

"I loved you," I whisper painfully. "You know?"

"I know," she whispers back.

"Did you?"

I know she knew. I said it repeatedly, hoping that words would speak louder than actions for once.

"Liam—" She's pleading with me with her eyes. Silently begging me to put us both out of our misery right now by, I don't know, leaving? Kissing her? Telling her that it doesn't matter if she won't ever love me and that I'll take anything from her? I don't know.

"Emerson—"

"You broke my heart." I already knew this, but confirmation, hearing it come from her lips, it hurts. It's a reminder that, at one point, I was almost the person to rebuild it.

"And you broke mine," I say.

19

EMERSON

Now

I don't remember the moment I fell in love with Liam.

It happened, though. We both let it happen unintentionally.

And maybe that's what I needed. I needed love to surprise me. I needed it to find me when I wasn't looking.

I wasn't looking for Liam that summer, but we found each other.

He was my best friend. I shared more with him than I did anyone else. Liam made it easy to be me. The closer we became, the deeper I fell.

One day, I woke up, and love was there. It was like I was a baby deer, a fawn trying to find its legs to stand on the ground, ready to face the world for the first time. Everything was new, everything fresh. I was discovering the smell of the grass, the colors of flowers, and the sounds of my surroundings for the first time. That's what it felt like that day. I was reborn, or whatever was blocking my eyes was removed, and I saw everything differently, anew.

I had never loved anyone before. I had sworn off it after watching how much pain it can cause in its wake, never letting myself get too close to the possibility. I didn't think I was good enough for it. . . and, ultimately, I wasn't.

I never told Liam I loved him. I didn't know how. Feeling it was one thing, saying it was another.

In hindsight, I realize I was waiting for years for him to tell me because I didn't want to be the one to risk themselves first. He finally did tell me, but hearing it wasn't everything it's chopped up to be.

But now he knows. He knows that I loved him.

We stand in the hallway, holding each other's gaze for minutes.

Liam breaks our eye contact, frustratedly pushing off the door. He keeps releasing deep, audible breaths, the type you hear in a yoga class. His feet pace back and forth in front of me before he spins toward the elevator and walks down the hallway.

He doesn't say a word to me. Or even bothers looking at me. This is why I didn't want to say anything.

I hear Liam grumbling over his heavy steps, talking to himself frustratedly.

"Did you want to rip your heart out again? You knew her answers."

"You shouldn't have pushed her."

"I should never have gotten that close to her."

I wish I could unhear all of it.

He's upset, and I get it, but nothing in me feels guilty about his behavior—he asked for it. He asked for it, and here it is, a repercussion of love.

As he waits for the elevator, facing the metal doors, Liam turns to his left, back toward me.

The look on his face is piercing. That new baby deer kind of love? His face is the hunter shooting it down. The full reality of tonight settling in and pulling the trigger. His eyes are broken, no longer being able to mask the hurt he felt—then and now. Glimmering behind the hurt is love, trying to push through. I know it is. I can see it. Trying to make the situation better. Trying to demand we say everything that we still aren't.

"Liam," I try to call out, but nothing comes out. Nothing. Instead, I feel the words I want to say clawing to get out. They long, desperately wishing that this was an entirely different situation. I wouldn't let him get on that elevator in any other situation. I'd run to him. Tell him how I can't stop thinking about him. How missing him drives me crazy. How I've dreamed of this moment and pictured it so vividly. Then kiss him, pull him back to my apartment, and never let us go again.

But Brandon. But Natalie.

But everything that happened that summer.

The elevator chimes. Liam's head drops, and he steps on the elevator without another look or goodbye.

Was this it? Was that my opportunity, and did I blow it? Is this how it all finally ends?

I don't move. Physically, I can't.

My back slumps on the door to my apartment. The solidness keeps me from completely falling apart. I keep staring at where Liam was, hoping maybe, just maybe, he'd come back.

I allow myself another moment before pulling out my keys to go inside. Halfway through the front entryway that leads to my apartment's main living area, my chest tightens. I feel like I can't breathe.

In and out. Inhale. Exhale. Repeat.

Coaching myself through something so human it's second nature, but my stupid self has forgotten how to do it.

I can't get Liam's face out of my mind. Trapping me only feet away, close enough that I could make out every cord of muscle and his rapidly beating heart. The fact that he asked me if I ever loved him. Or how he said my full name. It's as if my mind decided to hit rewind and play in slow motion the night, forcing me to relieve it as if I wasn't an active participant.

I slip my purse off my shoulder and drop it on the counter before I head to the bedroom closet.

Brandon stops me.

"Emme?" he asks.

"This is a pleasant surprise. I didn't think I was going to see you till Friday. What are you doing here?" I step toward him, rising on my toes to kiss him.

He pulls away from me, shaking his head. His arms crossed in front of his chest.

"Is everything okay?"

"I believe I should be the one asking you that." He snorts.

"What do you mean?"

"Liam isn't only an old friend, is he?"

I shake my head no. "I mean, he is—technically. We haven't seen or spoken to each other in over three years."

"But before that?"

"But before that, he wasn't just my friend."

"Or a summer fling."

Even though I know it will hurt both of us, I don't avoid the truth. "Liam was my first love, my everything."

"It sort of feels like he still is."

"He isn't." Is that the truth?

Brandon snuffs out a laugh. "How he looked at you last week clearly shows he isn't over you."

Is Liam not over me?

"Don't read into it. It was a surprise encounter," I say.

"I'm not reading into it, Emme. It's quite obvious," Brandon says sternly. "Do you love me?"

"You were," he nods as I finish speaking, "listening. What did you hear?"

"Enough to know that this," he points between us. "Is not what you want."

"That's not true. I want you; of course, I do. I want the future and life we've been planning with you." I try taking a step toward him, but he retreats backward another.

"Then why haven't we set a wedding date yet?"

"We need a venue first, and we haven't found one yet that we both like."

"Cut the bullshit, Em. We haven't found one you like. And you know what? I'm starting to think that's a load of shit, and you don't want to set a date because I'm not who you see a future with."

"Brandon," I sigh out his name.

"Tell me the truth right now, Emme." His voice is surprisingly calm.

"I do love you—" I play with the engagement ring on my finger. The feeling of it sitting there burns my skin. "—but not that way."

"I know I'm going to regret asking this. Do you think you ever could?"

I shake my head no. A tear trickles down my cheek as his heart hardens against me.

"What am I to you? What was I when we met?"

He's going to hate me, but I can't lie to him. He deserves the truth.

"A harbor from the loneliness I felt. You—there was something about you that filled the void he left. For the first time since Liam, I tried to let myself be in love. I tried to be in love with you."

"My mom was right about you. She saw through you and warned me. Told me that there was something about you that was cold and guarded. That you were using me, how hesitant you were when I asked you to marry me."

I chime in as he speaks, "We hadn't even spoken about the future yet."

"And the way your interactions were cold or distant at times. She didn't know how or why, but I refused to believe her. I went to bat for you every time she told me to call it with you because I love you and truly thought you felt the same about me. . ."

I don't bother to stop the salty tears falling down my face.

"I've been nothing but good to you."

I slightly cringe, ignoring how he is to me around his mom.

"I know, Brandon. If I," I tap my chest, "Was someone else, I could have loved you like that, easily and deeply."

Brandon shuts his eyes, scrunching his face in agony. "Do you love him?"

"It's not that simple."

"It is Emme. Either you do or don't." Brandon comes to sit next to me on the floor. "Love isn't complicated. It's rather simple, actually."

"How?"

"It just is. Stop guarding yourself, and you'll see." His voice is sweet and tender. A one-eighty from the ridgidness he exuded seconds ago.

"I don't know how to uncomplicate it. I watched it hurt and break people. It broke me before I ever got a chance."

"In life, some things deserve second chances. While love provides us the avenue for a second chance, you need to give the feeling a second chance. I wish I were that chance, not only for you, but for me, but we aren't."

"Did I waste your time?"

"Don't think that. We're twenty-eight. There is a lot of life left to live. These memories with you, maybe not this one, I'll cherish them forever. It may take me a moment to get over you, but you never wasted my time." Brandon takes my chin between his thumb and forefinger, pulling my face to look at his. "However, it'll be a waste of your time if you don't learn from this."

"Okay," I reply, my shoulders tense as I take in what he said. I have to learn from this—more than you don't have to say yes to a proposal just because it's public. "Do you need to leave right now?"

"It would be for the best."

"Can you stay? Not for the night, but for a little longer. I'm not ready for this to be over yet."

"Yeah, I can." I'm surprised he says yes. His anger is still radiating, but I don't think he wants this to be over yet, either.

Brandon scoots closer to me and puts his arm around my shoulders, drawing me closer to him. I lean my head on his shoulder as he kisses the top of my head.

"I'm sorry, Brandon."

We sit there for an hour, Brandon holding me while I feel way too much. It's quiet, but I think he cried too.

After our tears have dried out, Brandon picks me up, carrying me to the couch, placing me on it, where I curl up into the fetal position. He covers me with my favorite fuzzy blanket with dogs on it. I lay there, emotionless, eyes glazed over, exhausted from tonight as he leaves.

I climb off the couch, heading to my bedroom closet like I tried to do hours earlier before Brandon stopped me.

A box is on the top shelf, behind a basket of belts and scarves. I stand on my tippy toes and remove the basket. Stretching further to reach the box, I pull it forward and off the shelf.

My memory box.

As a girl, my mom started this, keeping artwork and trinkets from my childhood. At first glance, you would think it was a shrine to me, but now it's a shrine of my memories.

Letters Natalie and I passed in high school. Photos of us from middle and high school dances—our outfits are tragic; Natalie would die if they ever saw the light of day now. I put aside these memories.

Reaching for what I came here for. Inside this memory box lies my relationship with Liam. Photos of the places we've been. Images showing how happy and *in love* we were. Cards from my birthday and holidays. Little trinkets that he would send me with messages of 'this made me think of you.' The first book he annotated.

Three years ago in September, two months after we ended, I collected all of these items and placed them in this box. That night was the last time I allowed myself to shed tears over him. I closed the lid and put the box in my closet. I haven't touched the box since then—well, until right now.

On both hands *and feet*, I could count the number of times that I desired to open this box. My willpower was so short some nights that I would distract myself.

Tonight though? I need them.

I *need* to relive those years. I need the comfort of these memories. Even though pain will inevitably come with reminiscing, I know I'll be wrapped in a blanket of comfort from the best summers of my life and my favorite version of myself.

I undo the rubber band that is holding a stack of photos together. It snaps me in the palm.

The photo on top is of Liam, Callum, and George. They're smiling on the beach in Lagos. They had just finished a push-up contest. George was trying to prove he was the strongest, but I didn't mind the view. Callum ultimately won and didn't let them forget it for the remainder of the day. I laugh out loud, thinking about how easily they adopted me into their trio. Beatrix and Audrey, too. Joking with me as if I was one of them. In many ways, I was one of them.

Before looking through the photos, I pull out the book and open it up. On the dedication page, in his surprisingly nice handwriting for a male, it says: *You are enough, States.*

20

LIAM

Six Summers Ago

"Are you going to tell us why Beatrix is with someone else?" Callum interrogates George.

"Isn't she always with someone else?" George makes a face and takes a large drink of his tropical cocktail, complete with a little umbrella skewered into a slice of pineapple. "It's just how it is with us."

"But this is the first time she's ever walked away from someone else to be with you?" I chime in.

"I don't know, and I don't care," George lies. He does care; he always has. They can't figure their shit out. At first, they blamed it on George going to medical school, but I don't think her parents like him all that much. They see him below her, below their status and money. Beatrix lives for her parents'—a.k.a. dad's—opinion, but at some point, when is it too much and time to say screw off? *I did.*

"You do care. Otherwise, you wouldn't be a lovesick puppy dog right now wishing that Bea would have said yes to coming instead of probably off shagging her friend."

"Callum." I throw a warning look in his direction.

"What? He does!"

"I love her. I have since secondary school. I know she loves me, but this—this is us, and we are both okay with it. Please drop it," George says with more emotion than I think he's ever shown in the duration of our friendship.

"When was the last time you talked to her about a relationship?"

"A year ago," George replies to me.

"I think you should talk to her again. You might be surprised that she's changed her mind," I say.

"Yeah. Maybe I'll call her up when we get back to London. Now, can we please focus on a fun boys' day in Lagos?"

"Boys and Emerson," I correct him.

"Right, the cheeky brunette. Saw her in your bed when Bea and I got back. The door was propped open before you call me a gossip." George and Callum both bounce their eyebrows at me.

"And I was on the couch before you made me go into the room," I tell them. "Be nice to her." I toss back my drink.

"A please wouldn't hurt," Callum coos.

"Oi, Liam. Always nice to girls from America," George smirks at me and then orders another drink. "Can I have another one of these?" He points down at the drink using the pink umbrella.

Callum and I follow suit and order another round of drinks while we wait for Emerson to meet us in the lobby before heading to the beach. We fall into our usual banter around Premier League and Premiership Rugby.

Emerson finally shows up in the lobby. The sound of her sandals clicking on the floor has our heads turning toward her. She's wearing the same denim shorts from earlier, but this time, no shirt, only a seersucker teal blue string bikini. Her hair is up in a high ponytail.

I fucking love a high pony.

George pats me on the shoulder twice as he walks by. "Good luck with that one," he says quietly.

"Let's go to the beach-each, let's go get a wave. They say what they gonna say have a drink, clink, found the Bud Light. Bad bitches like me—" She points to herself and then toward us to finish the Nicki Minaj lyric as we walk up to her.

"Not that hard to come by," George changes the lyric and throws an arm around her.

The two of them walk out of the hotel, singing and dancing to the rest of the song together. I don't even feel jealous that his arm is around her, touching the bare skin of her back. What I am feeling is more of an unknown territory. Should it feel right that she's getting along with my friends this well?

***

The four of us head down to Praia do Camilo. At the top of the stairs leading down to the beach, I offer my hand to her. To my surprise, she takes it, letting me guide her down the stairs.

"Is everything in Portugal made of hills and stairs? I swear everywhere I turn, there is some damn incline." She tries to laugh, but it comes out as a strained pant.

"It is," I reply to her.

"Want me to carry you?" George says at the same time. Tossing us a smirk over his shoulder.

"Two perfectly good legs. I think I can handle it," Emerson jokes back, and I like it. I like her a lot.

We find a space on the beach several meters away from the water.

Immediately, Callum and George take off their shirts and launch themselves into the water. Emerson is making camp for us. In the bag she brought are four towels, I assume from the hotel. Emerson lays two out on the sand, tossing a third to me. She lays hers out and uses her bag and a book to hold down opposite corners. I walk around the other towels and lay mine down next to hers, closer than it needs to be.

"You should go join them." She peers up at me from the towel she is sitting cross-legged on.

"You sure?" She nods.

Reaching behind me, I grab my shirt collar, pull it over my head, and drop it on the towel. Walking toward the water to meet my mates, I feel something hot on my back—Emerson's gawking at me again. It makes me smile.

She enjoys watching people. What her intention is of it, I don't know. At first, it made me feel special, but I realized she does it to everyone, everywhere—granted, I don't know if she's trying to undress them in her head as her eyes do me. She doesn't make it strange either. Her soft eyes help that. Not in the soft, bunny-like way. They're gentle and warm, a welcoming contrast to her rather sometimes inhospitable exterior. Maybe that's why it's not weird or why I never want her eyes to leave me.

Once my skin is pruney and I've swallowed at least a liter of salt water, thanks to boys being boys, I peek back at the beach to where our towels are, wanting to check in on Emerson. But she's not there. A momentary freakout rushes over me that something happened to her. It goes away quicker than it arrives when I find her down the shore walking.

"Emerson is fucking fit," I hear George say behind me. The three of us all stand waist-deep in the ocean, watching her.

Whack. Callum playfully hits George upside the head. "Shit man. What was that for?"

"Be polite. He asked us to be nice," Callum says.

"I am being nice! We always talk about each other's girls," George barks back. "Don't act like you don't have eyes, Callum, or forget that you were talking about how gorgeous her ti—"

Whack. Callum hits George again.

"Liam doesn't even appear to care."

Whack. This time, it's me who hits George. I do care. I care more than I should for only knowing her this short of a time.

"Reminder! We have rules," George says to us. "Till you sleep with her, she isn't yours."

Callum rolls his eyes and shakes his head. "George, when was the last time we followed the rules?"

"School," I respond.

"So two years ago," Callum concurs.

Back at university, we made this rule, *stupid rule*, when all three of us liked the same girl—word of advice for anyone, never go for the same girl as your friends. The rule eventually applied to any girl. Whoever slept with her first, well, she was their girl then.

SLEPT! Who does that? We did.

Unfortunately for Callum and I, George was the biggest player on campus. If we discovered a girl, he'd probably already have been with her by the time we met her. During our third year, the female population caught on. We thought we were screwed, but that's when the real games began, and we really got screwed.

I throw a glare over my shoulder at George. "Rules don't apply in cities that start with L anyway." I make that up on the spot.

"Nice try," George chuckles. "We went to school in L-O-N-D-O-N! And we are in Lagos? Now, if you want her, you better claim her."

George dives underwater, swimming off from us toward a group of girls to our right.

I look back to where Emerson is walking toward us in the water.

She isn't just hot. She's beautiful.

If that's the only thing George sees in her, then he'd never win the game if there was one to even begin with.

21

EMERSON

Now

You up?

Callum: I am now.

I miss him.

Callum: You text me at 4:30 am to tell me that. Tell him that, not me.

Brandon and I called off our engagement.

Not even seconds after I spotted the delivered message appear under the last text I sent to Callum, my phone rang.

I pick it up on the second ring. "Callum?"

"Emerson, it's about time that's called off."

"Excuse me, but I don't need you confirming that."

"Come on, he was a buffer for your mind. A placeholder for—"

"That's not true. I don't tell you everything."

"I smelled through your bullshit, States. Brandon was barely easing the fact that you wouldn't let yourself be with the person you want to be with," Callum continues without acknowledging that I spoke.

"He asked something similar to that."

"Did he now?"

"I don't need condescending Cal right now," I say firmly.

I fill Callum in on Liam and I's walk home and how Brandon had heard our hallway conversation through the door. Then, how Brandon graciously bowed out of our relationship. I know he's hurt and mad, but he left me with a proposition and words I desperately needed to hear.

"Are you okay?" Cal asks.

"I will be. I'm more upset that I hurt Brandon than the engagement being called off and that it was Liam who sent it spiraling."

"You have to stop blaming Liam."

"Why? None of this would have happened if he hadn't asked to come upstairs. I would still be engag—"

"Miserable. You'd be miserable, Emerson. Yeah, Brandon overheard, but Liam didn't do anything besides tell you the truth. All he's ever tried to do is show you the love you deserve. In a roundabout way, he did that tonight."

"I hate it when you are right."

"Most do. Are you mad I didn't tell you about Liam being there?"

"Not anymore. I was at first, but I realized it was probably for the best. I get you were protecting me in a way." Is that the truth? I'm not sure. "As I texted you, a heads up might have been nice, though."

"It's not that I didn't want to tell you."

"Telling me would have given me the opportunity to determine what I wanted to do and prepare any lingering emotions."

"After a year, I didn't expect you two to run into each other." His voice is sincere.

"Kind of hard not to when he's with my best friend." Callum can't see my eye roll but can easily hear the sarcasm dripping from my voice.

"Wait. You know Natalie? She's your best friend? Is that why he was at your place?"

"Slow your horses, dude. Natalie and I have known each other since we were seven."

"This makes sense."

Is he delusional? In what world does any of this make sense?

"Oh! Care to elaborate on how this all makes sense? Because none of this makes sense to me!"

"Well, one night, her phone lit up with a text notification. Ya know me, let my eyes wander over. The name of the text was Emme. That wasn't what caught my eye. It was a picture. Natalie sitting on a boat, hugging a smiling brunette. I thought she looked like you, but she had sunglasses on and short hair. Haven't seen you in years, so how would I know what your hairstyle is now? I just assumed it wasn't you."

It's the same photo I used as my lock screen. The picture was taken on the Fourth of July last summer.

"Surprise, it was me."

"Yeah, I realize that now." Callum pauses. "Probably could have thought about the name being Emme."

"You've never called me that before." Honestly, Callum is the only one who even calls me Em of the London crew. I'm just States to everyone there.

"I'm sorry, States."

"Don't be. The world being small isn't your fault." I swiftly change the subject. "I heard you are coming here soon, too."

"I'm gathering some of the documents we need from London before I fly over to meet Liam. Probably will be there within a week. Latest, two."

"Fair warning: Natalie will want to set us up once she finds out."

"Should I make George come instead? He'd love this. Still wants his chance with you, States," Cal jokes.

"Liam wouldn't allow it, you know that." I sigh at the irony of it. Liam would die seeing me with one of his friends but is currently with mine. "Beatrix, either. I'm excited to see you."

"Were you excited to see him?" Callum's question is direct.

"If I say yes, will you judge me?"

"No."

"I couldn't decide if I wanted to kiss his face. . . with my lips or my hands. Callum, I thought I was over it. I told you I moved on. . . but seeing him last week and with. . . her tonight was salt in my Liam-shaped wound."

"And talking to me isn't salt?" Cal keeps with my lousy analogy.

"No," I breathe out. "Does he know you still talk to me?"

Cal hesitates for a moment. "There are some things better left as secrets, I believe."

There's a beat of silence between us.

"Every few months, he asks about you, though. I reckon he knows."

"What do you say when he asks about me?" I ask, nervous to know the answer.

"Don't ask about what you don't want to know." His phone beeps, another call coming in. "I've got to take this, but Em."

"Yeah?"

"They aren't dating."

"Are you sure?" I don't believe him.

"Positive." Callum wraps up our call, telling me he'll see me soon and to try to get some sleep.

That didn't help. I miss Liam more now.

I toss my phone on the bed and let out an agonizing groan.

The photos I was looking through before he called are still in my hand. I scoot backward, resting my back against the side of my bed.

With the photos between my fingers, I keep flipping through them. I stop five photos in, holding them as if I could somehow enter them and be taken back to that moment.

It's a candid picture of me and Liam. George was always sneaking my camera—several photos were taken that I wish I had never seen, but others like this, I wish there were more of them.

We were out for drinks after dinner in Lagos. Liam and I were walking back from the bar to our table. My camera was in George's hand. I was sure he was using it to zoom in on a girl's butt.

Liam leaned down to whisper in my ear. Full belly laughs took over me instantly, and I tripped over myself. Liam's hand, without a drink in it, reached out to catch me and bring me to him. The photo is of him holding me. My body curled into his. My head tilted up at him, smiling and laughing. His eyes locked on me. The expression in them that night was confusing. He kept looking at me as if he wanted me, but it was as if I had grown a second head in the next blink of his eyes.

Liam steadied me; my head was still turned up at him. He brought me closer. As we stood there, he focused his gaze on my lips, mere inches from each other. So close. A single movement from either of us would have caused a collision. His breath hitched as my tongue darted out to moisten my lips.

All I wanted was for him to kiss me.

But something happened when I thought he would lean in and do it. His eyes closed, and he pulled his head away. He released me from his arms and walked back to the table.

George captured the moment.

Our *almost moment* captured forever, in a stack with our *almost forever*.

22

EMERSON

Six Summers Ago

Today was one of those days that you remember forever. The type of day you tell your grandchildren about when you're reminiscing about what it was like to be young and dumb.

This would be my definition of young and dumb.

Alone. In a foreign country, spending the day with three boys I barely know. It also sounds like the start of the next *Crime Junkie* episode, but something deep inside me, so innate, is telling me to do it. Go there. Be with them—*be with him.*

In all seriousness, though, I couldn't have imagined a more perfect day.

My expectations were already low—anyone's would be if you thought you were going to be spending the next four weeks of your life alone. Not that I would have minded, but after having the most fun I've had on this trip, I'm grateful to subtract one day from those I'll spend solo.

"Does this place work for everyone?" Callum asks.

After dinner, we all agreed to go out.

We're standing in the middle of a cobblestone street. No cars can drive on the road, only bikes and pedestrians. The night is crisp, with no clouds and only stars in the sky. Neon signs from restaurants and bars illuminate our faces.

"You're one of us now, you realize?" George wraps an arm around my shoulders, squeezing me into him as we walk toward our destination. "Drink for a drink. Tit for tat. We pace each other, so you better keep up."

"Yeah?" I shrug out of his embrace. "You forget, I went to college in America."

George smiles at me with too much excitement, which scares me for wherever he's expecting this night to go.

"Ready?" Liam reaches for my hand, pulling me with him and into the place.

George grabs a round of shots from the bar while we find a high table. Eagerly, he raises them in the air as he makes his way to the table.

Callum and him seated on one side, Liam and me on the other.

"Cheers, mates!" We clink our glasses together before dropping back the shots.

My eyes shoot close, and the cold liquid, vodka, sends a shiver through my veins. I feel it to my toes, and they curl. Opening my eyes, I find Liam focused on me with a feline smile, and my toes curl again.

"Bar?" he asks me.

"Lead the way."

The guys gave us their drink order, which was beer, as expected. Everyone wanted a beer except for Liam, who ordered a Negroni with an extra shot of gin.

"Something stronger?" I eye him, brows raised in suspicion.

"What should I be drinking then? That piss water you just ordered? I'll pass."

"If you want piss water, you should come to the Midwest. This stuff"—I gesture to the glass bottle set down in front of me—"is much better. I promise."

"Maybe someday I will."

Maybe someday I will. Butterflies flutter in my stomach at the idea of seeing Liam again—more than today and in Chicago.

What would it be like to see him again? I think I want to.

George coughs once as we return to the table. I pass their drinks to them across the sticky table. He slides my camera toward me. It wasn't out when I left the table, but I swore I saw it in his hands when we were walking back from the bar. What he took a picture of, I don't think I want to see.

"Left ya a lil' surprise on there."

"Thanks?" I ask cautiously.

"Someday, you'll thank me for it." He winks.

Liam and I slip back into our seats next to each other. Me on the left, him on the right. He sat on the right at dinner earlier, too. Liam whispered into my ear at dinner that he noticed I am left-handed and figured it would make it easier for me to eat and have space without him bumping his right arm into me.

"So, States. Tell us about growing up over the pond," George says.

"Am I getting interviewed?" I ask snarkily.

"Easy, girl." His hands rise in front of him. "Only curious about where you are from."

"Indiana," Liam beats me to the answer.

"Good memory." I glance over at him, taking a sip of my beer. He looks proud of himself for knowing the answer. "I'm from Fishers, Indiana. It's a suburb of Indianapolis. Smack in the middle of the Midwest. If you were to visit, you'd get nothing like this or what I bet London is like. We have miles and miles of farmland."

"Cal here is used to the farmland. Aren't ya? He's from the town of Guildford in Surrey," George says.

"My grandparents used to be sheep farmers. Dad wasn't about it and moved to Sydney, where he met my mom. When we moved back, I loved spending parts of the break from school on their farm," Callum elaborates.

"It's easy to forget that even thousands of miles apart, some parts of life are so similar. That our worlds aren't all that different," I respond.

"This is why I enjoy exotic girls. They bring perspective, and I'm always interested in learning something worldly."

Callum spits out his beer after George's response.

He...what? My eyes flutter. "Exotic?"

"Aye, like you." George smirks.

"What's the minimum qualification, not being from wherever you are located?"

"Bingo!" George cheers.

"Got. . . it." I turn toward Liam, pointing the neck of my beer his way. He hasn't said a word. "What about you?"

"I don't like you because you're not from here, but it is a hot bonus." He winks.

"That's not what I meant." I swallow. My cheeks pink at the thought that he likes me.

"What about me?" he asks.

"Want to share with the group about yourself?"

"Grew up in London, went to school in London, and I live in London now. Doubtful that anyone could drag me away from living there. I don't think there is a me without London."

Callum and George roll their eyes. I already knew this; we talked about it earlier. I wanted an excuse to hear him speak.

"Any siblings?" I ask the table.

"Only child." Liam points to himself. "Cal has two older brothers and a younger sister. George is a middle child of two sisters."

"Callum's sis is a real babe, too. Audrey is finishing up school at Oxford now. Studying psychology."

"I'm going to pretend you didn't say that," Callum says.

"You aren't going to tell me that my sisters aren't babes? I'd be offended because my mum is stunning, and we all got our looks from her."

"I wouldn't call them babes to your face, man. He has one older sister who lives in Paris now, and the other is about to be at university."

Hearing them speak for each other about these details of their lives is endearing. It shows how knotted their friendship is, which reminds me a lot of Natalie and me.

Natalie. Wow, this is the first time I've thought about her since we arrived. And I haven't heard from her all day either. I figured I wouldn't be able to avoid thinking about her with the consistent texts I would be receiving, but she's been silent.

I fire off a quick text to her.

"Any sibling for you, States?"

"Nope. Only child."

"Damn, I've always wanted to cross off my bucket list, American sisters," George remarks. His tone is deadly serious.

"For fuck's sake George." Callum slams his bottle on the table, causing it to bubble up toward the top. "What is the matter with you?"

"Nothing." He shrugs.

"I'm sorry to disappoint. What if I find someone that looks similar to me? Would that work out that kink for you?"

"States, I'd rather just have you."

"I'm flattered, but you're not my type." I give George a quick wink to be sure he knows I'm only partially kidding and not out here trying to bruise his already large ego.

"He's everyone's type," Liam butts in. A scraping noise draws my attention to where he moved his chair closer to mine. The side of our knees barely touch. "If he's not, then what is?"

Smooth way to find out if he's my type. I know he's curious. I'm curious if I'm his too.

"If I said you, would you try to discreetly bring your chair closer to mine again?" I call him out. "I don't have a type, but if I did. . . it wouldn't be you either." I lick my lips, noticing he's staring at them.

Liam leans in toward me.

"Liar," he whispers in my ear. His breath is hot, traveling down the upper half of my body right to between my thighs. He leaves his mouth there, the touch of his lips on my skin is faint. My eyes close lightly. "I think I'm exactly your type. It's all over your face, States."

I pull my knee away from his. The spot is cold from the lack of skin-to-skin contact, but I need the cold. I need the cold to decrease the record-high temperature my body is pushing.

I don't bury the use of his nickname for me—well, their nickname for me. George and Callum have also adapted it. But it's the way Liam says it. He calls me it, and it makes me feel like I'm his. His in a way that I've never been anyone's before—but I'm not his. So why is there a part of me that thinks it might be okay if I was?

I blink rapidly, trying to rid myself of this thought and wash the look that is all over my face away.

"Didn't enjoy what you saw earlier today?" Liam slides his hand under the table, placing it on my thigh right above my knee. He gives it a slight squeeze as he starts moving it up. Higher and higher. "I bet if I were to keep going, I'd be able to tell exactly how much you liked it. Thus proving that I am your type."

"You wouldn't," I dare him. I'm looking straight ahead, giving him zero indication of exactly how wet I am for him.

"You're right. I won't because I respect a woman, and if she says I'm not her type, then I'm not her type."

Liam swiftly removes his hand from my thigh and places it back on the table.

"Unlike you, I won't lie. You are my type. Quite my type, Emerson." My name is a purr on his lips, the sound of it petting every plane of my body.

He's not leaning into me anymore, acting as if nothing just happened. Liam reaches for his drink, picks it up, and brings it to his lips. I watch as his throat bobs when he swallows.

I swallow. . . a little too loud.

Callum and George sit there pretending to ignore what is happening across the table when we all know they are well aware.

I return us to the conversation.

I'm trying not to let his words, the heat, or whatever went on between Liam and me linger.

Ignore it, and it'll all go away, right? Yeah, right.

We continue talking about growing up. When asked about our parents, both Liam and I avoided answering. It all ends with them sharing stories from college. I love hearing them talk about this, especially the stories about Liam.

The entire day, I craved to get to know him better. I want to know everything there is about him. Who he was as a kid and who he is now. How he started his company, and what his aspirations in life are. His favorites—foods, TV shows, books. How his lips would feel on mine.

I think he wants to know me too.

Every time I've spoken tonight, his attention has been devoted to me. He wasn't distracted like George or Callum, even though they asked a majority of the questions. Liam only listens. I kept sneaking peeks at him; his blue-gray eyes looked like they were processing and storing every piece of information about me as he did last night.

I've always appreciated the small things. Big gestures are one thing, but I think you see someone through small, intimate gestures, like remembering where someone is from. It doesn't take a lot to show someone you care about them.

If someone wanted to go back and tell my parents that, I would appreciate that, too.

Liam doesn't move his chair back to its original spot. Instead, he keeps moving it closer like I am a magnet, drawing him closer, the force too strong to repel.

We are close enough now that the whole side of my leg is touching his. My skirt has ridden up, revealing more of my bare leg to his touch.

The connection between our lower bodies is searing. If he were to put his hand back on my thigh now, it might put me over the ed—shit, I think he just read my mind. The palm of his hand is now firmly situated on my leg.

Liam is a magnet for me, too.

My upper body is inching closer and closer to him.

I almost forgot we have company at the table. That we aren't the only two at this table, in the bar, in this city, or in the entire world. I've somehow lost myself in him.

Callum and George are enthralled by their phones.

Liam and I are in the middle of our own conversation now. We are bickering about something important—what the best pizza toppings are.

Mine are banana peppers and honey.

His is pepperoni.

"You know that makes you boring, right? Only pepperoni."

"It's not boring. It's called consistency. Always good, and everyone is bound to have a pepperoni pizza on their menu. Boring is better than being a weirdo that wants to have sticky fingers when they eat pizza."

I would say Liam is like his choice in toppings, consistent, but he keeps surprising me.

"I'm not a neanderthal. I don't get it on my hands."

"No! Please tell me you aren't the person who eats pizza with a fork and knife." He's barely two inches away from me—mouth wide, with a playful look of disgust.

"So what if I do?" I lean my head in closer.

From the proximity of our faces, I can see the gray speckles in his blue eyes. Far away, it's easy to lose the gray in the blue, but right now, I can see the crystal the gray makes his eyes. It's as if the Atlantic displaced some of its water in his eyes. They are a shade of blue I've never seen before that has me leaning in closer for a better look.

"I take it back. You aren't my type then," he says.

The right side of his mouth raises, a half smirk plastered on his face. His ocean eyes dip to my lips. I pull part of my lower lip in between my teeth. Liam inhales sharply.

Carefully closing the remaining distance between us, I lightly brush a kiss on his lips, pulling away before he has the opportunity to kiss me back. "That's a shame, then." I pull the entirety of my body away from him. "For a minute, I thought you were mine."

23

EMERSON

Six Summers Ago

Callum and George bid us a goodnight, claiming they were tired and wanted to return to the hotel. Their fake yawns were theatrical at best.

It's only Liam and me now. This is our first time alone since I woke up in his arms this morning.

"Are you tired too?" Liam asks me. "We can head back if you are."

I'm exhausted, *but* I want this little bit of alone time together. It's potentially the last I'll get before we go our separate ways tomorrow, and I still have this itch to know more about Liam—all of him, really.

"No." I yawn. "Would you care to take a walk, though? It's nice out tonight."

We've already finished our drinks as the place gets busier. The bar is body to body, and people are waiting in the wind to snag our table the minute we leave.

"Let's go."

His accent still throws me occasionally. I'm not enamored with it; okay, that's a lie. I might be a teensy bit obsessed, but it's when he uses words or phrases that I don't know that it throws me. Or, like tonight, when he drinks, and it gets thicker and rougher, the sound of it is like morning stubble being brushed against my most sensitive skin.

I watch others around us, heading to dinner, drinks, or to get lost in the night. Everyone appears happy. We appear happy.

I am happy. I'm happy being here with Liam.

An emotion I'm slightly scared to admit to myself.

"If I haven't told you already, I'm sorry." Liam breaks the silence between us. "You look beautiful tonight."

Liam hadn't told me. I didn't need him to say it to know he was thinking it. He's looking at me the way he did earlier at the beach. I don't think I was supposed to see him looking, but I caught the glances between conversations, behind his sunnies, and when I was walking along the shoreline. Each time a seed of feelings was planted in my stomach, I'd shake it away but then catch him watching me again, and that feeling would blossom again. By now, I probably have a whole garden in there.

Have you ever had someone look at you as if they can see right through you to exactly who you are at your core? I hadn't till I met Liam. That's how he looks at me.

With eyes on me, backlit by the moon and stars, I think that maybe I could *love* him.

A cluster of laughs and recklessness barrels at us from the small convenience store to the right, startling me from that obscured thought. A group of six children, not paying attention to where they are running, and their trajectory unintentionally aims straight toward me.

They are going to ram right into me.

Liam reaches out, pulling me to him before they have a chance to trample me. He growls curses at them to watch where they are going, but they ignore him and run along. Liam doesn't let go of my waist once we are away from them down the street. He shifts his hand to the lower dip of my back, guiding us back toward the hotel.

"I had a great time today," I tell him.

"Me too." Liam leans his head toward me and smiles. His smile takes up the entirety of his face. I don't think I've ever seen someone smile so big or been this attracted to a smile before.

"You are a great friend to Callum and George. You know that?"

"They are great to me too. The two of them are the brothers I never had. Cal is the sensible one, as you can probably tell. And George, he's the pesky younger brother, always buggin' you and up to no good. I didn't have many friends like them till I got to uni. We've been through a lot together, and honestly—I don't think I would be here without them." His hand rubs my back in small little circles. "Tell me more about your friends and family. You didn't speak about them earlier."

"I always wanted a sibling—a big family. But my parents never wanted another child; thinking back, I see that it was for the best. They divorced when I was in middle school. Nat, the friend with whom I was on this trip, is basically my sister."

"I remember you mentioning that this morning."

"We went to college together—we didn't even apply to different schools—and we're moving to Chicago together at the end of the summer. Looking back on my life, it's always been the two of us."

"I think friends can be family. Sometimes, the best family we have is the one we find."

"I agree. She's kind of like George." We laugh at the comparison, even though he doesn't know her. "They are almost the same person. I swear they'd be two peas in a bed if they ever met."

"I owe a lot of myself to her. She's stayed around. A lot of who I am and what I do is for her. Losing Nat would be a heartbreak I don't think I'd ever overcome." I go on to tell him more stories about the two of us from growing up.

"What about your parents?" I ask him, over talking about myself.

"My mom passed away three years ago from a long battle with cancer."

"Liam, I'm so sorry." I squeeze his hand, which I interlocked with mine.

"It's weird when she passed, I was sad, still am, and don't think I won't ever be when I think about her, but I was relieved that she wasn't in pain any longer. The last two years were utterly brutal for her. She fought with everything in her, but it wasn't enough. Knowing she is in heaven and has a healthy body again is the joy I find in the situation. I'll see her again someday, I know." He tugs a tight, worn smile. "My dad and I don't speak much. He was angry that I didn't return to football after being injured."

"Is that what ended your career?" I ask him.

"No." Liam shakes his head, his tone slightly cold. "I could have returned, but I didn't want to. I loved the sport, but it became too much about my dad and getting to the professional level that I lost my love of it. As kids, coaches tell us to have fun, but I think people forget that at some point along the way. It wasn't fun living with his pressure. I used the injury as my way out."

"When did this happen?"

"I was starting my second year at university. At that point, several teams were bidding for me to join them."

"I guess. . . I don't get it. You were there. Practically, in the pros. Why not return?"

"Not my dream, States." He sighs.

"What do you mean?"

"It was my dad's dream for me to play professionally, not mine. I didn't want to disappoint him, so I lied and used the injury. He demanded excellence growing up, pushing me constantly, and as a kid, I thought I had to do what he wanted. I let his dreams confiscate my own till university and when my mom passed."

"What is your dream?"

"Travel. Hotels. Fun."

I tip my head up toward him, creating a space for him to elaborate—if he wants. He's given me the opportunity and safe space to speak freely. The least I can do is return the favor, but selfishly, I do it because I want to know more.

"I want Hayes Hotels to become a global hotel line. Luxury places to stay worldwide known for their community impact and incredible views, giving people an excuse not to stay home."

Liam continues telling me about Hayes Hotels. Without ever stepping foot into one, I feel as if I have. He talks about them and his dreams as if they are canvas and he is the painter, fluidly moving the brush, creating the most vivid picture. I can't help my gaze as it focuses on him, mesmerized by his rhapsodic smile and the childlike excitement in his eyes.

"I have two in London and am working on a third."

"That's incredible. Where is the third?" I can barely ask through the memorization of him.

"Edinburgh."

"Did you always want to do this?"

Liam chuckles. His cold tone is no longer present. It's replaced with lightness and passion.

"Oh no. From age five to ten, I was properly convinced I wanted to be a tube operator."

"A what?"

"The person who operates the underground train in London. I was fascinated with trains and thought the tube was awesome."

"I can picture it." I grin at him, trying to contain the laugh bubbling in me. "A striped denim cap on your head. Three-piece navy blue suit. Total Tom Hanks in *Polar Express* vibes. There is still time to change career paths," I tease.

"Sounds riveting, but I might stick to this." Liam pulls me closer to him. His mouth up against my ear, he says, "Unless that is. . . your type."

"Hmm. . ." I turn so that my lips are to his ear. "I'll pass. I think I like this Liam a lot."

"Is that so?"

I shrug.

"When did you buy your first hotel—wait, how could you afford that? I don't expect that to be cheap or something you casually fall into?"

"It's not. My mom is how I came into the money. Her parents had left her and me a trust. The terms of my trust from my grandparents gave me access when I turned twenty-one. When my mom passed, all of her possessions and money became mine."

"So you are rich?"

"I'spose. I've invested a lot of the money into my company."

"But you're twenty-four? You didn't do anything dumb with the money?"

"Didn't say that. I enjoy myself, but don't overindulge."

"That's why you didn't ask for me to pay." He nods. "Did someone teach you or help you?"

"I studied business at school, but a business professor of mine invested in me—time, money, and wisdom. He helped me create a business plan and then lay the foundation. In the fall of my final year, he invested in the company after I found my first property—a hotel that had already opened and was searching for new ownership. Hotel Magenta reopened two months after I graduated."

"He must be proud of his return on investment," I say, but I don't mean the money. I mean Liam. He's driven and brilliant, and despite his presumptuous behavior, he's humble about everything he's achieved. He's incredible.

We fall into a comfortable silence for the remainder of the walk back to the hotel.

Every so often, I pretend to miss a step, forcing his grip to become firmer, bringing me physically in balance but more emotionally unbalanced.

At the hotel, Liam walks me to my room.

Your room is below his. He has to pass your floor naturally. Don't read into this, Emerson, I have to tell myself.

In the hallway, we are standing outside the door to my room. I turn to face him. Liam reaches up and tucks a strand of loose hair behind my ear. His fingers graze my cheek in the process. He leaves his hand tucked in my hair, his focus dropping to my lips. Again.

"You're staring at them like you're trying to decide whether you should kiss me," I call him out.

Yes. Yes, you should kiss me. I try to tell him with my eyes.

He takes a deep breath.

His chest rises and falls.

"Tell me not to," he breathes out, fluttering his eyes close.

"I can't do that."

He doesn't move.

"It doesn't need to be anything more than it needs to be," I say with encouragement for the both of us. "It's just a kiss. A way to satisfy our curiosity, nothing more."

Except I know that it'll mean more, and I'll want more. A kiss won't be enough.

"Emerson—" His eyes are pleading with me to put an end to this, but his body is telling me a different story. It's a story I want to finish writing together and on the other side of the door.

Without thinking twice, I rise on my tiptoes and kiss him.

If he isn't going to do it, I might as well. Pressing myself against him gently, letting my top lip linger between his for a few seconds.

"Now, are you going to kiss me, or should I go get Geor—"

I'm unable to finish my sentence. Liam's lips fuse with mine.

He's fiercely kissing me as his body moves closer. My body hits the door behind me with a thud. He brings his free hand to cup my other cheek, holding me to him. Liam trails his fingers up my sizzling skin and into my hair. He leverages my head, tilting it to bring my mouth closer to him and deepening our kiss. I release a soft moan into his mouth.

It's good. A damn good kiss and no kiss should ever be this good.

My hands roam his back as I feel every curve and line of his muscles. They shudder under my touch.

There isn't much space between our bodies, but I push on him, trying to bring him closer because I need him closer.

Liam stops kissing me and removes his lips from mine. One hand falls to my waist, the other from my hair to my face. He drags his thumb over my lips until it reaches my mouth's center. "No one, and I mean no one else, gets to kiss these lips. They're mine.

I want you to be mine." He says it as if it's a question for me to answer.

Pulling his thumb down and catching my bottom lip, he stops when he reaches my chin, nodding in agreement.

The world around me goes quiet as Liam places both of his hands under my thighs. He picks me up, and I wrap my legs around his waist, putting us level. My hips ground into him as he sandwiches me against the wall. I thought the last kiss was good, but this kiss takes me to heaven. I've never gotten off from only a kiss before, but with his possession and precision, I might—not to forget the incredible hardening length that is supplying ample pressure to my core.

Our kiss breaks when the footsteps in the stairwell echo down the hall. I'm placed on the ground, watching in shock as Liam pulls away. Standing there, Liam's eyes roam up and down my body, watching as my chest rises and falls in tune with my heavy pants as I try to find air that isn't him.

His hands that were holding me are now firmly planted on the wall next to either side of my head. Liam extends his arms, putting distance between us. He, too, is panting.

The footsteps become muffled as they climb higher and further away from us. A quiet tension now looms between us. Unlike earlier, this silence is uncomfortable and feels weighted. I can see it in his eyes that he is contemplating what next.

Option one, we open the door and find out what else could be good—based on those kisses, I'm pretty confident it would be.

Option two, we pretend that this kiss didn't happen and go back to being strangers to friends.

I'm not positive there is a correct next move, but I know which one I want. Like I already knew, this kiss isn't enough.

I turn to face the door, scanning my door key.

"Do you want to come in?" I ask over my shoulder, glancing back to see that Liam already selected option two.

24

LIAM

Six Summers Ago

After arriving back in Lisbon from Lagos, the four of us parted ways to our respective hotels but with the promise that we would see each other later.

Emerson claimed she needed a nap after not sleeping much the night before. I couldn't help the pang of guilt that sat with me. Did she not sleep because of me? I can't say that I got much, either. The entire evening played back in my head.

After a cold shower, my hand, and the taste of her lips, the regret of walking away left me lying in bed, staring at the ceiling. It crossed my mind to go back downstairs.

Tell her I'm sorry I left her standing in the hallway.

Tell her why I walked away—even though she'd roll her eyes at the reason.

It wasn't the alcohol consumption last night that influenced my decision. It wasn't how she pretended to trip to force my hold on her to tighten or the taunt about getting George. It was the fact that in less than forty-eight hours, we would never see each other again.

That's why it would never be just a kiss—or one night together.

It's ironic how the time we have left is the same amount of time that it took for her to become someone to me. Someone that one night with wouldn't be enough. *A whole lifetime with her wouldn't be enough.*

Two days later, I want her as much as I did that night.

And that's the problem. Forty-eight hours became days, and now I'm debating going to Paris with her.

Except that Emerson didn't mention anything the morning after the kiss. She acted like nothing happened between us.

Today hasn't been much different.

"States is effing cool, mate." George draws my attention to him.

Emerson is sorting through painted tile coasters for her apartment in Chicago.

We visited Miradouro da Senhora do Monte, taking the trolley up to it earlier before walking through a market, hopping between food and souvenir stands. The guys and I have been tracking all over the city with her, making sure to cross everything off her Lisbon list.

"I know."

"Had an interesting chat this morning."

"Yeah? While I was running?" I raise an eyebrow toward him.

"Yeah. I might have asked her about you..."

"What do you mean about me?" My pulse picks up.

"Last night at dinner, the two of you had this weird tension-infested force field surrounding you."

"Force field. . . ?" George waves off my comment.

"That's not the point. I asked States about it this morning. When she met Cal and me in the hotel lobby for breakfast, I could sense she was nervous about being around us—turns out you, today."

"What did she say about me?"

"If you'd shut up, you'd find out."

I go to speak but close my mouth.

"She said you snogged her in Lagos, which we knew. She also said you left her standing there in the hallway when she went to invite you in, which we didn't know. States went on to ask about your past. Curious about how you are with other women and one-night stands."

I run my hands through my hair, tugging on the brown strands.

"I didn't want her to be just another girl I've slept with. She's not like that to me," I admit.

"Why didn't you tell her that?"

"I didn't want her to feel rejected or explain emotions I'm still trying to navigate."

"You're an idiot. It was still rejection either way. I think she would have understood."

"You do?"

"She seems reasonable. But when Cal and I glanced at each other, not knowing how to respond, she rolled her eyes and mumbled about this being another reason she doesn't believe in love."

Emerson doesn't believe in love? "What?"

"I was confused, too. A tad shocked after how she's been interacting with you. Cal tried to ask her about it, and she shut down."

How can anyone not believe in love? I swear I remember her mentioning that she loved her best friend. Or taking a bite of a Pastel de Nata and outwardly claiming her love for her new favorite pastry.

Is that feeling not the same? How can one love but not believe in it?

I watch her and Cal move to the next merchant stand. George, standing next to me, watching me as I try to figure her out.

***

The next afternoon, Emerson asked me to go with her to Paris, her next stop, and I said yes. I had already told her I loved Paris and created a non-tourist list of places to see, eat, and do.

Paris was one of my mom's favorite cities, and being back always feels like I'm visiting her. Business brings me here occasionally, but being in Paris with Emerson is like seeing it for the first time—and the best part, from her eyes.

I think I would be okay seeing everything from her perspective for the rest of my life.

We've checked everything off her Paris list, including a day trip to Versailles, an afternoon in the Louvre, and a visit to the Shakespeare and Company bookstore.

Being the Emerson Clarke I've learned her to be, she's benevolent at her core. After every item we crossed off, she asked me what I wanted to do, see, or eat. Every time, I told her I didn't care. As long as she's right beside me, that's what I want to do.

She's still under the impression that tomorrow is my last day with her. But while she's sleeping in, which is what I'm assuming she is doing because I have yet to have a knock on my door this morning, I finalize arrangements to finish her trip with her.

I plan to tell her tonight.

Cal: Anything else you need me to cover?

No. I'll call if there is. Thanks again.

Stepping away from the office for the next month to be with Emerson wasn't easy to coordinate, but it was an easy decision. I'll stay ahead on emails or whatever work I can, but I'm thankful for Callum handling everything in person. He's a tremendous friend-CFO hybrid. I return my phone to the bedside table, returning to my book. Ten minutes later, my phone buzzes with another text from Callum and George.

Cal: Don't fall too in love with her

George: I bet he already has.

I stretch out my arms. My mind slips to thinking about Emerson, as it has every other minute for the past ten days. I'm thinking about her sleeping. She's the most peaceful sleeper I've ever seen, not that I watch people sleep often or that I've seen her sleep except for our first night together. Her soft, pink lips part slightly, and she breathes so softly that you almost think she isn't breathing. It terrified me at first.

Like dominos, I fixate on her lips and kissing them again.

Everything about her draws me to her. I'm obsessed, and I've never been this obsessed with anyone or anything in my life. I consume as much as I can—time included. I know this trip will end, and our time together will expire. I'll head back to London, and she'll be back in the States, but until then, I want anything and everything I can get from her.

There's a knock on my door. Light, three times. Emerson.

Our rooms are next door to each other. Based on her original accommodations, she has two beds in her room, but I, *stupidly but respectfully*, insisted on getting my own.

"Good morning," her soft, sleepy female voice says as I open the door. Emerson is still in her pajamas.

"Good morning," I reply, tucking loose hair behind her ear and running my fingers through its soft strands. "Wanna come in?"

"That's why I'm standing here." She brushes past me with a smirk. "Can I use your bathroom?"

"Don't ya have one in your room?"

"Yeah, but I got up and came right here. Didn't have to go then."

"What's on our agenda for today?" I ask her as she exits the bathroom.

She walks over to the bed, joining me on it. Folding her knees beneath her, she gives me a gentle smile. "Well—" Emerson finds my eyes, locking her big green ones into my blue-gray. There's an idea turning behind them. "I had this idea. . . but you might think it's stupid."

Emerson bites her lip.

Those daydreams of her mouth from earlier this morning? They're back. I try to brush them aside instead of crawling to where she's seated and kissing them, focusing on what she's saying and not where the words are coming from.

"No stupid ideas, remember?" I remind her.

"We said no stupid questions between us, not ideas."

"Semantics."

"Not really—"

"Say your idea, but add a question inflection at the end. It's a question then."

She rolls her eyes at me, and her chest raises with a silent laugh.

"Okay then. What if we order room service, and then we flip a coin? Heads you pick, tails I pick? No set plans, we see where fate takes us?" Emerson tilts her head and gives me puppy dog eyes, working this whole question-thing. "My dad and I used to play this before my parent's divorce. It became our thing. Each game was a new adventure, leading us to places we knew and had yet to discover, even in my hometown," she tacks on.

I didn't need the explanation; I would have said yes to whatever came out of her mouth. Spending time with Emerson is enough for me. Getting to know this about her? Getting to share in one of these good memories of her dad? That makes today that much better.

Emerson doesn't talk about her parents. Whenever the topic comes up between us, she changes it. All I know is that they divorced when she was in middle school.

"Do you want to be heads or tails?" I ask her.

"Tails, always." Emerson gleams at me. "I'm going to change. I'll be back in thirty minutes, top. Can you order breakfast for us?" She jumps from her position on the bed and bounces out of the room.

"You got it, States."

25

LIAM

Six Summers Ago

"Tell me about your parents."

"What about them?" Emerson asks me.

"You mentioned they are divorced, but avoid them in other conversations."

It landed on tails during our last flip. Emerson decided on a bottle of wine and a snack in front of the Eiffel Tower. We picked up fresh bread, cheese, and fruit before finding a spot along the water.

"I don't like talking about them." She chews on a torn-off piece of baguette.

"I can see that. Why?" Emerson sighs. "I don't mean to pressure you." And I don't, but George's comment about her not believing in love isn't lost on me, and I've deduced it down to this.

Emerson takes a big drink of her wine, finishing it entirely.

"I was thirteen when he left. A year later, he remarried someone else. She has two kids, a boy my age and a girl four years younger. So, I guess I lied. I do have siblings if you count them, but I don't have a relationship with them. My dad didn't want custody of me." I'll never understand how a parent couldn't want their child. Even in my parents' divorce and estranged relationship with my dad, they both loved and wanted me. "Mom's lawyer was the one to negotiate—force him into one weekend every other month and split holidays. His new wife had split custody of her kids and coordinated it perfectly. I was never there at the same time. Only a handful of weekends and some holidays in the five years crossed over."

"How is your relationship with your dad?"

Emerson laughs. "You think I have daddy issues, don't you?"

"Should I?" I give her a concerned but puzzled look.

"No—both of my parents messed me up." *Oh.*

"Dad left, and Mom went into shambles. She tried, but she didn't know how to function without him. Mom first blamed herself until she discovered he was dating and the woman had kids. That's when she blamed me. Snide remarks here and there. Sarcastic jokes and little jabs that made sure I felt like I was the reason he left—that if I was a better daughter, then he would have loved me enough and wouldn't have needed not just one new kid, but two."

We both take a deep breath. Emerson's words knocked the breath away from me.

"Nat was the one who picked me up every time I cried," Emerson continues. "Her family let me come over for dinner or stay with them when Mom couldn't get it together enough. She became my family then. It took years for my mom to come around, but she did—sort of. She half-assed apologized. Our relationship is courteous now, but I can't help feeling that I lost out on fundamentals. That all of it affected me more than I've come to terms with."

Yeah, her childhood affected her. She's a people pleaser—and I think she knows it even though she does it subconsciously—who doesn't believe in love. I can see it in how she talks about her friend and why she always asks what I want. Emerson doesn't think she's good enough for anyone and believes she has to be a chameleon of their happiness to make them stay and love her.

I wish she knew that isn't true.

I properly fancy her for her.

"I used to love fairytales as a kid," she says.

"Is that why you can't remove your nose from books, and we've been to—" I count on my fingers all the bookstores we've had to go to. "Eleven bookstores?"

Nudging my shoulder playfully, Emerson smiles at me, and that's all I want right now. I know she doesn't enjoy talking about this, and I can see her drifting into herself.

"Yes." Her smile fades. "After my parents split, I hated them. Hated the idea of happily ever after. Everything about them felt like a lie. But that grew tiring—hating them so much. I might not believe in love, but I enjoy escaping my reality into worlds where it's safe to believe in it. Places and stories that allow you to be someone that is enough to deserve a relentless, written in the stars, type of love."

My eyes are watery. I keep blinking to keep them at bay, but all I can do is feel the weight of her confession on my shoulders.

How can someone this wonderful feel so much distaste? How is it possible for her to never feel enough?

"Wow." Emerson covers her face with her hands. "I did not mean to say all of that. To think you only asked about my parents. You probably think I'm messed up in the head, that it's no surprise no one loves her."

"You're wrong." I move her hands from her face, holding them in one hand. I hold her chin in the other, forcing her to look at me. "You are so easy to love, Emerson. I'm sorry no one has ever made you feel that way *before*." Before me because I don't want her ever to think that she isn't enough for me.

I let go of her hands. Without thinking, I brush a strand of hair behind her ear, leaning in to kiss her. I might not be in love with her—yet—but I can show her love. A love she's always deserved, a love that is real and does exist.

She kisses me back. Her bottom lip coming between mine. Its glorious fullness tempts me to bite down on it. Emerson lets out a soft moan before opening her mouth to all of me, letting my tongue roam into her mouth.

It's a cascade of small kisses till we're making out in front of the Eiffel Tower. It doesn't stop as we move closer together, and my hands grip the back of her head. I hold her to me because I never want to leave—leave this position, leave this place, leave *this girl*.

I don't know who pulls away first, but we do.

"One last flip? Whoever it lands on, the night is theirs to decide," Emerson asks.

Ideas are already running through my head: how to show her all the ways that she is capable of being loved—and how to get back into this position.

"The entire night?"

"Yes?" She stares at me, puzzled.

"Hand me the coin, aye. I'll flip." I take the coin that is in her palm.

I flip the coin, purposely dropping it to the grass. I quickly reach for it before she can. I don't want Emerson to call it.

It's on tails.

I wanted it to be heads.

I pick it up carefully, shielding the coin and my hands from Emerson. Slyly, I flip it over to heads. Reaching out my hand to her, I open my palm.

"Heads. You're up!" Her eyes go expressive.

"I hope you're ready for it." I wink.

"What are you thinking?"

"You'll see." As if I hadn't known exactly how I wanted the day to end.

26

EMERSON

Now

Do you know how hard it is to get rid of an indentation of someone? This isn't a foam mattress where the indentation goes away on its own, where in five minutes, you wouldn't know that someone was lying on it earlier. No, we're talking about a rough, callused, ridged indentation so deep that there isn't a ladder to climb out of it or a way to fill it in. All of this is from someone who, every time you see them, speak to them, and sleep with them, you are the one who makes it more profound.

Liam's indentation lies in my heart.

A recess the size of the Grand Canyon that I don't think will ever be filled because he took some of me with him. And I was the one to hand it over. How are you supposed to fill in the indentation when you don't have those parts of you to fill it back with?

I've tried.

I've tried my best to get over Liam Hayes. To fill the void. But getting over someone like him isn't that easy—it's nearly impossible. When I think I've made progress, some memory creeps into my mind and plays like a movie you can't tear your eyes away from.

Until yesterday, it was at least a dull pain. Subtly there. Easy to ignore with practice—and I've gotten damn good at practicing. At least, I thought.

You live day after day, knowing it's there, but you finally decide you enjoy it, so you stop trying to fix it. That pain becomes part of everyday life.

Missing and loving Liam is a part of everyday life.

The morning after we slept together for the first time, while we were twisted in the bedsheets, he let me know he made arrangements with work. Liam planned to join me for the remainder of my trip. He set aside everything to be with me. Liam chose me how no one else had.

My stomach dips and twists with thoughts about that decision and what transpired to get us here. Everything about Liam, that trip, and the years after is something you'd find in a book on my shelf.

My head throbs from crying all night. I don't think I slept for a minute. All because I thought I had finally filled that indentation in with Brandon.

I woke to a text this morning from Brandon. He said he'll swing by with my things from his place this afternoon. It won't be much, only a few articles of clothing and bathroom products.

Our lives were never thoroughly combined. Retrospectively, that was probably a sign that it wouldn't last.

He also said he's not angry at me, which is a relief because I'm angry at myself.

I'm angry that I've been so naive about these feelings I've harbored.

Angry that I hurt him.

Angry that I've wasted so much of my life on someone.

And I don't even know if I'm talking about Brandon... or Liam.

That's how I ended up with Chloe on our way to Natalie's.

27

LIAM

Now

"Hiya!" Natalie says as she opens the glass door to my office. "Care for a late lunch? Your assistant ratted and said you haven't eaten."

I peer up from my computer to see her leaning against the door frame.

"Starving. Give me fifteen minutes to finish this email, and we can go."

"I'll wait for you outside."

I meet Natalie out front of the building. When I checked the clock before heading down, I didn't realize it was already three.

The day had flown by. I was up early. I couldn't shake my conversation with Emerson, and a seven-mile run didn't shake it either, so I came in early. I picked up Joe & the Juice on the way in, but it sat on my desk untouched, and I have been behind my computer all day.

Our Chicago location's grand opening is in a couple of months. The remodel is well underway, meaning many contracts, blueprints, paint colors, and more to review. I threw myself into it without coming up for oxygen once today.

Emerson had also sent over an updated overview of the marketing campaign their team put together for the launch. It included a one-year plan detailing ideas for growth and visitor retention.

It had Emerson written all over it. When she first started, she used to call me to ask my thoughts or to review her plans. I learned the ins and outs of how her mind works, which I can see while reviewing our strategy.

It's brilliant, but I didn't expect anything less.

"Not planning on coming back after?" Natalie nods toward my work bag on my back.

"No. Decided to shut down the office early today. Told everyone to finish whatever they are working on and head out."

"That's sweet of you." She gives me a proud smile.

***

Lunch was good. I could tell Natalie wanted to ask about Emerson. She'd open her mouth to say something, then close it, taking a bite of her salad or a sip of her matcha. I didn't bother to bring it up. I know we need to talk about it, but do we?

Natalie and I are whatever. Emerson and I are barely even friends, so I don't know if there is any explanation that needs to be had. . . yet.

Afterward, we took the train back to her place.

"I wasn't expecting to get invited, but then—Chloe, what are you doing here?" Natalie says as we walk into her apartment. Chloe rummaging through the freezer.

"9-1-1. Used the emergency friendship key." Chloe points to the couch. Lying in the fetal position is Emerson. "Engagement is over."

Natalie bolts to the couch, picking up Emerson's head and lying it in her lap.

It takes everything to control my emotions from outwardly showing right now. *Emerson isn't engaged.* I'm ecstatic, selfishly. It's not that I want to be with her—that's a lie. Huge shitting lie. I do want to be with her. There hasn't been a day since we met that I haven't wanted to be with her. It used to make me cross that we weren't together.

I don't find pleasure in seeing her unhappy, though. If Brandon was making her happy—taking good care of her, treating her well, and loving her—then I don't want their engagement to be over.

"Ice cream is behind the frozen fruit in a pink container with no label."

Chloe shakes her head. "Why?"

"It was too tempting, and I kept eating it for breakfast. Now I don't!"

"Do you know what flavor it is?" Chloe asks Natalie.

"Chocolate. Liam, if you are staying, you'll need a spoon."

"No," Emerson says, sitting up from her position on the couch.

Our eyes meet, and the horror of the look she's giving me kills me a bit. Her eyes are bright green, rimmed in red.

"I want him to leave," Emerson deadpans.

Natalie's eyes are bouncing from Emerson to me. She probably wishes she had asked at least one question about us earlier.

"Liam," Chloe glares at me and sighs. I nod my head; she doesn't need to tell me. I'll leave.

"Going to use the loo, then I'll be gone," I say.

Walking down the hall, I try to listen to their conversation.

"What happened?" Natalie asks.

"It wasn't working. Brandon was upset that I said no to another venue and was disrespecting his mother's planning."

"You were disrespecting his mom? She hasn't listened to one thing you wanted for the wedding! She didn't even want me to be your maid of honor," says Natalie.

"I know." Emerson sniffles a cry. "At least we don't have to worry about her now—maybe. I'm surprised she hasn't called to go off on me about the split."

"Emme, it had been a year of plan. . ." Their voices drift off as I close the bathroom door behind me.

I didn't have to go; I needed to know what had happened.

Did I make this happen?

Stop being a prick. This isn't about you.

I flush the toilet and wash my hands to keep up with the optics. Opening the door quietly to extend my time in the hall before leaving, I run into Chloe.

"Fancy meeting you here again," Chloe sarcastically remarks.

"Chloe," I growl lowly.

"I know she's lying about why they called off the engagement. Her displeasure when you arrived with Natalie made it obvious that *you* had something to do with this. I don't know what, but I will figure it out. Now, if you'll excuse me, I am going to use the bathroom."

She pushes past me, shutting the door with *oomph* behind her.

I don't think Chloe likes me.

I take a deep breath before returning down the hall. Natalie and Emerson aren't talking, but the sound of a container being scraped clean fills the room.

I try not to focus on Emerson, but that's a challenge and one I'll always fail. There's a brief smile on her face, but it fades when she catches me looking at her.

"Liam, would you mind running to the store and picking up some more ice cream?" Natalie asks me. She spins the container, opens it toward me, and frowns at the emptiness.

"Yeah."

"A strawberry shortcake for me and Emme likes—"

"Cookies and cream," we both say at the same time.

"Yeah. . . how'd you know that?" Natalie asks.

"Good guess, I'sppose." I shrug.

"Hmm, okay. You can leave it outside the door when you get back." She looks over at Emerson, who is scrolling on her phone. "We appreciate it!" Natalie sings.

"Anything to help."

I leave without a final look. I grab the ice cream from Whole Foods at the corner of Natalie's block.

New markets are always woozy—never set up the same, even if they are the same brand. I meandered around the aisles until I found the ice cream. Then, I retraced my steps through them, picking up some of Emerson's other favorite snacks.

I return to my place after dropping off the food. My evening now free. I changed to weight train in the gym on the first floor of our building, before lying on my couch reading, when I decided to text Emerson. It's almost nine, and I figure she's probably no longer with Chloe and Natalie.

Emerson: Don't be. He deserves better than me, anyway.

Don't say that. That's not true.

Emerson: It is.

Emerson: I didn't love him as I should have; he deserves someone who does.

So do you.

28

EMERSON

Six Summers Ago

I promised myself two things the night I decided to stay at that table with Liam.

Promise #1: Do not go home with Liam Hayes—completely broken. Absolutely shattered.

Promise #2: Do not fall for Liam Hayes—not broken.

That's why I shouldn't be falling for him. *Right?*

Ten days with someone is not nearly enough time to fall for them. It's supposed to take more time than this, right?

But after today, how could I not fall for him? How am I supposed to feel anything other than—nope. *He said one nice thing to you, that doesn't mean you abandon your beliefs.*

I've never spoken about my parents like that to anyone. Not even to Natalie, and she lived through it with me, a front-row seat to the idiocracy that devoured my family, but I never said anything about how I felt.

And I told Liam all of it because I knew I could. I know I joked about him thinking I'm messed up, but I didn't mean it. I don't think he judges me at all. He's a safe space for me to be me.

And he then told me that I am easy to love. Like what?

You're wrong. You are so easy to love, Emerson. I'm sorry no one has ever made you feel that way before.

I don't know how he knows that when Liam barely knows me. Or does he?

Liam holds the door to the restaurant open to let me through while taking my hand to help me down the small set of steps. We walk hand in hand, fingers interlocked together.

We could get an Uber back, but we don't. It's not even a question between us if we should or not. We walk. We have every day since our walk home in Lagos. Small, nonsensical conversations pass between us, but it's the easy, comfortable silence that sits between us that I think we both enjoy. Words aren't always necessary, at least not with us. Our walks are intimate, a way to be together without questions or pressure of getting to know each other or need to be enough for anyone or anything else. We're simply Liam and Emerson on our walks.

Several blocks from our hotel, two people are playing music on the street—one on cello and the other on violin. An instrumental version of Taylor Swift's "Love Story" starts playing.

"Dance with me," Liam says, pressing a kiss to my forehead.

He pulls us into the street; the only people outside besides us sit on the patios of the restaurants nearby.

I take his lead, turning toward him. His other hand comes to the small of my back. Mine move to his back, pressing into his shoulder blades for support. We move in unison from side to side for most of the song. I can feel the muscles of his back tense and relax with each step. He removes his hand from my back, and he spins me out. My dress flows out from my body, riding up to where most of my bare legs show. While spinning back into him, my heel gets caught in the stones, and I slip. Before I can fall, Liam catches me.

My breath hitches as I look up at him. *He's so handsome.*

I blink, fixating my eyes deeper into his. They darken, and I can sense the heat and desire flooding from them.

My body is upright in a collision of our mouths.

"Take me back now," I pant out breathily. "Please."

Liam says thank you in French and drops a few euros in their cup before leading us back to the hotel.

It feels like my slip slipped us both into a different dimension. Our pace is rushed as we make our way back to the hotel. Stopping once in a dark alley to kiss—pushed up against a brick wall, leg curled around his back, neck exposed, warm lips finding my pulse.

The tension between us and between my legs increases as we climb the hotel's stairs. It's like the walls are closing in, pressurizing us to the point where the only solution is combustion.

But I may combust before that if we don't get to the room quick enough and his touch is all over me.

I slip my hand out of his after he pulls us into his room, taking a few steps away from him. It's dark, dimly illuminated by the moon coming through the windows.

I bend down to undo my heels.

"Stop." Within seconds, Liam is in front of me. He's not speaking, but I can sense the fire growing inside me, letting me know he's there. His breath is warm and trailing down my exposed skin. Taking a deep breath through my nose, I relish in his smell.

He bends down, kneeling before me, taking off my heels. Kissing the inside of my knees and thighs as he removes my shoes. It's gentle and tantalizingly slow. A precision to his tactics meant to drive me wild.

Liam stands.

He lifts his right hand to my shoulder, his fingers loosely playing with the ties to my dress. If he were to pull one of the strings, that side of my dress would fall, revealing part of my lacey, strapless black bra.

He takes another step closer; our bodies now flush together. He leans his head down, mouth level with my ear. "Emerson," he pants. My eyes shut, and my head leans into his touch and voice.

He pulls the tie, undoing the bow.

"Liam," I say back to him.

He drags his hand over my collarbone, his lips trailing kisses to the other shoulder, releasing that tie.

My dress falls to the floor, revealing my lacey, strapless black bra and matching lace underwear. Slowly, I lift my head to meet his gaze.

His eyes are beating down on me. Practically flush together, I can feel and sense his needs.

"My view was better with you on your knees," I say.

He takes a step back.

"Emerson," Liam groans. "Is that what you want?"

I nod.

"Use your words. Tell me, is that what you want." Liam is dragging a finger between us lazily up my thigh and over my center. The fabric of my underwear being a terrible barrier, I know he can feel how achingly ready I already am. He smirks.

"Yes."

Slipping two fingers into the waistband, he pulls them down. I raise each foot one at a time, and he throws my underwear to the side.

Liam returns to my body, on his knees, kissing up my right leg, lingering a kiss right on my hip; he pushes my legs apart. Running his hands up my outer thighs, the need inside of me is becoming uncontrollable.

A short and sweet beg leaves my mouth. "Please."

He lets out a laugh, and then his mouth is on me. Liam licks me from back to front. He acts like he didn't have anything for dinner, and I'm it.

Liam picks up his pace deliberately, I'm wet and burning frantically, and then he stops. Liam removes his mouth and replaces it with his fingers. One. Then two. As he glides his fingers in and out of me, he tries to lock his gaze with mine, but my head is thrown back.

"Look at me, Emerson," he demands. "You said this view was better. Watch me with those pretty green eyes indulge in this pretty pussy of yours."

I look down at him.

"What do you want?" He's wearing a smug grin. His lips glisten.

Barely able to communicate, I try to get out, "Mouth. Both," but it comes out short and quick. He interrupts my nonsense and starts devouring me again. The combination of his tongue and finger brings me over the edge.

"Liam!" I curse out his name.

He doesn't stop.

Liam waits to remove his mouth until every wave of my orgasm is nursed out of me. He stands and kisses me, allowing me to taste myself on him.

"You, my darling States, are mouthwatering," Liam says.

My mouth is back on his, ready for more—ready for all of him. I drop my hand between us and stroke him. His hands come to my bra, reaching around to the back; he unclasps it and tosses it to the floor.

Still kissing, Liam walks us backward until my legs bump against the bed. I climb onto it, leaning up on my knees. My hands move to his shirt, making quick work of the buttons. At the same time, his mouth is exploring me. He kisses my chin, the side of my neck, and behind my ear, working his way from one side to the next. His kisses travel down to my chest, above my breast, as I reach for his belt.

Pulling back, he removes his pants and underwear. Maybe it's the lighting, or perhaps it is just him, but he's cut enough that the V dips right into his. . . my eyes flare.

He's definitely muscular, large. . . and hard.

"I warned you," he says, recalling our conversation in Lisbon when he saved me from falling.

Liam's eyes roam the entirety of my body, now laid out on the bed. The reality of being completely naked in front of him hits me, and for a moment, I'm embarrassed. Quickly, I cover my stomach and body. Not wanting him to see my curves and not flat stomach.

Liam leans over me, reaching and taking hold of my wrists. "Never hide from me. You are beautiful. Every. Part. Of. You. There is nothing about you that you should be ashamed of." Liam's strong, sweet, and affirming gaze makes me feel as if I'm the only person in the world who matters to him.

"I'll try," I reply simply.

He leaves me with a smile before turning around and heading to the bathroom. He's rummaging through his toiletry bag and then returns with a condom in hand. Standing in front of me, I let my eyes look and absorb all of him. As I watch him, I hear foil ripping, and he rolls the condom on.

The nice moment we shared seconds ago is gone. Liam is on top of me, positioned between my legs, the tip of him rubbing between me.

"Tell me if it's too much," Liam tells me.

"It won't be."

Okay, it might be. I claw at his shoulders and gasp at the stretching feeling.

Liam chuckles, pausing to let me adjust. "It's almost all in."

He pulls out slightly before pushing in gently till all of him fills me.

"States." He swallows, breathing hitches, feeling how tight I am around him. "Is it?"

I shake my head no.

"Good girl," he kisses my forehead. "You're already taking me perfectly."

"This isn't my first rodeo," I say—matching mischievous smile form on our faces.

"And it won't be your last with me." Liam starts to move in and out of me. His thrusts are consistent at first but become faster and harder as my breath quickens, and I grasp at the smooth sheets with my hands.

I'm getting close again. The edge I want to barrel over with him is in sight, and the pressure within me is pushing me closer to it.

Liam must sense it. He reaches for a pillow, pulls up my hips, and places it behind the small of my back. The smallest change in angle giving him better leverage to dive deeper into me from on his knees.

My release is inevitable as soon as Liam reaches a hand down and pinches my most sensitive spot. My legs curl up around his back as he continues to thrust harder and play with me. My climax pulses around him. Liam follows with a cry of my name on his lips.

Catching our breath, he pulls out of me. Lying side by side, he wraps an arm around me, pulling me into him.

While we lay there, I can't contain the smirk that curls across my face. I let out a soft giggle.

"What are you laughing at?" Liam asks.

I giggle again. "Just that the British came."

Liam pinches my side. "Is that right? I won't warn you next time." I can feel him laughing through his arms that are holding me.

Liam eventually gets up and heads to the bathroom, letting me know he'll grab something to clean us up. I look up at the ceiling, thinking, trying to figure out how I will get through the rest of this trip without breaking another promise to myself.

29

LIAM

Six Summers Ago

"What time is your flight today?" I ask Emerson as she crawls up my body, out from underneath the sheets.

Laying on top of me, her arms resting on my chest, I use my thumb to swipe remnants of me from the corner of her mouth.

She sucks my thumb into her mouth. Circling her tongue around it while keeping eye contact with me.

Releasing my thumb, Emerson kisses me and climbs out of bed.

"Not until three this afternoon. I'm going to call an Uber by noon."

"Hours away, States. Hours away from now." I flick her a smirk. "Come back here." I pat the space next to me.

Across the room, she stops pulling out her clothes from the dresser. Only in my t-shirt, the one she stole the first night she stayed over, her hips sway in a teasing but lustrous way as she turns to face me. Her lips pout as she walks back over to the bed. Pulling back the white, cloud-like covers, she climbs in next to me, braiding her bare legs between mine. Her smooth skin is silk against me.

We've shared a bed since that night in Paris. Even in a room with two beds, I booked it on purpose after she recounted an incident from earlier in her trip, we'd cram our bodies into one. I loved those few nights when there wasn't space between us, and we were forced to be skin-to-skin. Emerson doesn't cuddle when she sleeps. She'll start curled up into me but eventually ends up wiggling her way to the edge. She says it reminds her of college and sharing a twin bed.

I tried not to think about who she was sharing it with.

Untangling our legs, rolling on top of her. I take hold of her hands, pinning them over her head. I'm inside of her as quickly as I watch her thoughts go everywhere else.

EMERSON

I enjoy being next to him. It's why I didn't mind when Liam rearranged all of my hotel arrangements. It doesn't hurt that he's in the industry and knows the best places to stay.

I like the proximity it forced us into.

Breathing in the same oxygen as him. *Breathing him in as oxygen.*

That's what it feels like right now.

I'm breathing him in.

Each thrust an inhale. Each release an exhale.

The air my body needs to function at the capacity of who I want to be when I'm with him—not just when we are in this position.

I'm not ready to go home. To leave all of this, *Liam* and *us*, behind.

My mind keeps drifting further out, like I'm in the ocean that separates us. We live on two separate continents, and after today, we will never see each other again. I'll return to my life breathless without the source. I'm nervous I'll suffocate. Gasping for air, gasping for this version of me that he's given life to.

I don't love Liam. I love me with him.

I try not to let the emotions get confused.

We finish, and Liam lies beside me on his side. We're facing each other. His fingers draw small circles on my upper bicep.

"What's running through that bright, exquisite mind of yours?" he asks me.

"How incredibly hot you are."

"You'd suck at poker," he teases.

I release a deep sigh.

If emotions are the lock, then I'm the key to a door of all the ways I'll never be enough for love. But that's not us. Since I've met Liam, we've never been the type of strangers to keep our emotions hidden.

"You can tell me, Emerson." His voice is gentle.

"I know. Easy answer? I don't want to leave." I release another sigh. "Truthful answer? I don't know how to go back to pre-summer Emerson."

"What do you mean?" His brow furrows with genuine confusion.

"If you had told me eight weeks ago, I'd have stayed in another country alone. I would have laughed in your face and told you how wrong you were. This," my hand gesturing to myself, "is not me."

"You mean lying in bed across from a fit and wildly charming male specimen?"

"Exactly." I roll my eyes at him, but he isn't wrong. I wouldn't have, ever. Well, ever isn't true. I would, but not night after night and spending the days in between together. "I wouldn't have allowed myself to fall for you. I know that's what you've been trying to do for the past four weeks. You were trying to show me that love is real."

"Did it work?"

"No." I shake my head. "But I'm open to the idea."

That doesn't satisfy him—his smile wavers.

"This girl, you know, isn't the girl who showed up here eight weeks ago. That girl was afraid—afraid to be enough for someone. I thought that to get others to like me, want me, and stay, I had to be the person they wanted me to be."

Liam doesn't say anything, only listens. His eyes don't leave mine.

"With you though. . . I'm finally the Emerson I want to be. This version of me is someone who is enough for you—enough for myself. At first, I thought I was crazy, but the more time we spent together, the easier it became to be her. Less guarded, more open to l—" I don't finish the L word. "I want to be who you've allowed me to be when I go home."

"Allowed you to be? States, I haven't done anything. You are this person already."

"Doesn't feel that way," I breathe out.

"Why?"

"I. . . I don't know. . ."

"Please don't get mad at what I'm about to say. But—" Liam stops talking. Eyes roaming my face. I think he's searching for a green light to continue.

"But?" I shift my head forward, urging him to continue.

"I'd never lie to you. . . or want to say anything to hurt you. But I think you allow your parent's divorce to haunt you. It altered your thoughts, causing you to believe that you'll never be enough for anyone. If you weren't enough for them, the people who are supposed to love you unconditionally, then why or how could you be enough for anyone else? It's dominos. That started it, and now you have this insistent part of you to put others ahead of you. Not in a compassionate or generous way—which you genuinely are, by the way—but ahead of who you truly are." He reaches out to brush away a tear I didn't realize was there off my cheek. "Appease me on something. That list of yours that we completed the past four weeks. Tell me which of those items were your ideas."

I stare at him, blinking away the additional tears forming.

"I was right, none of them. There's a reason for that." The intensity of his gaze is driving me wild.

"I'm assuming you are going to tell me the reason?" I don't doubt he isn't going to tell me. I'm trying to give myself the extra moment to prepare myself for another truth bomb Liam is going to detonate on me. Whatever he is going to say, I probably already know deep down. That's what sucks about all of this. I'm not oblivious to it. If a stranger can see it, I can see it.

"Your desire to be loved—which I know you don't *believe in,* so you say." I roll my eyes at him. "Allows you to be walked over.

Your friend? She's learned exactly how to get whatever the hell she wants. Using you because you believe that if you don't, she won't be there for you.

"You said it yourself: you think you must be someone you aren't to keep people. Those parts that make you *you* will go dormant at some point. Who is pushing you to be Emerson? Your ideas, interests, this side of you, Emerson, is fucking fascinating. Quite marvelous, truly."

"Even the sass?"

"Might be my favorite part of you." He smiles.

"How could you possibly know all of this?"

"Because from the moment I laid eyes on you, I knew exactly who you were."

My heart skips a beat. "That's not a valid answer. You just knew?"

"I couldn't take my eyes off you that morning, right?"

"Right."

"It wasn't only because of your beauty, which please, know you are the most. . . shit. . . beautiful person I've laid my eyes on. I could easily stare into your emerald eyes all day. Tangle my hands in your hair if I can get them away long enough from your delicious curves." He gives me a sexy smirk I know too well at this point. "If I could lose myself even more than I already have in you, I would." He leans forward to kiss me gently. "Your wall might be tough for others to crack, but I saw right through it. Getting to know you the past few weeks? That confirmed every remarkable notion I had about you. You are so easy to love, Emerson." It's precisely what he told me that day in Paris when I told him about my parents. And now, I get this tickling sensation that he might love me. "Anyone who doesn't know that, that's their loss. But you also have to give them the opportunity to love you for exactly who you are in there." He reaches out and taps my heart, then my brain, and then my mouth.

"Liam. . ."

"Don't. Let me finish. This woman that you want to be, no are, she's going to burn out." Ouch, that sounds harsh. True, but harsh. "And that would be a loss. She's in there. She's in you. You have to try. Shit, not even try—just be you, States. And if you forget, think about me. I'm case study number one. An exemplary example of what it looks like when someone loves you for who you are."

LIAM

That's because I love her. I love Emerson Clarke.

30

EMERSON

Six Summers Ago

Liam, surprisingly, was the one to drag us out of bed. I didn't go easy, but it was a battle worth losing. His flight to London was two hours after mine, but he insisted on going to the airport with me.

"Thank you," I say to him outside of my gate. My boarding group called over the intercom.

"See you later, States." He kisses me, then kisses me again before pivoting and walking away toward his gate.

I don't move. I stand there watching Liam walk away.

Is this really it? Is this all we'll ever be? Two strangers thrown together to be summertime friends, only to leave as strangers again.

He peers over his shoulder in my direction one last time. An exchange of smiles, the same smiles from the first time I saw him, are gifted to each other.

"Take a picture, it'll last longer." He winks and looks away.

I do, committing it to memory and tucking it away alongside the best summer of my life.

Time to go home.

***

"Emme! Oh my gosh!" There is a screech as I exit the airport. Natalie is standing there jumping up and down. I'm halfway to her when she sprints the remaining distance to me.

"I missed you!" Natalie throws her arms around me tightly.

"I missed you too. How was your grandma's funeral?" She loosenes her death hug enough that I can hug her back.

"Mom is dramatic." She rolls her eyes. "As soon as I got home, my dad told me I didn't need to leave you."

"I still agree with your mom that you needed to come home. You'll be glad later."

"Yeah, whatever. What I'll regret later is not seeing more of Europe with you." Nat boops my nose. She takes my bag from me and points toward where she is parked. "Tell me all the details! Dirty ones included." She looks over her shoulder at me, and her eyebrows dance.

"Dirty details?" I choke. Natalie knows the details of the trip. . . in detail. She texted me daily for photos and updates, and I shared enough to make it feel like she was right there with me. However, Liam may not have made it into any of the details.

My cheeks grow hot, probably red, thinking about him.

"Emme, please tell me you were *not* boring the entire time. Your head in books, walking around to take in the 'views', people watching, silly photos of strangers and random architecture." She's shaking her head like she's disappointed in me. "I should have stayed. I knew you wouldn't enjoy yourself."

Liam's observation from this morning has me viewing her and what she said through a different lens.

"Are you serious? That's mean and not true."

"I'm just saying, I know you." She's shrugging off the entire comment as if she didn't slap me across the face with her words.

"Actually, I had a great time. Best summer of my life."

She tosses me a look. One I can't quite decipher. She doesn't ask or say anything else about the trip. Sitting in the passenger seat, Natalie drives and tells me about everything she purchased for our Chicago apartment.

I don't listen to anything she says, annoyed with her.

Instead, I unlock my phone and flip through pictures from the trip, lingering a moment too long on the ones of Liam and me. We didn't take many, three or four if you include the one George took in Lagos, which is my favorite of us. However, my favorite picture of the trip is one of him.

We were in Amsterdam, our last stop. Liam admitted he had some work that he needed to attend to. I suggested we go to a café—I could read while he worked for an hour or two. We ended up spending five hours there, both reading after his work was complete. He'd never exuded such casualness in a white t-shirt, which was probably still more expensive than my entire outfit, but whatever. His hair was shaggier than when I first met him, the ends curling, and he hadn't shaved in a few days. I liked him with scruff.

I went to the bathroom. Walking back to the table, my eyes find him. Liam doesn't see me. He's ravishingly handsome. Pen sticking out of his mouth, head down with a couple of strands of hair falling in his face, such attentive focus I've come to enjoy, reading my book. I snapped a picture of him on my phone.

I sat down at the table. Liam closed my book and returned it to me.

On the plane, I pulled it out to read. Liam highlighted sections, wrote sweet nothings in the footer, and his review on the back page.

Looking at the photo now, knowing what he did, makes me love it even more.

A notification comes across the top of my screen.

A text message from Liam?

I blink a series, trying to ensure I see what I see. Liam's name is on the screen.

That's impossible. I didn't give him my number. Of course, it crossed my mind, but I chickened out.

I click the message open.

Liam: I'm not ready to find out what it's like for you to forget me.

Liam: Friends?

31

EMERSON

Now

A week has passed since that night in Natalie's apartment when she and Chloe nursed me back to sanity. Natalie has texted and called several times, asking if I wanted to take a workout class with her, go to the farmers' market, or pick up a new pair of sandals Gucci dropped and that she desperately needed after I bailed on our weekly margarita night.

By the time Thursday evening rolled around, I was over Brandon—mostly. That was going to end, and I think I knew it for months, so in a way, I grieved it as it was happening. I had moved on to my fixation on Liam, which meant Natalie.

I didn't know how to face them. So I stuck to myself.

I respond to her texts, knowing she'd be more concerned and panic if I didn't. Being 'busy' is officially running low in stock as an excuse.

Luckily, work has been busy, so avoiding her isn't entirely a lie. Nelson and Moore isn't normally busy this time of year, but in the past four months, we've onboarded eight new clients, including Hayes Hotels. My coworkers complain about working extra and how it's ruining their summer, but I've welcomed it with open arms. It's kept my mind off everything else for at least a week.

It was slow, the Liam recovery phase. After what happened in London three years ago, it took me a long time to get back together. Natalie and Chloe struggled to get me up off the couch for months until, one day, I decided I couldn't be that way anymore. It was my birthday, and there's nothing like deciding to stop wallowing in self-pity as a birthday present for yourself.

I went back to regularly scheduled girl's nights, picked up my camera again, and even went on dates that Natalie and Chloe set me up on.

The only thing I didn't do was tell them the full gravity of what occurred with Liam, who they nicknamed London Lover Boy.

Their help was great, and I'll always appreciate it, until they realized it was going in one ear and shooting right out the other. As much as I fronted that I was okay and moved on behind closed doors, I wasn't. What happened between him and I was deeper than a broken heart. It was a broken version of myself.

The tape I used to put the pieces back together is losing its stickiness, coming undone and unraveling me in the process.

My phone buzzes on my desk. Glancing over, I see a number on my screen.

> **+55 020 4561 8441: Don't ignore Natalie.**

In the haze of Brandon and work, I hadn't questioned why Liam's messages last week or today didn't include a contact name. I knew it was him.

After saving his number, I stare at his contact page, trying to place when I deleted it. I don't remember getting rid of it.

> **I'm not. I've been busy.**

> **Why do you even care?**

> **Liam: 1. You're her best friend.**

> **Liam: 2. She's suspecting something.**

Okay

Liam: Emerson. . .

Liam: You have to believe me that we didn't do this on purpose.

We?

Liam: I would never do anything to hurt you.

Good joke, you should be a comedian.

I'm furious.

I don't even care that he's texting me on her behalf. That is the type of guy he is. Liam is thoughtful to a fault and protects those he cares about. It's one of the things I loved about him. I don't care about the idea of him caring about Natalie, either. *Don't lie to yourself, Emerson, you do.* But I'm not furious about him caring for her.

I'm furious that he has had my number this entire time.

Three years.

I haven't heard from him for three years, and he texts me now?

No drunk texts. No apology. No groveling. No communication for three years.

Even I had accidentally drunk-texted him a few times in the couple months after.

His ability to go cold turkey on our relationship was unbelievable. Remarkable actually!

I'm trying to tame my temper, but it's roaring inside me like a lion. I made up reason after reason why Liam never contacted me, especially in those first few months. He deleted my number or lost his phone and my number with it. Or hell, he even blocked me because he was that upset about what happened that he couldn't bear to have anything in his life that correlated with me.

But he had my number. He still *has* my number.

This. Whole. Damn. Time.

One call—even a text! That's all it would have taken. I needed him to reach out first; I desperately needed it. Needed him to confirm and calm every idea that coursed through me after that damn day.

"Hey Emerson. Margot wants to see you in her office." Blake dips her head into the archway of my glass office. I look up at her, the interruption startling. "Everything okay?"

"Yup. Struggling with location ideas for an upcoming shoot for the new kombucha brand."

"What about the rooftop pool at The Hoxton Hotel," she immediately says. "Ben and I went two weekends ago. Immaculate views and their daybeds are this pool-ish teal blue, almost the same color as their new summer flavor."

"That's perfect, Blake. I'll call them after this meeting. Thanks."

"Have you tried their drinks yet?" Blake asks.

"No."

I click the side button on my phone. My screen goes dark, and I put it in my top desk drawer. Closing my eyes, I take a deep breath, re-grounding myself, and push my anger aside.

"I was surprised at how much I enjoyed them. Not normally a kombucha girly; it's too vinegary for me, but their strawberry kiwi flavor tastes like these juice boxes we'd get as kids. I'll bring you one tomorrow!"

Heading out of my office, I walk right past Blake. I'm a few strides ahead of her, my pace quick. When Margot wants to see you, that means you don't dilly-dally. It means you get there now.

Trying to catch up with me, Blake calls out, "You know if this doesn't ever work out for you, you could be a full-time photographer."

She's finally in step with me when my head whips in her direction, remiss by her comment.

If this doesn't work out. Is Blake serious?

She keeps going, "Your photos are incredible. Ben and I couldn't get over them. I've barely gotten any work done recently because I've been staring at them. You're extremely talented. I don't think I've ever met someone who can capture love like you can."

What a roundabout way to give someone a backhanded compliment.

Hearing her say I know how to capture love when I can't in my own life feels too ironic.

Well, I did once, but I was too oblivious to it until it was far too late when it became the weapon that took me down.

"Thanks." I give her a weak smile as we walk into Margot's office.

***

Margot is a bitch, but we all knew that already. Twenty minutes later, Blake, the rest of my team, and I exit her conference-style office. We were informed that we are being pulled from an upcoming campaign to launch Bamboo's new all-organic sunscreen line. Blake is devastated. Besides Hayes Hotels, this would have been her most extensive campaign yet. I'm pissed because I've been working with Bamboo for all of their product releases for the past two years. Margot didn't even give us a good enough reason for why we were getting pulled from the account.

"Shitty excuse for a shitty situation from a shitty person," Blake mutters quietly to me, and the lack of composure in words from her surprises me. "At least we can focus on Hayes Hotels more now."

Yay, how exciting. Like I need more time to focus on Liam.

With anger-colored glasses on, I grab my phone from my desk and slump into my chair. Mad at Margot, mad at Liam, mad at

Natalie, and mad at myself for feeling this way. I fire off a text without thinking.

> Do you know how often I thought about contacting you? Fighting with myself on whether I should or shouldn't reach out to you. I convinced myself that after every-thing, you'd reach out to me. That you would apologize. When you didn't, I had to con-vince myself that you meant what you said and hated me so much that you 'lost' my number or blocked me. I had to believe this so I wouldn't hurt myself all over again. Three years. Three years, and this entire time, you've had my number? If this was all part of your plan to get back at me, consider it a gold-star success.

Without wasting another minute, I type out another message and press send.

> You could have talked to me then, just like I could talk to Natalie now. Don't fight her battles when you couldn't fight ours. I need time. . . you just better hope for her sake I don't wait three years.

The rest of the workday was incredibly slow. After Margot's meeting, I threw myself into the current campaign I'm working on. Dotting I's and crossing T's, perfecting the campaign to the point where there is no question about whether my team should be pulled from another account.

I also hoped that work would rid me of this headspace.

My brain had other plans.

Graciously, it fixated on what I had sent Liam.

I was a bitch.

It was entirely out of line with everything I said. Liam doesn't reply despite my incessant checking for messages. I'm surprised my phone battery didn't die, considering how many times I tapped the screen or turned the volume on and off.

I don't think he will reply.

I don't deserve a response.

I'm making dinner when my phone rings. On the screen is Natalie's name and a picture of us from Halloween circa 2007, dressed as Candy Land characters that my mom made. She's, of course, Princess Lolly, and I was required to be Queen Frostine.

I checked that my sheet pan meal in the oven wasn't burning before grabbing my phone and answering.

"Nat! Hey. I'm sorry about this week. Work has been swamped, and I was pulled from Bamboo's new product launch, but that doesn't matter. You are my best friend, and I should always have time for you," I force out the half-truth quickly when I pick up the phone.

"This isn't Natalie," a male voice replies. "I didn't think you'd answer a call from me after your texts earlier."

"Oh—"

"Natalie is in the shower. I don't have much time, but we need to talk."

"About earlier. . . Liam, it was uncalled for. You weren't doing anything but being kind. I was fired up about work and took it out on you." I am sincere about my apology.

"You were right."

Liam catches me off guard. *I was right?*

Before I get a chance to reply, he continues, "Leave the ball in whoever's court out of this. This is on both of us."

"Okay. . ."

"But do you think I didn't want to talk to you? Countless times, I picked up the phone to call. I'd write entire messages and then delete all of them. Over and over again. I told you I loved you, and you rejected me. Then you told me not to contact you and to delete your number. My ego bruised and heart—my heart that I gave you—destroyed. I cared about you deeply. You were my best friend. In a way, I thought maybe you'd come back, you'd reach out. . . but you never did."

Words and emotions I know, but now, in a tense I don't want to accept.

"I did reach out."

"When your thoughts were impaired."

"Drunk thoughts are sober words."

"I wanted sober thoughts and words," Liam says.

"Okay, but I didn't tell you not to contact me," I hear him mumble, sighing. "I wouldn't do that. There's so much more to it."

"Enlighten me."

"I didn't reject you! I just didn't say. . . didn't say anything. Then, at the bar—"

"Please leave that out of this..." Liam begs.

"How can I leave this out of it? What you said to George about me?"

Liam scoffs. "I didn't mean it, and you know it."

"Do I? Haven't been told otherwise."

"You didn't give me a chance."

"I did. . ."

"Did you, though, Emerson?"

I don't respond. I'm unsure what to say, even if there were words to encompass what I'm thinking and feeling right now.

Liam breaks the silence that fell between us. "Look, we both can acknowledge that we didn't leave things the best. We messed up and are both to blame, but we can't change anything now. There are too many what-ifs. *Too. Many.*" He emphasizes those words. "Trust me when I say they consume a part of my brain daily." He sighs again. "Natalie misses you. She doesn't understand why you are avoiding her. She needs you in her life. . . we both need you in our lives."

I need them both in my life, too.

"I know," I respond. "I'm not trying to hurt her. It's—" I pause before I say what I'm about to say. It's a test to see how far gone Liam and I are. "I never thought I'd see you again, let alone with my best friend."

His voice catches. "Emerson," he mumbles, but I hear the curses after my name. There's a lingering tension between us on the phone.

"Neither did I," he finally says to me. "The shower shut off. Natalie will be out soon, so I need to go. Can we be friends? Not for me, but for her."

"Friends. Yeah, we can be friends, Liam."

The line goes dead.

32

LIAM

Three Summers Ago

Twenty minutes into *The* Royals' second episode, my phone rings. A glass of red wine and sushi takeout sit on the table beside my couch. This show, *The Royals*, is absolute garbage, but Emerson loves to watch it for whatever reason. I'm watching this rubbish for her. Add it to the list of ways I try to stay close to her, bridging the distance between us.

At first, I thought she watched it since it's a satire on our government till the first five minutes of the first episode when William Moseley appears on the screen—her childhood crush. I've never seen *The Chronicles of Narnia*, but she claims Peter was hot. Googled him. Can't say I disagree with her. Aging like fine French wine, too.

My phone rings again; this time, it is a FaceTime from Emerson. I swipe the screen and note the time in Chicago. It's three there; she must be on her way to her date.

"He canceled on me! This was supposed to be our third date, but he canceled!" She immediately talks, "And his reason. S-t-u-p-i-d. Stupid. Guess why he canceled?"

"Hello. I'm good, long day but cheery. How are you?"

"You aren't helping. Liam. Guess." Damn, she's cross tonight.

"He didn't like the restaurant that you picked out?"

"Noooope. He canceled because I didn't. . ." There's a pause before she answers. I can't tell if she's embarrassed or hurt by the reason. "Put out after our second date," she whispers closely to the phone. "A second date? Come on, everyone knows that you have to give it at least three dates, which is tonight! Ridiculous! He literally couldn't even wait four more hours to get lucky."

"Oi, you see, I thought you had to go to two countries and agree to spend the next four weeks with the girl to get lucky."

"Ha. Ha. You're so funny." Her mouth purses together, and she glares at me through the phone. She's genuinely upset, I conclude.

"I'm sorry that happened, States. You seemed excited about the potential with this one, yeah?" Immediately, I knew it was the wrong word choice. One? More like ten? She's been *dating* lately, or at least trying to. Emphasis on the trying. It's not going well, as you can imagine, based on her frantic video chat.

"Yeah, this one." She rolls her eyes and sigh-laughs.

"Don't roll your eyes at me." That warrants a laugh.

"You're right, though. Did you take a screenshot!?"

"Documenting the moment. Liam Hayes was right," I say.

Emerson shakes her head at me and rolls her eyes again.

"As I was trying to say, this one, just as I think that with every other one?" A look of despair washes over her face. "What am I supposed to do to have this excitement reciprocated?" She shakes her head. "How do I get a guy to see potential in me?"

Something in my gut stirs—and it isn't the sushi. I want to scream, sound alarms, or teleport through this phone to let her know I see potential with her. Always have since we met. The level of chemistry between us and the ease with which we function is rare. There's limitless potential with Emerson. This guy, hell, any guy, must be a twat not to see it.

I guess I'm also a twat then because I do see it and haven't done anything about it.

"We aren't doing this again."

"Then tell me how to make it stop!" Emerson demands.

"Want to know how to stop? Easy. Stop choosing dimwits on those dating apps." I've asked her before if I can log into her apps. She always tells me what a terrible idea that is and that she can't trust me with her password. That's probably true; I'd delete her profile.

"Aren't you on dating apps?" She asks.

"Yeah. And? I'm me."

"Oh, right. I'm Liam. I'm perfect. All it takes is one flash of my perfect smile and a wink of my perfect eyes, and she's in my bed and then down the aisle. Hmm, I forgot," she says sarcastically.

"Exactly," I joke.

"Don't let it go to your head, pretty boy. It can't get much bigger." Emerson winks at me.

"Did you want to sleep with him?" I ask her, circling back to an earlier statement that's taken up residence in my mind. He *couldn't wait four more hours to get lucky.*

Sex doesn't come up between us often. If it does, I'm usually with George when she calls. I don't know why she doesn't bring it up. I don't talk about it because thinking about her having sex with anyone else makes me jealous.

I don't enjoy thinking about her with anyone else ever. I only want to think about her with me.

"Easy or honest answer?" That's her thing with me. She gives me the easy answer first—the one she'd give anyone else—and then the truthful answer that's reserved for me.

"Always."

"Easy: yes. Honest: with him, I don't think so." She shrugs it off. However, her body language and the pink hue on her cheeks make me believe she's only horny. She wouldn't say yes unless she were. "There, for whatever reason, wasn't a. . . spark. Trevor was nice. We kissed on our previous date. It was just blah."

I break out in a bit of laughter. "Emerson."

"Liam."

"Are you horny?" I ask her.

"And if I am? It's not like you're here."

Right. I'm not. Even if I was, would we?

"Want me to fly to you? Or we could. . . ya know, once you get home."

"No. I'll be fine," she groans. I don't consider it rejection because I didn't think she would even go for it.

Her definition of fine includes her irrational fear of dying alone and not only being horny.

A couple of months ago, on the phone, Emerson told me she believes she's going to die alone. Since then, she's been on this dating kick, trying to find 'the one.' I'm happy she is—supportive friend reporting for duty—even though it feels wrong because I want to be the one.

"You sure?" I ask. "I can be there tomorrow."

"I promise," she replies.

Emerson rambles on about work, telling me about the new brand they signed today. Some luxury travel bag? I'm piecing together what she's saying. It's hard to hear her with the wind and the city in the background.

I miss her—so much that the Emerson fog is rolling in pretty thick today. Usually, talking to her helps clear the fog, leaving sunny skies. I don't think it'll clear up anytime soon, though.

"We should book our summer trip," I interrupt her.

"Liam, I thought I told you that I'm not sure if I can this summer," she reluctantly says. "I have three big shoots that I am traveling for, and this new client will add a few more."

"I know, but think about it, please." Why are you begging? I worry she can hear the desperation in my voice and probably see it on my face, too. "You are too busy. Doesn't a break sound nice?"

"Of course it does, but it also sounds like logistics, activities, food, etc. Why don't you and the boys go yourselves this year to celebrate the opening of your Madrid location?"

"They aren't going to like that."

"Them or you?" she pointedly asks.

"Them!" Me. "C'mon."

I'm trying my hardest not to beg, but in reality, that's precisely what I'm doing. I need to know I'm seeing States soon.

Being with her works as a system reset. I leave that week or two refreshed; my head is straighter than it usually is. It wears off over time, and then we see each other—our little life cycle. It's been this way since that summer. It's why I snuck my number into her phone. I knew when she boarded that plane home that she became a part of me, an organ I'd need to survive.

"I miss you, States."

"I miss you too," she says. "Can I think about it?"

I'll take that as a win. "Of course."

"Tell me more about your day?"

And this is the cycle of our calls. One of us calls with a specific topic. We go back and forth till we've been on the phone for hours. Most of the time, I stay up well into the morning, and Emerson falls asleep on the phone. When that happens, I whisper good night, tell her I love her, and then hang up.

My day was less than cheery. She listens, but I can tell it goes over her head. "It's too big businessy," she tells me.

"What does Bea think about George's new girl?"

"Eh. Won't talk about it. He's bringing her around more, and I think it's hitting Beatrix that it could have been her. I think we all thought they'd work their shit out by now."

"You don't think they will?"

"No, I don't," I tell her, hating to admit that about my friend.

His situation is beginning to resonate. Our situations are similar but different. I'm ready to commit to Emerson. I don't want to be only her summertime friend; I want to be her all-time friend.

"We were at Fabric on Saturday. . ." I tell her about their fight before Beatrix stormed off and how no one has heard from her since.

Emerson is quiet while I speak about the rest of my week

From the shaky video, she's still walking. The phone's angle captures her neck and chin. She's paying attention to where she's going and people watching—synonyms for each other in her world—but I know she's listening.

She brings her phone in front of her face, a smile appearing slowly.

I stop mid-sentence. "—What?"

"London."

"What about it?"

"I want to come to London. No big destination. London."

"Why London?"

"The whole time you were talking, I kept wishing I knew these places. Knew the smells. Knew what the commute to work is like for you. I want to experience your life. Actually, be in it. I want to come to London."

If I was looking for a way to clear the fog, this is it.

"I'd love that," and that's the truth. "You're coming to London." And I'm grinning like a fool.

It's past midnight once we coordinate plans, and my eyes are getting heavy. We've been on the phone for three hours at this point.

I bid Emerson a goodnight as she climbs onto her couch with a new book. It's the one I sent her last week, *A Court of Wings and Ruin*—some bay boys she's been obsessed with, but I must admit, the book was quite good.

As we hang up, I can't pinpoint what feeling is running through my veins.

All I know is Emerson is coming to London for me.

33

LIAM

Three Summers Ago

I've wondered what it's like to be loved by Emerson

I wondered about it when she doubled back for another look at the coffee shop. When she'd send me pictures of her day, in the mornings I'd lay next to her, when she'd send me an annotated book. And when we'd hold hands, always making sure our fingers were interlocked, rubbing the top of my hand with her thumb. I've wondered about it for years.

I've wondered about it because I want to be loved by Emerson.

I want to come home and kiss her. I want to wake up in the morning and Emerson be the first person I see. I want to go to bed at night and have Emerson be the last person I see. The first and last of my entire life.

I want to be loved by her because I know I'm in love with her.

The ache to have her in my life has become an insistent pounding. My heart beats rapidly, and I think I'm going to have a heart attack. That's what she does to me. No one has ever had this much control over me, consuming every part of my mind and body in every facet of it—no one but Emerson Clarke.

I called Callum and asked him to grab lunch at our favorite gastropub in Southside. He says yes. I called George to inform him of our plans.

We meet up an hour later.

"Was out with Audrey when you called." Cal gestures his head in her direction.

"And you so happen to owe me lunch." Audrey kisses my cheek.

"Auds, probably good you're here." They all flash confused glances at me.

"Me?" She points to herself. I nod.

We order drinks. Enjoy said drinks. Order another round and food before any of them decide to speak.

"Spill," George speaks bluntly, setting down his pint glass. A bit of the amber ale sloshes over the side. "Why'd you want to get lunch?"

"Do I need a reason to get lunch with my best mates and Audrey?"

No, I don't need a reason to see them. Frankly, we usually spend Saturdays together, anyway. They don't need a reason to see me, but today, I called them because I need them. I really need them. Need them to set me straight about Emerson.

Is it supposed to be this hard to know if you are truly in love with someone? If you should tell them?

It's the fork in the road you ignore, knowing it's there but ignoring it until you are forced to choose: left or right, A or B, this or that. There's no sign, no telling you what you'll find at the end of the road, just a force pushing you to choose one. You have to choose one.

I'm at my fork in the road with Emerson.

"You don't, but you called us." Cal gestures to the group. He and George look back and forth between each other and me.

"And you bailed on us last night," George adds. "Which you never do unless it's for her."

"I told you I was tired. It was a long day at the office."

"But not tired enough for her," George says, asks—can't tell.

"D'you forget I work with you? I can see your calendar," Callum says at the same time his sister speaks.

"Are you tired from work or her?"

Both.

"I also own the company. I deal with shit you don't know about."

"Like what. . ." He tosses me a look that says, 'prove it.' He's my number two, he knows everything. There isn't anything I keep from him because there isn't a reason to. He'll find out one way or another, so might as well skip the bullshit and tell him first.

"I was tired. Does it matter if I want to talk to her?"

"No, she's your best friend," Audrey declares.

"I thought I was your best friend," George scoffs, leaning back in his chair and rocking on the backs of two legs.

"You are, but she's Emerson. It's different."

"Oi! That's £100, mate." George rocks the chair forward, pushing Callum in the shoulder from across the table.

Callum pulls out his wallet, throwing bills in George's way. Sitting directly in front of me, Audrey is smirking at the two of them. "Idiots," she grumbles.

Audrey turns her attention to me.

"Did you talk to her. . . ?" she asks.

"Yeah." I finish my drink. "She got stood up on a date. States called to debrief."

"Huh. First person?" Cal asks weirdly.

"I'spose. Maybe? She didn't clarify the order in which she told her friends she was stood up, but I did assume it was only a few minutes after they were set to meet."

"She wanted a chat with you?" I've known Audrey a month less than I've known Callum. She came to visit him at school after our first term kicked off. She's. . . expressive. . . doesn't know how to hide any emotions or thoughts from being all over her face to a fault.

"Wherever you're trying to get, Auds, get there," Cal says.

"Gettin' there, promise. Does Emerson do this after every date?"

"Possibly?"

"Yeah, she's into you." Audrey picks up her empty glass and flags the waiter over. "We'll all have another."

No one comments. I think they are waiting for me to say anything.

"Which you already know. If you didn't, the two of you wouldn't be inseparable every time you're together," Audrey adds.

"I'm into her," I admit.

"We already know that," George says in between coughs.

"Then why are we here, Liam?" Callum asks.

"I think I'm in love with her."

There it is, said out loud. The sound is not as scary as I thought it would be. It came out easier than I thought it would, too.

"We already know that. . . too," George says again.

"You do. . ."

What are they seeing that I missed?

"You are hung up on that girl—so much so that Molly called me—Molly, of all people. You told her there was someone else," Cal elaborates.

Molly was the only girl at university I dated. She was a fit girl and extremely intelligent—it was just school, you know? We dated for a year before we decided to be friends. She came back into my life last spring and wanted to start things back up. I tried—trust me, I tried—but she wasn't Emerson.

"I couldn't lie to her."

"But can you sit back and do nothing about someone else who dates guys and tells you about them? Or when we see her, you two can't get enough of each other that it is disgustingly annoying for anyone in your presence?"

"I'm her friend. We talk about stuff, which may or may not include my opinions on the males she fancies."

"That girl wants you," Audrey tilts her head. "She does that because you are the scale against which she weighs them—their appearance, their actions, how they treat her, and how they make her feel. If they aren't you, they aren't good enough for her. I think she's searching for your approval by telling you."

"And you do the same, mate," George adds.

"I've never once told her about a single woman I have been with." Because I haven't been with anyone since her, there's no one else but Emerson.

"Maybe so, but you measure everyone up against her."

"Ya heard the saying actions speak louder than words? You don't need to tell her, Liam. You want Emerson for yourself, and you have since you met her."

George laughs and says, "Even when I tried to cockblock ya."

But Callum keeps going on. "It's pissing obvious, it's painful. Honestly, I'm impressed by your stupidity of being friends with her for this long."

"I didn't want to ruin anything between us." I still don't want to ruin anything between us now. That's the problem—it's not that I don't want her or am in love with her. That's becoming as clear as a cloudless night to me; all the stars point to her.

"Shagging her every time you see her doesn't do the trick?" George asks.

"That's. . . different." I sigh, dropping my tense shoulders.

"Different?" George laughs and takes another drink of his beer. "Do enlighten us."

Different? Probably not the best word to use. I'm actually not sure if there is a difference. I think we blurred our lines a long time ago and became too comfortable with the confines in which we work.

I don't respond to George. He rolls his eyes and flags down the waiter to clear our plates from lunch and order a final round.

"I don't know what it is about Emerson. She's—"

George cuts in. "She's hot. She's fit. She's fun. She's got a great rump. She makes fun of you." He's counting on each finger. "She's smart. She's mad cool. She's hilarious. She's—"

"We get it." Audrey stops him with her hand up.

Cal is snickering. "He's not wrong. Emerson is it for you."

"She's more than that. . . she's *everything* to me. Emerson lights up my life; she's the sun around which my every thought and heartbeat revolves. There is something about her I can't get enough of. She believes that I bring out the best version of her, but she brings out the best version of me. Shit, I watched her read for hours the second time I saw her just to memorize her in hopes that—that I'd be able to have her in my dreams. But the opportunity to have her, the real physical her, not only in my mind? It messes me up. I stop remembering how to act. Don't know who I am. She feels out of reach, slipping out of my grasp, and if she does. . . will I fall off my axis?"

The three of them stare at me—proper shock and amusement on my best friends' faces. None of us have ever confessed anything like this about a girl before. Callum reaches diagonally across the table and places his hand on my forearm.

"You've got it bad for States," he says.

"I do."

"Then these words are wasted on us. You should tell her." Callum locks eyes with me.

"Yeah, I'll just text her and say I'm in love with you; let's be together." I laugh off the vulnerability I'm wearing.

"Maybe something more romantic, but yeah, why not? If you feel this way, why are you holding back?" Audrey encourages me.

Once again, this is why I am glad she's here.

"Chivalry is still alive?"

"Fair, but—"

"Don't think she feels the same?" her brother talks over her.

"Yeah." I frown.

"As the only female present, I'm telling you she does. Knowing Emerson, hell, knowing you two together? You are it for each other."

"My sister is right. Knowing States, she will want, and need, you to tell her face to face."

"We aren't seeing her this summer—" George complains.

I don't let him finish the sentence. Hadn't gotten a chance to tell them about the change of plans since Emerson and I decided last night.

"About that. . . she's coming here."

34

LIAM

Now

I shouldn't have called her.

I stared at my phone for an hour before grabbing Natalie's to call Emerson. I knew she wouldn't answer my call, but her earlier message was heard loudly and clearly.

Talking to Emerson is immensely intoxicating. She's always been a drug to me. I've never been addicted to anything in my life except her. It's an addiction I haven't been able to quit since the first time I laid my eyes on her.

Waking up this morning next to Natalie after falling asleep thinking and dreaming about Emerson is wrong. This line I'm walking is becoming dangerous.

Everything I said to Emerson was true, except I want her to see past our past for me, too. Our lives might not be crossed romantically anymore, but they are crossed. I've ached to be back in her life. The same aching I felt before I finally told her I loved her.

Before last week, I'd take anything she'd give me. But how was I supposed to know that we both had unfinished business cooped up inside of us? That's a bloody lie. Unfinished business is our calling card, the award we'd each win in this life.

It seemed pretty clear after the summer that we split—Emerson moved on. I was hurt, thinking we meant so little to her that she could just get over it. I did my best to move on. It wasn't until meeting Natalie that I became remotely alive again. I guess it makes sense; she and Emerson are best friends.

"Oh shit." Natalie is up, glancing past me at the bedside table clock. "Why didn't you wake me up?"

"What's wrong?" I ask her.

"I have to be at a studio in the Loop. . . an hour ago! Shit."

"Isn't that on Wednesday?"

"It is Wednesday, Liam." Natalie rolls her eyes at me. She jumps out of bed, pulls on a pair of leggings and a cropped, ribbed black tank top, and rushes into the bathroom while slipping her arms through a V-neck sweatshirt.

"Won't you be hot in the jumper?" I ask her.

"No, the studio is always cold."

I can overhear her on the phone in the bathroom. "Dave, I overslept—completely my fault. Yeah, yeah, I will be there in twenty minutes tops." She's moving frantically, braiding her hair and cleaning her face and teeth. "Calling an Uber now." She releases a sigh. "Thank you for not being mad. Yeah, see everyone soon."

Natalie is unnaturally naturally beautiful. She knows it but still layers herself with makeup, hair, and clothes—industry and society pressure has to be it. Otherwise, I think she wouldn't even touch half of it, maybe her hair; she smiles bigger when doing it, even if it is only a braid.

"You look beautiful this morning," I tell her, regretting the comment as soon as it leaves my mouth because only moments ago, I was thinking about how beautiful Emerson is—her best friend Emerson, and Natalie doesn't even know.

Regret is starting to lose its meaning and ability to be black and white. It's a gray zone between regretting what I'm doing to Emerson and what I'm doing to Natalie. What am I even doing to her? What even is this between her and me?

We aren't dating. We've honestly never slept together, either. Tried, but Natalie stopped it. She won't tell me why.

I should call it, but that's an inner battle I'd rather not face this morning.

"Thank you." She smiles over at me, her cheeks blushing.

I slip out of bed and slip on my jumper before following her to the kitchen, where I find a bar stool.

"I'll be back this afternoon. I have back-to-back meetings this morning. . ." Her mouth and feet move at light speed. I can barely make out what she's saying because she's talking so fast.

"Cal lands today," I remind her when there is a break between sentences. "We're adding shopping to our already long list of fun things to get done."

"Shopping for new hotels isn't fun?" Her eyes widen in exaggeration.

"Shouldn't you be going? Don't want to be later than you are?"

"Dinner tonight? The three of us, or I can ask Emme if she wants to come." Natalie tosses about fifteen items into a tiny purse that must be a clown bag in disguise. "Wait—you never told me how your walk home with her went?" she asks, her tone turning methodical.

"Lovely. Emerson is—lovely." George's laugh rings in my ears at the word choice to describe States. Lovely.

"Told you you'd love her." *Yeah, yeah, I do love her.*

There's a mad sort of grin on her face. It's gone within a minute.

Natalie drops a kiss on my cheek before rushing out the front door.

Rummaging through her cabinets, I find a filter and grounds. I turn the bag to read it. Vanilla-flavored? Ew. Does no one prefer a plain black mug of coffee?

Emerson does.

Still, make a pot anyway. When the trickle of coffee begins brewing, I return to Natalie's bedroom to grab my phone. Shoot off a text to Cal first.

I try George. Haven't spoken to him much since he dropped news that Beatrix is pregnant on Callum and me when I was in London last. He was going back home to see his parents last he told me. Doesn't answer.

Something in me urges me to call the only person. . . whose ears must be burning because his name flashes on my screen.

My dad, Haymitch Hayes.

We don't talk often. An occasional text message here and there. Ever since my mom passed away while I was at school, he's been different. I guess that's what happens when you truly lose the love of your life.

Even though they were divorced, they were best friends and madly loved each other—which didn't make much sense to others, either.

I think it is possible to love someone but not be with them. Maybe that'll be me and Emerson forever. Caught in the dimension of the universe where that's plausible.

Grief overcame him. For the first few years after Mom passed, he turned to alcohol to numb the pain, the first time seeing my dad drink more than a pint or two. Knew her passing was inevitable—diagnosed with breast cancer when I was twelve, had two durations of remission, but battled like hell. The cancer came back a third time, spreading into her lungs and liver. She died within the year.

My father's grief, mainly the alcohol consumption, made him more distant than he already was. Not returning to football didn't aid the situation either. His distance fueled his disappointment and distaste for me.

I told myself he saw me thriving at school and in the initial phases of developing my company as me not caring about my mother. . . or that she was gone. Or the neglect of everything he gave me as a child to get me to where I was athletically. Reality? Throwing myself into that is how I helped myself heal; if I didn't. . . I'm not optimistic I'd be here. I didn't know how to handle all the grief I felt at first.

Grief. A foreign monster that wreaked havoc on my mind. As soon as I learned to handle (defeat) it, it reappeared in a new version. That's what they forget to tell you about grief. It has many faces, and there's no way to prepare for it.

I wanted to go to therapy, told my dad, and his reply was to man up. Our relationship became even more estranged, and then I lost both of my parents.

Cal and George knew about what I was going through and sat there with me in the hospital the day she died. As relieved as I was that my mom was no longer struggling, I still wanted her on Earth with me. They watched grief shift something inside me. Manned up, as my father said, didn't talk about what I was going through until Emerson. She listened, asked questions, and helped heal those final parts of me that success couldn't. Emerson also helped me, more forced, rekindle my relationship with my father. Something I'll forever be grateful for.

I pick up on the third ring. "Son. It's good to hear from you."

"I've been busy," I ask him. "How are you?"

"Good, we are good." He's referring to his girlfriend, Michelle. They've been together for the past four years. She's incredible, and I'm happy he has her. Michelle reminds me a lot of my mom. When I met her, it made sense why my father gravitated toward her. "How are you? Are you back in London?"

"No. I'm in Chicago."

"Going for the expansion?"

"That happened last year, Dad," I remind him. Rekindled, not fully restored relationship—let me clarify that here. "I invited you to the opening. You haven't RSVP'd."

I don't expect him to come. He hasn't been to any of the others. He'll talk to me about everything I've accomplished but hasn't come to a single one, even in his own backyard. Michelle attended the last one in London. She told me he was busy and wished he could have been there. Her soft smile told me she tried. I don't push the issue. It may sting still, but this is far better than anything I could have hoped for.

"I'm s—" he starts to say.

"Don't sweat it. I didn't expect you to come, anyway," I cut him off, not wanting to hear that.

There's a long pause between us.

"I'm proud of you, Liam," my dad says.

My heart is like a geyser about to blow. It doesn't matter our age; we always want our parents to be proud of us. . . and hear it.

Since forming Hayes Hotels, he's never once told me that. Honestly, I don't know if he's ever said those five words to me.

"Thank you, Dad. I appreciate hearing that."

"I know I don't tell you enough." *Or ever.* "But I am. You've worked extremely hard to get to where you are. Your mom would be proud, too."

"She would." I smile, thinking about her.

"How long do you plan to be there?" he asks.

"Undecided. At a minimum, through the opening and the month following. Cal and I'll decide the rotation of presence needed here," I respond, updating him on the other two locations we are eyeing in the area to try to make a name.

The coffee pot alarm goes off, and I pour myself a cup. I take a small sip—this vanilla isn't half that bad.

We catch up about Callum and George. I tell him George's big news, and like me, he can't believe it. He informs me that he and Michelle are heading to the Highlands this weekend. He asks for restaurant recommendations.

Our call lasted another ten minutes before I jumped to prepare for work. He told me he was proud of me again, and we hung up. At least some part of today should end on a high.

35

EMERSON

Now

It's nice being friends with Liam again. It's incredibly nice.

The day after he called, I went to dinner with him, Natalie, and Callum. I was amicable, trying to gauge how far we could lean into friendship without tipping Natalie off that we previously loved each other.

She was oblivious, making it easier for us to drift toward each other.

Over the past two weeks, we've been to drinks, brunch, and evening farmers' markets in my neighborhood as a group. Liam even attended a workout class with Natalie and I—we were partners.

Even working with him has become exciting. Callum, Blake, and our marketing team are present, but I don't have an anxious urge when we have to be around each other.

Like I said, it's nice being his friend.

However. . . being friends doesn't stop the surge of heat when our bodies brush. Fingers graze and linger when passing the pepper. Shoulders brushing getting into a car, or knees bumping when sitting near each other.

That's happening right now.

Everyone, as in our strange growing friend group—Natalie and Liam, Chloe and Seth, Callum and I—are out for dinner. We're rounding out our week at Parlor Pizza in the West Loop.

We're seated outside on the patio at a picnic table. On one side of the table are Cal, Natalie, and Liam. On the other, across from them is Seth and Chloe, leaving me directly across from Liam. Our knees bump because of his height.

As our drinks are delivered to the table, I keep sensing a set of eyes shifting toward me. I realize that Liam keeps glancing at me.

"Is there something on my face?" I give him a quizzical look.

"I like the haircut," he tells me.

I cut it today. I had the idea, but I didn't think it would last—all of my hair ideas are fleeting, so I called my stylist, and by the end of the day, my hair was five inches shorter.

"Oh, yeah. I—I got it done today." I tuck a loose strand behind my ear, acting like a nervous elementary school girl when her crush compliments her. "Thanks for noticing."

Liam's mouth lifts into a soft smile. "I always notice you."

"Have you and Cal decided whether you want to buy the old Morrison Hotel?" Liam tenses as I ask the question.

"Yes."

"That was quick? Do you usually make decisions that fast?"

"No. Didn't say we were going for it or not."

"Are you?"

"No."

"Alright then." I let out a sigh, letting my eyes go too expressive in his presence, giving myself away. He can tell I'm getting annoyed that he is being this short with me.

"What—"

"Remember this friend thing between us? It requires talking to me. Did I do something?"

"Didn't say that."

"You are acting like it."

We've caught Callum's attention. He's staring at us from his spot on the other end of the table.

"Cal said you two had lunch," Liam says quietly. We lower our voices to keep the conversation between us.

"We did yesterday." I keep trying to make eye contact with him, but now he's choosing to avoid mine. "Only to catch up."

"Like you did that summer?" His tone has a bite of jealousy—or is he hurt about us getting lunch?

I glance at Cal, who is still staring down at us two. My face falters. Did he tell Liam? He promised me he wouldn't.

"I don't know what you're talking about."

I lie. I know exactly what he's talking about. The year after that dreaded summer in London, I returned to London for work. It took the entire four days I was there to work up the courage to talk to Liam. In my mind, showing up at his favorite café where he gets coffee every Thursday morning was a bright idea, as opposed to texting or calling to say, 'Hey, I'm in London.'

I approached the café when I saw him sitting outside with someone else, a female someone else. I turned around, hurt that he had moved on. I already had plans to get lunch with Callum later that day. I tried to bail, but he wouldn't let me. Callum and I remained friends but set the rule that day that we wouldn't talk about Liam.

"You do, States. I saw you two," he whisper yells. Saw us? Shit, he probably felt as I did.

"I was there for work, and we are friends." I shake my head at him, pleading with him to believe the truth.

"Right, just friends. That's why you reacted the way you did at dinner last week at the idea of you two going on a date. Maybe Nat should set the two of you up."

My mouth drops.

"Why are you acting this way?" I ask, disappointed in his hurt behavior.

He shoos me off. That's fine; if that's how he wants to play, let's play.

"You know what, maybe she should. I did always think that he was more attractive and a better man. Somehow, I got stuck with. . .*you*."

Any ounce of emotion on his face disappears. His eyes flare and darken, not in the dark color that he gets when he's craving to be inside of me, but in a shade of hurt that I've only ever seen once before.

Why, Emerson? Why did you have to say that?

Shaking his head, Liam goes to say something but is cut off by the waitress standing at the head of the wooden table, ready to take our orders.

"Want to split the Honey Boo Boo? Or Burrata Be Kidding Me?" Natalie asks Liam. "We could get both if you join us, Emme," she eyes me.

"Sounds good." I nod.

"A pizza love triangle. Love it!" She shakes her shoulders and then turns to the waiter, giving her our order.

I watch Natalie. Liam is watching me. A love triangle this sure is.

I excuse myself to the restroom.

Chloe touches my arms as I get up. Leaning back, she looks up at me and asks, "You okay?"

"Yeah. . . yeah, need to pee."

She straightens out, jumping back into conversation.

***

Exiting the bathroom, my hand still on the metal handle, the heavy door closing behind me, I run directly into something solid. I don't need to open my eyes to know who it is. The aroma of cedar and vanilla filters into my nose, running through my veins.

I don't open my eyes. I do not even bother to acknowledge him as I try to push past him, but he's too sturdy.

I step back, flush with the door. Reluctantly, I lift my head to meet his gaze.

"Tell me you didn't mean it." Liam's voice is desperate as if he doesn't get the answer he wants, then he will explode. Strands of his hair are out of place like he's been tugging on it.

"Mean what?"

"Cal. Me. Our first summer together. That you just got stuck with—did you mean it?"

"I don't know, maybe I did. That was six years ago, can't remember." I let myself fall further into the door. "All of that is in the. . . past."

"It's not the past. Is it?"

"You asked me to look past it. I am."

Liam growls softly.

"Am I missing something?" I ask slightly sardonically.

"Tell. Me."

This is the second time he's demanding answers from me. Answers and conversations I'd generally avoid. I don't like talking about us. Then, because I was scared. Now, because the memories are ghosts that haunt me.

His gaze is hot beating down on me, making my thoughts and emotions revolve around him as if he is the sun.

His height is to his advantage.

Discreetly, I squeeze my legs together, trying to get rid of the heat that is gathering between them. I can't bring myself to continue looking at his face, so I stare straight forward into his chest.

"No—"

"Full sentences. Please."

"No is a full sentence. Didn't you graduate at the top of your year?"

"Emerson. . ." I'm getting under his skin. *Good.*

"No. . . no, I didn't mean it. You shouldn't have to ask that if you know me."

"Why say it? Why joke about us?" His right-hand touches the side of my face. Liam grazes it slowly down to my chin, holding it. "I do know you. . . more than I probably should. More than anyone, I bet. I shouldn't remember you the way I do—your favorite color, your freckles that appear when you are in the sun, or the way you smell. How you sneak out of bed to brush your teeth because you can't kiss anyone in the morning because of your irrational phobia of morning breath. The small scar just below your right ear." His hand touches it as I turn my head. "And I shouldn't remember that all it takes to get your pulse racing is to put you in a position like this. We both know you love to be up against a wall.

"Your pulse is racing right now. I can see it—you're simmering, thinking about the last time we were in a bathroom. How I pushed you up against the wall there, my hand covering your mouth so that no one else could find joy in your screams. You're trying to resist us. You're wondering what it would be like if you turned the knob that's currently digging into your back, pull us inside, and lock it behind you."

My eyelids blink in sync with my pulse. It's unfortunate how right Liam is. "Curious if we are still just as good." I swallow. Liam drags his head away from mine and watches how slowly it makes its way down my throat. "It would be. Wanna know why? Because I know you. And you know me. You know I'm thinking about it too," he says, looking past my eyes and into all of me.

"That's not what I'm thinking about."

He laughs, and I want to smack the smirk off his face. Maybe I was thinking about it. Is that wrong?

Actually, yes, Emerson, that is completely wrong. You are thinking about him in ways you can't think about him anymore. He hurt you. He hasn't apologized. He is your *friend*. We don't think about friends this way—except for Liam. You always think about him as more than a friend.

He was wrong about one thing, though.

I'm not curious if it would still be good. I know it would be. In this life, in another life, and in whatever life we found each other in, I know we'd be too good together. I'm not just talking about sex. I mean, in all facets of life, we would be too good together. Loving each other would have been too good, and that's why we could never be together.

"Sure it isn't. Then why'd you squeeze your legs, and your hands are clutching your skirt?"

I didn't think he noticed that.

"I notice everything about you. Haven't you figured that out by now?"

I roll my eyes and try to push past him again, but he doesn't budge. The electricity consuming my body is evolving from desire to frustration. Why is he doing this? Why does it matter that I made a joke? Would he have been jealous if I had wanted Callum back then?

So I ask him. "Why are you doing this?"

"Just because we aren't together doesn't mean that my entire being isn't consumed by you still. It's a bad habit I've had for years. Every thought of my every moment is *you*. Your contagious laugh, the way you squish your nose when you are embarrassed, your intelligence and ability to read a person's needs, how you try to order different things at a restaurant and then hate it because you are a picky eater. Shall I go on?"

My grasp on control is slipping. I'm starting to lose control of my heart—again—when he says things like that to me.

I can't speak. I can't stop Liam, nor do I want to.

There's power in knowing you are the source of someone's every thought.

"Even now, I can't seem to escape the thought of *you*."

My breath hitches.

He holds my chin where I can't look anywhere but him. A firm, warm grasp that might melt the skin right off.

"This whole time, I knew somehow, somewhere, we'd find each other again," he continues. His gaze shifts from my eyes to my mouth. Mine matches his. Liam rests his forehead on mine.

"Tell me you feel the same. We'll figure it out. Questions answered. No more hurting. I'll tell Natalie. It'll be over." His voice is pure desperation.

I'm frozen. I think my heart stopped beating because I feel nothing and absolutely everything simultaneously.

After several moments, I open my mouth to speak.

"Emerson. . . ?"

36

LIAM

Now

It's a female voice.

Sirens go off in my head. *Great, it's probably Natalie. This is one way to blow up things, Liam.*

They said Emerson's name quietly enough that it might have been Natalie. It's dark enough where they stand that we are all outlines of each other.

I'm praying it's not Natalie, or maybe I want it to be her. I want to end all of this here right now. I'm no longer hiding that I'm crazy about the girl standing before me, and I won't ever be able to feel the same about anyone else.

I push off the wall, releasing Emerson from my grasp. Her fortress wall snaps back into place.

I hear their footsteps get louder as they inch closer to us. The dim hallway light acts as a spotlight when they step into it.

Chloe.

"What the hell is happening here?" She demands.

"Nothing—" Emerson tries to say.

"Uh-huh. Sure looks like nothing is going on." Chloe turns to face me. "And I was just learning to warm up to you. I suppose you don't want to explain why you have the wrong girl pushed up against the wall, your face a misstep away from hers."

Wrong girl—she's not the wrong girl; she's the right girl, wrong time.

"She could be the right girl," I say under my breath. Emerson's eyes cut back to mine.

"Liam—" Her eyelids are fluttering.

"Could be, but you won't admit it. This was a mistake."

"Huge mistake," Chloe snidely remarks. I know she's protecting Emerson, and I appreciate her loyalty to her. But where's Natalie?

"Liam, stop—don't." Emerson reaches out for me.

Taking a page out of her book, I leave. She didn't stay then. I'm not staying now. The double meaning of walking away aside, I should walk away right now and go back to the table, turning this into our new unfortunate norm. Walk away from the feast of emotions that are on the table, too afraid to remove the lids to dig in and indulge them.

I'm halfway down the hallway before I turn back toward them.

"Don't what? Walk away? Leave? Learned from the best." I don't acknowledge their responses. I head back to the table.

"Did you see Emme back there? She's been gone awhile," Natalie asks me with concern.

"I didn't see her. Probably in the loo."

"Oh," she says as if she could see through my lie. "Chloe went after her. I hope everything will be alright."

I don't think anything will ever be alright. A conclusion I don't want to come to but might have to force myself to. She, Emerson, isn't letting this go. What I said, what she overheard. I hurt her in the one way that she's always feared.

Cal scowls down at me from the end of the table.

"Everything good?" he mouths.

I shake my head, picking up a slice of pizza that was delivered to the table while I was in the bathroom.

Emerson is walking back to the table, head and shoulders folded in. Chloe is a few steps behind her and looks. . .I think a look of confusion, maybe frustration. Her smokey facial expressions are hard to read.

Chloe sits back down. Emerson does not.

"I'm not feeling well. Think I'm going to head home," Emerson announces.

"Oh, no!" Natalie says first. "What's wrong?"

"Headache." Emerson's eyes swivel in my direction.

"Hm, okay. Do you want to take any food home with you? I can ask for a to-go box," Natalie offers.

"I don't have much of an appetite. You know how I get when I have a headache," she responds.

"Right."

"Feel better," I add.

Emerson doesn't acknowledge me as she picks up her purse and exits the restaurant.

37

LIAM

Three Summers Ago

Everything feels right having Emerson in London. *A little too right.*

I hadn't realized how much I missed her *or loved her*. We practically attacked each other—okay, I practically attacked her in the airport once she made it through customs. I didn't waste any time once she was in my arms and kissed her.

I couldn't resist it.

At first, when she didn't kiss me back, I thought I had made a mistake and read her wrong. Then she kissed me back, parting her lips for me, taking our kiss deeper and more desperate. Maybe she loves me, *too.*

Her side of the bed is cold when I wake this morning, but an aroma of coffee fills the air. She must be in the kitchen.

Emerson made herself comfortable—an understatement. She acts as if she hasn't been here for only three full days but rather that this is *our* life every morning. I climb out of bed, slip on the sweatpants she ripped off last night, and go downstairs to the living room.

My flat is perfect. Two floors, bedrooms upstairs, an open floor plan on the first floor connecting the living and kitchen space, and a downstairs bedroom that I use as a home office. Modern but traditional for Grosvenor Square. I've been living here for about a year.

From the bottom of the stairs, I catch a glimpse of Emerson dancing, wearing the old-school over-the-head headphones that I will never understand why she loves. She's in a tiny white tank, the brown of her perky nipples noticeable, and a pair of knit pajama shorts.

Quietly, I slide into the kitchen. I lean against the benchtop and watch Emerson.

She's so beautiful.

Enthralled by the woman dancing around my kitchen—for which she still has zero coordination—a giant smile can't help but form on my face.

Emerson's made herself a home in my apartment, just as she's made a home in my heart.

She grabs a mug from the cabinet and pours a cup of coffee. Then grabs another cup from the cabinet and sets it on the counter next to my coffee maker. The entire time, her hips are still moving from left to right.

I release a deep chuckle that catches her attention. She turns around and faces me, her lips lifting into a smile. She takes a sip of coffee and lets out an 'ahh.'

Emerson starts approaching me, shaking her hips, and asks, "You like what you see? There's more to these moves."

Then winks at me.

"Oh, I know there is."

She passes me; I reach out to stop her, drawing her to me. I lean down to kiss her forehead and then again a little lower, this time kissing her lips and dragging her bottom lip out from where she is biting it. She tastes like coffee. If this is how I could caffeinate myself, I'd never stop.

Emerson's eyes look up at me through her long lashes.

"I take that as a yes?" she teases me.

Pulling away, she returns to the coffee pot and fills the mug that she sat out. Pushes it to me across the counter.

"You know I like what I see, always." Always have, always will. "There's something I wanted to talk to you about."

Emerson waves me over behind her to the couch. We plop down. She leans forward and grabs the chunky knit blanket off the ground, pulling it over her as she curls into me.

"What did you want to talk about?"

I nervously take a sip of my coffee. Setting it down on the table, I open my mouth to speak, but the words I want to say aren't the ones that come out.

"Last day you get to claim all of me; I have to work tomorrow." I chicken out. "What's left on the list to do?"

While Emerson was adamant about not being a tourist during her visit, she certainly has compiled a list of the most popular things to see. It's as if she found the top ten touristy things to do, even though she won't admit it. We've tackled most of them, but it hasn't left us with time for the non-touristy things, which I'm okay with. It's been sort of nice. I can't remember when I last visited Buckingham Palace or sat and people watched at Big Ben. Emerson enjoyed seeing me as a tourist too. I told her she could do them this week when I was at work; she laughed it off. Unfortunately, this included an *I love London* t-shirt and top hat with England's flag on it. We streamed the *Friends'* episode when they went to London that night. I don't think I've ever seen her laugh so much when comparing a photo of me to Joey.

Luckily, Emerson doesn't leave until next Saturday. Booking her tickets gave me control of her stay; greedily, I planned it this way. I planned for her to have a long weekend teaser to be the tourist, for her to be with me while I was working, and for my work week to be light so that I could complete my list of places to see with her. I hope that if I show her my world, she might want to be a part of it forever.

"Remember that day in Paris when we flipped a coin to make decisions?" She peers over her mug, trying to hide the pink blush that's taking over her cheeks.

"Abso-fucking-lutely," I tell her. It's one of my favorite nights ever.

"What if that's what we do? See where the day. . . takes us."

***

Our most recent toss landed in my favor. I chose The National Gallery, an art museum. It was not the pick I would have gone with, but a storm had taken over the city, and I wasn't ready to head back to my flat. The gray skies should have been warning enough this morning when we left. Earlier in the day, we could dart between places, avoiding the light rainstorm. It would be impossible now that the skies have fully opened up.

There was also a storm brewing in Emerson; I could sense it. When we arrived at the museum, her eyes became cloudy. Her face became stoic, and I couldn't read it—I could always read her, even over video chats.

We explored hand in hand, but she felt far away, her touch non-existent.

"I'm glad you're here." I look down at her, giving her a warm smile, hoping to fill her with a bit of sunshine.

She doesn't speak. She returns my smile with a half-smile.

"Everything okay, States?"

She nods. Slipping her hand from mine, she draws it to her front. Crossing her arms in front of her.

"Mind if I walk by myself?" She asks me, but she doesn't need permission.

"Sure—"

Before I finish my thought, she's gone. I watch her walk away into a wing dedicated to the Renaissance period.

I give it fifteen minutes before I follow the direction she went in. She wasn't there. I make my way around the museum until I find her standing in a room all by herself, staring up at a painting, *Bathers at Asnieres* by George Seurat.

I come up beside her. She doesn't acknowledge me physically, but I know she knows I'm standing there.

"This makes me think about us that afternoon in Paris," she says.

"*Bathers* reminds you of that?"

"No. Sitting by the water, telling you about my parents." I watch her eyes flick over toward me and back to the painting. "What do you think these people are talking about? Do you think they are washing away their past in the water? Contemplating the decisions they and others have made that impacted their lives?"

"It's possible," I tell her, looking at the photo, really looking at it. "Him, right there." I point to the male sitting on the banks of the water, contemplation painted on his face. Stoic, frozen as a status, similar to Emerson right now. "It reminds me of you right now. What are you contemplating?"

"Do you think we are being cruel to ourselves. . . to each other?"

Emerson continues staring at the painting.

"Cruel?"

From the corner of my eyes, I can see her breathing pick up. She closes her eyes as if the words she's looking for are on the backside of her eyelids or she is giving herself an internal pep talk.

"Emerson, what do you—"

She cuts me off, "pretending that this week or two in the summer is enough?"

"It has to be," I say too quickly. I don't know why. This morning, I almost told her how I felt. I know it doesn't have to be this way, but this is what we wanted, right? No. I want her. I love her.

"Does it? Don't you ever wonder what it would be like if we—"

"If we were together? All the time. But this—this dynamic between us it works, yeah? You in Chicago, me here."

What the hell, mate? I'm cursing myself internally.

"I. . . I know, but I don't know if it's working for me anymore."

Wait. Is Emerson ending this? I'm second-guessing everything.

"Is that why you wanted to come to London? Do you want to friend break up with me?"

"No! Oh, Liam, no." Her head snaps in my direction and I turn my entire body to face her. She's shaking her head. "I think what I'm trying to say unpoetically is that it's becoming a lot harder only to see you once a year, to only have you through a phone. I want y—to know you."

"Come off it," I tell her off because that statement is ridiculous. "You do know me."

She almost said 'you.' Emerson was trying to tell me she wanted me, but instead, she said, *Know me*. She knows everything about me. I've never been one to keep secrets with those I care about. Whatever, whenever something has happened since the day I met her, I've told her. She gets every part of me, whether she realizes it or not.

"Do I?" she asks.

"What's my favorite color?" I quiz her.

Emerson rolls her eyes at me. "Green."

"Correct. What's my favorite smell?"

"Macadamia nuts. Which I still find odd."

"Correct. What's my favorite hobby?" My smile gets bigger with each question.

"Running. . . or reading. That's not a fair question. None of these count. Anyone could guess these."

"No, they couldn't because if they asked me about my favorite things, they would need to know you. To know me, truly, is to know that you are my favorite thing in this world. My whole world is you."

Emerson stutters. She takes a deep inhale. "Your whole world?"

"My whole world, States."

"That doesn't mean I know you, though." This woman.

"How could you not know me when I know everything about you so deeply that it became a part of who I am?"

Her breath catches like I've sucked all the life out of her. In ways, I wish I could because that would mean her life is in me, giving me life.

"Then why do we live in this bubble?!" Her shoulders drop. "Why do we let ourselves survive off the summer. . . because that's how I'm holding on. It's my life support. These fleeting moments of summer we get together."

"Because—"

"I'm not done. It hurts. Being with you these days hurts me because I know I don't get to have you the moment I board a plane, leaving us behind in this bubble—this stupid summertime friends bubble of ours."

This moment is equivalent to when my favorite football team scored a goal in stoppage time to win the Premier League four years ago. Everything Emerson says is precisely what I've needed to hear from her to not feel like I'm going mad.

Our time together or friendship isn't cruel—it's not admitting the truth to each other, that is.

"It would be nice if you could say something here." I guess I've been silent longer than I thought, taking in her confession.

"Pop it. Let's pop this 'bubble' you think we are in," I say confidently to her.

"But what if this is it? What if this is all we will ever be? How do we know if it's *enough*?" Her questions come out rapidly.

"We'll never know till we try. We can figure this out, Emerson."

"Figure it out? Liam, we could have figured it out this entire time, years ago." She shakes her head back and forth, pinching her eyes closed. "But we didn't. So what's different this time?"

I spin her body toward me. Using my hand, I grip her chin to raise her face to mine.

It's now or never.

Tell her. Tell her you love her.

Tell her the one thing she doesn't know about you. The one thing that is different this time. Keep her from retreating further into herself, backtracking on everything I know she's feeling.

"I love you, Emerson," I say. "This time, I'm in love with you."

She stands there, disbelief washes over her. Then, a wave of calmness crashes over her.

Emerson raises on her toes and plants a kiss on my lips.

38

EMERSON

Three Summers Ago

I'm type A—well, type A-ish. I like things organized, going a certain way, making a plan, and following it. I check boxes on to-do lists in every facet of my life, including other people's. I didn't check all the boxes for my dad or mom, so I try to ensure I check the boxes of others in my life.

That's why I need routines.

Coming to London, my second biggest fear was whether I could find a routine in Liam's life. Did I fit in? Do I check the boxes?

It was more than an 'I love you'. To have the relationship with Liam I want, I need to confirm that we'd work and that I would be enough.

Our lives are different. Different continents. Different jobs. Different upbringings.

On the page, they don't mesh.

Much to my chagrin, I've meshed right into his world. Okay, maybe four weekdays wouldn't be defined as a routine, but this is the fifth day doing it, and it's a routine enough for me.

Each morning, we get up and run together. After our morning run, we shower, and as Liam gets ready for work, I make coffee for us. Liam leaves pretty quickly after that to head to the office, which has been around seven. Liam's been working till four the past few days, but I know from experience that normally he'd work much later. I know he's leaving early for me, but I suppose he's the CEO, so he can make his own rules.

While he's gone, I pick up his place before packing a bag to head out for the day. In the evening, he takes me to a few of his favorite restaurants, and then we explore parts of London, showing me the places he grew up going to.

Today, I find myself at a park near his place—one he walked me through the afternoon after I landed. I've visited it the past couple of days. It's quiet and peaceful. I find a seat on a metal bench overlooking a series of others. I pull out a book and set it next to me while taking in my surroundings.

Across from me is a couple. They appear to be Liam and I's ages. Her legs are draped across his. He's leaning into her with his arm around her. Their heads are as close as possible, whispering to each other. The girl is smiling, giggling up at him. His eyes never leave her.

I wonder if that's what Liam and I look like. Do people look at us how I look at this couple and see a flashing, neon sign that reads they are in love?

Question after question, doubt after doubt, start drifting in. Unlike the blue skies above, my world goes gray. Clouds drift in, a storm of uncertainty, and cold raindrops regulate the temperature between Liam and me.

He told me he loved me. I couldn't say it back.

It wasn't the first time I'd heard those words, but it was the first time hearing them that they mattered and didn't feel like a lie.

That the person saying them meant them. No strings attached. No caveats. No boxes to be checked.

Liam hasn't asked why I haven't returned the sentiment. He hasn't pressured me to say it back. He hasn't acted like that's a problem.

But it's a problem for me. It's not that I don't feel the same way. I do.

It was there, on the tip of my tongue—I swear. I tried to tell Liam, but my whole mouth went dry. I wanted to tell him, but when I opened my mouth, I was mute. The words sucked into me like a vortex back into the depths of my soul, the dark part that is chaining me to my beliefs and holding me prisoner from accepting his love and loving him back.

I seized up then. I'm seizing up now.

My lungs seize up, my heart rate increases, my shoulders shake, and my thoughts run a million miles per hour, crisscrossing.

"Is she alright?" The couple across from me stares at me, concern flashing on their faces. The male's brows are tense as he asks the female.

"Are you okay?" She calls out to me from across the path.

I stare back at her blankly, but I don't see her or the male in whose lap she is no longer lying in. I'm thirteen again, seated under the covers of my plush, eggplant purple comforter; my arms are wrapped around my knees, squeezing them too tight. I hear the screams coming from downstairs—my mother's voice and then my father's. They go back and forth like a game of ping-pong, volleying threats back and forth at one another.

I ran up to my room when it started. My dad clattered his suitcase in one hand and two duffels in the other down the stairs. He must have left the items by the front door because as I picked up my head from my math homework, he looked me in the eyes, patting my shoulder, and told me he was leaving. My mom came flying down the stairs frantically. My dad bolts from me. They collide in the entryway to our house, where his bags are. She has her hands on them, refusing to let him go. That was when they were screaming. When I ran up the stairs, I tripped twice on the way up. Nausea rises in my throat as I enter my room. I throw up in the trash can in my room not once but twice. Climbing onto the bed and pulling the covers over me doesn't help quiet their screaming as it continues until it all goes silent. I climbed out of my bed, opening my door quietly. As if I were a mouse, I crept to the top of the stairs, where it opened up to our loft.

My mom was there sitting on the couch sobbing, not a sound coming out of her. I had never seen anyone silently cry before. It's rather terrifying. It pierced me to see her this way. A slam of a door snapped my attention to where my dad's bags used to be, but they were gone. He's gone, too. No goodbye. No explanation. No looking back at me. No, nothing.

This time, in the nightmare of the memory, I'm not only the little girl—I'm my mom. Liam's face and voice are those of my dad's. The memory is playing out in a vision of what I fear will happen to me someday. I can't—I can't let it come true.

I don't know how I ended up back at Liam's place, but I do. I don't remember getting up from that bench, collecting my belongings, or walking the few blocks.

I remember the ringing in my ears.

I remember my eyes going fuzzy.

I remember tossing up my breakfast.

I remember my brain going black.

Standing in Liam's flat, in the middle of his kitchen, it's as if the lights are turned back on. I take in my surroundings. I take in my body, starting with my feet, legs, stomach, arms, and head. The exact way my college therapist taught me.

I'm not in the nightmare.

I can prevent that nightmare.

I repeat the affirmations as I change into my running clothes, lace up my shoes, and exit Liam's flat again.

With the pounding of the pavement below my feet, the summer sun on my face, and the humid air coursing through my lungs, I'm hopeful that clarity will come.

I throw myself onto Liam's couch after when he calls me.

"Hey!" I answer the phone.

"Oi, love. I know we were supposed to get dinner with everyone tonight, but does tomorrow for brunch work instead?" he asks me.

"Yeah, of course."

"Figured I'll cook us dinner?" he asks. His voice is hesitant, or is that nervousness I hear in it? "Hold on, States."

Liam is talking to someone in the background. Chatter that goes over my head as they discuss something about an interest rate.

I enjoy seeing the interior of the places that Liam's company is inquiring about, but outside of that, I've told him before, it's in one ear and out the other.

"Still there?" I let out an *uh-huh*. "Dinner?"

"What are you planning to make?"

"You'll see." He laughs.

"What time will you be home?"

"Five latest. Gotta jump, but be hungry for dinner. . . and me." I roll my eyes. I know he can't see them, just like I can't see the playful smirk that I know is on his face right now.

"You better do the same."

"I'm famished. I love you."

"See you later," I say and hang up.

I kick my feet up over the edge of the couch, flipping through my book. Within pages, I fall asleep, dreams catching me quickly, exhausted from my run and panic attack.

"States, wake up," Liam says. He's gently shaking me. I rustle in the blanket. Fluttering my eyes open, I see him staring down at me.

"Fell asleep?"

"No. . ." I give a fake smile. "My run wore me out."

"You ran without me? And a second time today?"

"Maybe. . ." I sit up on the couch. Liam's training for the Berlin Marathon this September. He's deep into his training, longer runs than I could ever imagine running or would want to. What sane person wants to run twenty-six miles? When he began training, I started running. It was good to try something new.

Running together for the past five days has been a joy. It's comical to watch, I can only imagine. He looks like a horse on a slow trot, while I look like a cheetah at full sprint, yet they are at the same pace. Liam doesn't complain though. He doesn't worry about meeting his miles or speed when we are out together. It's sweet and makes me wish we could spend all our mornings like these.

"I run without you at home," I inform him. I don't say that I ran again today because it was the only way to escape myself and the nightmare—past and future. Until today, I only ran to stick to the plan he sent me and to be close to him.

Today, it was like I was running away from him.

"I know. I didn't expect it, that's all." He leans down and kisses me.

"What time is it?"

"Quarter to five."

I slept longer than I wanted to.

"Want to walk to the supermarket with me?" I nod, and he helps me up. Still in my athletic clothes from earlier, I put my sneakers back on. Liam doesn't change. He's still in his navy suit, fitted perfectly to his body. Every muscle, every curve accentuated. Even the color, a shade of navy, complements every feature.

He's handsome—I keep saying or thinking handsome to match the sophisticated way he's dressed, but he's Theo James level of hot. No, definitely hotter. Liam in a tailored suit, though? That does me in.

39

EMERSON

Now

Fidgeting for my apartment keys, my hand trembles as I open the door. I miraculously get to my room and lay myself down on my bed. I stare up at the ceiling and scream in the pillow I hold to my face.

"Why?!" I scream the word over and over.

Why did he say what he did?

Why do we hurt each other?

Why did I leave?

Why can't I return to that night?

Why has it taken us this long?

My phone is buzzing in my purse.

I grab it from the interior pocket. Chloe is calling me again. I've already sent it to voicemail five times.

She tried to get me to talk in the hallway before we returned to the table, repeatedly asking me to tell her what was happening. I told her it wasn't the right time. She huffed at me, annoyed, and walked back to the table.

Chloe texts me now.

> Chloe: Are you okay?

> Yes.

Chloe: Liar.

Chloe: Whatever that was, you aren't okay.

I don't know how to be.

Chloe: Talk to me.

I'm going to bed.

Chloe: Coffee tomorrow morning.

7:30 @ Lucky's work?

Chloe: See you there.

My phone buzzes again. It's probably Natalie or Cal checking in on me. Probably Cal. I'm surprised, annoyed, or maybe relieved when I see Liam's name on the screen.

Liam: Headache gone?

Hasn't left in weeks.

Probably won't go away for a while.

Liam: Can I help?

Are you kidding?

Liam: Can we talk about what happened?

No.

Liam: Please.

There isn't an amount of time that could change how I feel about Liam Hayes. Fated mates. An invisible string. I don't know what it is, but something is connecting us forever.

That first summer we spent together, he changed something in me. He showed me how to be the version of myself I wanted to be. He made me believe, for once, that I was enough.

Till I wasn't, we weren't.

In all my hurt and healing, how he felt didn't once cross my mind. Selfishly, I've been thinking about myself.

After we left that day in London, I thought he was fine. You had to be, to pack someone's bags. Then, a year later, he was with someone else, and I was still heartbrokenly his.

It hit me tonight that he was just as broken afterward, that I hurt him as much as he hurt me. It wasn't only me who thought everything was falling apart and was consumed by the emptiness left in the wake of each other.

And now I have the chance to have it all back.

But at what cost?

My friendship? A friendship that is decades old.

Trade the missing piece of my heart with Natalie's?

I don't care what anyone says. They might not be dating, but I know Natalie likes Liam.

What kind of friend would I be if I put her through what I spent years getting over? I have to pick her. I have to come clean to her.

***

There is a knock on my apartment door at seven.

"This is for you," Chloe says, handing me a black coffee and breezing by me into my apartment when I open the door. Tucker, her golden retriever, follows behind her.

"Thanks, Chlo. Why are you here? I thought we were meeting at Lucky's?"

"Changed my mind. I didn't want you to not show. Come sit." She pats the couch next to her.

"About what you saw last night. Did you tell Natalie?" I ask her as I walk over, sit down, and curl my bare legs under me. Tucker curls up on my dog bed for him in the corner.

"Do you think I want a death warrant out for the two of us?" She snorts.

"It's not what you are thinking."

She gives me an all-knowing scowl. I'm not escaping anything today.

"Are you sure? Because, to me, the guy Natalie likes had you cornered in the dark bathroom hallway, about ready to pounce. The look in your eyes? You wanted him too."

"It's not that simple."

"So you don't deny it?"

"Liam isn't only Natalie's whatever," I pause. "Liam is London—"

"Finally, you admit it!"

Taking a deep breath, I say, "Yeah."

Chloe spits her coffee out. I can tell by the look on her face that she's trying her best not to judge me or make me feel guilty about everything.

"Does Natalie know?" She asks quickly.

"Obviously not. . . or at least I'm not sure how she would know. She knows the exact amount of information as you do, which is minimal. Plus, Liam and I haven't said anything."

"Except you know every inch of each other." Chloe raises an eyebrow, giving me a knowing look. "Em, is he the guy from the bathroom you texted me about when you were in London?"

My cheeks go flush, then heat, turning pink, I know.

"Wow, okay, Liam!" Chloe smacks her lips.

"Don't remind me." My cheeks blush even more, thinking how history almost—like I wish almost—repeated itself last night. I rest my hand on my forehead. "He's really good at it."

"Or you just taste great." We burst out in laughter. "Why haven't you said anything to Natalie?"

"Look at her, Chloe. She's happy. When was the last time we saw her smiling and laughing like that about anyone? I can tell she cares for him. I couldn't ruin that." I release the breath I was holding as I said all that. "Liam and I had our shot, and it didn't work out. It's their time now, and I shouldn't be the one to get in the way."

Her face goes sour. It's the expression she gets when she knows a secret, more like anything that you don't know and wants to tell you but can't. It's why we never tell her about surprise parties. I tried to throw one for Natalie last year for her birthday and decided to recruit Chloe for help. Spilled the beans to Natalie a week beforehand at brunch after Natalie brought up her birthday. Chloe made the face, and then Natalie dragged it out of her in a matter of moments.

"You know something. Spill," I demand of her.

"What if it's going to change everything you are thinking and potentially feeling and could monumentally shake everything up? On the earthquake scale, it would be a five. Do you still want to know?"

"And you think having Liam waltz back into my life didn't already do that?"

"It's about him." Chloe bites her lip.

I'm intrigued now. I find myself leaning in closer to Chloe even though I can hear her perfectly from where I'm sitting.

"I don't think they are together anymore," she says slowly.

"Think or know?" There is a difference.

"Think. I overheard Liam talking to Cal last night when I was leaving. He was telling him that he was calling off what was happening between Natalie and him. That there's unfinished business he needs to tend to."

"He's ending it?" I ask, playing dumb.

"Don't quote me on it, but that's how it sounded." She takes a sip of her coffee. "I'm assuming the unfinished business is you."

Do people still change their relationship status on Facebook? If they do, mine should read Emerson Clarke is in an unfinished business relationship with Liam Hayes. Not 'it's complicated'. Not even 'in a relationship' because we weren't ever really in one either by standard definitions.

"I think unfinished business is the type of Band-Aid I've been using."

"Are you saying he's a bullet hole?" She rolls her eyes. Chloe hates it when Natalie and I use Taylor Swift lyrics as facts of life.

"He's more than that. He's—" How do I put this into words to her? Are there even words that summarize who Liam is to me? Do I even know what he is to me anymore? "Everything to me. I think he's the only love of my life."

"Then why haven't you been upfront with Natalie?"

I burst out in laughter, picking up my mug and trying to drink the coffee to stifle the laughter.

"What's funny about what I asked?"

"It's all ironic. Do you know what it's like to really be Natalie's friend?"

"Yes?"

"Now? Yes. Your entire life? No." I shake my head. "Growing up, Natalie was the girl every boy wanted. I became the bonus, the addition that she'd drag along to dances or on movie dates. It annoyed a lot of the boys she dated, but she didn't care. Finally, in our senior year of high school, I liked someone, and he seemed to like me back. He often asked about Natalie, and I thought he was simply interested in getting to know my friend. I was wrong. He liked Natalie and was using me to get to her. Happened again freshman year of college, furthering my fear of never being enough.

I dated around, but I held onto those instances in the back of my mind. That sliver of hurt was there but was easy to push aside because I was never interested in anything more with those guys. . . until Liam. It wasn't right away with him, but over time something clicked. Every limb, vein, hair—every part of me felt alive. He noticed me, wanted me, and made me feel as if I was enough for him. When I returned home, I didn't want to tell her about him because she was being a bitch. Also, for fear that she'd figure out a way to go after him, even though he was in London. Call it post-traumatic ex-boyfriend disorder. It probably would have stopped this from happening if I had told her about him."

"Probably." She reaches out to hold my hand. "I'm sorry you felt that way. That you felt the need to keep this big part of your life from her and, ultimately, me too."

"When you say it like that, it sounds even more stupid."

"It's not. I can't believe that's him. Well, actually, I can. I put the pieces together the night we watched Love Island at Natalie's. Now that I know it is, I gotta say it. . . he's HOT." Chloe fans herself off.

"Trust me, I know. Liam looks even better now than he did three years ago."

"You never disclosed why you two split. Will you tell me now?"

I spent the next twenty minutes filling in all the gaps from what I had told her previously. It was my own twisted version of Mad Libs.

What did my friends know? I met someone in Lisbon and became best friends, went on a couple of summer vacations together, fell for him, and it ended. What they didn't know? His name. Oh, and I never showed them a picture. Neither of us ever posted anything on social media.

You know the saying it's not you, it's me? I'm starting to believe that it's me, not them, and I can't keep tying these emotions and blame to Liam and Natalie.

"What are you going to do about it now?"

"Nothing. There isn't anything I can do."

"You're joking, right? You can't do nothing. If he's calling it with Natalie, this is your chance, Em. Second chances don't come around often."

"Before you walked up, Liam said he'd call it off with Natalie if I could admit to him how I feel."

"And. . . ?" She's looking at me dumbfounded.

"I think it's pretty obvious how I feel."

"Obvious doesn't cut it. You need to say it. How. Do. You. Feel?" Chloe asks, cutting through all of my bullshit.

"I-" I swallow. "I still love Liam. He's the love of my life. We could have had it all, easily. Those three years without him, I felt more alone than I did as a child. Being around him again is resurfacing all of those emotions I buried deep inside me. I can't decide if how I feel is what everyone else feels when they're in love or if what Liam makes me feel is unique. A type of love so intense that I think it's the very substance that makes up my bones and pumps through my veins. But he's been, is with Natalie. . . I don't know, ugh. I'm not going to hurt her by admitting how I feel. Him bouncing from her to me?"

Chloe sighs. "He's about to be the greatest loss of your life if you don't tell him."

40

LIAM

Now

I didn't sleep at all last night. Or the night before. Or the night before that.

Every time I closed my eyes, pictures of Emerson filled my head. Being awake isn't any better. At least when I closed my eyes, I wasn't regretting what I was about to do. If Chloe hadn't shown up when she did, I would have kissed her.

If she would have said yes, I would have taken States into the bathroom. Kiss the spot right below her ear that she loves, the same place I could feel her heartbeat, and breathe in my favorite smell. Letting my hands roam down her curves till they were at the edge of the temptatious sundress she was wearing. Sliding my hand up the bottom, I'd press the palm of my hand between her thighs, gauging how badly she wanted me too. From the fire in her eyes when I had my arms on either side of her, I knew she did. I'd kiss her again while my fingers moved her underwear to the side. I'd drink in every moan and breathy release from her mouth until she released down below, allowing myself to become cross-faded from her smell and sounds. Somehow finding the strength to pull away, I'd head to the door but not before glancing back at her, pulling her to me, and telling her, *"It's you and me. Forever."*

That's what this is. Or at least me being hers forever.

It's not like it would have been the first time we hooked up in the loo.

This would be a. . . tease. A blast from our damn good past that she decided we weren't enough for, so she wouldn't get enough to satisfy her three-year drought of me.

One time in a bathroom would never satisfy me.

Great. Now I'm straining against my zipper again, replaying another what-if scenario in my head.

You'd think I'd be used to these fantasies and know how to resolve the situation, but each time one crosses my mind, my body's response is stronger than any mental willpower I have. What's worse is that in these dreams, nine out of ten times, it's just us together—in a real relationship, her waking up in my arms, dancing around my kitchen, reading books in a café, and traveling the world.

My greatest fantasy is to be with her forever.

Callum draws my attention back to my unpleasant reality by throwing open the door to my office.

We are in the space we purchased last summer for our American office. It's on the forty-fifth floor in a building right off Michigan Avenue. We have three hundred and sixty-degree views surrounding us. One side lends views to the lake, the other to the river, and two to the skyline.

For the past two years, we've been working to get to this to this point. When Cal brought up the idea of opening a hotel in the US again, this time with a complete how-to-get-there plan, I knew that was the next step.

"Good morning, sunshine," Cal sings as he slides into one of the chairs in front of the oversized, angular glass desk. "Someone looks like they slept well." He's laughing.

"Shut it."

"You know, these views are great, but I think you can do better for your office." He's grinning at me with his, 'I want something' smile.

"You want this office?" I ask.

"Since you are offering. . . I accept." He raises his hand and brings it down in a cha-ching motion while mouthing 'yes.' I roll my eyes at him.

"We need to figure out the pool situation," I inform him.

"Do you think we should have the same food and drinks as Cleopatra or a different concept?" He flips through the stack of spiral-bound plans I handed him. "Personally, I think a separate concept and making the pool public would give us the potential for extra revenue and increase awareness for those who live in Chicago."

"I agree."

"Different food concept, then?" he asks.

I nod. "Yes. Blake, Ben's fiancé, had a suggestion when we were in our last marketing meeting. Bright colors and a tropical oasis give it a Miami or Ibiza-in-Chicago vibe. I had Carlos put together a potential food and drink menu. Take a look." I flip around the iPad I'm holding.

We review the plans, modifying a few cocktail names and recipe overviews, before sending them back to Carlos to get started. Callum also shares his thoughts about adding another rooftop bar with me.

"It would be another million dollars, at least," I remind him. "And we don't even know if we'll be successful here yet. Plus, it would potentially delay the opening."

"Why are you doubting us? You know we will be. I know it's a big investment right now, but think about it in a year or two. If we don't do it, and don't have the opportunity to seize it, would you regret it?"

Regret. A word and emotion I'm becoming way too familiar with.

Releasing a sigh, I nod in agreement. "Yes. And we have the budget?"

"Would I even suggest it if we didn't? Combining will save time and money with the pool. We can close the water after dark but leave the bar open, dining included," he says.

"And the space? We have it?"

"Of course. If it were separate, we would have the space; why wouldn't we if it's together?"

"True."

"Any names? Keep it on theme?"

"The Antony," I say confidently and quickly.

"The Antony?" Callum tilts his head, perplexed.

"Cleopatra and Marc Antony had an affair. They were legendary lovers, but they also had a drinking club together. They called it 'Inimitable Livers,' but that sounds rather terrible for a bar name."

Callum's eyes go wide, his brows raise. "What is your fascination with Cleopatra? The hotel design, restaurant names."

I shrug my shoulders.

"Hmm." He drops his suspicions, and we return to sifting through the plans. "What's going on, mate? You're physically here, but I can tell your head is somewhere completely else. Say with a brunette?"

Yeah, it's with Emerson, alright. I wonder what she's thinking, what she's doing, if she's feeling what I'm feeling, what she'll think of the hotel, and why I haven't called Natalie since Friday. I'm like a girl with all the thoughts prancing around my head. It's a wonder they can be great multitaskers.

I don't say any of that because I don't want to get in. Instead, I reply, "Decision fatigue."

"That much is obvious, aye." He runs his hand through his grown-out blond hair.

"Whatever you are trying not to say, say it. I'm not in the mood today."

"Probably won't help then. Does this have anything to do with Emerson?" He looks at me, holding my eyes hostage, and only the truth is going to let me regain my freedom.

"Why would you think that?" I ask him, trying to play it cool.

"I ran into her as she was leaving the coffee shop one block over. She's wearing the same demeanor you've had all morning. I asked her if she was okay. She shook her head no and kept walking. Are either of you going to tell me what's going on?"

"They both *failed* to tell me about each other. I've ransacked my brain for times she ever said Natalie's name. I can't recall. Natalie never mentioned Emerson. Neither of them said anything. It's like they mapped out this collision of my worlds and my heart. I didn't know."

Cal nods along.

"So when I run into Emerson, it feels as if it's fate until I'm at Natalie's, and she shows up. Emerson told me that Natalie never knew my name. She didn't know that we had already met six years ago, not six minutes ago."

I can't tell if Cal feels sorry for me or wants to laugh at me. It's the latter, as he breaks out in an obnoxious laugh.

"Wait, Emerson never told Natalie about you for the three years you were together?"

"We weren't together," I clarify.

"To-ma-to, to-mah-to. You two were together, no matter what the two of you said or did." I roll my eyes because he's right.

"Every time Emerson and I hang out, I can't keep my eyes off her. I find myself gravitating toward her, latching onto every word she says." I close my eyes, smiling to myself and thinking about her.

"For fuck's sake, please tell me you haven't acted on this." His hand is pointing toward me, making circles in the air.

"I might have." I crunch my face.

"Liam! You are her headache. And now, the two of you are mine."

"It almost happened, but it didn't. I'm making a mess of this."

"Are you going to tell Natalie?"

"I know I should."

"Do you like Natalie?" Cal asks me.

"Yeah, I did. I thought we were on the same page. I communicated my intentions going into last summer, but lately, something has changed in her."

"Then you need to tell Natalie. If you don't, you're dragging this on, and it will only get worse."

"You're right."

"Pause. We must remember this. August 3rd, you, Liam Hayes, told me I am right." "

"I tell you you're right more than I should."

"Tell Natalie." With that, he changes the subject back to our upcoming opening and final hotel details we needed to work through, including the remaining positions we need to hire for. Listing out the priority of what positions to fill.

By lunchtime, we have everything laid out. He lets me know that he's going to grab lunch with some girl he met over the weekend. Since Cal is leaving for lunch, I also leave, knowing exactly where I need to go.

41

LIAM

Three Summers Ago

Can grown men get butterflies?

When we returned to my flat, Emerson pulled the key I gave her out of her purse. Watching her unlock my door caused a kaleido-scope of butterflies to flutter in my stomach. I need to ask George. I bet he does. I can see it on his face when Beatrix is around.

"Need any help?" Emerson asks me from the barstool she's seat-ed in.

"No," I call over my shoulder.

She's humming along to the softly playing music in the back-ground. After a few songs, I hear her scoot back in the chair, her light footsteps crossing the wood floor to me.

"Are you making us breakfast for dinner?" She puts her arms around my waist.

In the pan, mushrooms are sautéing in a combination of spices. Using a wooden spoon, I push around the mushrooms to ensure none are burning or sticking to the bottom of the pan. Adding a pinch more of the spices, I place the spatula on the counter.

"A couple of days after we met, on the train back to Lisbon, I asked you what meal you could eat forever. You said breakfast."

"You remember that?" She sounds confused, but delighted that I remember such a small, trivial fact about her.

I turn into her, wrapping my arms around her. With both arms crossed on her back, I push against her back to bring her closer to me. The front of her body becomes one with mine. I love having Emerson in my arms, so much that I'd do anything to never let go.

"Growing up, Sunday mornings were my favorite. Mum would make breakfast. A proper, full breakfast. Never missed a week. She worked two jobs to be able to afford anything I needed. She wasn't home a lot, especially in the mornings. I was used to getting myself up, fed, and to school, but on Sundays, she was off. I'd wake up every week to the same smells as right now. Cartoons playing on the telly. We'd eat on the couch, and as I got older, she always let me have the bacon on her plate. 'Growing boy', she'd taunt me. We'd spend the rest of the day just the two of us, even entering university before the cancer took her. Most weeks, I still make this on Sunday and eat it on the couch."

"Thank you for sharing that with me." She isn't pitying me about my childhood or losing my mom as most people do. Her expression is warm and understanding. There is a kindness behind her eyes, thanking me for telling her but also letting me know she's there for me in my grief. "We should have done this on Sunday. You could have said that," she continues. Emerson tightens her hug.

"It's okay. I asked you what you wanted to do because I wanted to spend that day making you happy." Which is true. I want to spend every day putting a smile on her face and making sure she knows how incredible she is. "I've wanted to share this with you. I knew at some point this week, I'd make it for you. Breakfast might not be my favorite meal, but this is one of my favorite memories, and it's your favorite meal." I kiss the top of her head. Her classic smell is faint compared to the aromas filling my flat. "She would have loved you, Emerson. I know it." I place another kiss on her head, letting my lips linger. "Maybe, in a way, this is me introducing her to you," I say directly on her head.

"Thank you," she says to me, and I know she means it.

Her head tilts up toward me. She kisses me faintly.

When her gaze locks with mine, I'm pricked with curiosity. Does Emerson love me like I love her?

It's been days since we stood in that museum, and I told her I'm in love with her. I've said it every chance I've gotten. Seizing the opportunity because it's out there and I'm proud of it. I'm proud that I get to love her.

But Emerson hasn't said it back. She'll kiss me. She'll smile at me. But she doesn't say it back.

I've thought that's enough, but it's nagging at me. The wondering if she does or doesn't is nagging me like a bug that won't leave. I know that if I don't find out, it'll be as if the bug bites me, leaving an itching sensation behind. If she doesn't say it, I'll be itching to know if she loves me till, shit, who knows when with her.

"Do you love me?" I ask her.

She says nothing, of course. The soft smile on her face vanishes instantly, replaced with a face you'd make if you accidentally poured sour milk into your tea. I don't know if I expected her to say it back, but I expected at least some sort of answer.

She drops her arms and takes a step back. I ask again, "Do you love me?" Maybe she didn't hear me the first time.

She doesn't say anything again.

After a few moments, she stands on her tiptoes and kisses me. It's different from her earlier kisses.

The kiss is quickly followed by her turning around and walking away. I double-check that everything is turned off in the kitchen and follow her. In three strides, I quickly catch up to her and reach my arm out to clasp her elbow, stopping her from taking another step.

I can't let her go.

I can't have her not love me back.

42

LIAM

Three Summers Ago

Waiting for an answer from Emerson is like waiting for rain in a desert. I don't think there will be one.

Maybe it would be better if she didn't reply. Perhaps if she doesn't, we can rewind to before that moment. We can go back to how things were before I told her I love you, and she didn't say it back. I was happy with our situation—I think. We had each other in every way possible but one.

It was enough. It was enough till I knew I could have more. We could have more.

Telling her I love you was a release. A horse off to the races, and her love is the prize.

But am I going to be jockeying toward a prize that keeps getting farther away? I'll do it. It'll fuck me up in the process, but I'd do it. I'd do anything to have her. Anything to have her.

"Do you love me?" I ask for a third and final time. If she doesn't answer, I'll stop torturing myself and find a way to make peace with it.

Emerson shakes her head no.

I don't believe her. I don't believe that she doesn't love me.

"You're lying."

"Maybe." She shrugs her shoulders. There, I'm right.

"Why?" I ask through gritted teeth.

"Because I can't. I wish I could. If I did, I'd have the ability to feel all of this without it crashing down on me like a ceiling. You shouldn't have to ask if I love you. I should be able to sa—" she cuts herself off.

Her shoulders drop. My gaze drops to her hands. The nails of the pointer fingers of each hand are digging into her thumbs. It's not obvious to most, but it's a tiny tick that she does when she's anxious. "That's because you do. Emerson, you do love me. I know it," I respond to her.

Her head shakes from side to side. Turning around to face me, she's sucking in her lips, trying to do everything in her power to restrain herself from telling me.

I take a few steps backward, giving us space. Don't want to, but I do.

"You can. You have to try. I'm trying here, Emerson. Please try with me," I plead with her.

"I tried, but I can't," she says to me, her head still shaking.

Her tears and emotions overtake her body. I can see them raking through her, shaking her to the point that she collapses to the floor. Her knees underneath her, she falls forward, her hands catching her head in them. Emerson cries there on the floor in front of me.

"Don't say that. Don't do this."

I cover the distance between us in three strides. Dropping to the floor in front of her. My knees hit the wood floor with a thud, and brush hers. Too close, but too far away at the same time. I feel the rough texture of the original floors through the material of my pants. I know her bare knees will be scraped and red from them after this. I want to touch her. I want to reach out, but I don't right away. I want to pull her into me and never let her go, not let her do what I can see is coming.

How did it get to this? How did we end up on different emotional continents?

I thought we were on the same one. I thought we were finally moving in a direction together.

When she stood there on Sunday, what did I miss?

Emerson isn't speaking.

"Talk to me, States." I'm looking at the top of her head. Her brown hair is wild, falling to the sides of her face, shielding the remaining part of her face that her hands aren't covering from me"

"I—I found myself in you—but then I lost myself all over again," she stumbles over her words between tears. "Your love, I don't deserve—it—or you. I'm broken. I'm damaged. And I was wrong. This—" She leans back, her glossy eyes are like glass looking at me. Almost through me—"has to end." She gasps, elongating the word. "I can't do it anymore, not because we aren't right for each other, but it's messing me up. You deserve someone better than me and whatever I could ever give you."

"Of course, it's fucking you up!"

"See, you agree?"

"No. I'm not even close to agreeing with you. You're running from this—us, because, for the first time in your life, someone loves you unconditionally. You are enough for me, Emerson. My love for you is untamable. It's wild, demanding, compassionate, and *yours*. It's the type of love you've always deserved."

Her eyes soften, brightening momentarily like a shock of love electrocuting her. It doesn't last. It quickly fades back to the broken, tear glaze she's been wearing.

"Bu—"

"There are no buts. You are the only person I know who has relentlessly pursued being loved despite saying they don't believe in it. It's your marathon, and this is the finish line. We are at the finish line. Why are you slowing down? Why are you turning around and running back in the other direction?"

"I'm messing it all up," she repeats over and over. Emerson drops her head so that she isn't looking at me anymore.

I reach out, taking her chin in my hand. Her skin is ice-cold, our fire burning out within her.

"It's a mess that can be cleaned up," I assure her.

"I don't know how." Her lips wobble.

"You do, Emerson. Deep down, you do. And when you don't, which some days you won't and neither will I, we'll get through it together. We'll figure it out together. *Together.*" I emphasize the word, letting it come out of my mouth as a sucker punch.

I raise her chin, bringing her head in line with mine. Our eyes are holding close enough that I can see how green her's have become because of the tears. Their dark green is now a bright Peridot green. It compliments her brown hair and sun-kissed skin. Even with the hurt and agony behind them, they're beautiful. She's beautiful. She's the most beautiful person, inside and out, that I'll ever have the joy of loving. And if this is it—this is the last time I'll get to look at her—*stop. You can't think like this. This isn't it. You can't let it be it.*

"We can't. Not right now, at least," Emerson says. She bites down on her bottom lip, releasing it to speak. "I hope you can forgive me." We're frozen in this position, face to face. Her chin is in my hands. Neither of us move because we both know what comes next, that when we move it's over. She wants us to be over.

I lean forward and brush my lips against hers. Pulling away to look at her, then pressing my lips against hers again—a goodbye or a Hail Mary, I don't know.

Emerson reciprocates the kiss back.

My other hand moves to the back of her head, my fingers tangled in her hair possessively. It's not that I own her, but she owns me. All of me—my thoughts, heart, body, and mind.

Our kisses are intentional, savoring each other's touch and taste. Memorizing and committing it to memory—at least I am because there isn't anyone else who'll kiss me as she does. No one else whose bottom lip will pull in between mine like hers does. No one else that'll release a sweet, high-pitched moan when I bite down. No one else that mine are fitted to.

Not breaking the kiss because I don't want to allow her the chance to bolt, I guide her backward to the floor. My body is on top of her, throwing all of my love around us like a force field so that it's all she can see, touch, and feel right now.

"What are you doing?" Emerson asks me.

"Loving you," I reply.

She fuses her mouth to mine in an intense kiss. I break the connection of our lips, working mine to her chin and along her jaw. Then to her neck, right below her ear. I nip the skin there before placing a full kiss right over the spot. Kissing across her neck to the other ear, I do the same.

"Is that okay?" I ask through my lips on her skin.

"Yes," she says. If only she truly meant it. It doesn't matter how much I love her if she doesn't let me love her.

Her hands find the buttons of my shirt. She slowly starts to undo them. I push up off her, rising to my knees that are straddling her hips. I finish taking off my shirt for her before reaching for her tank top and pulling it up her arms. The built-in sports bra was a pleasant surprise, leaving her breasts bare and nipples erect.

I lean down, placing a kiss between her breasts, then moving to her right breast, sucking the nipple into my mouth. Twisting and pulling it between my teeth, Emerson's back arches, her breast pushed further into me. With a gentle bite, I release her nipple and trail kisses down her stomach, stopping right above the waistband of her iron blue spandex shorts.

Damn, these things are tight. How do women wear these all day? Does the suction not drive them mad? I barely enjoy my balls being trapped in suit pants for too long, especially when I'm pushing against the fabric.

She lifts her hips to help me slip them off her. Emerson's hands come to my waist. A leg wraps around me, and she flips us so that I'm now underneath her. Emerson's hair falls to my face, tickling me.

"How am I losing you?" I ask as I look up at her, a broken smile forms on my face.

"You aren't." Her hands undo my belt and then the button of my pants. I hear the sound of the zipper, and all I can think about is how that's what it'll sound like when she leaves—us zipping apart, cleaved back into our worlds where we don't exist together.

When she has me bare beneath her, between her legs, she lays on top of me, meeting my lips.

"I am," I heartbreakingly confess.

She shuts me up with a kiss. Followed by a series of them down my chest and abs till her plush lips are around my tip. She uses her tongue, making slow, taunting circles around it. The sensation is too good. Too fucking good. My head digs into the floor, my chin jutting upward with a groan.

With a quick surge of euphoria, I touch the back of her throat. Emerson's movements are deliberate from bottom to top, pulling up enough that I'm almost out of her before her warm mouth is right back down.

I work my hand into her hair, gripping the back of her head. I pull and push in rhythm with her. There is no need to control or change; she knows exactly how to make me come undone.

My other hand joins in hers. She brings it out to the side.

"Emerson," I groan.

That encourages her to keep going—faster, tighter. She's too good at this. Then she slows down, pulling her head upward until almost none of me is in her mouth, only the tip. She flicks her eyes at me, looking at me, knowing what she's doing to me. I'm not going to last.

"Emerson. I'm going to—" I can feel her smile around me. The sensation ignites my entire body and brings me dangerously close to finishing. "If this is the last time I get to have you, I want to be inside of you."

She releases me, moving on top of me and then guiding me inside of her.

She sighs, her eyes rolling to the back of her head as her body stretches to fit me. Emerson starts to move. It's not fast. It's fluid.

It's not feral. It's tender. Sex can be and mean a lot of things, but this, it's an I love you. . . and an apology.

Emerson repositions herself, angling her body just right, causing her head to be thrown back, panting. And if I wasn't as obsessed and in tune with her, I could have missed the quietest whimper of my name coming out of her mouth.

I let her keep at it for another minute before I pull her down and kiss her. I need more of her body on me. I need more connection. I couldn't last another second without feeling the weight of her on me.

"I love you," I whisper to her.

"I love you," I repeat it like it's bait, fishing inside of her for the feelings I know she feels, wanting to reel them to the surface so she can feel them.

Even if it's not me, I want it so damn bad to be me. To be the one that finally gets her to stop believing she'll never be enough. Because she is. She'll always be enough for me.

I grab her ass and pick up our momentum.

"Liam," she moans—this time, not a whisper. It's loud enough that I hope someone on the street outside can hear her—can hear precisely who she belongs to—who I belong to.

"More. I need more," she says.

Faster and harder—our movements, our pants. I'm barely breathing in between our kisses and the inferno that's burning between us. We could set the world on fire.

Her body clinches around me tighter, and I know she's close. I'm right behind her. "I'm close," she tells me.

My fingers are rubbing her between them, adding pressure that pushes her into that last level of pleasure with a cry. Her body lying on top of mine, movements slowing.

Nursing it out of her, I keep going. I feel her tightening around me again, and this time it's the both of us releasing together.

This doesn't feel like I just got off or another shag. No, it feels like releasing a part of me—the best part of me that I want her to have forever. Loving her, being with her, knowing her—that is the best part of me.

We come down from our high. Emerson lays beside me. I roll over to face her.

I tuck a strand of hair behind her ear as she says, "I should leave."

43

LIAM

Now

I rushed to Natalie's, hoping to catch her before she left for a shoot she has this evening.

"Nat! Natalie, are you here?"

"In here." I follow her voice, finding her in the bathroom washing her face. "How was your meeting with Cal?"

"Productive. We're moving forward with a different concept at the pool-bar area."

"Love! A new place for my friends and me to live at next summer. How long will it take to build out?"

"Since the pool is already finished, quicker than I anticipated. We already had a solid menu mockup, furniture, and everything. We should be ready for the opening."

"Nice," it comes out muffled while she brushes her teeth.

"There's something I wanted to talk to you about." Natalie lifts her head, finding my face in the mirror. She frowns around her toothbrush when she reads my expression.

"Oh."

She spits and rinses, patting her face dry with a towel, and then returns it to the hook next to her black-rimmed mirror.

Natalie walks out of the bathroom, past me, leaning against the door. Taking a seat on the edge of her bed, she pats the space next to her, inviting me to sit down.

"Figured I should sit down when I am about to be broken up with," she says.

I tell Natalie everything. I tell her how I know Emerson. I tell her how I was in love with her then and still am now.

Natalie doesn't speak the entire time.

For someone who doesn't know when to shut up, I appreciate her silence right now.

She doesn't look at me while I'm talking, though.

Natalie focuses straight ahead, staring at the door to her bathroom, keeping her eyes fixated on the only spot the sun is hitting: a small beam coming in through her window.

I've run out of words. Natalie knows it all, but she still isn't saying anything.

"Natalie, please say something."

"I should have known. You look at Emerson differently than me," Natalie finally says.

Her body language is hard to read. She appears to be. . . relieved?

I thought she'd chop my head off or something. She can be terrifying when she wants to be. She's all sunshine on the outside, but on the inside, she can be downright ruthless. I've experienced that side once and thought I was going to again this afternoon.

Shouldn't I be the one relieved that she's taking this better than expected? Instead, I am filled with a strange gut reaction that she knows more than she lets on.

"I—" I start to speak.

She puts her hand up to stop me talking.

"I need to leave but will be back in a few hours." She's heading toward her bedroom door. In the archway, she turns back to look at me, biting the inside of her cheek. "Come back later? There's something I need to tell you."

It's Liam.

Chloe: Hello?

Do you know where Emerson is?

Chloe: Why?

I know, you know.

Chloe: Know what?

About Emerson and I.

Chloe: Your point?

Please help me. I need to talk with Emerson.

Chloe: What do you want with her?

Her. . . she's all I want.

Then, now, always.

Please, Chloe.

Chloe: She should be on a run.

Chloe: Let me track her.

Chloe: Lincoln Park.

Thank you.

Chloe: Go get her.

44

EMERSON

Now

Mile five: loop around the park and head back, my inner voice repeats. I may or may not have gotten lost a few times while running. I even had to Uber home once.

"Emerson!" I hear my name called faintly.

The park is busy this morning, so I don't think much of it. I keep running.

"Emerson!"

I hear my name again, louder this time. I keep going, but I look around. No one I recognize is in my surroundings. They must mean a different Emerson.

"Emerson!"

I halt.

My name is loud enough to sound like it's playing through my headphones.

"Watch it!" In my sudden stopping on the pavement, I'm almost accidentally hit by a runner with a stroller coming in the other direction. Quickly, I jump out of their way onto the grass.

"States." I spin on my heels to catch an out-of-breath Liam keeling over.

An out-of-breath, shirtless, Adonis of a man. I swear he isn't even sweating, he's glistening. How is that even possible? Or fair! I come back from a run looking as if I ran through a storm in the rainforest, and my braided ponytail frizzes tripling the size.

My tongue darts out of my mouth, licking my lips. My effort in not gawking at him is a failure. I can't help myself. I've never been able to help myself, so why do I think I'd be able to now?

"Liam." Of course, my voice doesn't come off with confusion. It's breathy and oozes the dirty thoughts I'm having about him.

"You-you've gotten fast," Liam says, finally catching his breath.

"Or you have terrible stamina." I glower at him.

"We both know I have quite the stamina." He smirks.

I roll my eyes at Liam. "How did you find me?"

"Chloe." It's said with a wheeze. Liam stands up straight. "Can I join you?"

"Are you sure you can?" I ask back. "I'm sort of fast now." I mock him. He laughs at me and nods.

"I can keep up," he says.

We start running again. I don't turn my music back on, letting my retro headphones hang on my neck.

We run silently for a mile and then another mile, keeping pace with each other. Liam follows my gestures regarding where and when to turn.

"I qualified for Boston next year," Liam tells me.

"Ahh. So someone else has also gotten faster."

He laughs. "I always was. It was the baby giraffe I was running with who slowed me down."

"Is that what I looked like?" I can't help but smile, a small one that will unfortunately not go unnoticed by Liam.

"A beautiful one, but yes. When we'd run together, it was like your dancing, uncoordinated."

"Am I a grown giraffe now, then?"

"Sure, States." He glances at me at a stop light. I can't quite read the look on his face. There's a hint of anticipation and. . . it's the way he used to look at me. Those days in Lisbon and Paris, the ones that were the bridge to everything we became. The color is sharp, and I fear if I stare for too long, he'll hurt me again. "You've kept up with running."

"Sort of enjoyed it."

We're bouncing on the balls of our feet, shifting from one foot to the next. There are others around us—runners, walkers, bikers, and even a few rollerbladers. This is one of the reasons I enjoyed running, you aren't alone. Not that I actually feel alone, but there's a community of people surrounding you always. People smiling or waving as you pass each other, silently encouraging you to keep going one more mile, or up the sporadic Chicago hill.

But that's not why I've come to enjoy it—or why I kept running.

After Liam, well, I missed him. I missed that part of myself I was with him. Trying to navigate how to keep a tie to her—and him, I kept running.

When my feet hit the pavement and my breath is labored, I feel that connection to both people. So I kept running, and I learned to love it. I transferred my emotions into it—sort of like it's a conduit of power, and that power is called love.

"Told you. It's hard not to fall in love with it," Liam trails on.

That word, love, lingers between the two of us.

"Yeah... um, sure." I wallow.

There's a mile left to my apartment.

"So—" Liam says. "We need to talk."

"About what? Not sure there is anything left for us to talk about."

We haven't spoken since Friday. After I didn't hear from him over the weekend, I assumed he viewed our encounter as a mistake and was retracting the words that Chloe overheard.

"There is."

The light turns. We receive the little white man to cross. We take off running, moving to the outside of the pack that is crossing the street.

"And you choose right now during my morning run as the time to talk."

"No."

I give him a confused look.

"I wanted to spend time with you," he says.

"Do we need to talk or hang out?" I ask bewilderedly.

"Both?" he answers with a question.

"Okay?" I respond in the same tone.

"Why did you keep up with running?" Liam asks again.

I don't think now is the appropriate time to blurt out because 'I missed you'.

"Someone once told me I was good at running, figured I could at least get good at the actual sport," I say instead.

"I never meant it like that." Running beside him, I don't need to turn my head to know what expression he's wearing. It's remorseful. Liam promised me once he wouldn't hurt me. His words did, and three years later, we both haven't forgotten them.

"Then why say it?" I don't look at him, not because I don't want to; I can't. The closer we get to my apartment, the more people there are on the street. Weaving around them takes my full attention, and right now, it barely has half.

"We all say stupid things in the moment when we are hurt."

"I'm well aware of that." Earth to Liam, the whole reason we aren't together?

"I'm sorry for saying that about you. There isn't a second that goes by that I don't wish I could take back everything I said. Being hurt wasn't an excuse to exploit your insecurities and use them against you. I'm sorry, Emerson. Please forgive me."

Is there an expiration date on apologies, especially on ones that you've waited to hear for years? I don't think so.

"I appreciate your apology." I turn my head over my shoulder in his direction and smile. "Is that what you wanted to talk about?"

"Not entirely. Natalie and I are no longer." He grins like the Cheshire Cat.

"And?"

"It's you and me now, States. I want to be yours."

My heart stops, but my legs speed up.

Running in front of him, Liam trails after me.

I look back at him and say, "How about this time if I run, you catch me?"

We made it to the block where my apartment is. I slow my run down. Liam was still behind me the last time I checked. I figured I may have dodged or lost him in the sea of Chicagoans.

There is a tug on my wrist, spinning me into a hard, defined chest.

"I will," Liam says. "I'm not letting you go this time."

Then he leans down, seizing my parted mouth.

45

EMERSON

Now

I think wedding planning has officially gone to Blake's head. Not that it hasn't already. Two weeks ago, she set me up on a blind date with one of Ben's groomsmen, Alec.

Well-dressed. Crewcut blond hair. Sharp bone structure. Complete finance bro.

It went fine.

We've been on three dates. Correction: tonight is our third, I suppose.

Our first was happy hour with Blake and Ben. I'm not sure if that counts as a date, but for my purpose here, it does. Then, after work, we went on a walk to a small farmer's market. We grabbed dinner before the night was over. That's two.

Tonight he's coming out with my friends and me for my birthday.

Blake was being Blake setting us up and we both knew it. "Well, if you were attending the wedding, you'd probably go home with someone because you're hot and single. But now you're working on it. I thought if I set you up now, it wouldn't be weird if you went home with him that night." That was her reasoning.

She continued to inform me that I had this weird sexual tension going on about me and needed to get laid to fix it. A sexless bitch is what I believe she called me.

The next day, Blake asked me to grab drinks with her after work, bombarding me with Alec when I sat down.

She also slipped up about my birthday plans, and now he's here.

We walk into the club together. His hand is on my lower back as we locate my friends and make our way to them.

Sitting in a section toward the back, opposite the bar and dance floor, are Chloe, Natalie, Blake, Ben, a few other acquaintances, Callum, and Liam.

I didn't invite Liam. I invited Cal because we are friends, and I knew he'd bring Liam.

Liam's eyes find mine as Alec and I walk up to everyone. He fixes his gaze on where Alec's hand is touching me and I see his nose flare and jaw clench.

"This is Alec." I glance up at him with a fake grin. "You know Ben and Blake. This is Chloe..." I introduce Alec to everyone with their name and how I know them. At the end of the couch, the last is Liam. "...and this is Liam. We—"

I can feel the heated gazes of my two best friends, Cal and his, as they all wait for what I will say.

"Should be together," he cuts in.

***

I remove myself from the group when everyone is distracted with drinks or dancing. I catch Liam's eyes before I walk to the stairs.

The club is two stories. The upstairs is far quieter than the lower level. The music and energy of the lower level rise to this floor, keeping the ambiance alive. But it's darker, more intimate.

"Champagne and a Negroni, please," Liam settles up next to me at the bar.

He must have followed me up here. I wanted him to, but now that he's here, I don't know if I wish he'd turn around and leave or stand closer. Maybe pull me to him. Maybe hand me this drink and walk away.

He passes me my drink.

"You didn't need to do that," I say.

"A thank you would suffice." He smiles at me.

"Thank you," I say sarcastically, but it comes off more playful, almost as if I'm trying to flirt with him. Am I?

We leave the bar and walk over to the ledge that overlooks the lower level. There is a small counter at the top of the metal ledge with enough space to rest your drinks and lean on. We stand next to each other.

Looking down, it's easy to spot Chloe in her metallic sequin dress. She's a disco ball, the lights from the DJ booth reflecting off her. She's moving her body in tune with the beat, a man's hand wrapped around her waist and another in her hair. Chloe throws her head back. Her smile is big enough for all of her teeth to show. The guy leans his head into hers, whispering something to her that rewards him with another laugh.

"Chloe and Cal seem to be getting on," Liam says.

"She got over Seth real quick," I retort.

"When did they break up?"

"Four days ago. He cheated on her."

Chloe and Seth broke up earlier this week. Clubbing wasn't exactly what I had imagined for my birthday, but Chloe asked if we could. I said yes, deciding it was a good reason for everyone to get out, relax, and loosen up.

"Shit. That bloody sucks. They'd been properly together for what?"

"Under a year. Chloe had suspicions when Seth visited and finally confronted him over the weekend. I'm happy he didn't lie to her. It takes a lot of balls to own the truth." I take a couple of sips of my champagne. "Cal and Chloe do look good together."

"You and Alec looked good together, too." I turn my head to stare at him and find that Liam is already looking at me.

"Yep." My stare doesn't falter.

"He's friendly with you," he says bitterly.

I know he saw us walk in. Then saw us at the bar, where Alec's hand was still on my lower back, making idle circles on it. Then back on the couches, how close together we sat. There wasn't much space to begin with. Alec tried to have me sit on his lap, but that was pushing it. I didn't exactly want him here to begin with.

"Yeah, friendly," I respond.

"When did you two get together? Before or after I kissed you."

It's been two weeks since he finished it with Natalie, two weeks since he kissed me. This also means it's been two weeks that I've been ignoring every emotion and pull I feel viscerally.

I want him. I want Liam on my best and worst days.

But I'm trying to make sure I want an us too.

Speaking of Natalie. She has been watching the two of us like hawks tonight. However, her expression is hard to gauge.

I roll my eyes at Liam, shaking my head down toward the lower level.

"We aren't together, Liam."

"Just like you aren't actually with him."

My head snaps back in his direction. I open my mouth to refute his statement, but he beats me to it. "Why is he here, States?"

"I like him."

"No, you don't." He's shaking his head at me, an insanely hot smirk painted across his lips, one I want to kiss right off his face. "If you did, you wouldn't have been tense when you walked in. And it wasn't because you were staring at me. You didn't like his touch. And you didn't like it at the bar or when you sat down."

"Not. . . true," I say between catching my breath. Liam moves closer to me and places his hand exactly where Alec's was. An ice-cold shiver rushes over my body, but it doesn't cool off the heat radiating out from where his touch is. My body impulsively leans into the touch.

Liam doesn't say anything. Pulls his hand away, though.

I move closer to him, craving to have that touch back. I flutter my eyes several times, trying to clear out the images and thoughts of everywhere I miss and want those hands to be.

"It's my birthday," I say to him.

"I know." He inches toward me on the ledge. We're standing shoulder to shoulder.

"Aren't you going to wish me a happy birthday?"

"Is that what you wanted? Me to follow you up here to wish you a happy birthday."

Liam leans into me. I want him to kiss me again.

He doesn't.

His facial hair brushes against my cheek, and I shudder at the roughness of his movements. His mouth is next to my ear.

"Happy birthday States," he says. His breath sends a shiver down my spine.

Liam reverses his movements, placing a kiss on my cheek.

"You look sexy tonight," he says, kissing my cheek again.

Similar to Chloe, I'm also wearing a silver dress. Metallic denim, strapless, mid-thigh, and a zipper front that is undone enough that my boobs can breathe from being pressed up into each other. Matching silver heels and earrings.

"Liam," I sigh as he kisses my cheek again. Then my bare neck.

I want his mouth on mine. Not my neck. Not my cheek.

Not on anyone else.

I want his mouth on mine and only mine forever.

I reluctantly pull away from his touch, turning to face him. Finding his eyes, I see intensity rivaling my own, but I read what else they say.

Liam isn't going to kiss me again. I need to be the one to kiss him.

You shouldn't kiss him. You should kiss him. My conscience battles itself. *You shouldn't kiss him. You should kiss him.*

I want to. I need to. Screw it.

I kiss him. It's frantic and rushed before I change my mind.

Our kiss isn't soft. Neither of us is trying to be. Our lips move with passion and intention, laying claim to each other.

We pull apart.

Liam's eyes search my face as if he's trying to gain access to my present thoughts. I don't know why; he is my every thought. Right now. Six years ago. Three years ago. Every damn day.

I bring my hand to my lips, gently touching them, dragging my fingers down, and pulling my lower lip with them until they are resting there. I'm savoring the feel of his kiss. My eyes never leave his.

In a heartbeat, Liam's hands are cupping my face. He turns our bodies, pressing my back into the ledge.

Liam devours my mouth in a kiss, so satisfying it will be in the minds of everyone around us, not that I'm paying attention to them. I couldn't even if I tried.

I moan into his mouth as his tongue slides against my teeth and then licks the roof of my mouth. I kiss him harder. Liam lets me take control as his tongue retracts to his mouth.

He moans out a curse as I bite down on his lip, exactly the way he used to let me. Three years, and we still know exactly what buttons to push, where to touch, nip, kiss, and lick.

My hands drop from his hair to his back. Finding the hem of his shirt and then finding their way under them.

"Quite impatient." He laughs against my lips. "I've had three years to think about the things I want to do to you, States. No need to rush this."

"Show me."

My eyes sparkle with imagination.

"Not here," he says. "Not right now."

I remove my hands, letting them fall to my side. Liam takes them and puts them around his waist.

"It's about time!" someone yells at us. Liam pulls away. I glance over my shoulder to see that it's Cal. Chloe is sitting next to him, throwing double thumbs-up at us. "You might want to get a room," he yells again.

I look at Liam. He looks at me.

"Want to?" I ask him. Biting the corner of my bottom lip.

"Only if you can tell me you want us."

"What?"

"This." He points to me and then to him. "Only if you properly want us," he repeats himself.

I'm taken aback by what he's saying. Is it not obvious I want him? I kissed him. I'm roving my hands on his body. I'm liquid under his touch.

I want Liam. Is that not obvious?

Liam reads my expression. "Not only me, Emerson. Us. I told you what I wanted. I don't want one night of sex with you. I want you forever. If you don't want the same, then this can't happen."

I don't move. I'm frozen. By the confession? By the hurt? By the heat that eviscerated my body only moments ago?

"I'm going home. Be brave this time." He kisses me and then walks away. "Enjoy your birthday, States."

I watch from the upper level as he approaches Cal. Grabs his jacket and exits.

46

LIAM

Now

Cal was kind when he invited me to Emerson's birthday. It stung that she didn't invite me herself, and I tried my best not to read into it.

I shouldn't have assumed that confessing to her that Natalie and I were off, would put her and me on. It didn't. She went upstairs, claiming she needed to think.

What is there to think about?

In the past two weeks, we've texted, chatted after work meetings, and taken a couple of strolls during her lunch break, but that's it.

She doesn't want us. She wants me.

I saw that tonight.

It'd be easy to give in. To quench my thirst for her. A night together would do precisely that, but it wouldn't solve my problem of wanting her forever. I don't want to only be inside her for a night, but inside her life forever. I wish she wanted the same.

I had to leave before I gave in, and I would have been disappointed in myself if I hadn't.

Cal could see it all over my face when I grabbed my jacket. He asked if I wanted him to leave with me, but I shook my head no.

There's a pounding on my door. The knock is eerily like the one I heard every morning in Paris from Emerson, but with more force, almost frantic.

The knocks don't stop as I walk to the door.

I open the door while her fist is mid-pull back to knock again.

Emerson barges past me. "Cal gave me your address."

She's pacing back and forth in the living room.

"You are going to burn a hole in the floor," I tease her.

"What do you mean only if I actually want an us? You. . . you. . . you don't know what I want."

I walk toward her slowly, using the cautious steps you'd use to approach a wild animal. Her eyes are wild, and her chest moves up and down wildly.

"You're right, I don't." I take another cautious step toward her. "But I know what I want."

"And that warrants your ability to make decisions about us? That what you want is more important."

"No." I shake my head at her.

I take another cautious step. Emerson backs up a step.

"Why did you say that?"

I take a deep breath.

How she looks at me makes it evident that I could call my departure a lapse of judgment and take her any way I'd like—get my fix and figure it out later. But there's something inside of me—in my brain and heart—that feels like they are teaming up against me and forcing me to do the right thing. What even is the right thing?

"I want you, trust me, that's not a problem. I want you so much that it makes me mad, but I want us more." I cover 80 percent of the remaining space between us. Leaving enough distance for me to look at her without the ability for either of us to reach out and touch each other. I want to touch her, but that wouldn't be logical at the moment. At least, that's what I tell myself. "That's why I found you two weeks ago on your run and kissed you."

She blinks a million times. She does this sometimes when she's thinking and wants to get rid of whatever those thoughts are.

"Don't bury your thoughts. Tell me. What do you want, Emerson?" I say to her.

"You," she whispers.

"That's not enough. What do you want, Emerson?"

"Us." She stands taller and rolls her shoulders back. Emerson stares straight at me. "I want us. I want to be together."

A sweet symphony to my ears.

The remaining distance between us is gone.

My hands are in her hair, kissing her.

"I like this dress," I say, gazing down at her. My hands move up and down her body.

"It looks better off," Emerson says without skipping a beat.

"Good, take it off," I command. Dropping my hands from her body.

Holding my eyes, she reaches to the center of her chest where the zipper is, pulling the small metal tab down the dress. The dress opens and drops to the ground.

There's nothing underneath it. No bra. No panties. Only silky skin.

I release a cool exhale as my eyes roam her body. It breezes over her breasts, causing her nipples to harden.

Emerson is gorgeous. And she's mine. I'm hers. We're each others.

Emerson bends down to take off her heels.

"No. Leave them on."

I take her hand, walking her toward the stairs that lead up to my bedroom.

On the platform next to the stairs, I stop us. I'm the impatient one now. Spinning toward her, I pick her up and sit Emerson on the stairs. I kiss her lips, working my way to the spot below her ear. The skin is sensitive around the small scar she has here.

Her breathy moans are kindling to a fire, and that fire is me.

My hands are on either side of her waist on the step. I trail kisses lower and lower and lower.

Hovering over her, my hands grip the inside of her thighs. I spread her legs apart.

"You're so wet, States," I tell her as I lift my chin to look up at her. A finger slipping into her. "Have you been thinking about this for three years, too?"

Emerson swallows. She's watching my mouth and nods.

EMERSON

His mouth is on me. I know the feeling I can expect, but the immediate gratification of what he's doing is unexpected.

I think my muscles, bones, heart, brain, and lungs missed this. I missed him.

Having Liam back is a relief in every capacity.

His tongue drives every one of my senses wild. Circling, sweeping inside of me and back to my most sensitive spot. Pulling it in his mouth, biting down, and sucking on it at the same time.

He slides his right hand up my body, palming my breast in his hand, kneading it.

I keep trying to buck off the step, the pleasure already becoming too much. Liam's other hand comes to my waist, holding me still.

I wanted this.

I want his mouth on me. I want him inside of me.

I wanted this, but I want an us. I want us more.

This entire time, I've always wanted us.

Wherever he's been, wherever I've been, I've wanted it to be the same place. Whoever he's been with, whoever I've been with, I've wanted it to be us. Whatever his future holds, whatever my future holds, I've wanted it to be our future.

I've wanted us. And now I finally have it.

"I want us," I repeat to him.

He sucks harder. "Liam," I cry out.

He keeps going, not letting up.

Running my hands through his hair, I do the unthinkable and pull his mouth off me. Angling his head up toward my face, I can see myself glistening on his lips, and somehow, I become even more turned on.

"I've always wanted us." I lock our eyes and tell him. I want him to know that as much as I want this right now, we are more than any sexual attraction. More than our pasts. We are forever.

"I know," he says confidently.

He returns his mouth to me, and my orgasm hits me. A tsunami of pleasure and relief.

Liam stands up, pulling me with him.

"You said you had three years of things you wanted to do to me. Show me. Right now."

His eyes flick toward the kitchen and then me. He smirks and pulls me to the counter, turning me to where my stomach rests on the edge. The entire place is silent except for the sounds of a belt unbuckling, a zipper, and my ragged breath.

"What if Callum comes home?"

"Good, then he'll know you're mine, and I'm yours."

His hands come to my back, lowering me over the counter. My butt juts out in front of him. Liam leans down, placing his lips gently on my ass, then bites it.

I gasp, and he snickers. "I've thought about this, but over my desk overlooking Michigan Ave."

Liam holds me on either side, rubbing the tip of him between me before finding my entrance. Slowly, he pushes into me. Inch by inch until I'm full of him.

Liam pauses.

We both sigh. "You feel so good, Emerson. Exactly the way I remember. So perfect and begging for me."

He pulls out of me to where only the tip of him is there before thrusting back in all the way. Each time, it feels like he reaches a new place inside me. It's slow and deep. Liam continues like this for several strokes.

"Tell me what you want," he commands.

"So demanding of my wants tonight."

He snarls. "Tell me." Liam slaps my ass.

"All of you." He growls. Pushing inside of me hard. My breathing is unsteady. "More."

Liam listens and gives me what I want.

One of his hands comes to my neck, circling and squeezing it lightly.

"Liam," I whimper.

"Did you enjoy that?"

I turn my head. My cheek resting on the marble. "Yes."

I watch as he thrusts into me. His hand is still on my neck. Liam squeezes it again.

"Damn it, States. Keep watching me. Watch what you do to me and how you make me feel."

Nothing about this is sweet or romantic. It's feral. Everything about this is a reminder of the lost three years. Our frustration with ourselves and each other is poured out in heated movements and desperate touch.

I know that we'll find something sweet later, but right now, this is what we both want—we both need.

I'm like a dam that's about to burst, barely held together by the levy. Everything in me is being filled by him—the pleasure, the heat, the opportunity of a future together.

"Liam. I'm," I stutter. "I'm there."

"Let go. Let go for me," he requests. Despite his movements, his words are a gentle caress with double meaning.

He's telling me to let go of the guard I've had up, the fears I use as shields, the irrational what-ifs, and the words that tore us apart. He's asking me to let it all go for him.

And I do.

We let it all go together.

47

LIAM

Now

"We get it. You two are together, but this is a work meeting. Liam, can you stop eyeing Emerson for a minute so we can finish, and then you can go find his desk or one of the hotel rooms to finish yourselves?" Cal snaps at us.

"Blame him. He's the one that keeps trying to play footsie with me." Emerson glares over at me. Her hair sways over her shoulder, kissed with the sun. She's wearing a soft pink sundress today, which reminds me of a bloomed flower.

I shrug my shoulders. It's impossible to drag my attention from Emerson. Always has been.

Emerson wanted to take it slow after we got back together. We woke up the morning after her birthday, Emerson in my bed facing me. She still isn't a cuddler, but the faintest smile was on her face as she had her hand interlocked into mine. My hand was resting on her arm—I think we were both hanging onto the other, too afraid the night before was only a fever dream. Over coffee, I asked her to be my girlfriend, together properly this time. That was the opposite of slow, but I needed her to understand the capacity of which I am all in on us. It wasn't the L-bomb, so I figured girlfriend was slow enough.

Our relationship is a flower. It may have needed all those years of watering, but it's alive and thriving now. That's what matters, right?

"Get up." Cal gestures his hand up. "I'm sitting next to her. You are over here."

Blake, Ben, and a few others from our teams laugh as I play musical chairs.

"Happy now?" I ask Cal as I sit down, folding my arms across my chest and flicking my eyebrows up.

"We'll see."

"As I was saying," Emerson continues. "Opening the restaurant before the hotel's launch was a great idea. From that alone, you have reached 35 percent occupancy. Until the hotel opens, I recommend we raffle off one or two-night free stays a week; anyone who eats or drinks at Cleopatra that week is entered to win. The aim is to continue driving business there, which will also coincide with the hotel occupancy."

"What if we add in an additional entry if they book at least one night?" Ben asks.

Emerson looks over at me for a decision. It takes me a moment to answer as I think through the best options—*damn, she's sexy.*

"Make it a weekend and within ninety days of opening. They'll receive an upgraded weekend experience if they are already booked."

"Perfect. Johnson, can you note that for graphics and email? Moving on, did everyone review the list of influencers and the contract they will be signing? The minimum number of stories, feed posts, and videos is the same across the board. Blake, you will be managing these."

Watching her, what do the Americans call it, girl boss? Watching Emerson's girl boss is hot. Seeing her in the zone, commanding the room, and leading everyone with undivided attention is a hoot. She's intelligent. I already knew that, but how she orchestrated this together and presented it is remarkable—reason #87324 why I am ridiculously in love with her.

"Yup! Sending out invites and contracts this afternoon. Additionally, Ben gave me the list of people to invite to the opening. Their invitations went out this morning."

"On top of it, as always, thank you, Blake. Our digital campaigns to create buzz have been running for the past two weeks. I've included on page nineteen of the folder a review of the current analytics. Olivia will be reviewing those next. The last task item our team is working on is hiring a photographer. I've put together their creative brief and—"

"I want you to be the photographer," I cut Emerson off.

"Oh my gosh! Emme, you have to! Why didn't I think of that?" Blake squeals.

Ben shushes her.

"That's not my job," Emerson shakes her head.

"You do it on the side and enjoy it, yeah?"

"Yes." Her eyebrows are raised, silently asking me where I am going with this.

"Emerson, you are the only one who doesn't have a specific job for the weekend," Blake helps my case.

"Take the pictures. You are talented, and I would be proud to have you capture this." I stare into her eyes and ask, "Will you please be our photographer?"

Emerson bites the side of her bottom lip, contemplating my request. "Okay," she says softly.

Cal claps his hands. Blake and Emerson's team are beaming with a smile.

Olivia goes on about analytics. I hear what she's saying, digesting the numbers, but my focus is on the woman sitting adjacent to me. All I can see are the rosy cheeks on Emerson, and the excitement in her eyes to be behind the camera.

***

The marketing meeting for Hayes Hotel with Emerson and her team was the last of the day for both of us. She brought all of her stuff with her when they walked here from her office.

Emerson and I took Cal's suggestion before taking the train back to her place for the evening. My glass desk now has an excellent, sweaty outline of her body pressed up against it. I left a note for the custodians that I'll clean it tomorrow. But I might leave it. It's branded now.

"Are you going to tell me why you have a small suitcase with you?" She laughs. "Are you. . . moving in?"

"Not yet." I smile at her, rolling the carry-on-sized suitcase into her dining area. It's not a dining room, but her apartment has enough space that she can fit a round table with four chairs on the backside of her couch. I set the suitcase on the table. "This is for you."

She stares at me, confused. Big green eyes, and the corners of her lips uptick.

"Not the suitcase. What's inside of it," I clarify.

Last night, George appeared at my door. This suitcase and his in hand. Thankfully, Emerson wasn't over.

"What are you doing here?" I asked him.

"You asked for me to ship you a box of books. Do you know how many pounds that was about to be? Thought it would be easier to ship me!"

"We also heard from a little birdy that someone might be dating Emerson Clarke." Beatrix brushes by her husband, hugging me.

"Wonder who that is?" I speak loudly to get Cal's attention from upstairs.

I take the suitcase George packed the novels into, wheeling it behind me and shutting the door. Three years' worth of them, hand-picked and annotated for her.

The first one was for her birthday that year. I picked up a first edition of her favorite novel, *The Great Gatsby*, intending to send it to her, but I decided against it. They compounded from there. Anytime I saw a book she might like, I'd buy it, read it, annotate it, and write to her about what was happening in my life then, as I used to do on FaceTime.

There are twenty-three of them.

I've wanted to give them to her. Always knew I would. That's why I asked George to send them to me. A short-lived thought crossed my mind about saving them and slowly giving them to her, but I was too excited and too nervous that this chance with her might slip away.

"You can open it. It's not dangerous," I tell Emerson.

"Okay," she says slowly.

The sound of the zipper echoes in her place. She flips open one side of the suitcase against the refurbished table. The smell of books fills the space.

"Are these books?" She picks them up, one at a time, reading the titles out loud, flipping them over to skim the back. Emerson opens a few, flipping through the pages. Her jaw drops open as she turns to face me. "Are all of them annotated?"

"Yes," I kiss away the single tear falling down her cheek.

"Why? How?" She asks.

I tell her about the birthday book, catching her up to the most recent purchase, which was from the day we ran into each other at the coffee shop. It was a silly little second-chance romance that I thought was fitting. She giggles, informing me that she has already read the book and, like me, thought of us.

Emerson sets down the book clinched to her chest, draws me in close for a hug, and presses a soft kiss to my lips.

"Thank you," she says to me endearingly.

"I never stopped caring for you," I add.

She kisses my palm that's cupping her face, then walks out of my embrace, jogging down the hallway toward her bedroom.

She returns to the table, holding a box in her hands.

"This. . . this is my memory-shrine-box-of-stuff. It has all of my memories from growing up and from our summers together. . . and apart."

Emerson takes off the lid after setting it on the table next to the suitcase, pulling out photos, letters, field day ribbons, and small trinkets. I recognize some of them, but what catches my eye are news clippings and printouts of digital magazines in her hands.

"It also contains articles about you from over the years. About your new hotels or profiles on you, I'd keep them in here because I didn't stop caring about you either."

"How is it that we did these things to be close to each other yet kept ourselves so far apart?" I ask her.

"Anger, hurt, insecurities." She sighs. "I had a lot to figure out about myself. I'm not saying you were the martyr for me to change, but it took that summer in London to learn what I did."

"I don't feel that way, States," I assure her.

"I'm not perfect—Brandon is a testament to that, but I am trying. I'm trying to break these habits."

"I can see that."

"It's hard to unlearn twenty-eight years of life," she hesitantly chuckles. "But you are worth unlearning for."

I kiss the top of her head, holding her close to me. Picking up the box, we walk over to her couch and spend the rest of the evening reminiscing, laughing at her baby pictures, and *trying*.

48

EMERSON

Three Summers Ago

Cal picked me up twenty minutes later.

Liam and I laid there for most of that time. I almost told him I loved him, trying to salvage us, but my anxious what-ifs choked the words right out of me. Everything I've ever wanted was right there, next to me, holding me, and I couldn't do anything to stop myself.

When you lie to yourself enough, those lies become your truth. You realize they've become a truth the moment when you can't dissociate them from who you are. I decided twelve years ago that love wasn't real. A lie, I understand, that became this giant, monumental lie that I told myself.

I'm not worthy of love, and that became my truth.

For the first time in my life, there's someone I want to undo it all for, but I couldn't figure that out quickly enough.

I went to the bathroom to clean myself up. When I exited, Liam told me that I could crash at Cal's tonight, and we could figure out everything else with my logistics back to Chicago tomorrow.

I left my stuff there. Taking only enough clothes for the night and my toiletries. I hoped that this wasn't real, just a bad dream.

If it was, then tomorrow, now today, I could undo this.

Liam didn't say another word to me as I walked out his door. I brushed past him in the kitchen, once again with another sliver of hope that he'd stop me and wake me from this bad dream.

He didn't.

I stretch out my arm from the bed in Cal and George's guest bedroom, feeling around for my cell phone on the nightstand. It's only 7:30 a.m.

I could try to sleep for another couple hours, I tell myself.

Sleep. Ha. That's a joke.

Sleep was something I didn't do last night.

My head is throbbing, and my eyes are heavy and sore. Rubbing my face, I can assume everything is puffy without looking in the mirror.

Callum, the best friend he is, made sure I was comfortable before he left for his date last night. He offered to cancel it, but I can't ruin another relationship. I insisted he still go.

I ordered sushi from his couch, hoping it would make me feel better. The only place I knew was KENSU, Liam's favorite, which he took me to on Monday. By the time it was delivered, I was overwhelmed thinking about him. I cried myself to a restless and sleepless night.

This morning, my emotions haven't recovered. I'm still. . . confused and frustrated. That summarizes it well enough.

There is a knock on the door. Callum opens it carefully.

"You alright this morning?" he asks.

I sit up, leaning against the headboard.

"Do I look alright?" I ask back.

"I suppose no. Want a cuppa? Coffee?"

"Coffee, please."

"I'll put a pot on the stove. Take your time. . . just not too much," he says, and I think he means it differently, one that I'm not ready to unpack.

I shuffle into the living room, where I find Cal reading a book on the couch. He sets it down.

"Coffees in the kitchen. Mugs and milk are sitting out on the benchtop already." He gestures toward the small kitchen.

"Thanks." I try to force out a smile but fail.

"Remind me what time your flight is?"

I didn't wait for Liam to rearrange my departure. I bumped my flight up to today.

"Not until this afternoon. Only a few more hours of having to have me in your lives. States finally will stay in the States."

"Interesting. I don't remember saying I wanted you out of my life. Neither did Liam, if I stand corrected." Cal is giving me a don't-put-words-in-our-mouth smug grin.

"I need to get my stuff from his place. Liam should be at work by now—wait, shouldn't you be off already?" I ask him.

"Brunch this morning. All of us are—were going."

"Oh, right." I forgot.

I pour myself a cup of coffee and walk back into the living room. At the bottom of three giant, arched windows is a bookcase overfilled with books. In front of the wall are two oversized chairs facing the kitchen. I take a seat in one of them while window-shopping the bookshelf.

"Not George's." He confirms my curiosity about who these belong to. "My aunt is a writer. Growing up, every holiday or birthday came with new books."

"What's her name?"

"Mary Adamson."

"I've read a few of her books! The twists at the end are consistently unpredictable. I've never been able to predict a single book. The last one had me on the edge of my seat," I cheerily say. "I didn't realize you were a reader too."

"Few do. That's one of the things Liam and I bonded over."

"I know the feeling."

This is what I'm going to miss, and it will haunt me in the post-Liam phase of my life: all the ways we connected—shared common interests, shared different interests.

"Do you want to talk about it?" he asks.

"I—what—am I making a mistake?" I ask him reluctantly.

"Honestly, yeah." I'm happy he's honest with me, but it hurts to hear. Cuts deeper than I thought it would. "He told you he loved you, yeah?"

I nod.

"And you didn't respond—"

"You know the answers to these questions."

He shakes his head. "Wasn't asking a question, States." Cal rests his mug on his knee. He blows out air and tilts his head, staring at me as I believe an old brother would. "You don't need to say it back, but you shouldn't have said no. We both know you do. You've been leading him on. You can't play with his heart and think that he won't get attached."

"I would never do that."

"You've been doing it for years—"

"He's been doing it too!" I defend myself. "We've been doing it to each other."

"Are you sure about that?" No, I'm not.

Maybe he's right. I don't think Liam has ever led me on.

The gravity of everything Liam is to me compounds, rooting me down into the chair I'm sitting in.

"I never meant to bring him into my mess. . . or any of you by association."

"And you didn't have to let what hurt you become who you are."

We return to silence.

I turn my body towards the window. . . wondering if the answers to my problems are out there. They aren't. All I find is a gray, gloomy London morning, the sky filled with clouds like the weather is an extension of me.

You didn't have to let what hurt you become who you are.

Is that what I have done?

Is this who I have become twelve years later?

Something cold drips on my cheek. I raise my hand to it, grainy as salt. A single tear is falling down my face. I don't wipe it away. This one isn't for Liam, but for me—the younger me who was hurt and is still hurting. Unhealed and broken.

I thought I've been protecting myself by putting up these walls around my heart. Keeping myself close to people but not letting them get close enough to me to hurt me. In reality, I've been hurting myself all along.

I let what hurt me become me.

"Brunch is at eleven. Up to you if you want to come." Cal pauses, biting the inside of his cheek. "He'll be there. You should talk to him."

I drink the rest of my coffee slowly. Callum and I sit there in a peaceful quiet.

Rising from the chair, I walk over to Callum.

"Thank you." Leaning down, I kiss his cheek softly and turn, walking toward the guest room I stayed in last night.

"States," he calls after me. I stop walking but don't turn around. "Being enough for love and loving someone enough, means as much to him as it does to you."

49

LIAM

Three Summers Ago

Gliding through the entryway of the restaurant is Callum. *Alone.*

Everyone else is already here. I arrived first, purposely. Wanted a seat watching the door in case Emerson decided to show. She was invited, after all.

Plus, when she left, Emerson didn't take her stuff with her last night.

Which was a mistake. Her bags and that I should never have let her leave. I was her father 2.0—maybe not entirely; I may not have left, but I allowed her to walk out without a fight.

I thought I was giving her space—to think, to do whatever the hell she needed—but what I thought—no, what I knew she needed—was for me to have her stay, to keep fighting for us and prove that *we are enough*.

I was selfish and impulsive. When she wanted to leave, I said go. I needed Emerson gone. I was furious with her.

As everyone arrived, a sliver of hope formed in my heart. Maybe she'd come to get her belongings this morning. She didn't. Perhaps she'd show up now. She didn't.

That sliver waned with each step he took with no one behind him.

Callum shakes his head no as he gets to the table.

I push my chair back in disappointment. A dull red takes over my vision. Irritated that she's running. Irritated that she can't choose me, when I've chosen her.

"Trade me seats," I demand of Audrey. She does as I say, glancing between me and her brother.

"Switch him, Auds," Callum says to her.

My back is now to the door.

"Where's States?" George aims the question in my direction.

The red increases a shade darker.

"Not coming," Callum thankfully answers for me.

George follows up with, "Does that have anything to do with why she stayed at our place last night?"

Callum and Beatrix shoot daggers at him with their eyes. Even from where I'm sitting, I can see Beatrix's hand under the table squeezing his knee to restrain him.

"Doesn't matter where she slept; she wouldn't have shown up anyway," I bite back.

"That's not tr—"

The red increases a shade darker.

I cut him off. "Oh, come off it, Callum. You know she wouldn't have shown." I won't let him finish his lie.

"What happened?" Audrey's mouth frowns with uncertainty. The rest of her face follows—a look I've never seen her wear. She's the most certain person I know. Thoughtful, intentional, and a shit ton of words I would have described Emerson with.

"I told her I loved her, and she said nothing back."

Both girls' faces fall, their expressions telling me I look as heartbroken as I feel.

I pushed Emerson too far last night by asking her if she did. I could have survived with my assumptions and waited until she was ready to say it.

The red increases a shade darker.

"Was that last night?" Beatrix asks.

"Sunday."

Beatrix smiles. "No wonder you two were M.I.A. for an hour on Tuesday night. Those eyes weren't friend eyes you two were giving each other. The heat was pal-pa-ble."

"They've never been friends." George lets out a chuckle.

"Aye, neither have we," Bea says. George kisses her cheek.

"We always have been to her." I roll my eyes, taking a large drink of my Negroni. Flicking my gaze from the waiter to my drink. "She wears a damn good mask and knows how to lead someone on."

"I don't think she led you on," Beatrix says.

All of our heads turn to her.

"What? He just told her the other day. It's not like he said it years ago, and this is now happening."

I did tell her years ago. It was a roundabout way, but in Amsterdam, before we left, in bed, I told her I was an example of someone who loved her. I've loved her for three years.

"I disagree. States did," George says. "Cal does, too."

"Audrey?" Beatrix goes to her for support.

"I'm not making this girls versus boys. Why do you think she led you on?" Audrey asks.

"I saw everything with her, and she let me. Kids, a house here or there, a white picket fence, and dogs, if that's what she wanted. Life partners—all of it I saw with her because she's—she's—Too bad Emerson is fucked in the head. Doesn't believe that love exists."

They all sit there and stare at me.

"Who doesn't believe in love?" I ask rhetorically.

"For someone who doesn't, Emerson sure knows how to show it," George says. "And that's leading Liam on!"

"Add that to the list!" I slam my glass on the table. Run my hands through my hair. "When I look at her," my hands go to my eyes, then through my hair again. I think about Emerson. "I know she'd be the best life partner. She has no capacity to the amount or the way she can love someone. At least, I thought she did. Maybe this has all been a game to her. I'm the pawn. If that's the case, check-fucking-mate States. You win."

"Liam. . ." Audrey breathes out.

"Emerson knows it's real. At least you are the first person to make it real to her. She might need more time," Callum tries to tell me.

I roll my eyes and blow out a breath that feels more like a dragon blowing out steam.

"More time than three years?" I ask.

"It hasn't even been a week since you told her how you felt. She hasn't been processing it for years."

"You don't need to tell someone you are in love with them for them to know it. It's in the small gestures, the silence, and the mundane moments that I wanted her to know she is loved. Play back the past three years. I did everything I could to show her. I wanted her to believe in love not because I said it but because she could feel it." But I wanted—needed—her to love me back.

"But you never told her. She needed that. . . earlier," Cal says.

Why does it sound as if he knows her like I do? No one knows her like I do. No one loves her like I do, nor will someone ever love her like I do.

The red increases a shade darker.

"What about me?"

"Liam," George warns.

"She warned me. She told me she was fucked in the head, but I was blinded by her to see it. Didn't want to believe it, but I should have. Instead, now I am, too."

"Liam," Beatrix says cautiously.

"Loving her. . . it'll be the worst thing that ever happens to me. I wish I never met her." I shake my head, the red now the darkest shade I've ever encountered. There isn't a way for me to see past it. Or feel anything but it.

Across from me, Audrey's eyes go wide first. Then Cal's flare. It's like they are a game of dominos. George follows suit. To his right, Beatrix gulps.

"And I wish I never met you too," came a voice behind me.

That voice. Her voice.

Emerson.

She came.

Everyone is sitting there, staring at me and then staring at her. Cal's covering his mouth with his hand. George releases a push of air and runs his hand over his head. Bea and Audrey lean in toward each other. No one is saying a word, no movement.

Why is she here?

How long has she been standing there?

They were trying to warn me and prevent me from pushing my foot farther into my mouth.

This can't be happening.

Callum gives me a nod, a nudge to do something. I didn't realize how frozen my entire body had gone.

"Emerson, I didn't mean it that. . ."

I turn to look at her, but she's already heading out of the entrance. In a rush, I push my chair back and chase after her. I was always the fastest out on the football pitch, and I know from running with her this week that she isn't quick. I hope that I can catch her on the street before she's gone forever.

If I don't, that's what she'll be—gone forever.

Please, let me catch her.

"Emerson!"

The wind outside hits me, tussling my hair back. On the street, I swivel my head left and right to find her.

"Emerson!"

"Emerson!" I call out again.

To the right, I glimpse the top of her head. Even with the people on the street and the briefest snippet of her head, I know it's her. I take off in her direction.

"Emerson, wait. Please!"

She's moving quickly.

"Emerson!" My voice cracks.

She climbs into the backseat of a black car.

I know she can hear me. I'm close enough that there's no way she isn't hearing me call out her name repeatedly, begging her not to go.

Emerson doesn't acknowledge me when she closes the door. The windows are tinted, and I can't tell if she's looking at me, but she probably is.

She's probably glaring at me, on my knees and in tears like the idiot I am.

Emerson won't shed any tears. Why should she? What I said was the nail in the coffin of our relationship and confirmed everything she feared.

50

EMERSON

Three Summers Ago

Every minute I spend with him rearranges my life. Which is ironic because in the years we've known each other, we've spent barely two months together. Sixty days. One thousand four hundred and forty hours. Eighty-six thousand four hundred minutes.

But what about the time we weren't together?

That's one million five hundred-seventy-six thousand eight-hundred minutes that he's been changing me.

Everything I thought I believed and wanted is slowly changing. He's changing it. My trajectory is shifting, spinning, and re-aiming, pointing at him as if Liam, loving him, being with him, everything with him is supposed to be the trajectory of my life.

It might have taken me this long to realize that.

But it only took five minutes to ruin it all.

"Need to turn around?" the driver asks me.

"No," I tell him while I look out the window. Liam breaking down on the sidewalk, is finally out of view.

He didn't stop calling my name. Through the tinted window, I saw the regret pour out of him, how he ran his hand nervously through his hair, and the small trembles in his body.

"He grafting?"

"I don't know what that means?"

"Trying to win ya ova?" The driver's accent is extremely brash, making it hard to understand him.

"Oh. No."

"Shame."

Shame. I feel ashamed. Humiliated. I can't believe that's how he spoke about me to his friends. Embarrassed that I even thought to show up.

After pacing around Cal and George's place earlier, I decided to go and see him.

Callum had already left. He didn't know I was coming.

I didn't know the words I wanted to use, but I knew I wanted to tell him I loved him—in front of his friends. I love Liam so much that I was willing to say it publicly.

I was nervous when I showed up. I contemplated the decision a hundred times before grabbing the restaurant's door handle and walking in.

Tuning out my inner voice and listening to my heart, I headed to their table.

His voice carried a comfortable distance that rang in my ears when I heard it. It was like smelling chocolate chip cookies and instantly being transported to a favorite memory of home. His voice is home to me and drove my certainty about being there.

The confidence to tell him I love him. I no longer loved the feeling of being with Liam. I'm wholeheartedly in love with him.

My ears were a radio, hearing his voice but not what he was saying, till they tuned in, finding the station that cleared out all the fuzz.

I could hear Liam. Loud and clear.

I didn't believe it. I couldn't. I kept walking toward the table. The closer I came to their table, the worse it got.

She's fucked in the head.

I wish I had never met her.

I couldn't stay. I couldn't stand there with all of their eyes on me. Already an outsider to their group, I was curious if they, too, had thought this way about me.

As I walked out the doors, I had already called an Uber. I set the pickup for down the block just in case Liam came after me; I didn't want it to be easy for him to find me right away. It was the right decision, for once, because he did come after me, but not quickly enough. It could have been quick enough if he hadn't sat there like a coward who got caught.

I wish I could tell the driver that I agree with him. It is a shame.

"Best o'luck," he calls to me as I get out of the car after not speaking for the past ten minutes. Luck doesn't even come close to what I need.

Opening the door to his flat, my bags are at the bottom of the stairs.

LIAM

It's the worst day to have decided to drive my car to brunch. I used the valet when I arrived and am now waiting for them to return with my car.

Minutes I don't have being wasted. I need to get to my place.

That's where I'm assuming she went. My gut is telling me that she's there. And I'm going to trust my gut—I have to. Since the day I met Emerson, I had a gut feeling that she was the one, and I know I'm not wrong.

I'm still in disbelief that she showed up at brunch. Cal said he didn't know she was coming. I tried to get more information out of him, asking if she talked to him this morning. He wouldn't spill, which I respected. Was quite cross at first, but I understand now. His friendship with her is much like that of siblings, I realize.

I didn't mean what I said.

I didn't, even if it's hard to believe. I saw so much red that anger took over me. It was in the pilot seat of my brain, and steered it to an unknown destination.

Like the valet currently. Where is my car?

I have to get to Emerson. I have to talk to her.

They are taking forever. I should have called a taxi, or Uber, or ran.

I can't lose her.

Last night didn't even feel like losing her. It felt like a momentary pause for her to sort out her shit, and then we could hit play again, and damn it, she was coming to hit play.

I messed up.

I curse at myself as Cal drives me to my place. He didn't trust my state to be behind the wheel.

Three steps at a time, I sprint up the stairs of my building. There was no patience for the lift today. Cal is right behind me.

"Emerson!" I croak out as I throw open the door.

Inside my flat, I find her bags gone. The key I gave her on the coffee table.

I shouldn't have packed them. If I hadn't, she'd be upstairs right now packing. Or maybe she is up there now?

I sprint up the stairs, opening the door to my room, praying she's there.

"Emerson?"

No response. I check every room. She's not here.

Back downstairs, I lean against the wall, staring at the spot where her bags were sitting.

She had been here.

She had come to me and left.

She had come to my place and left.

She left. Emerson left.

She's gone.

Emerson's gone.

I slink down the wall. My knees come up in front of me, my head falls into them, and I cry. A flood of waterworks explodes from me, and I don't want them to stop. Callum sits next to me.

"Promise me," I say to Cal.

"Yeah?"

"Promise me you'll stay friends with her," I request.

Callum nods, and we return to silence. We sit there for an hour before George joins us, positioning himself on my other side.

Probably sounds messed up, but I want to remember this moment. Learn from my mistakes and when to shut my fucking mouth.

Loving Emerson consumes me.

Loving Emerson will never be a mistake. It might hurt now, but it was utterly glorious, riveting, and purpose-giving.

That's what I want to remember.

Since I laid eyes on her, she has consumed every part of my body. Her complicated smile and emerald green eyes, the way that when she laughs too hard, she snorts and hiccups simultaneously.

It's moments over FaceTime when I catch her cooking dinner with a glass of red wine in one hand and the spatula in the other, dancing to her not-only-shower shower playlist without a care in the world. Listening to and supporting me in chasing my dreams. Always willing to accept a call, even when the time difference was inconvenient. She brought out the best in me. A light on the grayest of London days. It was moment by moment, but I fell more in love with her each time.

There's an ocean of moments between us that remind me she's special.

You don't meet many people in your life like Emerson.

You don't experience love in your life like Emerson. Let me reassure you (and myself) that though she doesn't believe in it, she knows how to give it. She wouldn't properly call it love, but it is.

When people like her love you, you know you can't ever let them go.

And to think I'm being forced to let her go.

Getting over Emerson is going to consume me.

<h1 style="text-align:center">51</h1>

<h1 style="text-align:center">EMERSON</h1>

<h2 style="text-align:center">Now</h2>

Natalie sings to the tune of 'It's Friday' by Rebecca Black, a song that lived rent-free in our heads for about a year in 2011. She remixes the words to better suit our Saturday boat day.

Our sandals clack on the dock as we walk out to the boat we rented. Situated in Montrose Harbor, we'll leave from here and eventually link up with a few other of our friends' boats in the playpen, located off Ohio Street Beach. It's the best place to hang out after boating around. It's a no-wake zone with endless music and swimming—and hot, tanned, shirtless guys, which we are finally contributing to today—and one of our favorite parts of Chicago in the summer.

It was Cal and Liam's idea to go out on the lake today. They claimed they have a surprise for me, which slightly scares me. During the summer, it's typical for Natalie, Chloe, and me on the weekend to get lucky with boat invites, courtesy of Natalie's connections. There's always something or someone with a boat, and the three of us have never turned down a day on the water or a good time.

I love the water. Growing up in the Midwest, being on a lake within an hour is easy. I grew up water skiing and wakeboarding. Natalie's parents used to take us up to Central Lake, Michigan, for two weeks every summer. We'd sleep in a cabin but spend almost every waking minute in the water.

I toss Natalie my bag to put with hers on the boat when I hear my name called out behind me.

"Emerson!"

"I don't recognize that voice," Natalie says quietly to me. She stretches her neck to look over my shoulder to see who it is.

"I do." I spin around. "George!"

I take off running down the dock, losing my sandals in the short distance. I jump into his arms when I reach him. My legs wrap around him to prevent him from dropping me.

"Did she just Bachelor koala hug him?" I hear Chloe snicker to Cal.

"Koala, what?" he asks back.

"You know, throw her arms and legs around him like a koala hangs onto a tree. The girls on The Bachelor do it during one-on-one dates." Cal stares at Chloe, dumbfounded. "Never mind. Who is that?"

"It's George!" I say. He sets me on my two feet. "What are you doing here?"

"Oi, missed you, States."

"I missed you—Beatrix!" I'm surprised by the woman walking with Liam. He's carrying a large, bright orange Yeti cooler in his hands.

"Hi, Emerson," she smiles at me.

When they reach where we are standing on the dock, Beatrix and I hug.

"It's great to see you." She tells me as she rubs her stomach, her giant diamond blinding me.

"I'm sorry I didn't make it to your wedding," I apologize. I planned to go, even RSVP'd yes at first. Unfortunately, something with work came up, and I didn't go.

"You invited her?" Liam turns toward George.

"Needed to give the one person who would object the option to object," George jokes. Beatrix rolls her eyes at him with a huff.

"We understand," she assures me.

"Wait." I watch her keep rubbing her stomach. "Are you—"

"Pregnant? Yes. We're expecting a baby girl at the end of this year."

"Shut up. Seriously? Congrats!" I give both of them a hug, turning to Liam. "Why didn't you tell me?"

"It was your surprise."

"I thought that was going to be a dog."

"A dog?" Liam asks.

"I don't know. I've been thinking about getting one."

"We can chat about that later."

"Sorry to disappoint, States," George uses my words from our night in Lagos.

"This is nowhere near disappointing. You are going to be a dad, George."

"A girl dad, too." He smiles, but his smile becomes more prominent when he turns to Beatrix.

***

We docked in the playpen.

Sitting around the stern of the boat, Callum and George try to teach us how to play Ring of Fire when we realize it's their version of Kings. The skyline fills out the horizon behind us. Our music is fighting against other music coming at us from all directions. The combination is a mashup not even The Chainsmokers would use.

The water around us is calm except for the small waves when someone cannonballs in around us. Its' surface reflects the blue skies, making Lake Michigan appear bluer than it is, almost matching Liam's eyes.

When I joined them at the back, he pulled me into his lap and wrapped his arms around my waist.

I thought it would be awkward around Natalie, but it hasn't. She almost appears happy for us.

"So you two are doing this, yeah?" Beatrix asks Liam and I.

I glance up at him, catching the sparkle in the corner of his eye. His smile stretches from cheek to cheek as he answers, "Yeah."

"Good. Now pay up." She reaches her hand out to her husband, George—I still can't believe they are married and expecting. I keep finding my eyes lingering on her small baby bump and thinking about how they will be great parents. This little girl doesn't even know what awaits her when she tries to date.

I laugh softly, thinking about George talking to whoever she tries to bring home.

George rolls his eyes, drags out his wallet, and gives her two bills. Beatrix tucks them into the string of her bikini top.

"What are you laughing about?" Liam asks me.

"Oh, nothing." I laugh again.

Liam tickles my sides. "Just nothing?"

"Stop!" I plead with him between laughs.

"Tell me, and I'll stop."

"Ugh, fine." I give in. "I'm thinking about George being a teen girl's dad and how miserable he's going to make the life of anyone she brings home."

"She may never bring anyone back."

We both laugh at that.

"Their poor kids."

"My poor what?" George asks.

"Nothing," Liam and I say in hushed unison.

In my ear, Liam whispers, "You are going to be beautiful pregnant someday."

I used to not want kids. I was nervous that history would repeat itself and I would inflict the same pain on my children, or I wouldn't be enough of a mom for them.

The idea of that someday doesn't scare me. It doesn't scare me because someday will be with Liam.

With him, I can face anything.

I kiss his cheek and reply, "You'll be a great dad. I can't wait to have that with you, but I want you all to myself right now."

Liam leans in and kisses my nose.

"I'm all yours, States." He presses his mouth to mine. "Forever."

The game continues round after round until one of Chloe's turns, and the beer can cracks, and she is sentenced to finishing it in one drink.

"What cooler is lunch in?"

"The orange one," Cal responds to Natalie.

"Anyone want one?" Natalie asks the group, holding up sandwiches.

"I do," several of us say.

"I may or may not have packed you a peanut butter and pickle sandwich," Liam tells me quietly as the others pull out bags of chips and containers of veggies.

"You remembered that was my favorite type of sandwich?"

"It's impossible to forget a disgusting combination like that, but—" Our faces turn toward each other.

"Have you tried it? No. You refused!" I cut him off.

"But I remember everything about you, Emerson," he finishes saying.

"Why?" My head tilts and my insides ignite.

"Because it hurt more to forget you than to remember why I loved you—still love you."

"You still love me?" I ask with surprise. I assumed, but hearing it feels like winning the lottery.

He nods and then gives me an endearing kiss.

"I—"

Liam cuts me off with a swift kiss. "You don't need to say the words. I'm not going to ask or force you to this time. Take your time because I'm not going anywhere. I'm in this, and I love you more than enough for the both of us."

52

LIAM

Now

Emerson and I went to Traverse City, Michigan, for the weekend. It started as a work trip when our bar manager and cocktail curator-mastermind quit.

Ben was planning on visiting Traverstini, which is known explicitly on social media for its bartender, Flynn. We want him to work for us.

When I told Emerson about the situation, she asked if we could go instead.

We drove up on Friday morning and spent the afternoon and evening with Flynn. Saturday morning, we biked Sleeping Bear Dunes National Park before hopping around wineries in the afternoon.

You should have seen the smile on her face when a stranger randomly air-dropped a photo of us they took. I know she'll have it printed and in her memory box before Monday is over.

I had forgotten how much I loved traveling with Emerson. Yesterday, I kept picturing the places I wanted to experience with her. I have a list in the Notes app on my phone. Whenever I traveled, I found myself thinking about her. She'd enjoy this café, take a picture of this, want to visit this museum, try this food, and complain about this hilly city.

I'd write down the city, date, and memory in the note, knowing that one day, when we were back together, I would take her to those places and beyond. There isn't a part of each other or this world I don't want to explore together.

"States, I'm back."

I set two coffees on the kitchenette counter of our hotel room.

Walking through the hotel room, I laugh to myself when I hear the music coming from the bathroom. Emerson still has the same shower playlist from when she was twenty-two. Six years later, she hasn't outgrown her love for young Justin Bieber and 5 Seconds of Summer. It's cute.

The bathroom door is open, and the steamy air drifts from it. I slide through the gap quietly, dropping my running shorts and shirt to the floor.

I open the door to the shower, but a hand comes to my chest before I can step in.

"What do you think you are doing?" Emerson is smirking at me. The hot water runs over her. I watch as a droplet hits her chest and runs between her breasts. I have an urge to lick it off her.

I take a step forward, pushing her finger further into my chest. "Going to bathe you."

"No." There is a glint in her eyes when they flick down to my dick. Already hard just at the sight of her.

"Why not?" I push my tongue into my bottom lip.

"Thought we could play *our game*." Her smirk grows. "Flip the coin. Heads, you watch. Tails, you join."

Watch what? It wouldn't be the first time I've seen her shower.

"Coin is on the counter by the sink." She drops her hand from my chest, dragging her pointer finger down my abs. Her nail gently scratches the lines of my muscles, and my body shudders. Emerson stops when her finger is about to reach my dick. Holding my gaze, she runs her entire hand up me. My jaw clenches. Then she gently pushes me back toward the sink.

I grab the coin, flip it, and extend my hand to her.

Heads.

"Looks like you're watching."

"I've seen you take a shower before, States," I remind her.

"I'm not showering." Emerson's head tilts to the side, eyes burning into mine, as she steps back into the water. Her hand follows the path the water droplet took a moment ago, sliding it down her chest to her stomach to between her legs. "Feel free to. . ." She flicks me a look.

Oh.

I stumble backward at her confidence and, well, what she's doing to herself. Finding the doorway for support, I lean against it, making myself comfortable for the show.

Up against the glass, through the steam coating the panes, I see Emerson's body. Her womanly curves, erect nipples, and her head thrown back from the pleasure she's bringing herself.

One hand working inside of her. She alternates between pumping in and out and circling them inside.

Her other hand makes its way up to her breast.

I'm biting my lip, trying not to lose all control this minute. This is one of the hottest things Emerson has ever done.

"What are you thinking about?" I ask her.

"You." Her head rolls forward, and our eyes lock for a split second before her gaze drops to my dick, my hand slowly moving up and down. "I always think about you. I pretend that my hand is yours and that the fingers inside of me are longer, thicker, and stronger. Filling and stretching me more than I can."

I always think of you. I always thought of her, too.

"Liam," she whimpers.

I can't take this anymore.

I cover the distance from the doorway to the shower, turning up 'She Looks So Perfect' playing on her phone. It's probably the fastest I've ever moved in my thirty years of life.

"Don't finish," I command her. She listens and drops her hand as she turns around to face me. "Good, States. Now turn around and get on your knees."

She listens, sinking down onto the tile. "Hands, too." Emerson listens like a good girl. "Now crawl to me."

I'm on the opposite side of the shower. On all fours, Emerson starts moving towards me. Deliberately slow, looking up at me through her long, black lashes. Green eyes inflamed with desire. Water runs along the curve of her spine and off her ass.

I take an audible breath as she gets closer. Trying to refrain myself from releasing before I get to taste or touch her. She stops, rising to her knees in front of me.

"Let me see your hand."

"Which one?" Emerson asks playfully.

"You know which one."

She stretches her arm up, putting her hand in front of my face. I lean my mouth to her fingers, circling one of the two that were inside of her with my tongue before sucking the digit into my mouth.

I remove her hand, moving it in front of her face. Holding her wrist, I tell her, "Now you."

She takes her middle finger into her mouth. Cheeks hollow out as she imitates what I did to her pointer finger.

Her eyes flare, and she can barely cry out when I replace her finger with myself, thrusting into her mouth.

My hands are tangled in her hair as I get off in her mouth. Her eyes watch my movements. My eyes watch her take me so well.

Heads did win the coin flip, after all.

Emerson swallows and stands in front of me. Her mouth is on mine as if it wasn't even a thought. I place my hands on the back of her thighs. I pick her up, pushing her up against the black tiles. Her legs are wrapped around me as we kiss.

"Am I allowed to finish yet?" She says, mouth still on mine.

"No," I reply, bringing her down onto me. I thrust into her, picking up her pleasure where she left off patiently.

Emerson shifts her body down onto me. The sensation has my eyes rolling. "Whatever that was, do it again and you can finish."

She does. Again, and again, and again, until we are a mess of moans and us.

We shower off—I actually bathe her this time, then pack our bags to head back to Chicago.

***

There's an hour and a half left in our drive. My hand rests on Emerson's thigh, the other on the steering wheel. Momentarily, I remove my hand from her to turn down the music we've been singing to.

I glance over at her in disbelief that she's sitting here with me. It's been a month since her birthday, and we decided to be together—a month more than I ever thought we'd get.

"I still can't believe all of this was part of Natalie's elaborate scheme to get us back together," I say.

"Yeah, I'm happy we are back—wait. Natalie's what!?" Emerson's eyes flare, and she blinks rapidly.

Shit, did she not know?

"Natalie knew who I was when we met. . ." I speak slowly. "She sought me out."

Emerson brings her feet onto the seat, folding her legs in front of her.

"What are you talking about?" Her head spins in my direction. I don't look at her, keeping my eyes on the busy highway, but I know her brows are pinched, and her cheeks are heated.

"She told me she told you," I stutter over the confusion I'm experiencing. Natalie promised me she would tell Emerson—and I believed she would. Why wouldn't she? "I. . . I thought you. . . k-knew."

"Clearly not. I have no freaking clue what you are talking about."

"I didn't know."

"You also said that when you figured out Natalie and I were friends. Are you lying?"

"I didn't lie to you. I didn't know either time. I swear—"

"What the hell is going on, Liam?" She cuts me off. "You better tell me everything right now."

53

EMERSON

Now

My hand is in a fist—nails digging into the skin on my palm to the point that I know there will be crescent moons when I uncurl my fingers—and I'm pounding on Natalie's door.

"Open up, Natalie!" I keep pounding on the door. "I know you're home!"

The sound of her feet scurrying to the door echoes in the hallway—she's never been the quietest person. She opened her door as if she was expecting me. Probably does. I had Liam drop me off here with a festering amount of adrenaline and anger. Knowing him, he probably warned her about the fury coming her way.

"Emme!" She lunges forward, pulling me into a hug. Her arms wrap around me and squeeze tight—so tight I can't breathe or move.

"Nat, a little hard to breathe."

"Oops. Sorry, I'm happy to see you," Natalie replies. She looks me up and down. "You look hungry. I was making waffles." Waffles at two in the afternoon? She's compensating. She knows I know.

Natalie doesn't let me answer before grabbing my hand and pulling me into her place. She's in a peppy mood that I'm about to ruin.

"Do you want blueberries or chocolate chips? Screw it, let's have both."

I don't respond.

"How was your weekend away?" She asks me. "Has it been as good as you remember?"

Natalie is asking me about sex with Liam. You've got to be kidding me.

A new thought, much scarier than the ones that drove me here, passes through my head. Eyes go wide with terror. Did she have sex with him? Of course, she did. It's Natalie. How did I not think about this? *No, stop Emerson. Liam told you he didn't. But he also didn't mention this. Maybe he lied to you.*

I sit there and stare at her. Hands under my legs to help contain my anxious ticks.

"Did you sleep with him?"

She takes out two plates and places two giant waffles on each. Opening the containers of blueberries, she washes them before placing one in every other compartment of the waffles. In the other compartments, she places chocolate chips.

"Syrup?" she asks.

"Natalie," I demand.

"No."

"I don't believe you. You are the most sex-positive person I know. For the slimmest part of my sanity right now, tell me if you did."

"I didn't, I promise. It's a line I didn't want to cross." Natalie's eyes pinch.

"Seriously? That was the line you drew? You've got to be kidding me, Natalie. That is ridiculous, you know that?"

"Yeah. . ."

We eat—Natalie eats, I stare at her—in silence, my frustration fuming, and all you can hear is the clinking of the fork and plate.

"Soooooooooo," she comments behind her napkin, which she wipes her mouth with.

"Why'd you do it?" I ask directly.

"Emme, you have to believe I never meant to hurt you."

"That's what you start with? You never meant to hurt me." My eyes flutter. I laugh. "You've got to be shitting me, Nat. You can't even lead with an apology."

"You have to believe me—"

"Why? Why should I?" I shake my head at her, pushing my uneaten waffle to the center of the counter. "You lied. You manipulated him and our relationship for your own game. How did you not expect to hurt him or me in the process?"

"It wasn't a game."

"You could have told him the truth. If he loves me like he's saying, he wouldn't have needed you to fool him into coming back to me. What does that make me? Second place. A consolation prize of friendship, how wonderful. I should have seen it earlier. You've been doing this our entire friendship. You take advantage of my weaknesses to get what you want. You devalued the friendship I thought we had. And now, you devalued whatever the hell Liam and I were!"

After Liam confessed everything Natalie did, I told him I needed space and a chance to figure this out. I was hurt that he didn't say anything to me. I understand that Natalie promised she would tell me, but why didn't he bring it up? His excuse was that he thought I would freak out. Well, he's right.

"That's not true. How does this do that?" She's shaking her head at me like I'm the crazy one in the situation.

"Are you serious right now? How could I not think that if you knew who he was and intentionally did this? You did this for yourself. You always do everything for yourself."

"I did this for YOU!" she raises her voice. "Emme, you barely, BARELY, told me about him. I'm lucky I saw a glimpse of him three years ago to even know who he was."

"You saw him three years ago?"

"A photo. Your photos. On your birthday, when you were putting all that clutter into a box in your closet. I was awake that morning and could see the photos. I snuck back into your room later and looked at them."

"You snuck into my room?" My head jerks back at the audacity she has. "You were the one to tell him never to speak to me again."

"Yeah, I did. I was mad that you didn't tell me about him."

"I did."

"That's bullshit, and we both know it. You said you met someone and broke up. Nothing else."

"You kept Liam a secret and away from me for a year."

"We both kept secrets, Emerson." Natalie never uses my full first name.

"I didn't tell you because I didn't want you to steal him. Do you not think if you hadn't gone home while we were in Lisbon, you wouldn't have been the one to fall in love with him?"

"No, I don't," she genuinely says.

"Don't lie. Every boy always chose you, or you found a way to make them choose you." I start laughing. "I'm such an idiot. It didn't even matter. You still found a way to make him want you."

"You're being unfair. Will you please let me explain," Natalie begs.

"Think it's a little too late for that. You should have told me last summer when you met him. It's done. I can't do this. I can't be with him if he wants to be with you. If he couldn't choose me on his own. If I'm not enough..." I slump onto her couch. I didn't realize I had gotten up and was pacing her place.

Natalie gets up from the barstool she is sitting in, walks over, and sits beside me. I put my elbows on my knees and place my head in my hands. I'm overwhelmed with emotions, and my anxiety is almost at its peak. I don't even know what to feel right now.

She reaches out for me.

"Don't," I bite out. Natalie recoils her hand.

I stand up. Looking around her living room, I think about this summer, seeing Liam here with her and me curled up on the couch after my engagement ended. Every time we were all together, she knew. She knew and didn't care about me enough. I was willing to choose her—push down my desires and love for her, but she was never willing to choose me.

Natalie and I have been drifting apart. I think I knew this but didn't want to admit it. She's been more reserved since last summer, not talking about guys in front of me, encouraging me to make wedding decisions, and avoiding hanging out. I should have asked. Well, I did. She denied any accusation. I should have stuck to my gut.

"I'm going to leave," I tell Natalie.

"Are you sure?" she asks.

I head toward her front door. Once I reach it, I open it and take a step so that I'm halfway out. Turning around, I stare back at Natalie and say, "Yeah. I'm also done with you. Please don't speak to me ever again."

I close the door behind me.

54

NATALIE

Now

Emerson's my best friend. If I were to look in the dictionary for the word friend, Emerson would be the definition.

Or so I thought.

I felt this way until I knew she was lying and keeping a secret. We didn't do secrets, her and I. But she kept Liam from me.

After I saw her three summers ago putting away those photos, I thought back to our summer in Europe and when she returned.

She'd take a call, stepping away or running to her room. She'd return glowing. Emme would get a package and hide it, but a grin would be plastered on her face. Even her personality was lighter, as if she wasn't chained down to her past anymore.

All of it makes sense. It was Liam. Liam Hayes was the one who got my best friend to love.

After they 'split,' she took a few steps back, shifting into an in-between version of herself. I actually missed the in-love version of Emme from those summers.

I always wanted a way to get them back together.

I would have stolen his number from her phone, but I deleted it on her birthday three years ago. I was mad at her but wanted to protect her from being hurt by him again—a big mistake. I should have let her speak to him when he called to fight for her. I answered the phone and immediately acted on protection and anger.

When I met him, it was as if the stars aligned, giving me a chance to fix my mistake. Of all the people I could have met at a bar in Costa Rica last summer, I met Liam Hayes.

I'm buzzing after an incredible photoshoot earlier that day. The feeling of doing what I love with a brand that I had dreamed about working with for years had me on cloud nine.

The entire team from the shoot and all the influencers were meeting up for our last night together. My flight home wasn't for another two days, but most people were leaving the following morning.

Walking into the bar, I felt all eyes on me. Wearing my favorite green, sequined minidress, I noticed the lights reflecting off it. Showstopper Tinker Bell—exactly how I wanted it. I twist my hips to the music and smile, seeing the group I'm meeting across the place. Before heading to them, I stop by the bar to order an Aperol spritz. Call me basic, but at least it wasn't an espresso martini.

Turning from the bar to head to my friends, I catch a gentleman behind me staring down at me. I had never felt so petite in my life. I lift my gaze to meet his.

He's sexy. Tall, dark brown hair, and a jawline that looks like it breaks hearts. He has money and a good job, but his hair and outfit tell me he's here for a good time. His fitted t-shirt shows off the firm muscles underneath. Everything about him is beautiful but eerily familiar.

"I'm Natalie," I said without needing to be asked.

"I'm Liam," he replies. His British accent piqued my curiosity.

Huh, Liam. A British Liam. "What's your last name, Liam?"

"Hayes."

Liam Hayes in the flesh.

Haven't seen or heard that name in about two years. That phone call was the last time.

Seeing him now, he's even more attractive than the photos—they do not do this man justice. He's a drink of cold water on a hot summer day, an electric shock to the system that makes you want another. I can't take my eyes off him. He's the type of guy that will age like fine wine, and my girl missed out big time.

I never made it to my friends, but none came to find me. I spent the entire time with Liam, and it made sense why Emme was obsessed with him. And why she's been heartbroken since whatever happened between them.

"Your mood is better," Liam's friend George said to him.

"I guess so," he replied, eyes flicking toward me.

Liam and I were sitting next to each other at the table with his friends Callum and George. He leans down and whispers in my ears. "You remind me so much of someone I used to know."

Used to know a.k.a. Emme, a.k.a. Emerson.

I don't need to ask Emme if she missed him to know she did. If they both miss each other, there's no reason they aren't together.

At that moment, I thought about telling Liam who I was. I didn't, obviously. Instead, operation get-the-two-of-them-back-together was born. I thought I was some Machiavelian apprentice.

The plan? Great—kind of. I figured I'd invite both of them to dinner and surprise back together.

The execution? Not as great. My best friend now hates me and made that pretty clear as she stormed out of my apartment. And there might have been a few roadblocks.

I didn't see Liam after that night. On the plane home, we were seated next to each other. He told me about his hotel empire and expansion in Chicago.

I thought fate was going to do my job for me.

Till I landed and I had a text from Emerson. I'm engaged, it said.

I was shocked. I didn't think she and Brandon were at that stage, but I must have been missing something—I was.

I didn't think she and Brandon would last, so I kept a friendship with Liam. Waiting for the moment to strike.

My plan was working perfectly until one of the days, I felt a tingle.

We hadn't even touched, only flirted, but suddenly I wanted to.

I started feeling something for Liam. Absolutely unexpectedly and definitely wrong.

My feelings became conflicted. I wanted Emerson to be happy and to have Liam back, but I liked him. I didn't expect to care this much for him, but trying not to was impossible.

I changed my plan. If she didn't want him, then I'd take my shot, but as of then, it was all up to Emme. I waited to see if she'd call it with Brandon last summer and fall. She didn't.

Liam and I stayed friends and became friends with benefits slowly.

I'd lie to Emme. Coming up with excuses when boys would come up or I had plans with Liam.

I liked Liam. I do believe he liked me, but never in the way he loved her.

That night in my apartment, I saw them together and noticed how they kept sneaking peeks at one another. It was as if they were trying not to make it obvious—they were doing a terrible job.

Jealousy crept throughout my body watching them. Liam was 'with' me, but I was jealous of Emme. None of this was right anymore.

I forced Liam to walk her home because I had to decide whether I could do this anymore. Or would he end it himself?

At first, it didn't even cross my mind that I was literally handing him to her on a silver platter (which was the original plan). By the time it did, it was too late to rescind. While Liam was with Emme, I sat on my couch contemplating ending this entire charade. But would I end it to have him for myself or for them? He would have picked her. So, I decided not to end it at all. I didn't want to lose. With Emme, I always got what I wanted, and she never believed in love—and was engaged!—anyway. Jokes on me.

Emme avoided me for a week after she and Brandon called off their wedding. I knew she wasn't upset about the engagement but about Liam. I also knew the engagement was called off because of him, but no one wanted to confirm that for me. I just knew I was right.

But then something changed, and she was hanging out with us again. I assumed Liam had said something to her after I found a call to her on my phone that I don't remember making.

Our threesome of sorts went on for weeks: Liam, my unofficial-boyfriend-whatever, Emme, my very official best friend. Orchestratedly placing the two of them next to each other. Chloe came when she was free. Callum, too, once he was in town.

Liam introduced the two of them as if they hadn't even met before. No one needed to tell me they had with how attached to Emme he became.

The whole plan came crashing down that night at Parlor Pizza.

When Liam followed her to the bathroom, I knew something was up, but I did nothing. I never did anything; I let everyone think I was unfazed. I downed my cocktail and slammed the glass on the table slightly too hard. I reached over, took Liam's drink, and I downed that, too. It was disgusting. Chloe's head jerked to me and then to the empty side of the table. She was getting annoyed at me for my lack of care attitude.

Not even minutes after Chloe left the table, Liam came back. His face was flushed as if he had been caught—they were caught.

Liam confessed everything to me days later, and we called it off. At that moment, I was mad. I was furious that I was being played, yet I was the one playing him—playing them.

At work, my frustration settled. I wasn't mad at him for picking her.

I explained everything that night to him. Liam wasn't mad. He laughed about it. I clearly manipulated him, and the guy shook it off as if it was nothing. He must really love Emerson or is messed up in the head.

He loves her. That's what it is.

I was happy. I was proud that someone like him wanted to be with my best friend. Liam cares about Emme the way any best friend would want their best friend to be cared for. He wants her fiercely. He understands her needs and fears but isn't afraid of them. The way he sees her is beautiful.

If I were to have been with him, it would have been a loss. He never would have loved me as he loves Emme.

I can accept that.

What I can't accept is how she now hates me.

I guess I get it. I didn't tell her like I told Liam I would, but maybe Liam should have chatted with her about this before they decided to get together.

I don't know if this is entirely my fault. *No, it is, Natalie. You should have told her when you returned last summer.*

Emme is hurting, and it's my fault.

Not once did it cross my mind that she'd be this hurt. She feels betrayed by both of us now, betrayed by two people who love her, like a pawn in her own game of love.

And I'm not sure there is a next move.

55

EMERSON

Now

Why are there this many people grocery shopping on a Friday at 4:00? Isn't there work to be done or bottles of wine to be consumed? I shouldn't have to stand in front of the same display of avocados for ten minutes, waiting for a pathway to move.

It's taken me twenty minutes to move from the produce section of Trader Joe's to the dairy section. There are only four items in my basket.

I stopped on my way home from work, planning to pick up ingredients to make pad thai at home and enough snacks and wine to fill my weekend. I know it's going to be a lonely one. Chloe left this morning, traveling for work till Monday. Without speaking to Natalie or Liam, I'm not sure what I'll do besides run, read, and stuff my face with the peanut butter-filled pretzel nuggets I dropped in my basket.

Five days have passed since everything went down between Liam, Natalie, and me. I haven't spoken to either of them. Not for their lack of trying. Both have called and texted me enough that you could consider it stalking. Natalie even employed Chloe to try to convince me to talk to her. Without trying to put Chloe even more in the middle, I tell her that I need time. Because time can fix this, right?

Chloe is refusing to pick a side outwardly. I value that because I know she is seeing clearer in this situation than I am. However, I can tell if she were to pick one, it would be for me to get over myself and under Liam. She keeps telling me that he isn't to blame. After leaving Natalie's, I found Chloe at a tattoo shop getting a new tattoo that looks similar to one that Callum has on his butt. When I asked her about it, she smiled and shrugged her shoulders. Then went back to telling me that I was blowing Liam's part in all this out of proportion.

I told her everything. How the weekend was serendipitous. When looking at Liam, all I felt was an overwhelming sense of love and that I wanted to tell him. I planned on professing my feelings to him in the car, but Natalie came up instead.

There's an opening in the aisle I need to go down. Walking down the aisle with pasta and sauces, I accidentally bumped into someone's cart, who was paying more attention to the shelves than where I was going.

"Oh, sorry," we both say at the same time.

I look up to see Liam standing there.

My heart about jumps out of my chest seeing him. I've missed him.

I quickly look away and turn around to go down a different aisle. I can come back to this one later.

"You've been avoiding me," Liam says, following me.

I muffle a laugh. *Shouldn't have thought you'd get away from him, Emerson.*

It hasn't been easy to get away from him this week. Liam meant it when he said he'd catch me.

Flowers on my desk Monday morning.

Hot black coffee in hand, waiting outside my building on Tuesday to take the train with me to work. Giving me his umbrella when we got off because I forgot mine and it was raining.

I found a package in the mailroom on Wednesday containing a camera lens. I had told him last week I'd debated buying it. Attached was a note saying to use it for the opening of his hotel next week and that he can't wait to have me as a part of this big day.

On Thursday, I found him stretching in the lobby of my apartment building, waiting to join me for my run. When I walked up to him, he kissed me on the cheek and asked if he could join. He didn't talk to me during the run, and when we got back, he kissed my other cheek, told me he loved me, and kept running.

There hasn't been anything today, though I have been waiting. After Monday, I was eager to see what he would do next. Just because I needed to figure out how to work through the deception didn't mean I stopped loving him.

That's an impossible feat. Once I started, I never fully stopped. I may have let it go for some time, but it didn't leave me. When someone is the love of your life—or, like me, the loss of your life, I don't think it is possible to ever unlove them. You can pause, find someone else, or ignore the beat of your heart that is them—but that doesn't mean you don't have a microscopic amount of love for them. I'm pretty positive first loves are like this, too.

And I'm screwed because Liam is my trifecta. He will always be option D, all of the above.

I try to move around him, but he sidesteps to stay in my way, using his cart to block my pathway. We stand there fighting each other with our eyes. He stares into my soul, his lips rising into a smile as if it's his sword. Mine are a shield firmly placed in front of the entranceway into everything I'm feeling.

I lose the fight by breaking eye contact and waving the white flag with a single blink. "I haven't been avoiding you. I told you in the car; I don't know if we can do this."

"Emerson," he replies and reaches out to touch my cheek. I turn away from him, not wanting to feel the ache that will come from his touch.

"Liam, you lied to me," my voice sounds protective.

"I didn't lie."

"Semantics. You didn't tell me about Natalie."

"I already told you, Emerson, I thought you knew. You never brought it up, so I didn't."

"What then? We were supposed to go about together and you two would never have told me?" I let out a big sigh.

"I'spose. I don't see it as a big deal."

"Not a big deal?! My best friend and the guy I—you two had this whole plot, pulling strings you shouldn't have been pulling."

"Natalie's plot, not mine. Please don't lose sight of the fact that we are together. That's why it's not a big deal."

"If she never told you, who would you be with?" I ask boldly.

Liam stares at me. A beat of silence passes between us—I swear it could have been an hour—before he says, "You."

"That should have been a quicker answer for you. I knew this wouldn't work." I say pointedly. I let out an annoyed sigh.

"Am I not in the same relationship? This has been working. What do you mean?"

"I wasn't enough then, and sure as hell am not enough now," I say with a bite.

Liam shakes his head; the anguish he must feel is showing, and I know I'm the one who caused it. I've seen it before, the only other time I hurt him. Again, in mindless retaliation for him hurting me.

He raises his head, our eyes meeting. The gray in them is nowhere to be seen; they're the iciest shade of blue. "You're right. You aren't just enough. You are more than enough. I don't know how else to make you see that."

It's exhausting being the girl silently begging people to pick you, choose you, and love you. Our entire relationship, that's all I've wanted from him. I wanted Liam to pick me, but somehow, I blinded myself to all the ways he was. It wasn't loud or obnoxious. It was quiet and steady. Exactly the way I would want to be picked, chosen, and loved.

But as much as being that Emerson is exhausting, it's easy to fall back into her patterns.

"I guess I'm still fucked in the head," I throw the words out too easily, instantly regretting it.

"You aren't States. You never have been. Don't give up now, please," he begs. I peek at his cart, realizing there are ingredients to make breakfast—the meal I could eat forever. Liam remembered because he knows me—better than I think I know myself. "I was planning on showing up with dinner—to cook together. I want this."

"I'm not saying I don't want this either—"

Liam nods his head toward me, brows shooting up. "I believe your words were that you knew this wouldn't work," he says as I was thinking the same thing.

"I-I don't know." *Do I anymore? After everything, I still can't let him all the way in. What is wrong with me?*

I push my nails into my thumb, trying to feel a different sort of pain. Ashamed with myself and knowing I can't give him the answers he deserves.

"Okay. That—if that is what you can give, then I'll accept for now. But Emerson, please understand that I'm not going to stop."

"Stop what?" My eyes go big, slightly taken back by him right now. Me wanting to fight and push him away. Liam realizing that and still wanting to pull me closer to him.

Liam swivels his cart, pushing it next to mine. I hope we aren't blocking other customers. We are taking up the entire width of the aisle, the fronts of our shoulders touching. He looks over his shoulder and says, "Showing you how much I love you."

I pull my bottom lip in between my teeth. "Okay," I say in slight defeat. He's tenacious, and I'm tired of fighting this.

A slow smile stretches across Liam's face before he pushes his cart forward and walks away. I finish grocery shopping, catching glimpses of him, before returning to my apartment.

An hour later, dinner is waiting for me outside my door.

56

EMERSON

Now

Liam didn't stop his DRAGS or daily relationship affirmation gifts and acts of service, as Chloe keeps calling them. I figured it out after our encounter at Trader Joe's.

Chloe has genuinely done her best to keep me from being alone in my thoughts, but it hasn't fully helped.

It's not that I feel alone because there aren't people surrounding me. Chloe is practically glued to my side. She isn't allowing me to go through this heartbreak alone this time.

"What are you doing here?" I ask Natalie as I walk up to Chloe and I's designated meeting spot for our walk.

Tucker wags his tail as I approach. I bend down to pet his head and am met with a slobbery kiss across my face.

"I'm on my way to a happy hour at LUXBAR. Chloe and I ran into each other out here," Natalie replies. I know she's lying. That restaurant is nowhere near where we are. The walk from here to there alone is something Natalie would never do.

"You're lying, but whatever."

She shakes her head, disappointed in my response. If she was hoping for me to forgive her and act like everything was okay, she hoped for the wrong thing. Despite how I feel about my situation with Liam now, it doesn't change what she did or that she hasn't shown any remorse.

Chloe chimes in, "I love that place. Make sure you get their Mexican espresso martini. I had it when my mom was in town this spring. She thought it was too much of a kick, but honestly, it could have used more."

"Thanks, Chlo." Natalie glances between the two of us. "I guess I'll see you two later. Have a nice walk," she says with sadness. She turns around and heads toward the restaurant.

Chloe and I take off walking toward the Chicago Riverwalk. It's one of our favorite places to people watch. Our usual hot girl walks turn into hot girl people-watching. We'll make it maybe a mile before we sit down along the river. It also usually includes a glass of wine or two—or a bottle. Natalie is also usually included.

My heart slightly hurts when I think about that. Twenty-two years of friendship gone—but I don't know if Natalie was ever my friend.

"Have you talked to Seth?" I ask Chloe.

"Absolutely not. He called and left a voicemail the other day, apologizing. The apology was an extended elaboration of what he told me already."

"Was it not one time?"

"Nope! One drunken night led to a month of hooking up. When he was visiting, I thought it was suspicious that he was on his phone so often. He was texting her." I noticed that, too.

"Did you call him back?"

"And say what? You're an asshole and a waste of my time. Nah, he doesn't deserve a response. We are too old to deal with college-aged bullshit. I blocked his number." She claps her hand in a done-and-dusted movement. "And before you ask me, yes, I am okay, better than okay. I'm happy and ready to go fishing again."

"Seems like you baited an English boy?"

Chloe laughs. "Cal? No. Hot, but no. We are providing moral support for each other to deal with your shit. Which speaking of. . . are you ever going to hear her out?" Chloe asks.

"But I want to hear about you and Cal." I pout.

"You just did." She pokes me in the shoulder. "I've given you two weeks to be a bitch about this, but times up."

"Didn't realize I was on the clock for dealing with the betrayal of my longest friend." Chloe says betrayal is extreme as I keep talking, "It's not that simple, and you know it."

"Then what is it? Because to me, it looks like you are willing-ly losing the love of your life and your best friend. Tell me I'm wrong."

"They lied. Left out pertinent information."

"So did you," Chloe reminds me.

"That was different."

"How?"

"I didn't have some mastermind plan."

We're outside Tiny Tap when she halts and politely grabs my arm. Chloe turns me toward her.

"Look, Em, you're hurting, and it's obvious. Since we became friends, I've never seen you like this. You're a shell of the friend I *love*." I try to speak, but she puts her hand over my mouth to stop me. "I get it—or at least I'm trying to. Natalie lied, whether she had valid reasons or not, but I think—no, I know this was out of love."

"Out of love? That's what you are understanding? If she loved me, why would she let herself fall for him?"

"You can't control who you fall for," Chloe points out. I roll my eyes.

"Why would she keep this for a year? Why wouldn't she tell me, or you, when she got back last summer?"

"She probably thought you were happy with Brandon and had moved on."

I shake my head no.

"You have to talk to her about her reasons." We take a seat on one of the large stone ledges. "I know you've had your ups and downs with Natalie. I get why you're upset: Your biggest fear is happening in real time, but you are letting it happen. You could put a stop to this, you know? You are letting yourself lose by acting this way.

"You allowed yourself to live in Nat's shadow your entire life. You think of yourself as second place to her. That one wrong move would cause her to stop being your friend, and you'd lose her love. The truth? You could never lose her love—or mine. We don't love you for the things you do for us. We love you because of who you are. You are generous and never shy away from helping someone. You are fierce and loyal, protective of us. I wish Nat told you how much she looks up to you more often. We both do. Neither of us would be the women we are today without you. You consistently make us the best versions of ourselves by being you. We love you. But do you know when you were the best version of yourself?"

I laugh, "When?"

"The summers you spent with Liam."

"Chloe, you only knew me for two of those summers," I remind her. She didn't know Emerson before, so what grounds does she have to make the comparison? "How can you say that was the best version of me?"

"Because I know you *now*."

Am I different now?

Of course, getting your heart broken changes you, but I'm fine. I've added enough tape to put myself back together. Like anyone who was in love once, I falter some days, but I'm fine—I'm not fine.

Chloe puts an arm around my shoulders—a half-hug but enough of an embrace that I feel the love transferring from her to me. "You aren't kidding anyone with your I'm fine facade."

"I don't. . . I don't understand," I choke out.

"Take a guess," she says to me.

"I loved him."

"I think love is an understatement. I sometimes think he is your every breath. He's"—Chloe makes me sound like a love-drunk fool, but maybe I am?—"the missing piece. You were lighter. You were brighter. I'm not saying you haven't been yourself for the past three years. You haven't been the version of you that is truly you."

Chloe sighs. "You are infinite when you believe that love exists. Aren't you tired of being like this?"

"Yeah, I am," I reply. Looking out over the river, I'm contemplating how to escape this mess. "I think I really messed up this time, Chlo. How do I fix this?"

"Talk to him."

"I don't think I deserve another chance from him."

"There are a lot of things in life we don't deserve. You might not deserve another chance, but the two of you, together, deserve an actual chance. The secret to love is knowing you already have it. You already have his love; you don't need to earn it."

Liam would never make me earn it. I nod.

"Chloe, have I ever told you I love you?"

She chuckles. "Yeah, but you can tell me again." Chloe gives me a cheesy smile. I squeeze her into a tight hug. "I love you, States."

We continued our walk, catching up on work and any other topic that allowed her to avoid my continued questions about Cal and her.

The sun is setting as we decide to head to our places.

Reaching into her fanny pack, Chloe pulls out a small envelope with my name on the front. I recognize the handwriting. It's Natalie's. "I promised Nat I'd give this to you when you were ready. She gave it to me yesterday, and I think you're ready for it now. Not to forgive her, but to finally—"

I hug her, cutting her off. I don't need to hear the end of what she's saying.

57

LIAM

Now

"Negroni, please," I ask Flynn. My throat is parched from all the congratulations and talking I've been doing tonight, bouncing around the room from person to person.

Swiftly, he's passing the drink across the bar to me, already moving to the next couple to take their orders.

There's a tap on my shoulder. I turn around and find Emerson standing there. Damn, she looks good. My jaw drops in awe.

"Do you have a free moment to take photos outside for the press releases coming out next week?" Emerson asks me.

At first, I was thrilled to have Emerson on my arm tonight. That would have been a mistake. Seeing her behind the camera, moving around the room with such ease and control, I knew that's where she was meant to be.

In our final meeting yesterday, she asked me if I wanted to make any changes to the shot list she created. I said, "No. I want to see my hotel and the night through your eyes. I trust you." Which is true. I trust her, but I also want to see the hotel designed for her through her eyes. When we started developing this hotel, I wanted it to be a place that she was drawn to. Even if it were a cocktail at the bar, she'd be back in my world.

She's good at her marketing job, but photography is her superpower.

And she's a superhero dressed in green—a high-neck, low-back, floor-length satin dress. It's my favorite shade of green because it makes her eyes this wild, hypnotizing color. It is intimidating, and tonight, I know it's where all of her power is drawn from.

Her hair is pulled back into a bun with a few front strands loose, and the tightness of the bun accents her high cheekbones. Her makeup is light; her lips are painted a soft pink. As I follow her to where she wants to take the pictures, I watch the halter ties move with the sway of her hips.

I didn't know if it would be the optimal dress for her to shoot in, but when I saw it the other day in the store, I knew she would look beautiful in it. When she walked in, I was surprised to see her wearing the dress. She texted me thank you, but besides that and our meetings, she hasn't spoken to me.

It hurts to lose her all over again. And I've exhausted myself by replaying this summer. I am leaving for London on a redeye tonight and hope that it's the reprieve I need.

"And another one facing this direction." She moves my shoulders to a different angle. My hand reaches up to hers.

"You are breathtaking tonight," I barely get out as my breath leaves my body as I look at her.

"Someone suggested I wear this dress." She forces a smile. "Thank you again."

"You're welcome." My hand is still on hers; neither of us cares to move. Eyes locked on the only person I ever want to look at. Staring at her, holding her hand, it doesn't feel as if she's slipping away this time. I can sense her holding on—holding on to me just as tight as I am. "Tonight is impressive. This is the largest turnout for an opening, and Cal told me we are already at no vacancy for the next two months."

"I know." Of course, she does.

"Thank you for all of your work. I know you were reluctant to take this on at first."

"That's because I was nervous about seeing you." Her eyes drop to the sidewalk.

"And now?" I ask.

"I think you can hear my heartbeat." I can. It's loud and rapid. She's nervous now, too. "You don't need to thank me, though. All of this is because of you—your hard work, your dream. I'm proud of you. You've accomplished all of this, Liam. I'm happy I got to be a part of it for once."

"Me too. Are you done being cross with me?"

"I'm not mad."

"Then what are you—"

I'm interrupted by a whistling cat call from Chloe as she exits the hotel to find us on the street. "If I didn't know any better, the two of you look like quite the pair tonight."

I may or may not have bought a tie in the exact shade as her dress and made sure my suit corresponded. If anyone in there tonight looks like they belong together, it's us.

"Blame him." Emerson delicately rolls her eyes at me. She knows, but at least she shows no signs of displeasure.

"Let me take a picture of you two," Chloe demands.

Emerson grumbles about it being her job to take the photos, as I agree with Chloe. "That would be lovely."

Chloe reaches out, taking Emerson's cameras off her. I stand beside Emerson, wrapping my arm around her waist and bringing her into me. In her heels, her head is perfectly under my chin. I move my arm, adding the other around her shoulders and chest.

The flash goes off. I turn my head, leaning down slightly, and kiss her temple. The flash goes off again.

Emerson stumbles forward. "That's enough. I should get back in there." Taking her camera from Chloe, she's off.

"She'll come around, I promise. Whatever happened flipped a switch in her. Emerson is being Emerson. Processing and navigating—and fighting through the voices in her head. She's finally figuring it out. Don't stop showing up. Okay?"

"Okay."

Chloe hugs me. "Congrats on tonight." Then follows Emerson.

I head back inside, continuing to make my rounds. Give a couple of speeches. Hop in and help give a tour, and be the leading man Hayes Hotels needs me to be.

After a few more hours, as the night winds down, I know it's finally time to head to the airport.

I find Cal to say goodbye.

"Are you sure you want to go?" Cal asks me.

"Yeah." I nod, hugging him. "I'm proud of you. We wouldn't be here without you. Enjoy the rest of tonight and this next week."

"Thanks, mate."

Patting my best friend on the back, I say a few other goodbyes and then leave.

I pause before the doorman opens the large glass door. Turning my upper body, I glance back one last time at the party. Immediately, my eyes find her. Standing there smiling, she drops one of the two cameras she's using tonight at her side.

EMERSON

With my cameras slung across my back and hanging at my sides, I pick up two glasses of champagne from the waiter walking around with them. I make a round downstairs and then on the rooftop, searching for Liam to cheers the night properly.

Everything is going perfectly. Attendance, bookings, social media posts, and engagement—everything we worked on is surpassing our projected numbers.

I'm proud of my team, but I'm even more proud of Liam—of everything that he's accomplished. The memory of the night he shared his dream with me lives rent-free in my head. The vulnerability in everything he dreamed up, his worry of never getting there, and the childlike excitement—it's hard to think it wouldn't happen. With Liam's mind, he can accomplish anything. The pursuit of his dreams is relentless; me included in that list.

There's Cal. I spot him across the pool, walking up to the bar.

"Did you know Cleopatra and Marc Antony had a drinking club while they were together?" I ask him as I settle up at his side.

"I did. Liam told me that." Callum's eyebrows raise peculiarly. "Is he going around telling everyone?"

"Oh no. Don't tell anyone, but I kind of have a secret obsession with Cleopatra."

"Huh, you do?"

"Yeah?" I reply hesitantly.

"Interesting."

"What's interesting?"

"I think this entire place is designed for you. The names and interior design. . . I think Liam created all this with you in mind."

"But—but we weren't—"

"I know," Cal says in agreement.

This can't be all for me. That doesn't make sense. As I look around the bar and think about the rooms I photographed earlier, the lobby. . . I need to find Liam.

"Have you seen Liam? I came over here to ask you."

"He left."

"Do you know where he went? I need to speak with him."

"London."

"London?!" My pulse races. Concern and despair wash over my face. He's not here.

"The owner of a hotel we have been interested in for the past two years called us about purchasing it. He wants to meet to work out a deal. We were excited until he gave us a week's expiration date. If we don't come to an agreement by Friday, it's going on the market, and we will have to battle it out with everyone else."

"And you couldn't go?"

"Liam offered."

". . . Because of me?"

"Not everything revolves around you States." He finishes his drink and orders another. "He knows the guy personally. But if this partly concerned you, I wouldn't blame him."

"I thought you were Team Emerson."

"I am."

"Sure." I sigh-laugh-snort. I'm not sure what combination came out of my mouth. "I'm figuring it out," I tell Cal.

"Are you?"

"Yes, I am—"

"You've had three years and an engagement to figure it out, States," Cal says at the same time.

"Why does everyone keep acting like me, magically believing in love is supposed to be easy?"

"You are also blaming him for something he didn't do. Letting it set you back. States—"

"Don't States me, Cal. Be real with me. This isn't some game to me, and I'm working on it."

"By avoiding him?"

"I'm not avoiding him! I need space—I need to get out of his stupid gravitational pull for once to overcome this and stop letting it happen."

"He deserves to feel the same love that he gives you."

"Yes, I get that. It's not that I don't love him. I do. You know what? Forget it. I'm figuring it out, and that's all that matters. Do you want this champagne?"

I shove the glass toward him and leave.

58

EMERSON

Now

Nothing is better than taking off your heels at the end of the day. I release a deep exhale at the immediate relief when my feet touch the cold floor.

Leaving my camera bag and purse on the counter, I go to my bedroom to change. I thought it would be Liam to take this off me tonight, not me. My arms twist around my back, stretching to reach the zipper. I unzip the back of the dress before untying the bow at the nape of my neck and letting it pool at my feet.

Dressed in my comfiest pajamas—sweats and Liam's old soccer shirt- I return to the kitchen. Natalie's letter stares at me from the fridge as I make a cup of nighttime tea.

I'm leaning against the counter, steeping the tea bag in the hot water. Pulling on the tag lightly, the bag moves around in the water. I stare back at the letter, contemplating whether I should finally read it.

Taking a deep breath, I reach for it.

Curling up in my favorite blanket on the couch with the tea, I open her letter.

Emme,
I'm sorry. I'm sorry. I'm sorry. I hope you realize that I never meant to hurt you.
It wasn't supposed to be like this. The day I met Liam, I knew instantly who he was. How could I not? He was exactly the way you barely described him. And if I'm being frank with you, he looked like the photos you kept of him. I know I shouldn't have gone through your belongings, but I was curious and didn't enjoy feeling like you

were keeping something from me. We never kept secrets from each other.

When he walked up to me in the bar, I planned to tell him that night, but then I had this idea. What if I could convince him to come back here to Chicago with me and surprise you both? Well, he was already planning on coming, and then when I got back, you and Brandon looked happy.

I didn't expect to fall for him. It didn't happen right away. . . me falling for him. But it's too easy not to. I understand why you did. He's perfect.

And I didn't mean to make him fall for me (if that is even remotely a way to describe his affection for me).

Of all the people I know, you deserve a relationship like the one he can give you. After everything you've done for me, I wanted to do this for you. For the both of you.

When I told Liam, he was mad, fair, but quickly let it boil over and then laughed. He looked at me and said thank you. What guy on this planet would say thank you?

I told him I would tell you, but I chickened out because I didn't know how, and the more I waited, the more I figured it didn't matter.

You two were together—the way it's supposed to be.

Emme, you have to know he was in love with you then and is in love with you now. It's been evident since the night in my apartment when I saw the two of you look at each other. He's never looked at me like that. Never. Each time you were near each other, he was the most relaxed I've ever seen him. It's like his missing part (and you!) was returned to him.

Maybe this whole thing was simply getting him back to you. Well, it was. . . that was my plan.

I guess what I'm saying is that maybe my messing up has a purpose, like someone or something else had this plan all along. I think you two were always meant to get back to each other—one way or another.

I don't expect you to forgive me for this or for falling for him, but I hope you can move past that. Whatever happened happened. I hope that the biggest mistake of my life allows the two of the most incredible people in my life to be happy. I want you to be happy. This love you feel? The one you keep denying and lying to yourself about. It's going to be scary, and it's not always going to be perfect, but it shows you know it's real, that it's true.

If you want to believe it, start with the reason you stopped. Talk to your mom.

XO Nat

I drop the letter on the couch, wiping away the tears on my face. Pulling out my phone, I send a text.

Hey. Want to come to the city?

And then I send another.

Can we talk?

Liam: I'll call you tomorrow.

59

EMERSON

Now

When I arrive, she's already sitting there. I haven't walked through the door yet; I'm standing on the sidewalk outside. But I know she's there. I can see her sitting at a table underneath the 'eat now caffeinate' sign. Her back is facing the window, but it's the haircut and denim jacket I recognize.

Her chestnut brown hair is cut short, about an inch above her shoulders. Ever since Dad left, that's been her signature cut. She said something about how her long hair felt too much like a security blanket for the old her and then rambled on about how Dad 'loved' her hair that way. New chapter, new cut, I guess?

The light blue chair she's sitting in covers most of the jacket. I can only see her shoulders and the moments in time that cover them. I love that jacket and all the stories that go along with it. My mom, Susan, got matching jackets with her best friend Clarissa during their sophomore year of high school. Before my dad, they were inseparable, similar to Natalie and I. Music festivals, trips across the world, and college; everywhere they went or anything they experienced, they'd get a patch, a pin, or stitching to commemorate it. Their friendship slowly dissolved once my mom and dad got together. Clarissa never liked my dad and always told my mom that he'd end up breaking her heart—not sure if she was a fortune teller back then because she was right. Even though their friendship came and went, she still wears that jacket. I think it's her version of a 'you were right' because she'd never come clean to Clarissa.

I'm standing on the sidewalk and second-guessing my invitation to the city for lunch. When she immediately texted me back, yes, I was in shock. I had assumed she'd say no and didn't want to make the three-hour drive.

I stop at the counter to order before I go to her table. Ordered the huevos rancheros tostadas and then an iced strawberry matcha. Then to comfort the conversation I need to have with her, I ordered a slice of carrot cake Mom's favorite.

"Mom," my voice comes out small, weak.

I touch the back side of her shoulder as I step around to the other side of the table.

Placing the cake between us, I pull out the chair and sit across from her.

"Oh, honey. It's so good to see you." Her arm reaches out across the table and squeezes my forearm. "I miss you."

"I miss you too, Mom." I do miss her, but it hurts too. It feels like I'm letting myself down by missing her.

I've missed both of them, Mom and Dad, since that night when I was thirteen. Dad might have physically left, but Mom emotionally left.

And I've I've added Liam to that list.

The list of people I miss, but don't miss. We all have one, right?

"When was the last time I was in the city? Oh, I know! Christmas after you and Natalie moved here. It was bitterly cold and snowed all day that we missed our tickets to see Hamilton."

"Yeah, I think so."

She cuts into the piece of salmon on top of her kale Caesar salad. "How's work?" Mom asks me.

"Good. Yeah, good." I nod my head. "Busy with a few new companies coming on board, but good."

"I wish you'd quit."

"Mom!"

"What? You are wasting your true creative talent working there. You should go full-time with photography. Do you know how much money is in the wedding business?"

I roll my eyes at her.

"You could make over six figures a year."

"I don't care about the money."

"So?" She rolls her eyes back at me. "It's more than what you are making now—"

"I don't even enjoy shooting weddings."

"What do you mean? You love photography."

"Right, photography. Not weddings." She gives me this look of confusion. "I want to take photos of places, people, animals, and moments—not weddings. Think travel and leisure."

"That's not consistent or easy. Weddings are always happening. Just look at your father. Some lucky photographer got two gigs out of him."

"Seriously?"

"What?"

"You know what." I glare at her.

They deliver my food and drink. Using the interruption to get off that subject, I indulge in my food. My mom follows me, cutting another bit of her salmon before forking a bite of kale.

"What is Natalie up to today? I had assumed she'd be joining us for lunch."

"She had a prior engagement. She says hello." I lie. I won't be telling my mom about my fight with Natalie. A fight—ha, that's an understatement.

"Oh. I texted her that I was going to be in the city. Maybe I can catch her before I take off."

"How long were you planning on staying?" We hadn't discussed this.

"A day or two."

"Oh."

"Don't look too excited. I wasn't planning on confiscating anymore of your time—I wouldn't dare." She laughs and smiles. You know, the kind of laugh that is a bit nervous, but you cover it up with a smile so the other person doesn't realize. She's got that mastered.

"Okay." I take another drink of my matcha. "I wanted to talk to you about something, Mom."

She nods her head and smiles this time. It's motherly and safe. It throws me back into the past when I was a child. It is the face she used to give me before life threw itself at her.

"Did you—" I pause. "Ever love Dad?"

"Yes, of course. Where is this coming from, honey?"

"I don't know." *You do know, Emerson. You can do this.* "Sometimes, I think about you two and us as a family before Dad left. It's hard to remember the two of you in love."

My mom laughs out two breaths.

"Did Dad ever love you?" I ask her.

"I like to believe so," she tells me, and I think I believe her.

"What happened?"

"Your father and I loved each other the best that we could. When we met, our attraction was chemical. The fall into bed five minutes after meeting sort." Huh, I understand that, unfortunately. "We were impulsive to get married and had you quickly after. It all happened quicker than we expected. I loved—I still love him in ways and always will. For years, our dynamic worked. And it was enough—till then, one day, it wasn't, and there was a sense of his wild youth that he wanted back."

"You were thirty-seven when he left?"

"I know. " She laughs. "How you get back your twenties when you are almost forty still doesn't make sense to me."

"Yeah," I concur.

"Why are you asking about this?"

"You told me it was my fault," I finally admit.

That statement hangs there between us. Her face falters.

"Honey," she says, taking a deep breath. "That's not true; you know that, right?"

"I was thirteen, I didn't know. How was I supposed to?"

"I guess. . . Oh, I'm sorry."

"You went on for years with that story. Abandoning me, treating me poorly. I know you lost your husband, but I lost my dad and mom."

"That's—"

"Not true? It is. After that night, it was like neither of you wanted or loved me."

"Emerson, we've always loved you." Her eyes are watery, probably matching mine.

We both look at each other. We breathe, blink, breathe, blink—over and over for, I don't know, how long.

"Because of the two of you, I thought there was something wrong with me, that maybe it was me who was unlovable, and that's why love didn't exist in my universe. Why didn't you two work out? Why didn't you two love me? It didn't matter in high school. Didn't matter in college. At least as I got older, it became easier and easier to build up a wall around my heart. I'd place people at a distance without letting anyone get close enough to even dare climb that wall."

"Emerson—"

I shake my head at her, silently telling her to stop talking and just listen.

"It wasn't till six years ago that I met someone who dared. He climbed and climbed and climbed and then tore down that wall. With everything in him, he loved me, and I couldn't allow myself love him back. I was so scared that we'd become the two of you or that I was like an infectious disease, that somehow he'd realize he didn't deserve me and destroy me."

"What happened between the two of you?"

"I left—ironically, like the night Dad left. He yelled out my name, begging me not to go, and I didn't look back as I got in the car to leave."

"What is his name?

"His name is Liam."

"Where—where did you meet?"

"That summer, I was in Europe. I met him the day Natalie left."

"Oh, the young man that traveled with you. I remember Penelope"—Natalie's mom—"telling me about that. Did you love Liam?"

"Yes." I finish my matcha and then sip from the glass water cup. "He's back."

"Well, that is fantastic!"

"It's not because I still can't allow myself to be with him fully. To actually fucking love him."

"Language, honey," she whispers like I'm ruining the children's ears around us. "Is that why you wanted to get lunch? To figure out a way to unlock your heart?"

I nod. Those watery eyes? They are pools now, and a single tear overflows. Quickly, I wipe it away, not wanting to show too much emotion in front of my mom. I hate being a crier. Actually, no. I love how much I feel.

"First off, please know that I love you. Being your mother is the best thing that ever happened to me, and I'm sorry that for years, I made you feel anything but that. You were not the reason your father left, and I should never have said that. I hope you forgive us both one day for how we treated you, even if it takes the rest of our lives, but please understand now that we love you bigger than the whole sky, always."

She brushes a tear away from both of my cheeks.

"And look, the thing about love is that it's not perfect. I could recite to you all the love is kind, love is patient, love is whatever, but I won't. I'm not saying that's not true; it is, but love is so much more," Mom continues. "Love is messy, and it can fail us, but it also reminds us that we are human. We are designed with love inside of us—it's a chromosome. That's what makes it real. It's not a fairytale, made-up romance. It's a feeling. It's a decision that we get to choose daily to act on. But even when we don't, that doesn't mean we still can't feel it." She gives me this knowing look, another reminder that she may have failed to act on her love for me, but she still felt it.

I'm quiet, smiling and staring at her. Her words pour into me, and my brain soaks it all in like a sponge. I can feel the neurons inside my brain firing and rewiring themselves. Mental images of the future, all the possibilities that come with believing love exists, show up in them.

My what-ifs are changing from what if we fail or what if I'm not enough to what if we have kids or what if we celebrate fifty years of marriage?

I can finally feel and see all of it so clearly. And it's all with Liam.

"Do you want to be with him?" My mom asks.

"Yes."

"Then be with him. Tell him how you feel. Show up each day ready to choose love. And ready to learn because that's another thing about love: it's unique to each of you. It evolves and shifts. To make it work, you have to be flexible with it. Sometimes, the circle has to go through the square hole. Loving him and letting him love you will sometimes feel like that, but that's when you stay. That's when you choose love the action, not only love the feeling. Right now, I think you need to do some acting."

Some? More like a lot.

"Thanks, Mom." I smile at her.

"Of course, honey. I love you."

We smile at each other, and for the first time since I was thirteen, I don't just hear her. I believe her and feel it deeply like it's always been there.

"I love you too."

60

LIAM

Present Summer

Once upon a time, at the beginning of this summer, I ran into a girl who I didn't know how I would ever see again. In my mind, there wasn't a doubt that we'd be back together by the end of the summer. Even an engagement—yes, I am that confident that nothing would stand between us—or friends with benefits would keep us from falling together. I dreamed of returning to London with her. A redo from our summer that tore us apart.

This time, we'd get it right. I'd tell her I love her, and she'd say it back.

Returning by myself had to happen. I knew it wouldn't be for nothing. Emerson confirmed that when she called me the morning after I left.

"I need some time to sort this out by myself," she told me after apologizing for overreacting and blaming me for the whole Natalie situation.

"Are you upset with me?"

"No." I'm not cross at her needing space. I'm happy to be finally in her realm. "There's no rush States. Today, tomorrow, or next year. I love you now, and I'll love you then."

She said, "Okay," and then hung up. We've spoken. I wait until she calls, trying to respect the space she requested.

I know she's been hurting. She's been hurting for sixteen years and has chosen now to figure out how to stop. It wouldn't be fair for me to think it could magically go away. I did that once, and it imploded things, pressurizing her to the point where she was fizzing out like a champagne bottle.

I meant it when I told her I loved her enough for both of us. I love her as she is now, but if taking this time to figure herself out finally is what she needs and gives us a fighting chance, then I'll keep loving her from afar. I mean, I'm already quite good at it.

Even if she never figures it out and we age, my hair goes gray, and I forget about everything else in my life, I'd never forget her. I'd never stop loving her.

But I have a feeling I won't need to wait that long.

I thought I would return to London for a week or two and then fly back to Chicago. Staying for a month did not cross my mind anywhere in my plan.

The day after I landed, I met with Edward Blyton, owner of Hotel Royal in London and several other locations across the continent. By the end of the week, a contract was with our legal team for review for every location.

During lunch with Edward, he informed me that his wife has stage four breast cancer and was given a year or two to live. They are in their late sixties but look and act like they are far younger. He wanted to sell a majority stake in his company. We worked out a deal that his locations will become a subsidiary of Hayes Hotels. We will retain majority ownership, but he will have a minor role.

I asked him why he wanted this.

"Time with her. I want to commit this version of myself to her and do everything I can to make her happy and feel loved. When people look back on my life, I don't want them to think of my career or achievements. I want them to think of the way I loved her. I'd give up everything if it meant one more minute or year with her."

I understood everything he wanted. That's how I feel about Emerson.

"Why my company?"

"Do you remember when we met? We were both on vacation in the BVIs. You were walking into the lobby with a young woman. You stepped away to introduce yourself, but over your shoulder, I watched the way she watched you. She had this expression on her face—a face you only get when you are in the presence of your true love. I saw my wife and I in the two of you."

"Emerson," I mumbled under my breath.

"Yes, that must be her. I picked Hayes Hotels because I know you'd do the same if you were in my position."

Leaving that lunch, I felt lucky. I already knew I didn't care how long Emerson took to figure it out; I felt fortunate that I was the one she was figuring it out for.

It would have been easy to make Callum come back here to work on this, but Emerson wanted space. And Edward was right; I'd do the same. Working on this deal was specific and personal.

So I stayed.

We completed the deal and the quick takeover. Everything moved fast, but it was important, and I was proud to be able to do it. Every early morning and late night was worth it.

An hour or two passed from when I put myself horizontally on the couch. It was post-run, and I had nothing to do on this rainy Saturday but watch the Premier League when there was a knock on my door. I waited to answer the door, assuming it was the lunch that I ordered for myself. The match has only two minutes left of play, and Arsenal and Chelsea were tied. I left specific notes to leave it at the door, anyway.

Whoever it is at the door knocks again.

EMERSON

Emotions from the last time I stood outside his door flood my system.

Pushing those anxious emotions and memories aside, I remind myself that I'm here now. Mistakes in the past, this is our now, and with my whole heart, I believe he'll see it that way, too. Like they always say, the third time's the charm. Right?

But I tell myself this is actually the first time because I'm finally ready—completely there, completely in it.

Taking a final breath, I lift my hand to the door before I chicken out. Quick, fleeting thoughts of self-doubt cross my mind.

What if he's not here? You wait.

What if he doesn't love you back? Stop joking around. Liam loves you.

What if he turns you down? Then we'll pick ourselves up and move on, being proud of ourselves for finally going after what we want.

This is it, Emerson. Don't be a coward.

Folding my hand into a fist, I knock on his door.

There's no response.

I knock again.

I know he's here. There is a tingle in my body, my heart rate picking up the way it does whenever he's near. It intensifies as I hear footsteps amplifying. The sound of a lock being flipped echoes in the hallway.

This is it.

The door opens.

I lift my head, and our eyes lock.

"Hi," I say.

"Hi," he replies. A massive smile slowly appears.

I stare at it, getting lost in how much I love his smile. How much I love him.

"States, what are you," Liam can barely get out before I drop my bag and wrap my arms around his neck. Slipping my hands into his soft brown hair. I push my lips to his.

Liam kisses me back. My lips part as his tongue finds mine. Like they were only ever meant for each other, our kisses move as mindlessly as the act of breathing. His hands come to my lower back, and he guides us inside his flat. Removing one hand, he shuts the door behind us and pushes me against it. My bags are still in the hallway, neither of us giving an ounce of care. Liam returns his hand to me, cupping the right side of my face. The gentle caress on my face is warm, and I lean into it instinctively. We keep kissing, neither of us wanting to pull away except for desperate gasps of air that aren't each other. But if I had it my way, he's the only thing I'd breathe for the rest of my life. We're like two stupid high schoolers who just discovered kissing and can't get enough of it. Liam pulls my bottom lip into his mouth and bites down, causing me to moan softly into his mouth. He groans in response.

With the satisfaction of knowing that there will be plenty more of this to come, I break our kiss.

Staring into my eyes, Liam pushes a loose strand of hair behind my ear. I break our kiss, satisfied that there will be plenty more of this to come.

"States, what are you doing here?" he asks.

"I'm done pretending that I don't love you." There is no need for the fluff. "You're everything to me. I wish I could tell you I knew it from the day you walked into my life, but the day I walked out of that door made me realize how much I care about you. I loved you then, and I love you now. I'm in love with you."

"You are?"

"I am," I say confidently.

We move to his living room. He sits down and pulls me onto his lap. I turn to straddle him. An intimate position we've been in countless times, but this time, I only want to see him. Really look at him while I finally admit to him how I feel.

"This. Us. Everything is on me. I've been in my head, and I'm sorry. I never meant to hurt you by letting everything get in the way—the distance, my parent's divorce, Natalie, my anxiety. Whenever I thought I loved you, I allowed these excuses to get the best of me. It took me a while to learn that I can love you despite them and because of them. In the end, whatever excuse, trigger, or anything else that comes our way doesn't matter to me anymore as long as I get to choose you. And I do. I choose you. I'm not perfect.

I'm still figuring it out, but my love for you is so loud that it quiets the insecurities."

I lean forward to place a gentle kiss on his lips. Liam is quiet, allowing me to own the moment, own my feelings, and finally have the bravery to take what I want.

"I realize now that it's been you and me all along," I continue. "Wherever I've been. Whoever I've been with. Whoever I am. Memories of us are memorized in my mind. Time and time again, they'd replay the cruelest or sweetest moments. Each time, reminding me of everything we could be. My mind somehow always knew, using those memories as barriers to make sure I never moved on. There were days I was desperate to forget, to let you go and be free. But there were days that I wished I was brave enough to do whatever it would take to get back to you."

"You're brave enough now." Liam brushes his knuckle against my cheek. I close my eyes, longing for his hand to stay there forever.

"Tell me it's not too late. Please." My please comes out broken. A crack that reveals the desperation behind it because I wouldn't blame him if it were. "Please," I beg again when he doesn't answer.

Liam laughs. Laughing?

"You're laughing? I'm serious right now."

"States, if it were too late, then that kiss or how much I want to undress you right now would be wrong, aye?"

He's still laughing, and it vibrates through my entire body. He brings his hands to either side of my face, holding my face mere inches away from his. We're so close that I can feel his breath and smell the same cologne from that night in Paris.

"It'll never be too late for us. There's no place you or I could go or people we could become where we wouldn't find our way back to each other. It's always been us, and it will always be us," Liam says with the purest sincerity I've ever experienced.

It's not too late. Everything that happened is in the past. Scratch that. It's not just in the past. It is our present. A chapter we finished that led us to the one we are writing now.

There seems to be nothing left to say but "I love you, Liam Hayes."

"I love you too, Emerson Clarke."

He reaches out for me and pulls me into his chest. His warm embrace and the smell of him feel like home. It is exactly where I'm supposed to be—with him and in love with him.

Natalie was right. We were meant to find our way back to each other.

EPILOGUE
Liam

Six Months Later

I love the summer, but springtime in London is quite exceptional. Mild weather but full of color–blooming magnolia trees, the greenest grass, and parks full of daffodils. Full of Emerson. Maybe that's why this has been my favorite season.

Emerson moved to London officially in January.

She quit her job, deciding to bet on herself as a photographer full-time. She'll always have a job with Hayes Hotels and any future location we open, but since September, her photos have blown up. The photos she took at our opening were featured in Entrepreneur, GQ, and US Weekly—the list is long. She's on a waiting list; the demand for her is that high—every sort of gig and all over the world.

I'd like to take credit—in an interview, they couldn't get me to shut up about her. Luckily, they ran all of it—but this is all Emerson. Remarkable talent. Remarkable girl.

My phone buzzes in my hand.

Chloe: Did you do it?

Callum: Seriously. Chloe is becoming a pain in my ass.

Chloe: Shut up. I am not.

George: She is. We are waiting.

Beatrix: I dragged a crying baby out today. Hurry the fuck up. We've already waited years for this.

George: Someone's hormonal. Baby #2?

Beatrix has removed George Eaton from the group chat.

I'd wait even longer for her. Now, goodbye. I am busy.

I push either side of my phone to power it down.

As much as I would wait forever for Emerson, I hope I don't have to wait as long this time for an answer from her.

I'm proposing to her. Today. Any minute now, really. I'm waiting for her to return with black coffee for us.

Sundays are my favorite days with her. Work is a drag and occasionally pulls us into working most days; however, we keep Sundays reserved for us. No exceptions.

A morning run if we aren't exercising other parts of our body. Breakfast like my mom used to make. Cartoons are replaced with books. And then *our game*. Heads, I pick what we do for the day—which usually involves us exercising those parts of our body.

Tails, she picks. It's been months, and Emerson still behaves like a tourist. Dragging me to who knows where.

Today didn't start any differently.

The coin landed on tails, and she asked to go on a long walk, flipping it along the way. I agreed—quite overzealously accidently. Emerson's brows pinched in response to my eagerness.

I watch her walk out of the café with coffee and a glowing smile. It's still wild to me to think that when we met, I would have done anything to see her smile, and now, it feels like it's a frozen expression. Or maybe that's just me.

"One black coffee for you." Emerson hands me my to-go cup.

"No black coffee for you?" I ask her.

"Iced oat milk latte with honey." She extends the coffee for me to try.

I take a sip. "That's...I'll stick to my usual. Why the change?"

She shrugs, and her smile falters. "I miss Chloe." We haven't been back to Chicago since she moved here. Before that, we went back and forth to see each other. I had offered to fly us back; I had plenty of work there, but Emerson wanted to adjust to living here. Chloe and her speak on the phone as much as possible. But from experience, time difference can be a bitch.

Chloe was the first person I called when I decided to propose to Emerson. She stalked Emerson's Pinterest account to find a hidden wedding one. At the bottom were photos of rings she liked. Chloe sent them to me, and I instantly knew the perfect ring for her: my mom's.

Emerson doesn't know Chloe is in London with our friends waiting for us. I should probably end their misery and get around to the whole one-knee thing.

"I know. We are going back next month. Her birthday sleepover is planned?"

"Yeah," Emerson replies. "I'll see her then."

We walk a few meters before I stop. "Next flip?"

Emerson nods. I hand her a coin—not the one we'd been using, but a special one. I had it custom-made to read 'Marry Me' on each side.

She trades me her coffee for the coin. Without looking at the coin, she tosses it in the air and catches it in her palm.

I set our coffee on the ground. Reaching into my coat pocket for the ring.

Emerson slowly opens her palm.

"Hea—what?" Her eyes flick between mine and the coin, sparkling with something between disbelief and excitement. Her cheeks turn the most radiating shade of pink. "Marry me? Marry...m-marry me?" she stutters in confusion.

I nod at her, smiling as big as I can. Then I get down on one knee, pulling the ring out of my pocket.

"Marry me, States. I've loved you for years, and there isn't anything I want to do more than love you forever. I promise to choose you. I promise to bet on us. Just say yes. Say you'll marry me."

She bites her lip before leveling herself with me.

"You have to flip for my answer," she says. I give her a look. "I'm kidding. Yes, yes, yes. I'll marry you, British Isles."

I laugh at her tacky nickname.

"Good, now will you kiss me, or do I need to get George," I joke.

"Oh, shut up."

Emerson's lip touch mine. She kisses me in a way that promises she'll love me forever–no doubts, no checked boxes, just unconditionally.

Acknowledgements

First off, to you, the reader—THANK YOU! Thank you for taking a chance on my book and me. Because of you, authors like me take risks and do what we do. Keep reading, keep loving (obsessing) characters, and keep being the best community out there.

I hope you loved and enjoyed Emerson and Liam's story as much as I loved getting to write it. If you did, I would appreciate and be forever grateful if you left a review on Goodreads and Amazon. A positive review is a small gesture that authors love, and so would Emerson.

To my grief, it's weird to write, but this is because of you. Not many know, but writing this book helped me work through parts of my dad's passing. Even though some of those original storylines didn't make it into this version, working through those emotions in characters helped me process and find peace.

Dad: I miss you. There are no other words to convey that. Even though you aren't directly involved in this, there are so many characters floating around in my head that I see parts of you in. I hope one day I can be brave enough (and not selfish) to share them, but until then, it brings me joy to share your life trope in a book: second chances.

To my family, thank you for supporting me through this process and not judging me when I said I was going to write a book. You've always told me I could do anything, and your support lets me do that.

Shay and Rachel: I love you both. This story wouldn't be complete without you two. Thank you for holding me to my personal deadlines and allowing me the space to never shut up about the book.

To Callahan, your immense love and support throughout this process kept me going on the tough days. Thank you for beta reading and keeping up with my crazy ideas.

To Emily, thank you for being a great beta reader, grammar police, sanity manager, and encouraging every bit of spice.

Alanna, I'm so happy we both got back into reading simultaneously, even though it was Harry Styles fanfiction. That love and obsessive compulsion to always be reading got me to this point.

An honorable mention to BRM. You've got a great rump, too.

To my once Summertime Friend, Casey, this wouldn't be possible without you. Thank you for believing in me, giving me the space to fulfill this snowball dream, and blabbering about writing or books. I'm forever grateful that I get to do life with you. Oh, and an addition to my vows: I promise never to stop taking over our living room as my personal library. I love you endlessly.

Lastly, to myself: You did it. You wrote a book and published it. I hope that you remember the feeling of this accomplishment forever. Never be afraid to do something and chase a dream, no matter how small or big.

About The Author

Hannah Hamrick is a romantic at heart who believes everyone has their own happy ever after. She writes swoon and giggle-worthy romance novels filled with real-life emotion and characters. A Midwest girl at heart, she lives in North Carolina with her own Summertime Friend and two fur children, Barrett and Archie. When she isn't writing, you'll find her with a book in hand, traveling, or watching reruns of Survivor. Current vibes include indulging in Diet Coke, laying in the grass with her dogs, and uncoordinated dance moves to Taylor Swift.

To stay up to date on Hannah's upcoming books, connect with her on social media, @authorhannahhamrick.